# 编 委 会

**主　编** 朱世宏　杜柯伟

**副主编** 彭　翊　夏　娟

**策　划** 廖　飞　陈滔伟　陈　立　高　媛

**编委会成员**

- 四川大学
- 电子科技大学
- 西南交通大学
- 四川农业大学
- 西南石油大学
- 成都理工大学
- 四川师范大学
- 西华大学
- 西南科技大学
- 乐山师范学院
- 成都大学

**编辑组** 杨　几　李益众　郑佳洁　陈　敬　赵　敏
雍晓燕　黄瑾悦　陈甜甜　王　琦　唐　虹
彭之梅　夏　婷　杨汪蓝珺　杨玉清　张学敏

**英文翻译、审稿** 姚　键　黄　鸣　孙张静　熊亭玉
张　岚　郭粒粒　杨　蓓　周怡乔
黄　曦　王利华　樊　皇　周　悦

# 四海之纽 川山有约

Taking the World as a Link to Study in USA—For the 10th Anniversary of CSC–SUNY 150 Program

写在四川"CSC–SUNY 150 奖学金项目"十周年

主编：朱世宏　杜柯伟

Editors-in-chief：Zhu Shihong　Du Kewei

四川大学出版社
Sichuan University Press

项目策划：段悟吾　张　晶
特邀编辑：Rebecca Zhou（周明倩）
责任编辑：段悟吾
责任校对：周　洁
封面设计：墨创文化
责任印制：王　炜

## 图书在版编目（CIP）数据

四海之纽　川山有约：写在四川"CSC-SUNY150奖学金项目"十周年 / 朱世宏，杜柯伟主编. — 成都：四川大学出版社，2019.3

ISBN 978-7-5690-2822-5

Ⅰ．①四… Ⅱ．①朱… ②杜… Ⅲ．①纪实文学—作品集—中国—当代 Ⅳ．① I25

中国版本图书馆 CIP 数据核字（2019）第 042330 号

**书名**　四海之纽　川山有约：写在四川"CSC-SUNY 150奖学金项目"十周年
　　　　Sihai zhi Niu Chuanshan You Yue：Xiezai Sichuan "CSC-SUNY 150 Jiangxuejin Xiangmu" Shi Zhounian

| | |
|---|---|
| 主　编 | 朱世宏　杜柯伟 |
| 出　版 | 四川大学出版社 |
| 地　址 | 成都市一环路南一段 24 号（610065） |
| 发　行 | 四川大学出版社 |
| 书　号 | ISBN 978-7-5690-2822-5 |
| 印前制作 | 成都墨之创文化传播有限公司 |
| 印　刷 | 成都市金雅迪彩色印刷有限公司 |
| 成品尺寸 | 170 mm×240 mm |
| 印　张 | 22.25 |
| 字　数 | 551 千字 |
| 版　次 | 2019 年 5 月第 1 版 |
| 印　次 | 2019 年 5 月第 1 次印刷 |
| 定　价 | 98.00 元 |

◈ 读者邮购本书，请与本社发行科联系。
　电话：(028)85408408/(028)85401670/
　(028)86408023　邮政编码：610065
◈ 本社图书如有印装质量问题，请寄回出版社调换。
◈ 网址：http://press.scu.edu.cn

四川大学出版社
微信公众号

# 讲好中国故事，继往开来，携手推进中美人文交流

## ——为中国"CSC-SUNY 150 奖学金项目"实施十周年纪念书

### （教育部中外人文交流中心）

    2008 年发生的"5·12"汶川特大地震转眼已过去整整十年。大灾给汶川及其周边地区的人民带来了巨大的伤痛，大灾也引来了国内外各界的关爱。在世人携手绘就的感人画卷中，由中美双方合力促成的"CSC-SUNY 150 奖学金项目"（又称"中国 150 项目"）就是其中浓墨重彩的一笔，十年过后依然鲜亮如初、令人动容。

    十年前，也就是"5·12"汶川特大地震后一个多月，美国纽约州立大学总校向我方提出，希望邀请 150 名来自地震重灾区的四川高校大学生赴美学习一年。这一提议立即得到国务院领导、教育部、四川省教育厅的高度重视，在中美双方各级政府、使领馆、教育主管部门以及四川相关高校的倾力支持、共同努力下，不到一个半月即完成 150 名四川高校大学生的选拔和派出工作。这批优秀的大学生在美国一年期间得到纽约州政府、纽约州立大学及其接待家庭、在美华侨和中国驻纽约总领馆等无微不至的关照。许多感人的故事，已成为中美民众友好交往的佳话。"CSC-SUNY 150 奖学金项目"成功实施所产生的积极效果，也让中美双方看到了中美在文明互鉴、民心相通方面的迫切需要和巨大潜力。

    就在该项目结束后的次年（2010 年），中美人文交流高层磋商机制在北京正式启动。迄今，中美之间共举办八次高级别人文交流机制大会及相关配套活动，协力推进教育、科技、环保、文化、卫生、社会发展（涵盖体育、妇女、青年、

社会组织）、地方人文合作七大重点领域的务实合作，为双方增信释疑和友好交往贡献了绵薄之力。

2018年，中国迎来改革开放40周年。改革开放的成就举世瞩目，为中国带来了历史性巨变。40年来，随着改革开放的不断深入发展，中外人文交流已成为党和国家对外工作的重要组成部分，是夯实中外关系社会民意基础、提高我国对外开放水平的重要途径，对"一带一路"建设和人类命运共同体构建具有十分重要的作用。

"CSC-SUNY 150奖学金项目"既是中美教育交流史上的重要事件，也是中美人文交流发展进程中的生动案例。当年的大学生们如今大都已成家立业，正在各地努力打拼，经营着各自精彩的人生。相信大家会继续肩负推进中美人文交流的历史使命，发出中国声音、讲好中国故事、贡献中国方案，以更多实际行动，服务于家乡经济建设与社会进步，服务于四川与纽约之间的省州合作，服务于中美人文交流的蓬勃发展，服务于人类命运共同体的构建。

# To Further Promote Sino-US People-to-People Exchange by Telling China Stories Well

—Preface to the 10<sup>th</sup> Anniversary of the Implementation of CSC−SUNY 150 Program

(Chinese and Foreign Humanities Exchange Center, Ministry of Education of the People's Republic of China)

It has been ten years since the 2008 Wenchuan Earthquake. Although the catastrophe has brought great pain to families in Wenchuan and its surrounding areas, it has attracted the attention of all walks of life at home and abroad. Among the moving picture scrolls painted by numerous people, the CSC-SUNY 150 Program (also known as the China 150 Program) launched by China and the United States was just one of the most important touches. And ten years later, it is still bright and heart-warming as ever.

Just more than one month after the Wenchuan Earthquake ten years ago, the State University of New York offered to invite 150 students from affected universities in Sichuan Province for one year of study in the United States. This proposal was immediately attached great importance by the leadership of the State Council, the Ministry of Education and the Department of Education of Sichuan Province. With the full support and joint efforts of the Chinese and American governments at all levels, embassies and consulates, the competent educational authorities, and the relevant universities in Sichuan, 150 university students in Sichuan were selected and dispatched in less than one and a half months. During their one-year stay in the United States, these outstanding students received great attention from the State Government of New York, the State University of New York, the host families, overseas Chinese in the United States and the Chinese Consulate General in New York. Many moving experiences, brewed in time, have become a good story of friendly exchanges between the Chinese and American people. The positive effect of the successful implementation of the China 150 Program has also caught the attention of the leaders of China and the United States to the urgent need of and great potential in mutual learning of civilizations and people-to-people exchange between China and the United States.

In 2010, one year after the completion of the China 150 Program, the US-China High-Level Consultation on People-to-People Exchange was officially launched in Beijing. Since then, China and the United States have held eight high-level meetings on people-to-people exchange and related supporting activities. They have worked together to promote practical cooperation in seven key areas of education, science and technology, environmental protection, culture, health, social development (including sports, women, youth, and social organizations) and local programs of people-to-people exchange, which has contributed a continuous impetus to the friendly exchanges between the two sides by enhancing trust and dispelling doubts.

The year 2018 is the 40th anniversary of China's reform and opening up, whose achievements have attracted worldwide attention and brought about great changes in China's history. With the continuous deepening of reform and opening up over the past 40 years, it has become an important part of the work of the Party and the state to promote Sino-foreign people-to-people exchanges, an important way to consolidate the foundation of social and popular will for Sino-foreign relations and enhance the level of opening up to the outside world, and a very important role in the construction of the "Belt and Road" and the building of the community of shared future for mankind.

The China 150 Program is not only an important event in the history of Sino-US educational exchanges, but also a vivid case in the development process of Sino-US people-to-people exchanges. Now, most of those students of the China 150 Program in those days have already established their families and businesses, working hard everywhere and managing their own wonderful lives. We believe that they will continue to shoulder the historical mission of promoting Sino-US people-to-people exchanges by spreading China's voice, telling stories about China well and contributing to China's solutions, and they will do more to better serve the economic construction and social progress of their hometown, the cooperation between Sichuan and New York, the vigorous development of Sino-US people-to-people exchanges, and the construction of the community of shared future for mankind.

# 前言

朱世宏

流光易逝，不知不觉中，距离"5·12"汶川特大地震已过去了十年。2008年8月，应美国纽约州立大学邀请，150名来自我省地震重灾区13所高校的大学生抵达美国，分赴纽约州立大学22个校区，开始为期一学年免费的学习与生活，开启了我省13所项目学校与纽约州立大学的交流与合作。在这宝贵的一年里，在国家领导人、中国驻纽约总领事馆及各界华人华侨的关心下，在美方老师、同学的细心照顾和帮助下，这150名同学刻苦学习、虚心求教。2009年5月底，同学们完成一学年的学习回到了祖国，回到了家乡。部分同学在美经历的点点滴滴被汇集成册，收录于《纽约·我心飞扬——四川地震灾区150名大学生在美国》一书中，向世人展示了中美两国人民之间的深厚友谊和感情。

而今，寒来暑往，斗转星移。十年过去，破碎的废墟上早已实现了新的站立。缅怀和告慰逝者最好的方式，就是生者努力前行、尽如所期。灾难带来的巨大伤痛已变成镌刻在人们心底的坚韧和刚毅，时刻激励我们不忘初心、砥砺前进。当初应邀赴美留学的150名同学一直努力着，奋斗着，做家乡、祖国的建设者。

十年岁月沉淀，十年牵挂惦记。那一年的赴美留学经历，让150名灾区学生抚平了伤痛，打开了眼界。他们用知识提升能力，充实自我。不同文化背景下，全新的学习、生活方式对他们自身的发展产生了潜移默化的影响。陌生国度丰厚的文化土壤，老师、同学间点滴相处积累的真挚情谊，滋养着离家万里的游子，在他们的心田悄然埋下希望的种子。跨越国度，150名学生以留美之行为交汇点，

在各自人生画卷上描绘出绚烂的成长轨迹。他们在五湖四海，从事各行各业。有的至此爱上旅游，成为航空公司的管理人员；有的深耕在三尺讲台，传递和播撒知识的种子；有的折服于语言的魅力，默默探索文学的堂奥……他们带着满满的收获，专注于自己的兴趣爱好，一步一步实现梦想。

以梦为马，不负韶华，150 名学生在各自的岗位和平凡的生活里，于灾难后的重建中品味生命的欢愉和喜悦，于跨越文化、地域的交流中收获美好的情谊和回忆。回首来路，十年不改，他们各自沉淀出人生的真实与沉稳，平淡却不平凡，以自己力所能及的力量，向世人昭示生命最原始的颜色和温度。

我们将参与"中国 150 项目"赴美留学的部分学生这十年的成长经历辑录在这本书里，隔着辽阔空间和悠悠岁月，与过去那一群怀揣着希望和梦想奔赴他乡的亲历者遥相凝望：希望借此向读者传递这份跨越国度的情谊，向世界释放出最本真的柔软与善良。十载同心，前行依旧，爱心永存，希望永存。

# Preface

By Zhu Shihong

---

How fast the time flies, and unconsciously, 10 years have passed since the May 12 Wenchuan Earthquake! In August 2008, at the invitation of the State University of New York, 150 students from 13 affected universities of Sichuan Province arrived in the United States and went to 22 campuses of the State University of New York for a free academic year of study and life, and this initiated the exchange and cooperation between the 13 universities in our province and the State University of New York. Concerned by the state leaders, the Chinese Consulate General in New York and overseas Chinese from all walks of life, and with the attentive care and help of American teachers and classmates, the 150 students studied hard and sought advice modestly in that precious year. Having completed an academic year of study there, the students returned to their motherland and home at the end of May 2009. Some of the students' experiences in the United States have been collected in the book, *New York, Let Our Dreams Fly!: Experiences in the US of 150 University Students from Sichuan Earthquake Areas,* which shows the profound friendship and feelings between the Chinese and American people.

Nowadays, things have changed a lot. The past ten years have witnessed a new rise from the broken ruins. The best way to remember and comfort the deceased is for the living to try to move on as expected. The tremendous pain caused by the disaster has already turned to be the tenacity and perseverance engraved in people's hearts, which always inspires them to keep their original intention and forge ahead. Now, the 150 students who were invited to study in the United States have stepped from young people with high spirits into a stable and quiet middle age, striving hard to work as the builders of their hometown and motherland.

Ten years of sedimentary accretion and ten years of memory with concern—the experience of studying in the United States that year have eased the pains and widened the horizons of the 150 students from the disaster-stricken areas. With knowledge, they have improved their abilities and enriched themselves. The brand-new learning and life styles under different cultural backgrounds have exerted a subtle and profound influence on their own development. The rich cultural soil of a foreign country and the sincere friendship accumulated between teachers and students have nourished the young people thousands of miles away from home, and quietly sowed the seeds of hope in their hearts. Thanks to the good edification and education while staying at the other side of ocean, the 150 students, taking the American trip as their common start, have made their own brilliant growth trajectories on their life scrolls. Now they are scattered in every corner of the world and engaged in all walks of life. Some of them have become managers of airlines because of their love with tourism; some have continued to plough deeply on the classroom platform delivering and planting the seeds of knowledge; some have silently explored the supremacy of literature as they succumbed to the charm of language... They have started their life journey from their experiences in the United States with full harvest, concentrated on their interests and hobbies, going forward step by step to their dreams.

Taking the dream as the direction and driving force and being worthy of youth in their posts and ordinary life, the 150 students have enjoyed the joys of life during the post-disaster reconstruction, and harvested good friendship and memories in the exchanges across cultural and regional barriers. Looking back, they have still stuck to themselves for the ten years. They have kept the most basic sincerity and calmness of life, plain but not ordinary. With their own strength, they have presented to more people the most primitive color and temperature of life.

In this book, we have collected the growth experiences of some of the students of the CSC-SUNY 150 Program, gazing at that group of witnesses who went to study in the United States with hopes and dreams years ago. I hope that this book will convey this cross-country friendship to readers and release the most genuine softness and kindness to the world, and that they will forge ahead as usual with their common goal of ten years, with their eternal love, and with their persistent hope.

# 语丝 /Quotes

### 成都理工大学 / 艾玲

理想是人生的太阳，当你没有借口的那一刻，就是你成功的开始。从成都理工大学到布法罗大学，我跨越两个国度，增长见识，拓宽眼界，认清了自己的专业需求。改变，从 2008 开始。

*Chengdu University of Technology/Ai Ling*

Dream is the sun of life, and you will get a successful start once you rid yourself of excuses. From CDUT to UB, I have crossed two different countries, enriching my knowledge, widening my horizon, and knowing better my professional needs. Change started from the year of 2008.

### 成都理工大学 / 代婷

及时当勉励，岁月不待人。转眼十年过去，水牛城的时光还历历在目，仿佛就在昨天，我们一行人背着行囊，辗转二十多个小时奔赴理想的彼岸。我始终坚信上帝总是偏爱努力和随时做好准备的孩子，善待他人，善待自己，尊重生命和自然。我依然是那个奋斗且幸运的女孩。

*Chengdu University of Technology/Dai Ting*

Even ten years later, the memory of my days in Buffalo is still vivid as if it were yesterday, when all the program members carried heavy luggage and traveled more than 24 hours to arrive in Buffalo. I firmly believe that God prefers diligent and prepared ones, and I will be good to others, be good to myself, and show respect to life and nature. Also I believe that my hard work will pay off.

### 成都理工大学 / 李欣

理想与现实之间，动机与行为之间，生活总是火热的。只有深入地了解一个国家，才能学习其优秀的地方。拓宽自己的视野，提升自己的创新能力，与不同文化背景的同学相处，克服困难，锻炼自己。留学过程中有三点最重要：独立的生活能力、坚强的毅力和乐观的心态。

*Chengdu University of Technology/Li Xin*

To study abroad is quite different from travelling and business trips. A comprehensive cultural experience would deepen one's cognition, innovate one's creativity, polish one's problem-solving capability and broaden one's vision. From my perspective, I have learnt three important capabilities from the one-year study abroad program: independence, perseverance and optimism.

### 成都理工大学 / 舒玉婵

十年离散人未惆，常思量，自难忘。

万里春藤，感恩系心上。

纵然奔忙应未联，年如轮，自感伤。

暇中思绪返时光，稚如黄，眸无旁。

相见如家，渊识怀万象。

愿得来日首再会，忆往昔，义流芳。

*Chengdu University of Technology/Shu Yuchan*

Ten-year separation would not weaken my thoughts
On the people and life experience in United States;
The gratitude in my heart is ten thousand mile long ivy,
Connecting the unforgettable past and prominent future;
I am looking forward to a reunion in the near future,
Sharing the joy of a lasting friendship.

### 成都理工大学 / 王映雪

怀着敬畏之心去奋斗，怀着感恩之心去善待。整整十年，时光如梭，容颜会变，唯有爱不变。十年前的项目改变的不仅仅是我的人生轨迹，更塑造了我的品格，让我学会了如何去爱人，爱生活，爱这片土地。

*Chengdu University of Technology/Wang Yingxue*

Struggle with awe and be good to others with gratitude. In the ten years, time went fast, and faces have changed, but love remained unchanged. This program ten years ago has not only changed my life trajectory, but also shaped my personality; it let me know how to love others, love life, and love this land.

### 成都理工大学 / 袁玥

时光飞逝，十年如一梦。梦里梦外，连接着我跨越两个国度的理想和追求。永远心怀感恩，永远在路上行进，独立自主，我心飞扬。

*Chengdu University of Technology/Yuan Yue*

Time does fly. The past ten-year life experience continuously motivates me to pursue my dream in both nations with gratitude, critical thinking and independent mentality.

### 电子科技大学 / 谈天

生活需要感恩的心来创造，感恩的心需要生活来滋养。十年弹指一挥间，这份经历带来的感动与感恩，必将影响我的一生。愿中美两国人民的友谊长存，愿我们有再次相聚的那一天。

*University of Electronic Science and Technology of China/Tan Tian*

Life needs to be created with a grateful heart, while a grateful heart needs to be nourished with life. Ten years has passed in an instant, but the affection and gratitude brought by this experience will definitely influence my whole life. I hope that the friendship between the Chinese and American people will last forever. May we meet again one day.

### 电子科技大学 / 孙辰

回首十年初心不改，展望未来继续前行。经历过往事种种的我，更懂得感恩生活的幸福。那些记忆深处舍不得忘记的美国好伙伴、好导师，梦回 2008 年，依然那么熟悉。

*University of Electronic Science and Technology of China/Sun Chen*

Ten years later, I still stay true to my aspiration, and I look forward to moving forward. After experiencing disasters, I am more grateful about the happiness of life.

Those good partners and good mentors from the recesses of my memory are still so familiar in my dream back to 2008.

### 电子科技大学 / 王磊

有多大的思想，就有多大的能量。人们常说经历过的事情总会潜移默化地影响你之后的生活，所以经历过美国的学习，我更喜欢让自己的思维发散，多角度地去分析问题和课程内容，思考更多，收获也就更多。

*University of Electronic Science and Technology of China/Wang Lei*

The energy expands as the thought goes. It is often said that one's experience will affect one's life hereafter. So after the stay in the United States, I prefer to radiate my thought, analyze the problem and course content from multiple angles. By doing so, I could think more and get more.

### 电子科技大学 / 易青颖

世上最快乐的事，莫过于为理想而奋斗。我想，人生的价值不需要金钱和地位来衡量。在每一个当下我都做了自己认为有意义的事情，对社会产生了一点点的益处，那便足矣。

*University of Electronic Science and Technology of China/Yi Qingying*

The happiest thing in the world is to fight for the ideal. I don't think that life can be weighed by money and status. At every moment, I do what I think is meaningful and beneficial to the society, and that is enough.

### 电子科技大学 / 杨永益

回首这些年的人生选择，受美国之行的影响，我从一个性格比较腼腆内向的大男孩变成了一个更渴望国际化视野的毕业生。"CSC-SUNY 150 奖学金项目"让我开启了一段不平凡的旅程，在这个过程中我获得了更多的经验和能力。我深知，回报这些感激的最好方式，就是在这片土地上创造更多的价值。

*University of Electronic Science and Technology of China/Yang Yongyi*

I can say that the life path of mine has been deeply influenced by the trip to the US. I grew up from an introverted and shy boy to a newbie graduate who was longing for an international view. I would like to thank CSC-SUNY 150 Program for providing me a chance to start a unique adventure, gaining tons of experiences and abilities. I truly believe that the best way to reward those helps and caring is to create my own value on this land.

## 电子科技大学 / 钟灏

山路曲折盘旋，但毕竟朝着顶峰延伸。接触了不同的文化，感受了不同的生活方式，我的视野开阔了，不愿再纠结于生活中一些鸡毛蒜皮的小事，生活中遇到难过的事也会快速调节自己的情绪。积极处世，是美国之行给我最大的馈赠。

*University of Electronic Science and Technology of China/Zhong Hao*

The mountain road twists and turns, but after all, it extends toward the top. Because I have contacted different cultures and experienced different lifestyles, my vision and pattern have been improved. Thus I have learned not to be entangled with trivial things in my life, and adjust my mood quickly when I come across something sad. Such kind of positive attitude toward life is the greatest reward to me by the trip to the United States.

## 电子科技大学 / 张锐

我不去想是否能够成功，既然选择了远方，便只管风雨兼程。十年回首，早已枝繁叶茂，所有的过往和心路历程，那些心中珍藏的人和事，早已成为我人生中不可或缺的一部分。

*University of Electronic Science and Technology of China/Zhang Rui*

I don't want to know if I am going to be successful or not. I will march forward regardless of any hardship since the destination is right there. Ten years witnessed the flourish of my life. But all the memories and experiences have been related to my special journey. Those people and experiences have become part of my life.

## 乐山师范学院 / 邓霞

鱼知水恩，乃幸福之源也。去了美国之后，我学会了从另一个角度看世界，我深刻地感受到独立思考的重要意义，只有自己亲自去尝试，才知道这个世界的精彩纷呈。

*Leshan Normal University/Deng Xia*

Being thankful makes a happy person. After I studied in the US, I have learnt to look at various ideas from different perspectives, from which I have understood the significance of independent thinking. At the same time, I have realized that if I want to do something, I must take actions immediately, do it in person and finally I can enjoy my life in such a wonderful world.

## 乐山师范学院 / 冯叶婷

生活充满着选择，而生活的态度就是一切。在美国的学习和生活，让我知道了独立的重要性，也让我明白认识自己有多么重要，而更重要的是要做一个有梦想的人。

*Leshan Normal University/Feng Yeting*

Life is like a box of chocolate and the attitude towards life matters. My life and study in the US enables me to understand the significance of independence as well as the importance of self-realization, most importantly, a person with a dream.

## 乐山师范学院 / 黄清华

别人只能给你指路，而不能帮你走路。自己的人生路，还需要自己走。每每回忆起那时走过的路、吹过的风，感动的热流仍在心间流淌。那些笑容在我的记忆里一如昨日，暖意融融。那年青春年少，那年岁月正好，那年我们的生命荡起涟漪。

*Leshan Normal University/Huang Qinghua*

Others can only show you the way but cannot substitute you to be the one on the road, because we play an independent leading role in our own life. Now, in retrospect of the roads we once walked along, the wind blowing in our face, I still felt pretty touched. All the smiles were in my mind, so fresh and warm to me. That year, we were quite young, the days in the US were so wonderful, and our life was so exciting.

## 乐山师范学院 / 何文

如果一个人不知道他要驶向何方，那么任何风都不是顺风。这些深藏在我记忆里的故事，帮助我塑造人生观、价值观，深深地影响了我此后的人生定位，成为我人生中最宝贵的财富。

***Leshan Normal University/He Wen***

If one has no goal, his or her way of life may be full of various obstacles. All of these stories buried in my mind have changed my philosophy and values influenced me on my later development, and will be precious fortune in my whole life.

## 四川大学 / 陈晨

我时常在想："CSC-SUNY 150 奖学金项目"到底给我们留下了什么？是更开放、自信的心态，是同情心、同理心、包容心，是辩证的世界观与人生观，是感恩的心，是爱。十年，又是一个新的开始。我们一直心存感恩，希望可以贡献更多。

***Sichuan University/Chen Chen***

I often wonder what the CSC-SUNY 150 Program has left for us. In my opinion, it gives us a grateful heart of love with more open and confident mentality, compassion, empathy, and tolerance, and a more dialectical view of the world and life as well. Ten years is another new beginning. We have always been grateful and hope to do more.

## 四川大学 / 姜藜藜

十年之前，我不认识你，你不属于我。十年之后，我们存在于彼此的生命里。当年在纽约遇见的人与事，不仅成为我学术兴趣的起点和原动力，更让我感受到生命中温柔的力量。这份温柔可能在外人看来微不足道，可是在我心里，她强大到足以击败自然的冷漠无情和文化语言的重重障碍。

***Sichuan University/Jiang Lili***

Ten years ago, I didn't know who you were, and you were not mine. And ten years later, we are part of each other's life. Those people and things that I had fortunately met in New York have not only become the origin and motivation of my academic interest, but made me feel the gentle power in life. The gentleness may seem to be trifle for others, while, in my mind, it's been strong enough to defeat the apathy of nature and all the obstacles of language and culture.

### 四川农业大学 / 何世鸣

人生中的每个"第一次"都意味着成长。2008 年的第一次留学经历，既是疗伤之旅，也是感恩之旅、梦想之旅。回望十年，有些情感永不褪色改变。

***Sichuan Agricultural University/He Shiming***

Every "first time" in my life symbolizes growth. The first time of studying abroad in 2008 had become a journey of healing, gratitude, and dream. Looking back to the past ten years, some of the emotions will never fade away.

### 四川农业大学 / 李锦

心怀感恩的人，将被命运赐予更多。无论贫富，走出国门，才会更加懂得和珍惜自己中国人的身份。当走出国门，用比较的眼光来观察中外文化，才能更清楚地看清中国文化的轮廓，保持热爱祖国、团结同胞的初心。

***Sichuan Agricultural University/Li Jin***

The one who is always thankful will be blessed by destiny. No matter how poor or rich you are, you'll truly recognize how important it is to cherish your identity as a Chinese once going abroad. When we go out with a high recognition of cultural identity, observing the differences between China and the rest of the world in a comparative perspective, we'll get a crystal clear picture of our own culture. Only with the excellent quality can we stay true to our original mind of patriotism and solidarity.

### 四川师范大学 / 陈韵旭

生命不息，奋斗不止，未来还有无限可能。2008 年的那个夏天，一次跨越两个国度的梦想之旅，把中国人民和美国人民的心连接在了一起。精彩不只过去的十年，也在未来的每一个十年。

***Sichuan Normal University/Chen Yunxu***

Cease to struggle and you cease to live. The future holds infinite possibilities. In the summer of 2008, a dream trip across two countries connected the hearts of all the Chinese people and American people. The past decade was full of excitements, and the future will also be so.

### 四川师范大学 / 杜畅

加倍努力，挑战冒险，生命将证明我想要的并非空中楼阁。青春不只是学业，也要抓紧机会让自己开阔眼界。非常感激在我人生最有活力与激情的 20 岁，能遇见一群同样出色的年轻人，在一个美不胜收的小镇，度过了一段丰富有趣的大学生活。

*Sichuan Normal University/Du Chang*

With the double efforts and endless challenge, I believe my dream will come true. I got to know that apart from the education we get from schools, there are always more things waiting for us to explore. I am grateful that in the height of my youth I had the opportunity to see the wider world and meet a group of excellent young people, and had the richest and the most interesting university life in a small foreign town.

### 四川师范大学 / 秦誉心

不渴望一跃千里，只希望每天更进一步，拥抱生活。我像爱丽丝一样一不小心掉进那个兔子洞，开始了一段奇幻冒险。沿途的风景时而美不胜收，时而光怪陆离，让我目不暇接，忘却伤痛，迎接崭新的人生。

*Sichuan Normal University/Qin Yuxin*

I don't believe that I could jump into success with one leap. I hope I am making progress and enjoy my life every day. I was dragged into a completely different world, just as Alice accidentally fell into that rabbit hole and started a fantastic adventure. The scenery along the way was so beautiful and sometimes even bizarre to my eye. I was busy digesting everything that leaped into my sight and the sorrow was taken off my mind for the time being.

### 四川师范大学 / 唐兴林

"CSC-SUNY 150 奖学金项目"是中美两国政府和社会各界爱心人士一起用心编织的一张网。把对我们 150 名学生的关怀和支持，在这张网上汇集成"爱"和"力量"，鼓励我们努力成长，迎接更为广阔的世界。

*Sichuan Normal University/Tang Xinglin*

The program, CSC-SUNY-China 150, is just like a web, diligently woven by the Chinese and American governments, as well as caring people from all walks of life. This is a web of "love" and "strength", to show their care and support us 150 students, encourage us to strive on and embrace a bigger world.

### 四川师范大学 / 文欢

回望 2008 年，这是一份抚慰，也是一份惊喜。这一年，改变了我的一生。一个十年已经过去，在接下来的十年里，希望我们"CSC-SUNY 150 奖学金项目"的每一个人，都朝着自己的目标努力奋斗！

*Sichuan Normal University/Wen Huan*

I take a look back at 2008, and feel that year was a comfort and a surprise because it has greatly changed my whole life. A decade has passed. I wish a brighter future for everyone in CSC-SUNY 150 Program in the next ten years.

### 四川师范大学 / 杨轲

时间如白驹过隙。眨眼间，如今的我已来到三十而立的人生路口。回首过去，距离 2009 年 5 月 25 日回国已经过去了 3 440 个日夜，点点滴滴仿若一场梦。美国之旅让我树立了一个人生准则：做一个乐观通透、积极向上的人。要对身处困难之中的人伸出援手，把这份属于"CSC-SUNY 150 奖学金项目"的精神财富不断传承下去。

*Xihua University/Yang Ke*

How time flies! With a blink of eyes, I am standing on the intersection of life at my age of 30. Looking backward, I have spent 3,440 days and nights since I came back to China on May 25th, 2009. All stories that happened there resemble a dream. This journey to USA helps us to establish a code of life in our mind: to be an optimistic, honest and active person. We need to lend our hands to people trapped in the difficulties and carry forward the spiritual legacy of the CSC-SUNY 150 Program.

### 四川师范大学 / 周涛

遂早有，蜀地多沃野，蜀人为乐民。沉吟间抚昔，仰首后望今：

庭中，桑叶桃枝沃若生；屋内，浅笑和语日日密。更有举国相倾来助，万人合力来援，物力齐聚，思心合一，幽幽别恨，已去大半。 蓬勃心志，暖如青阳之谷风，流连此间；盛如朱明之赤日，照临四方。别后有重聚，劫后生新息，清心得道，多难兴邦，人间至理矣。

*Xihua University/Zhou Tao*

Since the ancient time, Sichuan has enjoyed abundant lands and optimistic residents. Nowadays, in the yard, mulberry trees wear full green leaves and peach trees wear full fruits. In the house, there are always laughters and smiles. United as one, people from all walks of life in our country brought assistance and goods to help us rebuild hometown, so that we almost forgot the grief and sadness brought by the disaster. Those undoubtedly brought a vigorous energy to us as warm as the gentle wind and the warm sunshine. Since then, we have had a reunion after being parted and a rebirth from the disaster. A simple philosophy of the world is that a pure heart makes a just cause, and much distress regenerates a nation.

## 西华大学 / 陈玲

因为美好的感情，我们舍不得离别；因为纯真的友谊，我们更加懂得珍惜。时间很短，故事很长，感谢为整个项目付出的每一个人，正是有了你们的付出才有了温暖的 "CSC–SUNY 150 奖学金项目"。下一个十年，我们不忘初心，感恩前行！

*Xihua University/Chen Ling*

Because of good feelings, we were not willing to leave; because of true friendships, we knew how to cherish them. It is impossible to pour out the whole story within such short time. However, I would appreciate each and every one who has made contribution to this program. It was his or her efforts that made the "CSC-SUNY 150" come true. We need to keep our original intention to go further with thanks.

## 西华大学 / 王隆攀

从一名 21 岁的青涩大学生成长为 31 岁的成熟青年，十年前的那段时光仿佛已经离我很遥远，但有时又仿佛近在眼前。这趟美国之旅，让我认识到人类其实是社会性的群体，我们的个体成长也是

四海之纽

Taking the World as a
Link to Study in USA
川山直说

社会的一部分，"既然接受了这次宝贵的机会，那么就要勇于承担这份责任"。

*Xihuan University/Wang Longpan*

Time of 10 years ago seems to be far away from me, but sometimes, it lingers on in front of my eyes. And I have grown from a 21-year-old young university student into a 31-year-old mature young man. This American trip has made me realize that human beings are social groups, and any individual growth is just part of the society. "Since you took this precious chance, you must shoulder the responsibility. "

## 西南交通大学 / 蒋沥辉

岁月给了我很多，也让我成长了很多。生命是一段旅程，需要我们每个人用心体会，也需要我们学会自己去丈量。希望我们每个人都坚守内心的准则，用爱、用宽容、用包容去对待身边的所有人和事，也愿我们每个人都能被生活温柔以待。

*Southwest Jiaotong University/Jiang Lihui*

Time has given me a lot and made me grow up a lot. Life is a journey. It needs every one of us to experience it carefully. It also needs us to learn how to spend it. We hope that each of us will stick to our inner criteria and treat everyone and everything around us with love, forgiveness and tolerance. I also hope that each of us can be treated gently by life.

## 西南交通大学 / 吴丹

这十年，从一个家庭变成一个人，是长大；这十年，从一个人变成一个家庭，是成熟。在平平淡淡的生活中，收获一个纯良的自己、诚恳的自己、磊落的自己、热忱的自己。在平凡的生活里，笑出勃勃生机。

*Southwest Jiaotong University/Wu Dan*

Over the past ten years, I have grown up from being with my family to living independently; over the past ten years, I have become mature from a single person to having a family of my own. I hope that I can end up finding a kind, earnest, bright and passionate self and laughing out vigorously in my plain life.

### 西南交通大学 / 杨然

十年前，"CSC–SUNY 150 奖学金项目"是我们梦开始的地方。这十年中，我们都在为梦想积蓄能量，在十年后或者不久的将来，我希望"CSC–SUNY 150 奖学金项目"可以一起实现梦想，不忘初心，不负众望，回报社会，让这个世界更美好。

#### *Southwest Jiaotong University/Yang Ran*

Ten years ago, "CSC-SUNY 150" was the place where our dreams began. In the past ten years, we have been preparing for our dreams. After a decade or in the near future, I hope that students in this program can realize our dreams, and never forget our original intention, always meet expectations, repay the society, and make the world a better place.

### 西南交通大学 / 郑渝鹏

十年之后，再回首，"150"之行并未止于2009年的那个毕业典礼。在这十年之中，那些温暖和爱如同种子一样慢慢破土，滋养着我们，鼓舞着我们，将我们凝聚在一起，把这些温暖和爱播撒开来，相信下一个十年，这些爱和温暖将会孕育出更多的种子。我们静待花开。

#### *Southwest Jiaotong University/Zheng Yupeng*

Ten years later, when I reminisced, I realized the travel to US didn't end with the commencement in 2009. During the ten years the warmth and love have been nourishing us, encouraging us and holding us together. And with the warmth and love spreading, we believe in the next ten years those love and warmth will bear more seeds. What we need to do is just wait for the flowers to bloom.

### 西南科技大学 / 陈冰

当年的经历，就像电影片段历历在目。人生能有几个十年，时间似乎过得很快，但却又好慢。未来的路还很长，希望在未来的十年、二十年，甚至更漫长的时光里，我能在越来越成熟的同时不忘初心，在某个领域发光发热，将爱的精神传续下去。

#### *Southwest University of Science and Technology/Chen Bing*

When reminiscing, that experience is like movie clips. Life can have a few decades, and time seems to pass quickly, but it is also very slow. There is still a long way to go. I hope I can become more and more mature in the next decade, two decades and even longer. At the same time, I will never forget my original intention and I hope I can make a difference in a certain field and carry on the spirit of love.

### 西南科技大学 / 丁勇

总结过去的十年，是最初留学期间培养起来的兴趣、毅力和眼界改变了我的人生轨迹，也是这些力量让我在曲折的路程中始终朝着一个方向不懈前进。过去的十年记忆以"CSC-SUNY 150 奖学金项目"开始，它的美好和珍贵永远不会结束。回忆往昔，我无比感恩遇见的老师和同学，他们是这份美好记忆中不可或缺的一部分，坚持信念，砥砺前行，我将一如既往，搏击海浪。

*Southwest University of Science and Technology/Ding Yong*

To sum up the past ten years, it is the interest, perseverance and horizon cultivated during the initial study abroad that have changed my life track, and it is also these forces that have made me make unremitting progress in one direction throughout the tortuous journey. The memory of past decade starts from the CSC-SUNY 150 Program, and its beauty and preciousness will never end. Recalling the past, I am extremely grateful to the teachers and classmates I met. They are an integral part of this beautiful memory. Holding on to faith and moving forward, I will continue to fight against waves.

### 西南科技大学 / 马洁好

"CSC-SUNY 150 奖学金项目"带给了我太多成长的经验，让我学着去尊重和理解人与人、文化与文化的不同。美国的老师和同学给予我无私的帮助和真挚的友谊，这些美好与感动至今温暖着我，让我一直心怀感恩与善念，也激励着我，让我更自信、更勇敢地去拥抱生活，热爱这个奇妙的世界。

*Southwest University of Science and Technology/Ma Jiehao*

The rapid growth brought by the CSC-SUNY 150 Program is hard to describe in words. I learned to respect and understand the differences between people and cultures. The students and teachers from SUNY also gave me unselfish help and sincere friendship, which still move me and warm me, making me always be grateful and full of good thoughts, and inspiring me to be more confident to embrace life and love this wonderful world.

### 西南科技大学 / 杨颖

这个十年已经完结，下一个十年即将开始。下一个十年，我希望成为一个更好的妻子、女儿，为我的丈夫和父母带来幸福，也希望能成为一个合格的妈妈，用自己的实际行动让孩子为我感到骄傲。更重要的是继续探索、挖掘从"CSC-SUNY 150 奖学金项目"学到的一切，成为一个更好的自己。

*Southwest University of Science and Technology/Yang Ying*

This decade is over and the next decade is about to begin. In the next decade, I hope to be a better wife and daughter, bringing happiness to my husband and parents. I also hope that I can become a qualified mother and make my child proud of me. More importantly, I should continue to explore what we learned from the CSC-SUNY 150 Program, and become a better self.

### 西南科技大学 / 余海意

不懂感恩，就不懂真正的美德。对于"CSC-SUNY 150 奖学金项目"的感谢，千言万语道不尽。这一路走来，要感谢的人太多了，许多人都在我生命中的重要节点教会我很多，帮助我很多。我将不忘初心，一路前行。

*Southwest University of Science and Technology/Yu Haiyi*

One who is not grateful does not know what true virtue is. Along the way, there are so many people who have taught me a lot and helped me a lot at the important points in my life. My gratitude for CSC-SUNY 150 Program is beyond my words. I will keep making progress along the way without forgetting the original intention.

### 西南科技大学 / 张维维

生活不能停留在过去，人的一生很长，会遇到各种各样的挫折和磨难，我们不能让自己沉浸在过去的伤痛中停滞不前。我接受了别人真诚的帮助，学会了感恩，也将继续怀着一颗虔诚的心，帮助需要帮助的人。

*Southwest University of Science and Technology/Zhang Weiwei*

We cannot always stay in the past. In the long lifetime we would encounter many types of setbacks and tribulations. We can't stick in the past pain. Having got a lot of help from others, I learned to be grateful and I am also ready to help others when they are in need.

## 西南石油大学 / 张绵

这是一份超越了国界、种族和宗教信仰的爱，这种大爱、博爱让我们更加相信，世界和平是永恒的主题。作为"CSC-SUNY 150 奖学金项目"的参与者，我们荣幸地跨出了一步，用自己的勤奋、才华、包容和友谊，赢得了尊重和喝彩，也让更多的美国朋友开始真正了解中国、关注中国，星星之火，可以燎原，期待未来。

*Southwest Petroleum University/Zhang Mian*

We have brought back love from the kind American people. This love is boundaryless in terms of countries, races and religions, which makes us strongly believe that peace is an eternal theme of the world. As one of members of the CSC-SUNY 150 Program, I won respects by my hard working, talents, inclusiveness and friendship and helped more American friends to learn about a real China and understand China. As the Chinese saying goes, a little fire can kindle the forest. I hope that our members of the program can continue to work out a more glorious story in our own field.

## 奥尔巴尼分校 / 陈凡平

看到现在你们依然快乐和美丽，我很高兴。作为现任系主任，我谨代表东亚研究系祝福你们永远快乐和成功！

*Albany/Professor Chen Fan Pen , Ph.D.*

It's good to see you so pretty and happy still. As the current Chair of the Department, I would like to represent the Department of East Asian Studies in wishing you continued happiness and success in whatever you do!

## 法明戴尔分校 / 丹尼·阿尔切里

什么是重中之重？世界和平！无他。我们在一起就可以拯救世界，这绝不是夸大其词。

*Farmingdale State College/Danny Arcieri*

What's at stake here? World peace! Nothing less. And I do not think I am exaggerating when I say together we may have saved the world.

### 法明戴尔分校 / 凯西·科利

他们尊重他人、与人合作、热爱生活，这些表现都让人赞赏。尽管在地震中遭到不幸，损失惨重，但他们依然乐观。

*Farmingdale State College/Kathy Coley*

Their respect for others, ability to work cooperatively and their love for life was inspiring. In spite of the tragedy of the earthquake and the enormous losses, they were resilient and optimistic.

### 詹姆斯敦社区学院 / 纳尔逊·加里菲

他们使我们认识到，世界各地的人们有许多共同之处，包括希望、恐惧和价值观，但其中最重要的是在全球化社会中，善待彼此，将对方视为同胞的愿望。

*Jamestown Community College/Nelson J. Garifi, Jr.*

They helped us understand that people from all over the world share so much in common including hopes, fears, and values—but most of all the desire to be kind and see each other as fellow citizens in a global society.

### 奥斯威戈分校 / 箫

十年是一段不长也不短的日子，很高兴大家都过得平安。你们现在是社会成长的动力，加油！

*Oswego/Xiao*

Ten years neither too long nor too short. I'm glad that everyone lived safe and sound. Now you are the impetus for the improvement of society. Go for it!

### 奥斯威戈分校 / 玛丽·安·霍根和安迪·纳尔逊

看到他们在杰克的植物企业所表现出的对自然的专注，看到他们为追求更高的学历所表现出的对教育的专注，看到他们为自己及孩子营造充满爱的环境所表现出的对家庭的专注，我们为这些年轻人的不断进取而感动。

**SUNY Oswego/ Anne Hogan and Andy Nelson**

We are impressed with the ways these young people have moved their lives forward by focusing on nature as in Jack's botanical enterprise and education as they pursue higher graduate studies and family as they create a loving environment for themselves and their children.

# 目录
Contents

## 电子科技大学

## 四川农业大学
Sichuan Agricultural University

## 四川师范大学
Sichuan Normal University

四海之纽
Taking the World as a
Link to Study in USA 川山首纽

成都理工
大学

Chengdu University of Technology

# 人生第三个十年，因你而精彩

## My Third Decade Fantastic Life Because of You

艾玲 / 成都理工大学　纽约州立大学布法罗分校 [1]

Ai Ling / Chengdu University of Technology　SUNY at Buffalo

2008 年 6 月的一天，"5·12"汶川特大地震后一个月，成都理工大学材料学院的党支部书记肖老师打来电话，简单地跟我说了"CSC-SUNY 150 奖学金项目"的情况，表明学院计划推荐我去参加校内的面试，话未说完，电话断了，也许是震后通信信号不稳定的原因。

挂了电话之后，我蹲在一堆土砖上，望着周围的泥土、破砖瓦、朽木，生锈变形的锅碗瓢盆，还有被雨水泡烂后发臭的衣物，那一刻我心里空落落的，双脚像被混凝土黏在土砖上一样，无法挪动。

Ten years ago, one day in June 2008, about a month after the quake, Ms. Xiao, party branch secretary of College of Materials of Chengdu University of Technology (CDUT), gave me a call and simply illustrated the situation of the CSC-SUNY 150 Program. She told me that the college had planned to recommend me to take part in the first interview. Words were not finished before the phone was disconnected. Maybe it was because the communication signals were unstable after the quake.

After I hung up the phone, I squatted on a pile of earthen bricks and looked around, only to find nothing but dirt, broken tiles, rotten wood, rusted and deformed pots and pans, and smelly clothes soaked in rainwater.

At that moment, my heart went blank, and my feet could not move as if they were glued to

---

1　纽约州立大学布法罗分校（SUNY at Buffalo，简称 UB），也被称为纽约州立大学水牛城大学。

这时，妈妈拖着一辆装满建材渣的小推车在我面前停了下来，擦了擦汗，说道："发什么呆，别蹲太久，灰尘这么大，去帐篷里找一把铁铲来。"

我突然清醒过来："妈，学院给我打电话，说是有个机会可以出国交流一年，让我回学校参加面试。"

那天一家人一边忙着收拾只剩下围墙墙根的院子，一边催促我赶快去学校了解情况，抓住这次难得的机会。走时妈妈也不忘安慰我，让我放心去，家里没有大问题。

接下来的一个月，我忙于面试、准备材料、出行前培训。临近离开，也未能跟家人好好道别。还未来得及做好充分的心理准备，我便踏上了飞往纽约的飞机，不知道接下来会度过怎样的一年。

说实话，那是我人生第一次坐飞机出国，看着飞机慢慢滑过太平洋上

the adobe when my mother pulled a small cart, which was loaded with construction debris and stopped in front of me. She wiped away the sweat and said, "What are you thinking about? Don't squat too long for it's so dusty. Go to the tent and find a shovel out..."

Before she finished her words, I came around suddenly. "Mom, the college told me that there is an opportunity to go abroad to study for a year if I can pass the interview."

That day, I only remembered that the family was busy managing the yard course, which only had the corner of the wall left. They urged me to go to school to figure out the situation and seize this rare opportunity. When I was leaving, my mother did not forget to comfort me that there was nothing difficult at home, I could go without hesitation.

In the following month, I was busy with my interview, preparing materials for going abroad, and taking training class before departure. I even failed to bid farewell with my family with the departure day approaching, nor to be well-prepared for the upcoming year abroad before I boarded on the plane for New York City.

To be honest, that was the first time in my life to go abroad by plane. When I saw the plane

空，一片未知的土地，一座未知的城，一群未知的人，在等着我们，伴着强烈的耳鸣，我睡着了。

### 布法罗的家，别样的温暖长存

我在美国一年留学生涯中给我印象最深的非"Capen 411"莫属。"Capen 411"是布法罗大学国际学生管理办公室，里面坐着的都是一群可爱可亲的人，包括乔、马维斯、史蒂文、雷蒙和埃伦。

乔在我们眼中是一位典型的商务型男士，每次见到他都精神抖擞、精力充沛，工作节奏如同他的步伐一般，稳健而轻快。但处理我们的问题，他总会放慢脚步，时常让我们去他的办公室聊聊最近学业和生活上的事情，像父母一样关心我们的课程学习情况，有空就驱车带我们去逛中国超市，购买家乡味道以解我们的思乡之苦。

马维斯是办公室的财务，每月准时给我们发放生活补贴，总是嘱咐我们出门注意安全，少带现金。她是三个孩子的母亲，与我们聊天时，总能透出母亲对子女的关爱。她时常驱车带着我们出去游玩，车内播放着轻快的音乐，像母亲带着自己孩子出行一般，哼着音乐扭动着身体，让我们在紧张的学习后放松身心，享受生活。

glide over the Pacific Ocean slowly, I knew that an unknown land, an unknown city, and a group of unknown people were waiting for us. With a strong sense of tinnitus, I drifted off to sleep.

### My Lovely Home of Different Style at Buffalo

If you ask me to name a person or a thing that impressed me the most when I was studying in the US, it must be Capen 411 without second thought. Capen 411, the international students' management office of SUNY at Buffalo State University (UB), was filled with a bevy of lovable people including Joe, Marvis, Stephen, Ramon and Ellen.

Joe was a typical business man in our eyes. Every time we saw him, he was full of energy and vigor. The pace of work was as steady and brisk as his pace. But when dealing with everything about us, he would slow down, and let us go to his office to talk about the entire recent academic and life matters. He cared about our study as much as our parents did. When he was free, he would drive us to the Chinese supermarket to relieve our homesickness by purchasing the food with our hometown flavor.

Marvis was the financial accountant of the office. She granted the monthly living allowance to us in a timely way, and always told us to be

史蒂文是一位慈祥和蔼的老爷爷，每次见面都给我们大大的拥抱，也会像邻家老爷爷一般带我们到他家后院一起打理草坪，除草浇水。

雷蒙与上面三位相比，要年轻许多，跟我们年龄相仿，我们大多只会跟他说一些我们这个年龄段的玩笑话，他也会跟我们分享在布法罗的生活经验，算是一位没有距离感的大哥哥。

埃伦的办公室不在"Capen 411"，跟我们见面的机会不多，但也在默默帮助和关心我们，偶尔也会抽出时间带我们逛博物馆，或去附近公园散心。

这么介绍下来，不难发现，布法罗大学国际学生管理办公室已然成了我们在布法罗的家，有家的地方温暖长存。每逢过节，他们都会为我们举办聚会。最难忘的要数那年冬天的春节，他们找了一家温暖的中餐厅，

careful when going outside and not to bring too much cash. As a mother of three children, she liked chatting with us, always bringing us a feeling of motherly care. She often drove us out, playing lively music in the car, humming tunes and shaking her body. It was almost a trip between mother and her children, which relaxed us a lot especially after the intense study.

Stephen, a kind grandpa, always gave us a big hug every time he met us. He also took us to his backyard to do the lawn care together such as weeding and watering.

Ramon was much younger than the previous three people. He was about our age, so we could tell peer jokes to him. He also shared his experience in Buffalo with us. A brotherly friend he was.

Ellen's workplace was not in Capen 411, so we couldn't see her very often. However, we received many helps and much care from her. She would, sometimes, take us to museums and nearby parks to relax too.

With the introduction, it wouldn't be difficult to find that the office of international student management at UB had become our home, our sweet and warm home. They always

我们"一家人"围坐在大圆桌旁，就像过年在家一样，举杯畅饮，欢歌笑语。这样精心营造的节日气氛，让我们格外感动，特别是席间还收到了他们准备的红包，让我们觉得这样细致周到的节日小惊喜带给我们的不只是温暖，还有他们对我们满满的关爱。

## 追求所想　勇敢付诸行动

刚开始我们 150 位学生根据专业背景被分到纽约州立大学（SUNY）的各个分校，我和同校的代婷、西南交通大学的杨然、四川大学的阮田园一起被分到了工科实力很强的布法罗分校。布法罗，又称水牛城，是美国纽约州西部伊利湖东岸的港口城市，也是纽约州第二大城市。

初到布法罗，下飞机见到乔、雷蒙和一名女学生，他们帮我们拎着行李，一路从机场开车到我们入住的布法罗分校南校区的"Good Year"公寓。相比纽约，布法罗人很少，建筑也相对稀疏，但天气非常好，大片大片的草坪和蔚蓝色的天空让我对这座城市有了最初的好感。

后来在乔和雷蒙的帮助下，我们顺利选择了自己的专业课程和选修课程。带着激动的心情，我们第一次踏进一间一半是美国当地人、一半是来

held parties for us on every festival. The most unforgettable memory for us must be the Spring Festival in that winter. They found a Chinese restaurant full of warmth, and we, like the "family members", were sitting around the big table, toasting and laughing just like every family gathering in spring festivals. In such an elaborated festive atmosphere, we were moved deeply, especially when we received the red envelopes they'd prepared. These exquisite and thoughtful gifts did surprise us, and what's more, we were touched not only by the warmth but also by great care from these people.

### Putting My Desire into Action

At the beginning, the 150 students of us were distributed to various campus of SUNY according to our specific majors. I went to UB, with my schoolmate Dai Ting, Yang Ran from Southwest Jiaotong University and Ruan Tianyuan from Sichuan University. Buffalo, also known as City of Buffalo, is a port city on the eastern shore of Lake Erie in western New York State. It is the second largest city in the state.

When I first arrived in Buffalo, I got off the plane and meet Joe, Ramon and a female student. They helped us to carry our luggage and drove from the airport to Good Year Apartment in the southern campus of UB. Compared to New York City, Buffalo was relatively sparsely populated and built, and the weather was excellent. Large lawns and azure skies initially impressed me well of this city.

Later, with the help of Joe and Ramon, we successfully selected our major courses and favored elective courses. With excitement, I stepped into a classroom for the first time, where

自世界各地的学生的教室，找了一个不起眼的角落坐下来，心里忐忑不安。果然不出大家所料，前阶段的课程我们根本听不懂，完全跟不上。一下从母语完全切换到全英文的专业授课对我这种从小到大接受母语教育的人来说实在太勉强了。

因为跟不上教授的节奏，我越来越不自信了，以前对专业知识的浓厚兴趣慢慢减退。但这样下去也不是办法，我想到了场外求助。后来去乔的办公室聊了很久，他给了我很多有用的建议，我也在课后鼓起勇气去找授课老师说明自己的困难。让我意外的是，授课老师不仅没有嫌弃我语言没过关还选择这样难度的课程，反而鼓励我以后上课尽量坐前排，不懂的地方一定及时找他讨论，还让我以后上课前务必预习当堂课程的所有内容，这样就能有针对性地找出不懂的地方。

一段时间后，在不断加强专业词汇学习的同时，坚持每周练习数小时的口语后，我发现自己又重拾信心，开始主动找授课老师讨论问题，与同学组队完成课业项目调研报告。一学期下来，总算顺利完成了学分绩点，到第二学期，课程学习就轻松了许多。一年的学习过程中，我经历了从听不懂课程到主动找到问题的状态转

half of the students were Americans whereas the other half were international students like me from all over the world. I found a humble corner and sat down with worries. As expected, I could not understand the previous course, nor keep up with the pace at all. The sudden switch from our mother tongue to an all-English environment was beyond the reach for us who grew up in a full native-language education setting.

I became less confident as I couldn't catch up with the professor. My previous keen interest in my major knowledge was gradually diminishing. However, it was not a way to go. I thought of getting some help. Then I chatted with Joe in his office for a long time. He gave me a lot of useful advice. I got up the courage to talk to the professor about my difficulties after class. What surprised me a lot was that he didn't blame me on my poor language competence to this difficult course, but instead encouraged me to sit in front of the class and asked me to discuss with him on the problems that I didn't quite understand. I was also suggested to preview the course content in advance so that I could find my particular problems.

After a period of time, with constant study of the terminology and weekly practice of oral English with my English partner, I found that I regained confidence. I began to discuss problems with my professor actively and complete the project research report with my classmates. After a semester, I finally succeeded in accomplishing the credit grade points. In the second semester, course learning turned to be much easier for me. During the one-year study, I experienced the transition from being unable to understand the course to actively finding problems, and this change has assured me that persistence makes

变。我确信很多事情坚持下去就会有收获，勇敢自信地跨出第一步，就会让自己获得源源不断的惊喜与收获。这样的经历让后来回国后的我确信，我的人生应当有所改变，追求自己所想，并勇敢地付诸行动。

那年冬天，我们应邀赴美国首都华盛顿哥伦比亚特区度过了难忘的几天。在为期一周的领导力项目培训中，我们见到自纽约一别半年未见的其他"CSC-SUNY 150奖学金项目"的小伙伴。大家变得开朗健谈了许多，脸上的疑惑和迷茫也减少了许多。我们在一间会议室里交流这半年来的学习生活经历，也针对这次培训内容各抒己见。那时我才真切感觉到半年时间里我们收获了很多，包括美国大学的课堂文化、校园文化以及社会文化。我们的改变小到对人对事的见解，大到对自己的人生规划，都受到周围事物潜移默化的影响。这或许正是我们人生轨迹慢慢开始发生改变的时刻。

## 坚持在科研的道路上走下去

从纽约州立大学布法罗分校回国以后，我被顺利推免进入中国科学院继续深造，开始了我的研究生新生活。在2010年至2015年读博期间，我曾在研究生课题研究工作中遇到不少困

harvests. In many cases, if one can be brave and confident enough to take the first step, endless surprises and gains will be generated. After returning back to China, these experiences have convinced me that I should change my life, pursuing what I aspire, and acting boldly.

In the winter of that year, we were invited to visit Washington, D.C. for a few days, which I will never forget. During the one-week Leadership training program, we met the other participants of the CSC-SUNY 150 Program we had not seen for half a year since leaving New York City. We became more outgoing and talked a lot while the confusion on our faces decreased. We sat in a conference room, talking to each other about study and life experiences in the past 6 months, expressing opinions of this training program. I truly realized that we had gained a lot in better understanding American universities, their classroom culture, campus culture and American social culture. Our changes varied from views about different people and things to our life planning, which were influenced by the surroundings in an unconscious way. It was probably the time when our life path began to change.

### Stick to Scientific Research

After returning from UB, I successfully entered the Chinese Academy of Sciences with exemption of examination for further study and began my new life as a graduate student. From 2010 to 2015, I encountered a lot of difficulties in the research work of graduate students as a candidate for doctor. The experimental progress and the pressure of publishing papers often made

难，实验进度和论文的压力时常让我喘不过气来。多少个黎明我站在实验室门口迎来清晨的第一缕阳光后，又转头埋进实验室。我曾多次气馁，多次想过放弃。但每次一想到留美那年那个坚持和勇敢的我，我便告诉自己困难总会过去的，再坚持一下，终会看到希望的曙光。

后来，在这种精神食粮的慰藉下，我如期毕业，并获得了当年的优秀三好学生是称号。博士毕业，我如同重获新生，外壳更坚硬了，抗压能力也更强了。考虑到专业需求，我继续留在宁波材料技术与工程研究所（简称宁波材料所）从事博士后研究工作。宁波材料所于2004年建所，是中科院为数不多的新所之一，科研平台完善，实力雄厚，科研氛围浓厚，对于像我这样的青年科研人员来说，这个发展平台有很大的竞争优势。我从2010年来所读书以来，见证了其快速的成长，这也是我选择继续留下来深造的原因之一。

2017年年底，我在职称晋升答辩中，获得了研究所领导的认可，顺利晋升为副研究员。一路走来，虽然磕磕绊绊，倒也还算顺利。目前的科研工作以基础研究为主，日常工作主要包括项目申请、课题实验开展、文献阅读、文章撰写及专利申请。此外，在与相

me breathless. I stood at the door of the laboratory in many dawns, being greeted with the first light of the day, and then turned back to and buried myself in the laboratory. I was discouraged and thought of giving up many times. But every time when I recalled the persistence and bravery of mine in the US, I told myself that the difficulties would finally pass.

With all this spiritual comfort, I successfully graduated in time as an Outstanding Merit Student of that year. After graduation, I was just like a whole new person with harder shell and bigger pressure resistance. In consideration of the professional requirements, I continued to work as a postdoc in Ningbo Institute of Materials Technology and Engineering, one of the a few new institutes under the Chinese Academy of Sciences, with complete scientific research platforms and great research competency and favorable environment for scientific research. For young scientific researchers like me, the development platform has excellent competitive advantages. I have witnessed its rapid growth since I came here for study in 2010, which has been one of the reasons why I chose to stay for further study.

Fortunately, at the end of 2017, I got the

关企业的合作过程中，我也会了解企业的技术需求，并提供一定的技术支持。相信在不久的将来，我会更好地发挥自己在团队中的作用，找准定位，制订适合的目标，在科研这条道路上坚持下去。

## 认清专业需求，不能盲目出国

在我近十年的学习和工作生活中，我遇到了很多来自世界各地的国际留学生，常常从他们身上看到我当年的影子，也更能理解在异国他乡的他们需要怎样的关心和帮助。我和我们的"Capen 411"大家庭至今仍然保持邮件往来。乔时常会来中国出差，有机会就跟我们见面，聊聊彼此近期的发展和状况。

关于赴国外留学，我认为取决于个人的专业需求。对科研人员来说，最忌讳闭门造车，而是要实时了解前沿科研动态，所以必须参加各类国际学术会议，与国内外专家交流学习，这样才能让自己的专业有所突破和提升。随着我国科研水平的迅速提升，出国留学已不再是唯一的选择，在国内我们也有具有世界先进水平的设备和科研平台，我们也有一流的科研人才和技术人才，很多非常棒的团队为社会技术的进步做出了巨大贡献。我

approval by the leaders of the institute in the defense of professional title promotion and became an associate researcher. The journey has been bumpy all the way through, but I finally have survived. At the moment, the scientific research work is mainly based on basic research, and my daily work includes project application, project experiment development, literature reading, paper writing and patent application. In addition, in the cooperation with relevant enterprises, I will get to know the technical requirements of the enterprises and provide certain technical support. I believe that in the near future, I will give a better play to my position in the team, position myself properly, set good goals and stick to the road of scientific research.

### Go Abroad Based on Professional Needs

I have met many international students from all over the world in the past ten years both in the academic field and in daily life. Most often I could see my reflection in them. It would be easier for me to understand their needs as foreigners in this strange country. The Capen 411 family and I are still keeping in touch via email. Joe often comes to China for business trips. He will meet with us if he gets a chance and we all like to talk about what we're doing.

As for studying abroad, I think it depends on special requirements for different majors. As far as the nature of scientific researchers' work is concerned, it is taboo to work behind closed doors and never go out. It is necessary to know the latest scientific trends in real time. Therefore, we have to attend various international academic conferences, exchanging with both domestic and

们鼓励有需要的师弟师妹出国增长见识、开阔眼界，但一定要认清自己的专业需求，不能盲目出国，还要制订明确的学业目标和计划，这样出国才能学有所成。

最后，感谢当年为"CSC-SUNY 150奖学金项目"付出过的所有老师和工作人员，愿自己不辜负大家的信任。

foreign experts so as to make breakthroughs in our special areas. With the rapid rise of China's scientific research level, studying abroad hasn't been the only choice. In China, we have advanced world-class equipment and scientific research platforms, and top scientific research talents and technology talents. Many excellent teams are also making great contributions to the progress of society and technology. We encourage the students with academic need to go abroad to increase knowledge and broaden their horizons. But the premise is that they must recognize their professional needs; never make random decisions to go abroad. They're supposed to formulate clear academic goals and plans, so that they can be successful in studying abroad.

Last but not least, I would like to thank all the teachers and working staff who have contributed for the CSC-SUNY Program. I wish to live up to your trust in me.

# 十年后，仍在奋进的水牛城大学学生

## The Striving Forward UB Student during 2008-2018

代婷／成都理工大学　纽约州立大学布法罗分校

Dai Ting / Chengdu University of Technology　SUNY at Buffalo

2008 年，突如其来的"5·12"汶川特大地震无情地就摧毁了我美丽的家乡——彭州，可是并没有摧毁我们四川人克服困难的决心和斗志，我们怀着感恩的心继续努力生活。

正是在这一年，我的命运也悄悄地发生了改变。盛夏时节，我接到了当时就读的成都理工大学老师的电话，知道了学校推荐我参与"CSC-SUNY 150 奖学金项目"，该项目旨在帮助 150 名来自地震重灾区的大学生到美国纽约州立大学学习和生活一年。

经过层层选拔，很幸运，我成了这150 名学生中的一员。很快，同年 8 月，我第一次踏上了大洋彼岸的土地——纽约。

在这里，我看到了曾经在电影、电

The 2008 Sichuan Earthquake ruthlessly destroyed my beloved hometown—Pengzhou. However, the determination of the people in Sichuan in overcoming the disaster was not harmed at all, who restored their lives with efforts and gratitude.

2008 was also a life-changing year for me. I was informed by a faculty of Chengdu University of Technology through a phone call that I was recommended by the university to participate into the CSC-SUNY 150 Program. This program aimed to endorse 150 college students to study abroad in the United States for a year, whose hometowns were severely stricken by earthquake.

After a series of interviews and selections, I honorably became one of the one hundred and fifty. In August 2008, I set my feet on the ground of the other side of the Pacific Ocean— New York City.

视里出现的时代广场、帝国大厦、自由女神像……还有我最爱的纽约州立大学布法罗分校。纽约州立大学有6个分校，纽约州立大学布法罗分校是其中一所综合性很强的分校。当它真切地出现在我的面前时，我对这片土地充满了期待。

这个完全陌生的城市里的一切，对我来说都是新鲜的。我好奇这里的一草一木，好奇每个面带微笑、长着和我不一样面孔的人们。繁华喧闹的街头，拥挤的地铁，步履匆忙的上班族，数不清的摩天大楼，看不尽的车水马龙……在这个包容的城市，我知道属于我自己的纽约故事即将上演。

## 点滴变化都值得珍藏

2008年，我收获了很多。到了美国，我的口语提升了，眼界也开阔了不少，还结交了很多朋友、同学和老师，我的人生路突然宽了不少，我明白，可以用我自己的努力做一些改变。

那一年遇到了很多人、很多事，每一点一滴都值得回味。让我至今都感到遗憾的是，几年前电脑硬盘坏掉，那些珍贵的照片全都消失了，让我心疼了好久。那段日子里，每一个人、每一件事都是特别的。

来到美国，我首先要面对的挑战就是语言，以前我一直自认为英语还可以，

Times Square, the Empire State Building and Statue of Liberty were used to being scenes in movies and TV programs for me. But now, I watched them all with my own eyes. The University of Buffalo is definitely my favorite place in the United States. The SUNY system has six comprehensive universities and UB is one of the most comprehensive ones. Therefore, the first day of my arrival in UB filled me with so much hope and expectation.

In this exotic foreign city, the bustling and busy streets, crowded subways, hasty commuters, countless skyscrapers and constant rush of traffic and almost everything can easily arouse my curiosity. In the City that Never Sleeps, I started my life and study.

### Every Bit of Change is Worth Cherishing

In the year of 2008, I made great progress in my conversational English, and my vision was greatly broadened and acquainted with quite a few of faculty and friends. With persistency and motivation, I clearly knew that I could expand my horizon and make a change.

During my stay in UB, every day was special and unique; every clip of memory was worth to cherish. But unfortunately, the biggest upset of mine in recent years has been a hard disk drive failure, which crashed all my files and photos in UB.

Upon my arrival in the United States, language became my most significant educational barrier. I used to have mal-

但是到了美国，才明白实际运用与应试完全是两回事。在学习中，自己完全听不懂心理学老师的课，因为他有很重的口音，我的辅导老师约瑟夫就建议我在课堂上录音，课后再反复听，这个方法虽然稍显笨拙，但却十分有效。习惯了老师的发音后，上课便没有了障碍，在小论文中居然还得了高分。在会计课的学习中，因为是大课，很多专业的英语词汇和知识点自己完全没有接触过，一堂课下来很多都没弄清楚。这门课的教授和她的助教都很和善，课后主动问我有没有问题，耐心地解答我的疑问。

那一年很多人问我美国和中国有什么不同。我想，在大学时光里，国内我们不存在语言和文化背景的差异，所以能和同学、老师无障碍地沟通，学习起来基本没有太大的压力，平时老师和同学的关系也走得比较近，有助于沟通和互相了解。课程设计和课堂风格，国内课堂相对传统，但老师们都很负责。而美国的大学是典型的宽进严出，学生必须有很强的自律性和学习主动性才能有效地完成学习任务。同时学校注重沟通、团队合作、表达，虽然本科课程设置内容没有国内复杂，但是对学生的要求要高很多。这也是我面临的最大挑战，我也很珍惜这点滴的变化，这对我今后的人生也起到了很多积极的影响。

在生活中，也有很多令我难忘的事。

confidence in my language capability. My study experience in UB proved that I had an incorrect language study motivation-learning for examination but not for application. I had a hard time in the class of Psychology, for the professor of the class talked with a heavy accent. My academic advisor Joseph suggested that I could record in class and take the script as a perfect material for listening comprehension after class. It was a clumsy but effective methodology of language study. The outcome was quite fruitful—a better comprehension in the class and a satisfactory score of the term paper. The class of Accounting was a big one and the financial terms in the class lecturing confused me a lot. Fortunately, the professor and TA were very amicable and helpful. They were always there for me after class and clarified my questions patiently and effectively.

During my days in UB, people often asked me about the major differences between American and Chinese universities. In a Chinese university, professors and faculty are amicable and responsible, the relationship between professors and students is relatively close, the curriculum and classroom atmosphere relatively conservative and traditional; in an American university, students shall study in a fully-motivated and self-disciplined manner in order to complete one's academic tasks and maintain one's academic competence, and the characteristics of the curriculum are simplicity and an emphasis on collaboration. Adapting the academic study in UB was a challenge I had to take and a change I had to make. For me, every bit of change in UB is worth to cherish

感恩节、圣诞节都有当地的寄宿家庭邀请我们去做客。为了不让在外学习生活的外国人感到孤独，到了冬天，他们会邀请我们去滑雪；学校老师会邀请我们到家里去做客，品尝当地的美食；新认识的同学、朋友，会邀请我们参与很多有意思的活动……渐渐地，初到学校的很多不习惯也慢慢消失了。

在水牛城的日子里，最值得期待的还是每个月和几名同学不定期地在寝室吃火锅的时光，这是解思乡之苦的良方。

这是学习和生活都很丰富的一年，我感受到了当地老师、同学及很多很多人的善良与友爱。当然，我们这群幸运儿也时时刻刻被国内的老师、同学牵挂着。作为这个项目中的一员，我真正懂得了尊重和善良。

刚到水牛城的时候，语言、环境、课程都不熟悉，学习压力很大，我一度比较沮丧。后来被逼无奈，抱着一本本英文原版书和一台电子词典，在图书馆里待了几天，终于找到了感觉，找到了正确的方向，同时也爱上待在图书馆学习的感觉。不管是自己学习做作业，还是和同学朋友一起讨论，我逐渐爱上了在水牛城那种努力学习逼自己进步的感觉。现在我也比较喜欢尝试不同的事物，每次觉得很难或者是想放弃偷懒的时候，我就想当时那么厚的英文书都啃完了，现在再坚持一下吧。

and has had a positive impact on me.

My life in UB was unforgettable—celebrating Thanksgiving and Christmas with local host families, skiing with American friends in winter, visiting professors' houses and enjoying the local food, participating in interesting cultural fairs and activities. My incompatibleness with the new environment gradually disappeared.

Moreover, to enjoy a hotpot dinner with my roommates was definitely a monthly special event, which was the best way to sooth our homesickness.

2008 was a productive year for me both in learning and living. I was embraced by the UB faculty, students, Chinese teachers and friends with consideration, love and hospitality. Being a member of the one hundred and fifty, I learned the essence of respect and kindness.

In the first few weeks of my days in UB, I was frustrated and almost overwhelmed by

## 十年之后，我仍继续奋斗

短短一年的学习生活，使我渐渐地融入了这里，但却要面对第一次分离。为什么说第一次分离呢？我坚信我还将回到这里，再看看我曾经一待就是一天的图书馆，看看曾经帮助过我的老师和同学。

转眼十年过去，曾经的水牛城的时光还历历在目，仿佛就在昨天，我们一行人背着行囊，辗转二十多个小时奔赴理想的彼岸。

大学毕业后，我怀揣梦想来到广州，在一家外企从事供应链方面的工作。那家公司很好，当时我应聘的职位在整个亚洲只招 16 个人，我的留学经历和在纽约锻炼的语言能力给了我自信，最终我脱颖而出。

初出茅庐的职场"菜鸟"，很幸运地遇到了很好的老板。他给了我很好的平台和机会，对我后来的职业发展也很有帮助。再后来，我回到成都，在一家公司从事采购工作，几年的职场生涯继续丰富着我的人生。

如今的我不再是"菜鸟"，而且在所在的行业也取得了一些小成绩。我想，这和我在水牛城的经历应该是有关的。目前，我的生活状态比较符合自己的预期，但我仍朝着更好的方向努力着、拼

the stresses brought by the unfamiliarity to course curriculums, classmates and language. Instead of immersing in disappointment, I forced myself to spend hours in the library, practicing and polishing my language capability through reading and writing. Surprisingly, these diligent library study experiences put me into the right track and I fell in love with the feeling of making progress step by step. It has become an intrinsic drive that motivates me forward in cope with difficulties and challenges.

### The Striving Forward
### UB Student 10 Years Later

To integrate into the circumstances of living and study in Buffalo was hard, but to say goodbye to Buffalo was even harder. I firmly believed that I would pay a revisit to the UB campus, faculty and friends someday.

Even ten years later, the memory of my days in Buffalo is still vivid as if it were yesterday when all the program members carried heavy luggage and traveled more than 24 hours to arrive in Buffalo.

In the year of my graduation from college, I went to Guangzhou with my dreams and was recruited by a prestigious foreign venture company in the field of supply chains. The company only recruited 16 employees in Asia. I successfully stood out with my one-year privileged study abroad experience in SUNY Buffalo and my excellent language capability.

My initial professional development was guided by an experienced supervisor,

搏着。我始终坚信上帝总是偏爱努力和随时做好准备的孩子，善待他人，善待自己，尊重生命和自然。我想我依然是那个奋斗且幸运的女孩，我也相信我的努力终有回报。

如今，我与十年前一同参与此项计划的同学仍保持联系。在成都安家立业的我们，也时不时相约吃饭聊天，共同回忆我们在美国的点滴时光，每一段记忆都值得我们好好品味和珍藏。我们曾经开玩笑说，以后拖家带口再赴美国，肯定有不一样的感觉。

现在国家有很多助推中美人文交流的项目，有很多帮助中国学生走出国门的机会，也给了很多国外大学生申请到中国高校学习的机会，比如在世界各地逐渐发展壮大的孔子学院、汉语桥，国外留学生入住中国的寄宿家庭等。我想，随着中国与世界的互通，中国学生出国深造特别是进入名校的机会会逐渐增多，出国学习不再是很多中国家庭的一件"大事"，而是成为中国学生获取资源、增长见识的一种方式。

who provided me with opportunities and platforms of training and collaborating. Then, I returned to Chengdu for further professional development. Now my major job responsibility is purchasing, which has greatly enriched my life.

Because of my study abroad experience in UB, I have made remarkable contribution in my professional field and have been moving towards to my professional goal day by day. I firmly believe that God prefers diligent and prepared ones, and I will be good to others, be good to myself, and show respect to life and nature. Also I believe that my hard work will pay off.

I still keep in touch with the program participants now living in Chengdu. We often gather together and recall these wonderful days in the United States. Every moment is worth to cherish and look back to. We even make a joke that it will be a quite different experience if we pay a revisit to the United States with our family members.

Now, the number of Sino-US cultural exchange programs is growing. It has been much easier for Chinese students to have an overseas study experience. Of course, the communication is mutual, and more and more foreign students are now pursuing their higher education in China with the scholarships and opportunities provided by the platform of Confucius Institute, Chinese Bridge (Chinese Proficiency Competition for Foreign College Students). I am fortunate to be an eyewitness of cultural exchange improvement, which enables more and more Chinese students to go abroad, get acquainted with more people and expand their insights.

# 适应与克服，让每一天都有成就感

## An Everyday Sense of Accomplishment:
## Adapting & Conquering

李欣 / 成都理工大学　纽约州立大学石溪分校

Li Xin / Chengdu University of Technology　SUNY at Stony Brook

2008 年注定是不平凡的一年，当时我还是成都理工大学的一名学生，从没想过会遭遇一场突如其来的灾难。更让我没有想到的是，在中国政府和美国纽约州立大学的资助下，我能免费出国留学一年，这一年我收获良多。

如果用两个词语来总结那一年我的学习情况，我想是"适应"与"克服"。因为学业很重，每天都需要早起并且做好一天的计划，这样才能有效完成当天的学业任务。这对我后来的生活帮助很大。因为形成了规律的作息习惯，做完每天的事情后心中很有成就感，这给完成第二天的任务带来很大的动力，形成了良性循环。刚到美国

2008 was an unforgettable and productive year for me. I was an undergraduate student of Chengdu University of Technology, when the earthquake hit my family and me unexpectedly. Surprisingly and fortunately, I was endorsed by Chinese Government Scholarship Council to study abroad for one year in the State University of New York at Stony Brook, the United States.

I would like to characterize my one year study experience in Stony Brook as adapting and conquering. In order to complete the academic tasks in time and effectively, every day I got up early and strictly followed a neatly scheduled daily routine. The great sense of accomplishment became my intrinsic drive and motivated me forward in my following college days. I formulated the self-disciplinary habit during my days in Stony Brook, which benefited my academic performance and my professional development after graduation.

需要适应美国的教学方式和繁重的课程，泡图书馆甚至熬夜是常事。这一年，我取得了优异的成绩，这为我后来的大学学习提供了充足的动力。

## 拥有自由规划未来的权利

在这一年中，我深刻体会到美国教育与中国教育的不同。当然这没有谁对谁错，我们可以在吸取别人经验的过程中求同存异，取其精华。在我看来，多样性的选择是美国教育的一个显著特点。

这首先体现在学生群体上。美国学生有很多是读完高中直接读大学，但也有很多是工作后再读书，或者一边工作一边读书。这种现象在美国很普遍，大家也习以为常。但是在中国，可能很多家长会不太认同，认为这样会耽误很多时间。我认为这是个人的选择和自由，孩子有规划自己未来的权利。

我现在还记得，当时就有一位年近六十的男士和我上同一门统计课程。后来得知他以前是做金融工作的，因为在工作的过程中发现自己对统计很感兴趣，所以又进入大学深造。还有一位怀孕的妈妈，挺着大肚子来上课，精神饱满，也学得不亦乐乎。我当时就暗自佩服，渐渐明白，其实学

## The Right of Planning One's Academic and Professional Future

I was deeply impressed by the diversity of the American educational system, which is quite distinctive from the Chinese educational system.

Firstly, the college students came from diversified backgrounds. Most of the students had an immediate college enrollment after high school graduation, but there were also students who continued their study with professional experiences and took non-credit courses. I was deeply impressed by the right of planning one's academic and professional future.

One of my classmates in the class of Statistics was a 60-year-old gentleman. He shared his financial professional experience with me and deepened my interest in the study of statistics; a beaming pregnant woman was also my classmate, who has won my admiration in her capability in balancing personal life and academic study. Their enthusiasm perfectly illustrated the sustainable effects of education to people with diversified backgrounds.

Students from across the nation and the world choose American universities for a number of reasons. From my perspective, the inclusive campus climate is the most attractive characteristics of American education.

The course assessment system in American universities constitutes of quizzes, participation, examinations and final examination. It is a comprehensive assessment on student's learning motivation and capability. Moreover, with a purpose of prohibiting cheating and plagiarism, American universities encourage the students to perform and speak from their own experience,

无止境，这与年龄没有关系，只要你想，社会就会给你提供机会。

来自不同国家的大学生求学目的各不相同。我认为，美国多元的校园文化是吸引世界各地学生来此求学的一个原因。

美国大学一学期的最后成绩包括很多方面，它是综合能力的体现。比如平时的作业、平时表现、各个考试成绩都会占一定的比例，这样会促使学生重视平时的积累和练习。另外，美国大学十分重视学生学术纪律问题，鼓励学生用自己的经验、知识来充分表达，避免作弊或者抄袭等问题。这样能够培养学生的版权意识，尊重他人的研究成果，有利于营造良好的学术风气。

## 心怀感恩　大爱延续

2008年的地震摧毁了我的家庭，这次不可思议的美国学习经历却改变了我的人生轨迹。我从一个懵懂的女孩变成了一位常怀感激之心的母亲。我希望帮助社会，传递爱的火炬。

简夫妇是学校的一对教职员工，他们收养了两个中国小女孩（当时她们一个3岁，一个5岁）。他们夫妻俩非常热心，得知我们是"CSC-SUNY 150奖学金项目"的学生，特地邀请

knowledge and reading. It is an effective way of promoting intellectual property education and preventing infringement.

## Be a Torchbearer of Love and Generosity

Though the 2008 Sichuan Earthquake hit my family and me unexpectedly, the miraculous study abroad experience has greatly changed my life. From an inexperienced college student into a little boy's mother, I have become a grown-up with gratefulness and gratitude. Then, I hope I can pass on the torch of love and benefit a larger community with my own contribution.

Jane and her husband were faculty of Stony Brook and they were very benevolent to the students of CSC-SUNY 150 Program. They often invited us to their house on weekends to meet their two adopted daughters from China (who were 3 and 5 years old at that time). The couple raised the children with delicate educating, caring and love. They expected that their daughters could formulate an objective perspective on their heritage and master the Chinese language.

Out of my interest in children education, I planned to develop my professional life in the field of education and to work in a K-12 school near my residential community. I would like to benefit a larger community and make my contribution through introducing Chinese culture and

我们去他们家里，他们把两个小女孩照顾得很好，还希望她们掌握中文。

出于对儿童教育的浓厚兴趣，两年之后，我计划申请到家附近的一所学校工作。这是一所从幼儿园到高中的全日制学校。我希望在了解美国基础教育的同时，还可以向这里的孩子介绍一些中国文化。

出国留学是一次深入了解一个国家的机会，这和旅游或者出差是不一样的。只有深入地了解一个国家，才能学习它优秀的地方。留学会拓展自己的视野，提升自己的创新力，开阔自己的心胸。我觉得留学过程中有三点很最重要：独立的生活能力、坚强的毅力和乐观的心态。

我希望更多的中国大学生走出去，保持开放的心态，把我们的国家建设得更加繁荣昌盛！

volunteering.

To study abroad is quite different from travelling and business trips. A comprehensive cultural experience would deepen one's cognition, innovate one's creativity, polish one's problem-solving capability and broaden one's vision. From my perspective, I have learned three important capabilities from the one-year study abroad program: independence, perseverance and optimism.

I strongly recommend the young people in China to go out and see the outside world. Be insightful and be contributive! It is beneficial to one's life and the future development of China.

# 万里春藤，感恩系心上

## Ten Thousand Mile Long Ivy: Gratitude in My Heart

舒玉婵／成都理工大学　纽约州立大学布法罗分校

Shu Yuchan / Chengdu University of Technology　SUNY at Buffalo

"对于我们这 150 个学生来说，'CSC-SUNY 150 奖学金项目'可能是改变命运和改变自己未来生活轨迹、工作轨迹的一个机会。我觉得我们是带着使命去的。我肯定不能为国家丢脸，我得注意我的行为，我的一举一动代表的是中国。"这是十年前的日记里我写下的一段话。

"For the 150 students of CSC-SUNY 150 Program, it is a life-changing opportunity. I shall go with a mission that I must live and study in a decent and diligent manner, for I act on behalf of China." This is a quotation from my diary written in 2008.

### 把喜欢的事做到最好

转眼"5·12"汶川特大地震已经过去了十年。回想起十年前在美国度过的那段时光，我印象最深、对我最重要的人，是比尔，我当时寄宿家庭的主人。他是一个非常勤奋努力的美国人，我在他身上学到了坚持的

### Merits Learnt from My Host Family: Hospitality and Gratitude

It has been ten years since the occurrence of 2008 Sichuan Earthquake. I often recalled my days in United States and found that Bill, a diligent gentleman in my host family, greatly impressed me. I learnt from him the quality of

品质，对自己喜欢的事情认真去做，而且要做到最好。他用心对待身边的人，那种温暖的感觉可以辐射到身边的每一个人。比尔会在周末或者节假日把我们接到家中去体验当地人民的生活。由于他的工作业务和范围涉及中国广州沿海地区，所以他对中国文化也很感兴趣。他常在家中泡茶请我们品尝。

　　我们一直保持联系，2015 年我结婚时邀请比尔来当证婚人。他从美国飞到中国，在我的婚礼上做了证词，他对参加传统的中式婚礼感到非常开心。

　　在美国的这段时间，在做人方面，我学到的最重要的一点就是感恩。翻看曾经断断续续写的日记，自己提到的最多的关键词也是"感恩"。拥有这个学习机会，我要感恩；遇到的所有人和事我都要感恩，因为他们本可以不这样做，但是因为他们有爱，所以才有了现在的我，才有了我的那些难忘的经历。我一直怀着感恩的心看待这段经历，我也希望之后我可以尽自己的努力去帮助更多的人。

## 自由、自律的学术环境

　　在 2008 至 2009 年的日记中，我做了好几个自我规划。为了实现我的

persistency. Bill attentively treated the people around him with kindness and hospitality. With his guidance and introduction, we had so much exotic cultural experience in the United States. Bill had several business contacts in Guangzhou and he showed great interest in Chinese culture. He often made cups of Chinese tea in his house and invited us to join him.

I have kept in touch with Bill after I returned to China. In the year of 2015, I invited Bill to attend my wedding as a special guest, who was overjoyed by the authentic Chinese traditional experience.

The other merit I learnt from my host family in the United States is gratitude. Gratitude was a high frequency word in my diary of 2008. With the one-year study abroad program and the kindness from the people, I became even more mature and have made my own contribution in helping others.

### A Free But Well-disciplined Academic Circumstance

In my diary from 2008 to 2009, I made

学术梦想，我在学校图书馆度过大部分的时间。

以前在国内考试，有开卷和闭卷，开卷是答案可以在书里面找，闭卷是背诵要点再在考试的时候写出来。去美国后，有一次做作业，我以同样的方式，将书本上的内容抄写在了作业纸上交给老师，之后没过多久就被老师叫到办公室，说我这是抄袭。抄袭在美国是一个非常严重的问题。我当时很懵，觉得这在我们国内每个人都这样做作业，怎么到了国外就成了抄袭呢？在同学的帮助下我终于明白了，抄袭被认为是学术上的不诚信。我开始意识到知识产权的重要性，抄袭行为会涉及侵权。

美国课堂氛围轻松，国际学生、残障人士都受到尊重，感觉舒适。记得我当时上了一门课叫多元饮食文化。当时那个教授竟然坐在讲桌上给

several self-contemplations on my academic plan, goals and application plans. In order to contribute and excel in my study abroad experience, I spent most of my after-school hours in the library.

Still, I confronted an academic difficulty and learnt a lesson on ethical offense. According to my experience in China, the approach of assignment completion can be categorized into two ways: completed with the reference book or without it. During the process of completing a class project, I relied heavily on other people's work and the professor severely criticized my plagiarism. I was so confused at that moment and finally got clarified with the assistance of my classmates. Plagiarism is considered as academic dishonesty and my wrongful appropriation was a great offense to the course professor. I started to realize the importance of intellectual property rights and learnt plagiarism may meet some legal definitions of fraud.

The inclusive classroom climate in the American classroom makes the international students, disabled faculty and students feel respected and comfortable. I was impressed by the professor of the course of Multicultural Food, who sat on the table and instructed the class in a light-hearted way.

我们上课，我印象很深。在美国学习期间，我的组织能力、沟通能力和表达能力得到了训练和提升。

## 过有仪式感的生活

我在美国的学习经历，使我特别希望毕业后可以到一家外企工作，当然我也如愿以偿。这份工作让我学会系统地去思考问题，同时也培养了我的工作模式和工作态度。

从毕业到现在，工作也有差不多八年时间了。我经验丰富，成长为一名职业女性。我认为生活要有仪式感——精心筹备，细心体会来自家庭和朋友的爱。

关于留学，我建议年轻人持客观、包容的态度，迎接多元文化。

## 尾声

十年离散人未惘，常思量，自难忘。
万里春藤，感恩系心上。
纵然奔忙应未联，年如轮，自感伤。
暇中思绪返时光，稚如黄，眸无旁。
相见如家，渊识怀万象。
愿得来日首再会，忆往昔，义流芳。

During my study in the U.S. my capabilities in organizing, communicating and articulating were well trained and escalated.

## To Live in a Ritualistic Manner

My one-year study abroad experience motivated me to develop my professional path in a foreign venture. Fortunately, I realized my professional plan after graduation. My professional insights and philosophy are well trained under the mechanism of Multi-national Corporation.

After eight years of professional development, I have grown into a young woman with matured mentality and excellent professional experiences. I believe the essence of life is to live in a ritualistic manner—celebrating festivals with delicate preparation and cherishing the affection from one's family and friends.

My personal advice to the young people who would like to study abroad is to be objective and willing to accept the diversity.

## Epilogue

Ten-year separation would not weaken my
    thoughts
On the people and life experience in the United
    States;
The gratitude in my heart is ten thousand miles
    long ivy,
Connecting the unforgettable past and prominent
    future;
I am looking forward to a reunion in the near
    future,
Sharing the joy of a lasting friendship forever.

# 我想让他们真正认识中国

## I Want Them to Really Know China

王映雪 / 成都理工大学　纽约州立大学波茨坦分校

Wang Yingxue / Chengdu University of Technology　SUNY at Potsdam

　　我叫王映雪，是成都理工大学英语专业 2006 级的学生，2008 年我参加了"CSC-SUNY 150 奖学金项目"，与"5·12"汶川特大地震灾区其他 149 名同学一起赴美学习。在美国我度过了非常忙碌而充实的一年，直到今天我都非常感谢当年的"CSC-SUNY 150 奖学金项目"。

　　感谢当时负责项目的陈滔伟老师，他为我们尽心打理出国前的一切事宜；感谢中国驻纽约总领事馆的叔叔、阿姨们的热情招待；感谢唐人街侨胞们的慷慨资助；感谢我在美国的寄宿家庭；感谢我的美国朋友、老师。他们无微不至的关怀，让我即使身处异国他乡也不觉太孤独，让我快速适

My name is Wang Yingxue, an English major of Chengdu University of Technology. In the year of 2008, I participated in the CSC-SUNY 150 Program and studied in the United States for a year with 149 other college students whose hometown were severely stricken by the 2008 Wenchuan Earthquake. I spent a busy and productive year in the United States. Until now, I am still very grateful to the CSC-SUNY 150 Program.

I would like to express my thankfulness to the program coordinator Chen Taowei, for his advice,

应美国的学习和生活，融入这个友好的国度。

## 抓紧时间充电，弥补差距

十年后，回想过去很多记忆都变得杂乱而模糊。当别人问我"你在美国印象最深的是什么"时，我一时语塞，因为满满的温暖和感动，是难以用语言来表达的。

相信 2008 年对于我们这 150 个学生来说都是永远难忘的一年。刚经历了一场重大灾难的我们，还未从悲伤的情绪中走出来，却意外得到了赴美留学一年的邀请。我们所有人都又惊又喜，因为当时出国并没有像现在这样容易和普遍，我们都非常珍惜这难得的机会。

在美国的一年，我积极参加学校的社团组织，周末和同学一起聚会，想更加全面地感受美国的校园生活。因此我结识了来自世界各地的朋友，

preparation and consideration before we studied abroad; thanks to the warm reception from all the personnel in Chinese Consulate General, New York; thanks to the generosity of the Chinatown folks; thanks to my American host family, faculty, friends and everyone who worked and contributed for this program. Their kindness and caring quickly dismissed my homesickness and loneliness, enabled me to settle down in America and integrate into this friendly nation.

### Recharged with More Knowledge to Close the Gap

A decade later, my memory about my days in America has become quite cluttered and blurred. When I was asked, "What's your most impressive experience during your stay in America?" I was tongue-tied, for the warmth and affection that I received in America was indescribable.

We, a hundred and fifty students, would never forget the year of 2008. Right after we experienced a catastrophe and were not relieved from the grief and sadness, an unexpected invitation—to study in United States for a year—made us shocked and happy. For ten years ago, going abroad was not as convenient and easy compared with present time. We were going to the United States and we all cherished this rare opportunity.

During my one-year study in the United States, I actively participated in the extra-curricular activities and hung out with my classmates on weekends. I want to experience the diversity of American college life. I got acquainted with friends from the United

我们一起欢度圣诞节，一起打雪仗，一起在公园划皮艇，我们敞开胸怀，学习不同的文化。

在美国的学业一点也不比国内轻松，甚至更难，很多课程注重精读和写作，而我之前接受这方面的训练比较少，这是我的弱点。我每天花在图书馆的时间超过8小时，抓紧时间充电，以缩短我和美国同学之间的差距。

美国的大学教育系统和国内还是有很大不同。第一，在美国没有"班"的概念，自然也没有班主任和辅导员，每个学生都是独立的个体，不属于哪个班或者哪个班主任管辖，这也特别考验学生的自主学习能力。第二，在课程设置上，美国学生大一、大二只上基础课程，到大三才开始选择专业课程，可以选修喜欢的课程，根据选课情况，每一学期同学都会变化，所以有很多机会认识新朋友。

我感受最深的地方，是美国的大学特别注重培养学生的独立和实践能力。我学的是商务英语，老师会让我们独立完成一份几百页的项目计划书。这份项目计划书必须是实地考察、调研之后为企业量身定制的，从选择商家、调查市场，到制订出合适的商业计划，整个项目特别考验学生的独立思考和操作能力。

美国学校虽然上课的时间很短，

States, Germany, Japan and Switzerland, etc. Celebrating Christmas, snowballing in the open air and kayaking in the park, these cross-culture experiences enabled me to broaden my vision.

To study in the American university has never been an easy task. Many courses required the students to be very capable in reading and writing. Compared with my native speaker classmates, I was competent in neither of them. In order to make up the academic deficiency and defend the diligent reputation of Chinese students, I spent 8 hours in the library every day.

Moreover, the Sino-US educational systems are quite different. Firstly, there is no concept of "class" in United States, nor there are faculties or teachers responsible for the class, and this situation requires every college student to be an independent and self-disciplined individual. Secondly, according to the curriculum, freshmen and sophomores remain undeclared in the previous two years of their college life, and this arrangement enables them to acquaint with more contacts through diversified course study and assists them to finally figure out the major in the junior year.

I was most deeply impressed by American college students' capabilities in critical thinking and knowledge application. I registered the course of Business English. My professor required us to complete a hundreds-page long business proposal independently, which should be specially tailored on the basis of a thorough fieldwork, customer survey and market research of my own. The proposal itself is a strict scrutiny on the student's capability in critical thinking and application.

Every day, after I finished my class at 3 p.m., I worked diligently in the library, took part in the

下午 3 点便放学了，但是我下课后不是在图书馆预习课程，就是在开会，或者在做市场调研，整整一年我的学习紧张而忙碌，这段学习体验极大地锻炼了我的实践能力。课后做项目遇到难题需要和老师打电话约时间单独沟通交流，同学之间也时不时会有合作，所以美国的师生、同学之间的关系非常融洽，老师会经常邀请学生到家里聚餐、过节。

## 让他们更了解中国

我因为在学校表现比较突出，绩点较高，有机会被学姐介绍到一家不错的美国公司实习。公司主营跨国服务，我比较了解中国的情况，又有美国学习的经历，所以负责打理中国市场。按规定公司不招收应届生，但因为我的经历比较丰富，实习期间也很努力，被公司破格录用了。

在公司工作几年后，我利用积累的资源和人脉在 2013 年创办了自己的跨国医疗服务公司，生活变得非常忙碌，经常辗转在中国、泰国和美国之间。我很享受这样的生活状态，就像当初享受美国之行一样。

这十年间，我真切地感受到中美关系越来越紧密，美国人对中国的认识也越来越客观。记得刚到美国学习

meeting and the group work and committed the market research. Never have I had such working efficiency and productivity in study and learning! Certainly, the one-year study abroad experience has greatly strengthened my motivation and capability in critical thinking and application. My interpersonal skills are also greatly polished through class project communication and festival celebration with professors and classmates.

## Let Them Know China Better

Through the one-year study, I had developed excellent academic acquisition skills and a remarkable GPA. Therefore, I was honorably recommended by an alumna and interned in a prestigious American corporation, which provided cross-border services. My professional skills and responsible mentality won admirations from supervisors and colleagues, and the internship was soon extended into a full-time job—to work in its China branch.

In the year of 2013, I resigned and committed entrepreneurship, focusing on cross-border medical service in China, Thailand and the United States. I am enjoying the productivity brought by my start-up experience, just as I did ten years ago in the United States.

In the past ten years, I have truly experienced the progress of Sino-US relationship. Upon my arrival in the United States, I was frequently consulted with hilarious questions like "Do you have Walmart in China?" "Do you have printed books in China?" "Do you have electricity in China?", which greatly upset me and put me into contemplation—communication is indispensable.

With the development of my start-up innovation in the field of cross-border medical

时，有的美国同学会问我：中国有火车吗？有沃尔玛吗？有电吗？有书本吗？这类问题让我觉得非常荒谬。他们对中国认识的匮乏，让我感到难过和无奈。

近年来，我一直从事中美医疗服务业，经常邀请美国的行业专家来中国开讲座，促进中美服务业之间的交流和互动。

经济的快速发展和中国人民消费能力的提升，直接导致不少美国人对中国态度的转变。我刚进入跨国服务行业那几年，美国人和我们谈判交流时，认为我们保守、不敢创新、市场份额低，不值得投入太多时间和精力。但随着我国经济不断发展，国内消费市场不断增长和扩大，很多美国人越来越重视开拓中国市场，他们找我合作，并愿意主动做一些商业调整来迎合中国的市场，这在十年前是很难看到的情况。

如今中国已经在国际上树立了非常好的形象，无论是出国留学还是商务合作，都比十年前容易了许多。虽然出国留学不再稀奇，但是如果有机会我还是建议同学们多走出去看看，去尝试不同的生活方式，去一个陌生的环境锻炼自己的生存和适应能力，同时，要看到更多的不同之处，对世界的发展变化做出更快的反应。

service, I have made my own contribution through business seminar and traveling.

With the development of China's economy and the rising of Chinese people's consuming capability, the image of China has been gradually changed in the eyes of Americans—from out of date, difficult to communicate with and conservative in innovation and collaboration. These positive improvements have also resulted into an up surge of foreign venture investment and specially-tailored business projects.

In the year of 2018, to study abroad and to do businesses in overseas markets are nothing special for Chinese. With a purpose of cultivating one's adaptive capability, I highly recommend the young people in China to go out and see the outside world.

### Ten Years Later, Only Love Remained Unchanged

On May 12th, 2018, the Memorial Day of Sichuan Earthquake 2008, I was traveling on business in the United States. Though I was far

## 十年，唯有爱不变

2018年5月12日，我正在美国出差，看到微博上很多人转发"5·12"汶川特大地震十年纪念日的博文，不禁泪流满面。

十年前我们150名大学生被满满的爱意包围，那些来自陌生人善意而无私的关怀，改变了我们的生活，如今我们分布在各行各业，想把这份爱延续下去。

近几年我一直在做慈善活动。去年，一名我长期资助的凉山女孩考上了大学。还记得刚得知这个消息时，我非常开心，认为自己做的事是非常有价值的，于是今年我又继续资助了一名年龄稍小的学生。

我想我正在做的不过是爱心的接力，是尽自己最大能力去回馈社会，将当年我们得到的关爱传递给更多需要关爱的青少年。

十年前的项目改变的不仅仅是我的人生轨迹，更塑造了我的品格；不仅让我每一天怀着敬畏之心去奋斗，怀着感恩的心去善待每一个人；更让我学会了如何去爱人，爱生活，爱这片土地。

away from my hometown, the mourning and throwback on the social media made my eyes brimmed with tears.

We, the 150 former college students, now work and study worldwide in different professional fields and academic institutes. In the past ten years, we have been filled with love and generosity from the people we have never met; rebuilt and changed by the unexpected study abroad opportunity. So, it is time for us to make the warmth and education sustainable.

I have been supporting two poor students from Liangshan Yi Autonomous Prefecture for years. Last year, one of the girls successfully enrolled into university. The good news encouraged me to continue the educational endorsement even more affirmatively.

I am very fortunate and grateful to be educated and nurtured in both nations, which enable me to feedback the people and society in a more sensible and responsible way. This program ten years ago has not only changed my life track, but also shaped my personality; it has not only encouraged me to struggle with awe every day and be good to everyone with gratitude, but also taught me how to love others, love life, and love this land.

UESTC

电子科技
大学

University of Electronic Science
and Technology of China

# 一段非凡的旅程

## An Extraordinary Journey

谈天／电子科技大学　纽约州立大学杰纳西社区学院

Tan Tian / University of Electronic Science and Technology of China　SUNY Genesee Community College

经常地，我会梦见自己重返校园：中学、大学，以及 2008 年在美国的那段时光。

十年前，"5·12"汶川特大地震给四川带来重创。全国人民万众一心，众志成城，给予四川人民莫大的支持与帮助。与此同时，很多外国友人也在尽自己的力量援助四川。其中，美国纽约州立大学提出了一个特殊的计划并付之行动。

纽约州立大学把眼光放在了灾区大学生的教育问题上，他们热情邀请地震灾区的大学生到州立大学学习一年。在中美两国政府高效率的合作以及无数人的帮助下，150 名学生在 2008 年 8 月 15 日登上了前往美国纽

I often dream of returning to school: the middle school, college, and the life in the United States in 2008.

Ten years ago, the May 12th earthquake caused incalculable damages to Sichuan. The people of the whole country were united as one, and offered great supports and help to the Sichuan people. At the same time, many foreign friends also did their part to aid Sichuan. Among them, the State University of New York proposed a special plan and put it into action.

The State University of New York focused on the education of college students in the stricken areas. They sincerely hoped they could invite college students from the earthquake-stricken areas to study at the State University for one year. Then, with the efficient cooperation between the Chinese and American governments and the help of countless people, 150 students from nine universities in Sichuan boarded a flight

约的飞机。从此，我们这群人有个共同的名字："CSC-SUNY 150 奖学金项目"。

## 初来乍到：热情化解乡愁

位于纽约市的州立大学分校海事学院热情地为我们举办了欢迎晚会，旅途的劳累和时差的不适应都被兴奋与激动取代。我对美国人的第一印象就是热情好客、真诚幽默、容易相处。当然，在那之后我对美国有了更多新的认识和更深入的了解。在纽约市短暂停留之后，150 人随即前往各自所在的分校，开始了一段不平凡的他乡之旅。

我所在的分校位于纽约州西部，名字是杰纳西社区学院，位于一个名

to New York on August 15, 2008. Since then, we have had a common name —CSC-SUNY 150 Program.

### Warmth Melted the Homesickness of Us New Comers

Maritime College, a campus of SUNY in New York City, hosted a welcome party for us warmly, which drove away our tiredness of the journey and the inconvenience of jet lag, and we all felt excited immediately. The first impression the Americans gave me was that they were hospitable, sincere, humorous, and easygoing. Of course, I would have more knowledge and deeper understanding of the United States after that. After a short stay in New York City, the 150 students went to their branch campus respectively and began an extraordinary journey abroad.

My campus, Genesee Community College, is located at Batavia, a small town in the western New York State, about a 9-hour drive from New York City. The school staff warmly received us

为巴塔维亚的小镇上，距离纽约市大约9小时的车程。刚下车，我们就受到了学校员工的热情接待，当地社区很多人也来迎接我们，并递给每人一个袋子。里面有糖果巧克力、介绍资料、文具，甚至还有一个别具风格的盘子，最让人感到惬意的是一张小卡片，上面写着：欢迎来到杰纳西。当然，对于美国人来说，任何时候一面国旗都是必不可少的，由此也可以看出他们对自己国家的热爱和自豪。相应地，对于中国的热爱和自豪也将陪伴我度过这段旅程，并将一直陪伴下去。身在异乡，这种感情尤为强烈。

## 课堂内外：师生共同进步

可能对于我们来说，这都是第一次走出国门，所谓的文化冲击是不可能没有的。虽然对于成长在互联网时代的我们来说，对国外文化多少有所耳闻，但是当真正置身其中的时候，仍然有很多让我们感到新鲜甚至惊奇的东西。

首先，国外课堂的灵活性很大，可以说十分自由。在课堂上，学生可以在任何时候提问，再简单的问题，老师也会耐心解答。和国内一样，老师都很喜欢爱问问题的学生，考试成绩不是最重要的，补考的条件也比较

when we were just getting off the bus. Many local people also came to welcome us by handing each of us a bag full with a lot of candies, local brochures, some stationery, and even a stylish plate. The most pleasant thing was a mini-card with the words "Welcome to Genesee." For Americans, of course, a national flag is indispensable at any time, from which we might see their love and pride of their own country. Accordingly, the love and pride of the motherland would accompany me through this journey and will continue accompanying me hereafter. Such kind of feeling is particularly acute while abroad.

## Mutual Progress of Teachers and Students in & out of Class

For all of us, it might have been the first time that we went abroad. It was impossible for us not to be buffeted by the so-called culture shock. Although we knew many foreign cultures since we grew up in the Internet age, there were still many things that made us feel fresh and even amazed when we were actually in a foreign country.

First of all, overseas classes always offer very flexible teaching and a very free atmosphere. In class, students can ask questions at any time, and the teacher will answer questions patiently no matter how simple the question is. The situation is almost the same as in China, in which teachers are very fond of students who are willing to ask questions, the test scores are not so important, and the qualifications for make-up examination are also relatively loose. That is to say, it is relatively simple to get credits.

Teachers placed great emphasis on the

宽松，也就是说想拿到学分是比较简单的。

老师最看重的是学生学习的过程，平时的小测验、小考试，涉及计算机的一些小项目在总成绩中占很大比重。国外学生的动手能力普遍比我们强，一方面是因为老师的严格要求和对实践环节的重视，另一方面是外国学生自身的兴趣使然。论成绩分数，特别是理科，我相信中国学生在任何地方都是优秀的。但是在做实验或者课程设计的时候，我们往往不是第一个完成的。慢慢地，我开始思考学习的真正目的，上大学的真正目的。在大学里收获知识是基础，而个人素质修养、思维的灵活性、解决问题的能力等，这些才是使我一生受益的东西。

在美国的那一年里，我始终能感受到来自每一个人的善意。我印象最深的，是我们的英语老师博伊德先生。他在课堂上非常热情地向我们介绍美国文化，课外还开车带我们去当地的

process of student learning. The usual quizzes, the small tests, the test reports, and some small projects involving computers accounted for a large proportion of the total score. I found that the practical ability of foreign students was generally better than ours because of not only the teachers' strict requirements and emphases on practice but also more interest foreign students had in it. In terms of scores, especially those of science, I believe that Chinese are the best in any place, but as to the experiment or curriculum design, we are often not the first to complete it. By and by, I realized the true purpose of learning and the real goal of going to college. Besides the basic task of acquiring knowledge, cultivation of personal qualities, flexibility of thinking, and ability to solve problems would really benefit me the whole life.

In fact, I constantly felt the goodwill from almost everyone during the year in the United States. What impressed me most was Mr. Boyd, our English teacher in the United States. From the very beginning, he introduced American culture to us enthusiastically in class, and drove us to the local historical sites and various interesting places out of class. What touched me most was that he warmly invited us to visit his home when we were about to return to China and introduced each family member to us, including his seven or eight pet dogs and cats. While sharing the delicious food with us, as an Irish-American, he told us his family and history in excitement. Immersed in such atmosphere, I gradually realized that the family should be placed in a more important position than before.

Just the same as in China, university classroom study only took us a small part of time

历史名胜和各种各样有趣的地方游览。最让我感动的，是在我们即将回国时，他热情邀请我们去他家做客，向我们介绍每一位家庭成员，甚至还包括家里的七八只宠物狗和猫。在与我们分享美味食物的同时，作为一名爱尔兰裔美国人，他还兴奋地为我们讲述他的家庭与家族史。现在想来，置身这种氛围之中时，我渐渐意识到，家庭应该放在比以前更重要的位置上。

大学课堂学习的时间只占很小的一部分，在国外也是一样。平时大部分时间是和朋友、室友一起度过的，这时候沟通和交流的能力就显得格外重要。这次具有特殊背景和意义的留学生活，让我们每一个人都肩负一种责任，那就是成为联系中美人民的使者，尽自己所能向他们展示中国近几十年来翻天覆地的变化。

每当中国的传统节日到来时，我们都会在学校组织一些活动，向大家介绍中国的文化和历史。另外，我们也向学校申请在课余时间开设中文课，让学校的学生、老师以及社区的人们更多地了解中国文化。同时，学校的老师、同学也以他们的热情感染着我们，让我们对美国文化有了更深的了解。

在美国的学校里，比起知识的收

in foreign countries. Since most of my time was spent with friends and roommates, the ability to communicate was particularly important. This study abroad life with special background and significance endowed each of us with a responsibility, that is, to become the messenger between the Chinese and American people, and to show them the earth-shaking changes in China in recent decades as much as possible.

Without mutual understanding, there is no common development. Therefore, whenever a Chinese traditional holiday came, we would organize some activities on campus, introducing Chinese culture and history. In addition, we also applied to open Chinese classes in our spare time, through which students and teachers in the school and people in the community, by means of Chinese study, could learn more about Chinese culture. At the same time, the teachers and classmates of the school also moved us with their enthusiasm, and let us have a deeper understanding of American culture.

In American schools, I benefited more from the understanding that the attitude towards knowledge and the learning ability are more important than the gains of knowledge itself. As an accomplished scholar, our physics teacher was very responsible for the students even

获，令我受益更多的是明白了对待知识的态度以及学习能力的重要性。我们的物理老师是一位学术造诣颇深的学者，即便是在杰纳西社区学院这样的小学校工作，他对学生也非常负责，再简单的作业也会认真谨慎地批改。每周两节物理实验课，锻炼了我们的实践动手能力，让我明白学会运用知识、自主学习新知识的重要性。

与"CSC-SUNY 150奖学金项目"相关的参与者和支持者有来自政府的工作人员，有来自民间的华侨华人，有来自世界各地的老师和同学，他们让我感受到来自各方面的关怀。我最大的感触就是要学会感恩，同时也要尽力去帮助周围需要帮助的人。

因为有了州立大学、纽约总领事馆、大使馆和华人华侨的支持，我们在寒假期间得以前往华盛顿进行了一次意义非凡的学习之旅。华盛顿很多建筑都是古希腊建筑风格，庄严肃穆，丝毫没有纽约那种热闹繁华的景象。美国虽然是一个相对年轻的国家，但是在华盛顿让我们切身感受到美国人对历史的尊重、对自己国家的责任感以及对政治的热衷。

when he worked in a small school like Genesee Community College. He corrected our homework carefully, no matter how simple the assignment was. Thanks to the flexibility of his two physics lab classes per week, I also understood the importance of applying knowledge and independent study of new information.

Outside the school, through contact with the relevant participants and supporters of CSC-SUNY 150 Program, I felt much care and help from those people we had never met before, such as government staff, civilian overseas Chinese, and teachers and classmates from all over the world. With them, I had the greatest feeling that I should learn to be grateful and try my best to help others in need.

Thanks to the support of the State University, the Consulate General of New York, the Embassy and the Chinese overseas, we were able to make a meaningful learning journey to Washington D.C. during the winter vacation. Most buildings in Washington are of ancient Greek style, giving a sense of solemnity and with no signs of the bustling New York. Although the United States is a relatively young country and lacks of a heavy cultural heritage, the American capital allowed us to feel the respect of Americans for their history, the sense of responsibility for their country, and their enthusiasm for politics.

## 学成归来：努力工作 回馈社会

回国完成大学学业后，我选择继续在本校完成研究生学业。国外的学习生活，开阔了我的眼界。在研究生阶段，我赴新加坡交换学习了 7 个月。在遇到困难时，我可以用更开放的思维来思考问题，同时也可以换位思考：换成我认识的或者见过的更优秀的人，遇到相同的问题时他们以什么方式来应对？

转眼十年过去，到了而立之年，现在我已结婚生子，过着比较稳定的生活。我工作了四年时间，在民航领域的一家研究所获得了助理研究员职称，从事的部分工作是与国际合作密切相关的。国外留学经历在一定程度上潜移默化地影响我的工作，特别是与外国同行直接接触沟通的时候，这种经历会给你带来便利。目前，最突出的一项成就就是作为沟通协调的角色，我促成了单位与欧洲一个同类型研究机构的广泛合作关系。

我现在从事的工作与赴美留学有直接关系，虽然生活中充满着各种约束，但我心里仍然希望未来生活能有所改变，我想在找到并实现自我价值的同时，去影响更多的人，让人生之路更宽广。

现在赴美留学的学生越来越多，

## Working Hard to Give Back to the Society with My Abroad Study Achievements

Having completed my university studies after returning to China, I chose to continue my graduate studies at my university. That studying and living experience abroad definitely played a pioneering role in my vision and thinking, including my 7-month experience of exchange study in Singapore. When I encountered difficulties, I could regard things more open-minded or from the perspective of better people I met or I knew. In this way, I could figure out their possible responses when they met the same problem.

In the blink of an eye, ten years has passed, and I am now married, have one baby and lead a relatively stable life. I have been working for four years, and I have obtained the title of assistant researcher in a research institute in the civil aviation field. In fact, part of the work is closely related to international cooperation. To a certain degree, the experience of studying abroad has exerted a subtle influence on my work and benefited me a lot, especially when I communicate with foreign counterparts directly. It has been so far my most outstanding achievement that I, as a middleman of communication and coordination, have successfully promoted the building of a broad cooperative relationship between my unit and a research institution of the same type in Europe.

My present job is directly related with studying in the United States. Although life is full of various constraints, I still hope that life can be changed in the future. I hope to influence more

在留学的前几个月，一定是充满新鲜感的，特别是对于从未踏出过国门的学生来讲，更是如此。在感受异国他乡的文化的同时，需要充分理解并尊重不同文化背景的人，与人为善。同时，牢记初心，让留学生活充满意义。

最后，感谢中美两国政府对"CSC–SUNY 150奖学金项目"的关心和帮助。当我们远在大洋彼岸的时候，感谢祖国给予我们的温暖关怀，也感谢将我们视为家人的华人华侨同胞。这个项目的成功离不开你们的支持。

十年弹指一挥间，这份经历带来的感动与感恩，必将影响我的一生。愿中美两国人民的友谊长存，愿我们有再次相聚的那一天！

people and let my life path go wider and further so as to fulfill my self-worth.

Now when more and more students go to study in the United States, they must be full of freshness in the first few months of studying abroad, especially for those who have never been abroad. However, it is necessary for them to fully understand and respect people of different cultural backgrounds and be kind to others while experiencing the culture of a foreign country. And at the same time, stay true to our aspiration and make the study life abroad meaningful.

Last but not least, I would like to express my appreciation for the concern and help from the Chinese and American governments to the CSC-SUNY 150 Program. My gratitude first goes to my motherland for the warmth and care to us when we were far away on the other side of the ocean, and my gratitude also goes to the overseas Chinese who regarded us as their family members. Without the support of any one of them, this project would not have been so successful.

Ten years has passed in an instant, but the affection and gratitude brought by this experience will definitely influence my whole life. I hope that the friendship between the Chinese and American people will last forever. May we meet again one day!

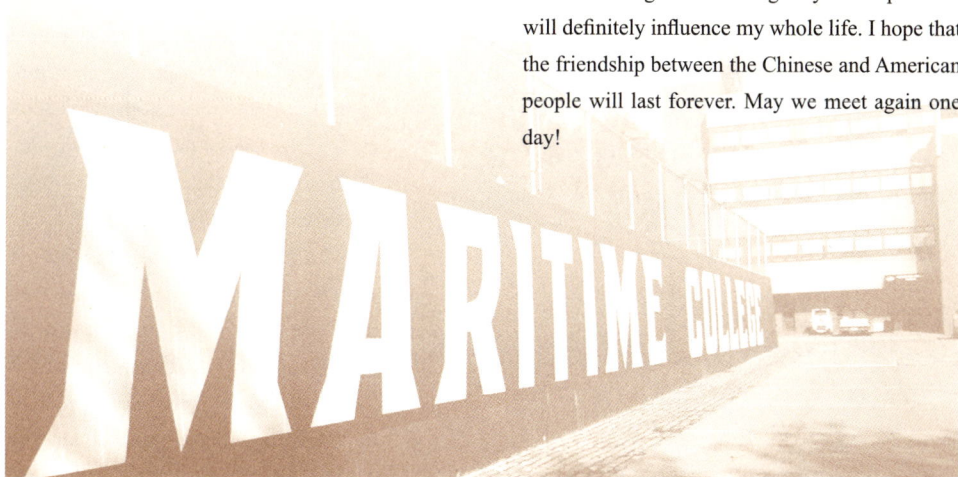

# 归来仍是那个少年

## Return with a Young Heart

孙辰 / 电子科技大学    纽约州立大学杰纳西社区学院

Sun Chen / University of Electronic Science and Technology of China
SUNY Genesee Community College

### 回到熟悉的 2008

### Back to the Familiar 2008

"Hi! Tom Jones, do you remember me, I'm Sun？" 一通越洋电话，又把我拉回了十年前。能够认识汤姆·琼斯，还得感谢改变我人生轨迹的 2008 年，感谢"CSC-SUNY 150 奖学金项目"，感谢纽约州立大学。

作为一个来自少数民族地区、从大山深处走出来的藏族小伙，我深深地知道，在灾难袭来之际，是在党和国家的关怀下，来自大洋彼岸的美国人民伸出援手，才使

An oversea call, "Hi! Tom Jones, do you remember me? I'm Sun", pulled me back to ten years ago. The chance to know Tom Jones owed to the year 2008 that greatly changed the course of my life. My heartfelt gratitude also goes to CSC-SUNY 150 Program and SUNY.

As a Tibetan young man from a mountainous minority area, I knew well that, when the disaster stroke, it was the Communist Party, our country, and the American people from the other side of the ocean that offered great support and

我有了这样一个机会，到美国继续学业，立志报效祖国。

得知"CSC-SUNY 150 奖学金项目"的消息时，正是我因家乡遭受灾难而处于消沉之时：父母作为政府工作人员，奋战在抗震救灾的第一线，而自己却心有余而力不足。这个消息让我感到振奋——一方有难，八方支援，我获得了一个机会，一个提升自己并更好地回报家乡的机会，我认真准备，经过层层选拔，坐上了飞往大洋彼岸的飞机。

在地球的另一端，我有一些激动，更多的是不安，电影里的街景、文化的冲击，是我对美国的最初印象。

当然那段时间最怀念的还是川菜，在这里我也友情提示：留学的四川学弟学妹，辣酱一定要多带；在美国朋友面前尽量不用汉语交流，这会让他们觉得受到排挤。

美国人民的热情友好，很快化解了我的不安。他们就像我的家人一样，让我在离家那么远的地方，感受到了家的温暖。

和蔼可亲的博伊德先生，像一名慈父，总是笑盈盈地为我们讲述美国文化，也是一个少见的会吃辣的美国人，他做回锅肉的悟性真的超高。美丽时尚的艾米，是我们喜欢的大姐姐。作为留学生顾问，她为我们制订

help to us. Since I got such an opportunity to continue my study in the United States, I was determined to serve the motherland when I came back.

I was informed the news of the CSC-SUNY 150 Program when I was depressed for the disaster in my hometown. My parents, as government staff, were fighting in the front line of relief in the disaster areas, yet I was unable to do something helpful. The news of the CSC-SUNY 150 Program and the helps from all sides spirited me up. I obtained an opportunity to improve myself and give my hometown a better return. On the basis of my careful preparation, I successfully passed through layers of screening and examination, and finally got on the plane to the other side of the ocean.

On the other side of the earth, somewhat excited, I felt more uneasy, as my first impression of the United States came from the streetscape from the movies and the shock of culture.

Of course, what I missed most then was Sichuan cuisine. Here, I also have a friendly reminder for fellow students who will study abroad: bring more chili sauce when you go to the United States, which will give you a longer transitional period before you get acquainted with your new residence. Also, try not to communicate in Chinese in front of American friends; otherwise, you may make them feel marginalized.

My uneasiness was soon melted with the warmth and kindness of the American people, who, just like my family members, made me feel the warmth of home even though I was far away from home.

Mr. Boyd, like an amiable father, always told us about American culture with smile.

日程、打点生活都是那么干练。豪爽耿直的克里斯，和他一起打球真的是有飞一般的感觉。他教我的俚语还有打招呼的姿势我到现在都还记得很清楚，有时走在路上还会对着空气复习一遍呢！还有那么多美国的好伙伴、好导师，梦回 2008 年，依然那么熟悉。

## 我的美国机遇　且行且珍惜

在美国的日子里，印象最深的，应该就是汤姆·琼斯吧。我们叫他老汤，我们的物理老师，上课非常有趣，实验做得非常好。虽然我们在国内都学过大学物理，并且得到不错的分数，但听老汤的课，看老汤做实验，总是能让我们对过去背过的公式有更加形象、实用的理解。

不过，给我印象最深的，却不是老汤在课堂上教授给我们的知识。

那一年圣诞假期，纽约州遇到了十年一遇的大雪。我们开始还很兴奋，但是渐渐地，雪越积越多，足足有两三米高，平原的公路两边都是雪墙。我们住的公寓是两层楼的，第一层的门窗完全被堵住，二层变一层。

说实话，当时我们还是挺害怕的，毕竟假期中，学校没有员工，没有补给，我们开始脑补"坐吃山空"的场景了。后来，我们听到有发动机的声

He was one of few Americans who could eat spicy food, and learned how to cook Twice-cooked Meat quickly. As an international student consultant, Amy, a beautiful and stylish elder sister we all liked, was always in high spirit in making schedules and managing our life. Chris, a straightforward and upright guy, made me feel like I was flying while I played basketball with him. He taught me proverbs and greeting postures, which I can still speak fluently and rehearse them sometimes even when there is no one on the road. There were so many good peers and good mentors in the United States. When I dream back to 2008, everyone is still so familiar.

### My American Opportunity to Be Cherished

In the days of my stay in the United States, the person who impressed me most was Tom Jones, whom we called Lao Tang. He was our physics teacher, whose class was very interesting, and whose experiments in good order. Although we studied physics and gained high scores in China, Lao Tang's class and experiments always visualized the formula we memorized and helped us understand the practical function.

What moved us most, however, was not what Lao Tang taught us in class.

That Christmas holiday saw the heaviest snow of the decade in New York State. We were very excited at first until more and more snow gradually piled up to two or three meters high and formed snow walls on both sides of the highway in the plain. The doors and windows of the first floor of our two-floor apartment were completely blocked only with the second floor visible.

音，往窗外一看，是一辆铲雪车开到了楼下。

"终于有救兵来了"，我们都很激动。一看，从车上拿着铁锹走下来的人，居然是我们的物理老师老汤！老汤向我们招手，告诉我们不要担心，便开始铲我们门口的雪，那一刻真的很感动。

圣诞节，本是老汤和家人团聚的欢乐时光，但他惦记着我们这群从中国来的学生们，冒着严寒，在门口倒腾快半个小时，才把门口的雪清空。我们赶紧到门口迎接，给了他一个大大的拥抱。老汤回到车上，还给我们拿了一大盒意式红肠，说要给我们做比萨，我们十分感动。

国内的课堂是两百人的大课堂，美国的课堂是二十人的小课堂。国内上课对学生自觉性的要求很高，美国

To be honest, we were pretty scared at that time. After all, during the holidays, there were no employees in the school, and there were no supplies. We all started to imagine the scene that we consumed all our food. Then, we heard the sound of the engine, and saw out of the windows a snowmobile drove down to our apartment.

"Help arrived at last," we were all excited. Fancy that the person out of the car with a shovel was our physics teacher Lao Tang! Waving to us and telling us not to worry, Lao Tang began to shovel the snow at our door. What a touching moment!

Christmas Holiday was meant to be a happy time for the reunion of Lao Tang and his family, but he was concerned about the safety of us Chinese students. In order to reassure us, he braved the cold to come and cleared all the snow at the door for about half an hour. We rushed to the door to greet him with a big hug. Lao Tang returned to the car and brought back to us a large box of Italian sausages. He said he would make pizza for us. I was so touched, really.

The essential difference between our class

的课堂上，讲师可以追踪到每一个人的表情，看表情就了解这堂课学生们的吸收程度怎样。课程设计上，咱们是按学分要求设计，社区学院是按学生需求设计，更像是购买课程和享受教育服务的过程。授课内容上，美国社区大学更注重知识的应用，这一点对于我们工科学生来说很重要。可能我念本科时理解还不深，研究生做芯片设计时，导师告诉我写文章和看书的时候，一定要抓住内容的实用意义才能融会贯通，从此我才开了窍。其实导师这句话，和美国的授课方式殊途同归。

怎么说呢，不能以既定观念甚至是传言去做判定，如果你要对一件事情做出自己的评论，那么亲身经历后才好发言。中美之间的相互理解，又何尝不是这样？

## 千年之后隔岸相望　我们继续前行

留美这一年在学习上的见闻，让我感到知识上有太多需要实地挖掘的地方，我想有更多的时间去充实自己，所以回国后我选择继续深造，读了研究生。工作后，抓住转型变革的机遇，从网点到渠道管理，再到省分行，再到公司业务，再到金融科技，我做的始终是最新的业务，为单位吃了多次

and American class first lies in that of university and community college, second in our big class of about two hundred students, which requires better self-discipline of students and the American small one with ten to twenty students, where lecturers can get to know how much the students absorb in the class by tracing the facial expression of each student. In terms of curriculum design, our curriculum design is made in accordance with the credit requirements and that of the American community colleges based on students' needs, an enjoyable process of purchasing courses and educational services. Finally in the content of lectures, in which American schools attach more importance to the application of learning because it is very important for our engineering students. Perhaps I didn't understand it deeply when I was an undergraduate, but when I did a chip design as a graduate student, my supervisor told me that it was possible to achieve mastery only through grasping the physical meaning of the content either in writing or reading. I have been enlightened from then on and realized the instruction of my supervisor and the goal of American teaching methods just through different paths that lead to the same destination.

Well, you can't make judgments based on

"螃蟹"。虽然目前还是普通员工，但相信自己会有更好的未来。

十年后的今天，对你们只有想念。多想给你们斟上美酒，唱嘉绒藏族的祝酒歌："阿拉羌舍哟，哦阿拉果牟羌舍……"想让你们知道，当年的少年，现在已经是有担当的男人，我的家乡、我的国家都在蒸蒸日上，感谢你们对我付出的所有。

现在的我，已经成家立业。我相信命运与缘分，我的爱人是一名来自北川，从十年前灾难的废墟中坚强站起来的羌族姑娘。经历过灾难的我和她，更懂得感恩生活的幸福。我们在生活中相互体谅，工作上相互鼓励，事业、生活蒸蒸日上。我向她讲述了在美国的见闻，并约定一起到美国我曾经生活学习过的地方走走，见见我的美国亲人。

我热爱自己的祖国，喜欢在四川

established concepts or even rumors. If you want to make some comments on something, you will have no say unless you experience something yourself. This is also the case with the mutual understanding between China and the United States.

### Keep on Moving in the Recent Ten Years after Returning

Through the experience of studying in the United States, I felt that much of my current knowledge still needed to be improved and I could have more time to enrich myself, so I chose to study in a graduate school after I returned to China. Upon my employment, I caught opportunities of transformation and invariably did the latest business of the company in the banking outlets, the channel management office, the provincial branch, the company business, and in the field of financial technology. Although I am still an ordinary employee, I believe I will have a better future.

Ten years later, I still miss those of my American friends very much. How I wish I could fill them with a cup of good wine, and sing the toasted songs of the Jiarong Tibetans to them! I wish I could let them know that the young boy then has grown into a responsible man, and my hometown and my country have become more prosperous. Thank them so much for everything they did for me.

Now I have gotten married and started my career. I believe in fate and chemistry. My wife, a woman of Qiang nationality from Beichuan, survived the earthquake ten years ago. Since both of us experienced that disaster, we are

的生活。祖国蒸蒸日上，我让自己忙起来，并十分享受这样的节奏和状态。相比娱乐休闲，个人的提升和家庭的美满更使我满足。留学的经历，让我看到了太平洋彼岸的精彩，也让我更加珍视祖国以及亲人和朋友。

文化冲击客观存在，我也是亲身经历才之后明白它的威力。我认为求同和融合是交流之道，我们都爱NBA，都爱熊猫，都听 Rap，都看功夫片，三明治可以夹"老干妈"，大饼也能卷热狗……我们发现共同的爱好，组合咱们的文化，既新颖，又亲密。

未来十年，我希望将祖国和美国人民的这份爱传递下去，在工作上进一步体现自己的价值，为社会做出更大的贡献。

more grateful about the happiness of life. We understand each other in life, and encourage each other at work. Our work and life are thriving. I told her about my experience in the United States, and promised her to visit together the places I lived and studied in the States and to meet my American relatives one day.

The United States is great, but I love my motherland more and enjoy the life in Sichuan. I want to be a part of the booming China. I busy myself with life and work, and enjoy such kind of pace and state. I am satisfied with the self-growth and a happy family rather than entertainment, leisure and indulgence. The experience of studying abroad has not only brought me the wonderfulness of the other side of the Pacific Ocean, but also made me value my motherland, my family, my friends and my loved ones at home more.

Culture shock is present, and I know its power because I experienced it myself. I believe that it is the correct way of communication to seek common ground and integration. We all love NBA games, pandas, rap, and *kungfu* movies. Sandwiches may be mingled with chili sauce, while sausage may be coated with Chinese pancake. It will be novel and intimate to find common hobbies and fuse different cultures into the one of our own.

In the next ten years, I hope to pass on this love from the Chinese people and American people, realize my own values at work, and make greater contributions to the society.

# 温暖与感动常怀心间

## Warmth & Gratitude Always in My Heart

王磊 / 电子科技大学　纽约州立大学詹姆斯敦社区学院

Wang Lei / University of Electronic Science and Technology of China　SUNY Jamestown Community College

一晃离"5·12"汶川特大地震已经过去十年，我从詹姆斯敦社区大学回来也有九年多了。这些年，我经历了读研、工作、结婚、生子，每次都想写点什么，谈谈最近的工作和生活，回忆一下在美国的那段时光，见见当时和我一起出去留学的可爱的人，以及那些帮助过我的老师和同学，尤其想给詹姆斯敦社区大学的老师们说说近况，但自己的懒惰总是占了上风。

### 收获爱情和友谊

转眼这么多年过去，虽然在工作上我没有取得很大的成就，平平淡淡，但是这段美国学习经历不仅让我

It's been ten years since Wenchuan Earthquake, and I have been back from Jamestown Community College for more than nine years. Over the years, I went through postgraduate study, employment, marriage, and the birth of children... My sloth always prevailed whenever I wanted to write something about my recent work and life, to recall the time in the United States, or to meet those loving people who went abroad with me and teachers and classmates who helped me, especially to report my current developments to the teachers at Jamestown Community College, so there are almost no connections.

### Harvesting Love & Friendship

So many years passed in the blink of an eye. Although I have not achieved any great achievements in the work nor do I have a wonderful life, I've learned a lot and harvested love from this experience. Both my wife and I

学习到了更多，也让我收获了爱情。当时我和我现在的妻子是一起参加"CSC-SUNY 150奖学金项目"的，我们俩从那个时候走到现在，家庭和睦，幸福美满。

我们会聊到参加过"CSC-SUNY 150奖学金项目"的同学，以前大家的样子和有趣的故事，以及他们现在的生活状态和工作，虽然联系不多，但一直关注着。包括之前的副校长玛里琳·扎格拉博士、校长格里高利博士、我们的任课老师，以及经历过的那些事情，我现在都记得清清楚楚。特别是有一个同学叫本·拉森，那时候关系很好，我现在也还特别关注他。我还去他家和他的家人一起过圣诞节，我仍记得，圣诞树上挂满了雪花、袜子和小礼物，大家互赠圣诞礼物，吃着烤火鸡，其乐融融，很温暖，很亲切。

## 一次有仪式感的生日

最近生日又要到了，不由得想起在美国时凯瑟琳老师给我过的特别生日。在那之前每次我的生日都是平淡无奇的，爸爸妈妈跟我说，今天是你生日，祝你生日快乐，没有礼物，也没有大餐，没有惊喜。

生在农村的我那时比较特立独行，又远在他乡，所以那年的生日是

were members of the CSC-SUNY 150 Program. From then on, we've been together with a harmonious and very happy family.

We would talk about the classmates who have participated in the program, the way they used to be, the interesting stories, and their current state of life and work. Although there are no frequent contacts, they have always been our concerns. Clearly remembered were those things we experienced and people, including the former Vice-Chancellor Dr. Marilyn Zagora, Principal Dr. Gregory T. DeCinque, and the teachers who have helped us. I have paid special attention to a classmate named Ben Lassen, who got on the right foot with me then. I went to his home for Christmas with his family. I still remember that the Christmas tree was covered with snowflakes, socks and small gifts; people were exchanging Christmas gifts and eating the roast turkey in such a happy and warm atmosphere.

### A Birthday of Ritual Sense

My birthday is coming again, which reminds me of the special birthday my teacher Catherine gave me in the United States. Before that, my birthdays were always ordinary with just the reminder and greetings from my parents instead of gifts or big meals. So the joy of birthday was very insipid to me.

Born in the countryside, I was a bit "maverick", and plus being far away from home, I spent my birthday alone that year. The only thing that could distinguish the birthday was the tradition of my hometown that I observed: cooking an egg on birthday, eating it and throwing the eggshell into the river. I have got no

自己一个人过的。唯一能记得老家过生日传统是要煮一个鸡蛋，吃完后蛋壳要扔河里。我到现在都不知道这有什么含义，但生日那天还是照着做了。其他的就完全和平时一样，没有蛋糕，也没有蜡烛，我也习惯了这种简单的过生日方式。

我们几个同学到詹姆斯敦社区大学后，许多老师都对我们特别照顾，热情邀请我们到他们家里去做客，请我们吃好吃的，感受一下地道的美国家庭是怎样的。

印象最深的是凯瑟琳老师。我还记得在她家和她的家人一起吃各种派，还有火鸡等。聊天时，她问我们各自的生日。当她得知我的生日刚过

ideas about what it means even now, but I still did it accordingly on my birthday. Except this, it was just as usual: no cake or candles. I probably got used to this simple way of birthday.

When we came to Jamestown Community College, many teachers, no matter whether they taught us or not, took particular care of us. They invited us to their home warmly, entertained us with delicious food and wanted us to feel what an authentic American family looked like.

The most impressive teacher was Catherine. When we ate pies and turkeys in her house with her family, she asked us about our birthday. When she learned that my birthday just passed and there was no birthday party, she was shocked because Americans paid more attention to the festival ritual. Then she said, "You should make up a birthday."

I thought she was just showing her courtesy, so I didn't take it seriously. Until one day, a call from Catherine said that she had reserved a table in a restaurant in downtown and wanted to make up a birthday for me. I was so confused that how could there be such a genuine person at first, but then was deeply moved. It was beyond my expectation that someone would celebrate my birthday for me abroad. Perhaps this is the sense of ritual that Americans have on their holidays. Anyhow, it was an unforgettable invitation.

Then Catherine and her husband, Anton, drove to pick me up. This was my first time to have a big dinner of authentic beef steak in a restaurant abroad. At that time, there happened to be the Christmas Parade and I saw the parade float for the first time. It was warm and touching that someone abroad held a birthday party for me. It was quite special and unbelievable for me even until now.

不久，并且没有生日会时，她很吃惊，因为美国人都比较注重节日的仪式感，当时她就说我应该补过一个生日。

我那时也就当作客气话，听听罢了。后来有一天，我突然接到凯瑟琳的电话，她说在市中心的餐厅定了位，要给我补生日。我一下懵了，觉得怎么会有这么较真的人，但随之而来的就是感动。在异国他乡有人给我过生日，还真期待呢！

后来凯瑟琳和她丈夫安东驱车来接我，我第一次在餐厅享受了正宗的外国牛排大餐。当时还刚好遇上了圣诞游行，第一次看了彩车。那天既温暖又感动，在异国他乡有人为我过生日，挺特别的，我到现在都觉得有点不可思议。

## 发散思维让我更有创造力

在美国学习这段时间，我注意到国内外教育上的差异。比如，对我影响最深的应该就是批判性思维，特别是在写作中。作文课要写，体育课也要写。写文章的时候，老师要求我们正面和反面都要想到，而且必须进行论证。这让我平时看待事情会尽量全面地去分析，而非单方面、片面地去看待。

美国的学校学生少，所以我们和

**Greater Creativity with Divergent Thinking**

During the study in the United States, I found there were many different things between education home and abroad. For example, what affected me most was critical thinking, which could be felt at almost everything you did, particularly when writing articles. We were required to write essays not only in composition classes, but also in other courses, including physical education classes. When writing, the teacher asked us to put both the pros and cons into consideration before demonstrating them. It taught me to look at things in a more comprehensive way, rather than on the basis of the unilateral analyses.

The number of students was small in a university of the United States, so we had a lot of opportunities to communicate with our teachers. I could feel the great care for us from teachers' hearts, which made me warm while abroad.

American education paid special attention to practical ability, so there were many tools in school. As long as the course had practical parts or when there were events for actual

老师的沟通机会很多。老师关心我们每个人，身处异国他乡，这让我觉得很温暖。

美国的教育特别注重动手能力，学校有各种各样的工具，只要是实践的课程或者遇到有实操性的事情，都会让我们去动手操作，当时我自己也做了很多东西。

人们常说经历过的事情总会潜移默化地影响你之后的生活，所以经历过美国的学习，我不再像大学一年级那样，照搬高中的学习模式——老师上课我认真听，课后自己去自习理解——而是更喜欢让自己的思维发散出去，多角度分析问题和课程内容。这样我思考得更多，收获也就更多。这一点对我之后的研究生学习和工作起到了很大的作用，我更有创造力。

这些年虽然与詹姆斯敦社区大学老师们的联系变少了，但詹姆斯敦社区大学的各种事却留在我心里。非常感谢他们，是他们让我拥有那影响我一生的难忘的美国之旅！

经历了大地震以后，我也更加珍惜现在的生活，感恩所有帮助和支持过我们的人。

performance, we were allowed to operate. So I made a lot of stuff at that time.

It is often said that one's experience will unconsciously affect one's life hereafter. After my experience in the United States, I did not copy the high school learning mode as I did when I was a freshman. Instead of listening attentively in class and digesting the lecture by self-study after class, I preferred divergent thinking, analyzing the problem and course content from multiple angles. By doing so, the more I thought, the more I would gain. Divergent thinking also played a major role in my graduate study and work, making me more creative.

Although there have been fewer contacts with teachers at Jamestown Community College over the years, I often think of things at Jamestown Community College. I really appreciate them for that unforgettable trip to the United States, which will affect my whole life!

After the earthquake, I cherish my present life more, and I am grateful to those who have helped and supported us.

# 那一年后，我把整个人生都留在校园里

## Since That Year, I Have Devoted My Whole Life on Campus

易青颖 / 电子科技大学　纽约州立大学詹姆斯敦社区学院

Yi Qingying / University of Electronic Science and Technology of China　SUNY Jamestown Community College

我是易青颖，本科、研究生就读于电子科技大学，毕业后留校工作，目前从事国际交流方面的工作。我是个特别爱吃甜食而不太能吃辣的成都人。如果问我喜欢什么甜食，我会回答我偏爱美式甜品。

这应该源于 2008 年至 2009 年，在美国度过的那一段时光。

I am Yi Qingying, graduated from the University of Electronic Science and Technology with a bachelor's and master's degree. After graduation, I continued to work at my university and engaged in work related to international exchanges. I am a native of Chengdu, but prefer sweets to spicy food. If someone asks me what sweets I like, my answer would be American desserts.

This answer stemmed from the time spent in the United States from 2008 to 2009.

### 回首

### Retrospect

记得接到辅导员电话的时候是在 2008 年的暑假前，得知有一个"CSC-SUNY 150 奖学金项目"，我并没有抱太大的希望，没有觉得自己会成为其中的一员。在两周内快速

I can remember that I received a phone call from the counselor right before the summer vacation and got to know the CSC-SUNY 150 Program. I didn't take it seriously because I didn't feel that I would be part of it. Then, in two weeks, I went through rounds of interviews

地经历学校、中国留学基金委员会的各轮面试，马不停蹄地办理护照、签证，接下来记得的就是在飞往纽约的飞机上了。

离开成都时，心里还有对刚认识一年的大学同学的不舍，但很快取而代之的就是初到纽约的强烈兴奋感。那个时候，我刚17岁，可能是"CSC-SUNY 150奖学金项目"里最小的成员。在纽约市短暂而又充实的几天很快过去了，150名成员分别前往纽约州立大学的不同校区学习、生活。我和另外4名同学一起到了位于纽约州北部的小镇詹姆斯敦，开始了为期9个月的交换生生活。

也许是因为我们都还是一群孩子，对一切都充满好奇，在詹姆斯敦的那段时光过得快乐而充实，并没有太多的不适应。我们和美国同学一起住在学校的宿舍里，相处得非常融洽。现在回想起来，似乎一切都还历历在目。

詹姆斯敦在纽约州的北部靠近水牛城，尼亚加拉瀑布所在的城市，离加拿大很近。让我印象最深的就是，才10月这里竟然就开始下雪，让我们这几个来自中国南方的小孩特别兴奋。不过雪下久了，我们也就腻了，每天出门都裹得厚厚的，担心滑倒。而詹姆斯敦的雪一直到来年4月才完

with the school and China Scholarship Council quickly, and rushed to apply for my passport and visa. After that, all I remembered was that I was on the plane to New York.

When I left Chengdu, my emotions were mixed with reluctance to part with my college fellows I had just known for a year; but this mood was quickly diluted by the excitement of arriving in New York. I was just 17 years old then and probably the youngest member in the program. The short and substantial days in New York City passed quickly, and we 150 members went to study and live on different campuses of SUNY. I, with other four students, went to Jamestown, a small town in northern New York, and started a nine-month exchange student life.

Maybe, because we were still young, and curious about everything, we had a happy and rich time in Jamestown, and did not feel very unsuitable. We lived in the dormitory with American students harmoniously. In retrospect, everything was still vivid.

Jamestown is in the north of New York State and near Buffalo, the city of Niagara Falls, and is close to Canada. The most impressive thing was that it started to snow heavily in October. At the beginning, the snow made us southern Chinese feel very excited. However, we got bored of the snow when it lasted for a long time, because we had to wrap ourselves in thick clothes every day and worried about slips on the snow. Not until in April of next year did the snow in Jamestown would cease. In this period, the happiest time was to be notified that school closed due to the blizzard. Our fondness toward this quiet town didn't faint even if the winter lasted for nearly half a year. We enjoyed the beauty of the town

全消停。中间最开心的时候，就是收到因暴风雨而停课的通知。当然，长达近半年的冬天，也并没有减少我们对这个宁静小镇的喜欢，我们见过它每个季节的美，也知道哪条街道上有好吃的比萨和布法罗鸡翅。

对于一个地方的记忆，往往都是跟人有关的。我的概率课老师里克，是一个胡子花白的大叔。每天开着一辆皮卡来上班，住在离镇上挺远的一片森林里。每年冬天他会打猎，邀请我们去吃鹿肉。一次我们在他家客厅坐着吃鹿肉的时候，门外刚好来了一头鹿觅食，那种奇怪又复杂的感觉至今难忘。情人节的时候，里克带着我们一起做心形饼干，包装好之后拿去售卖，把赚来的钱捐给当地社区的慈善机构，那应该是我第一次对做公益有了切身的体会。他每年还会自己做枫树糖浆，我们临走时送了每人一瓶。在我回国后的很多年，我们还保持联系，他告诉我今年詹姆斯敦又下了多厚的雪，给我看他今年打猎的成果。我告诉他我本科毕业了，研究生毕业了，工作了，恋爱了，换工作了，分手了……他像是个遥远而又温暖的港湾，即使知道也许再也不会见面，但是却可以分享一切。

还有负责我们留学生事务的约翰，一个胖胖的特别搞笑的可爱的人。

at each season and we knew in which street we could buy delicious pizza and Buffalo wings.

The memory of a place was often related to people. Rick, my teacher of Probability class, was a white-bearded uncle. He lived in a forest far from the town and drove a pickup to work every day. He went hunting every winter and invited us to eat venison. While sitting in his living room and eating venison, outside the door came a deer for food. Those strange and complicated feelings were still unforgettable. On Valentine's Day, Rick taught us how to make heart-shaped biscuits and sold them after packaging. The earned money was donated to charities in the local community. That was the first time I started to experience affairs of public welfare. He also made maple syrup himself every year and sent each of us a bottle to take home before our departure. In these years after I returned to China, we still kept in touch. He told me that Jamestown had another heavy snow this year, showed me his hunting results this year. I told him that I graduated from college, graduated from graduate school, worked, fell in love, changed jobs, and broke up... He, like a distant and warm harbor, knows that we may not meet again, but can still share everything.

There was also John, a chubby, funny and cute guy. He was responsible for our international

他最大的特点就是节约，会告诉我们哪儿买面包最便宜，哪儿买水果最便宜，总之就是掌握一切打折信息，最充分地使用各种优惠券。没过多久，他换了新工作去了华盛顿，大概是因为薪水高些吧。第二年我们春假去华盛顿玩，约他见面。他带我们去了当地的酒吧，当然也是因为"Happy Hour"时段可以五折！

我是一个记忆力不太好的人，但回首这一年，很多事情都记得特别清晰，具体到每个人、每件事。当然，最难忘的是这一年在美国增加的十多公斤体重，并且让我成了一个重度甜食爱好者。

## 十年

十年过去，好像一切都没有变，却又都变了。因为工作的关系，我没有离开过校园，似乎还一直以一个学生的样子生活着，所以有时候会觉得生活并没有多大改变。

在美国的学习结束后，我的口语水平有了很大的提升。我虽然是一名工科生，但一直对英语很感兴趣。回国后，我参加了很多活动，如参与各种国际会议、国际赛事，担任志愿者，有时候也会受邀主持一些国际交流活动。研究生期间，我加入了电气和电

student affairs. His strongest trait was thrift. He would tell us where to buy the most inexpensive bread or fruit. In his hands were all the discount information and the best way to use various coupons. Shortly afterwards, he had a new job in Washington, perhaps due to the higher salary there. The next year, we went to Washington in spring break, and met him. He took us to the local bar, of course, in the Happy Hour with a 50% discount !

Although my memory was poor, many things happening that year are still vivid in my mind, including everyone and everything. Of course, the most unforgettable thing was that I put on weight of more than ten kilograms in the United States that year, and became a heavy sweet tooth.

### The Ten Years

Ten years later, it seems that nothing has changed, but everything has really changed. Due to my work, I haven't left the campus, and still live as a student. That's why I don't feel much change in my life sometimes.

At the end of my studies in the U.S., my spoken language was improved greatly. Although I was an engineering student, I had always been

子工程师协会学生分会，并积极参与各项活动。2013 年，我获得了"IEEE Computer Society"颁发的"Richard E. Merwin Student Scholarship"，该奖项每年在全球范围授予 16 名在学术及社会活动中表现优秀的学生会员，同时我也成为 IEEE 亚太区的学生大使之一。2014 年，我从电子科技大学研究生毕业，获得了"四川省优秀毕业生"称号。毕业之后，我最终选择了留校工作。今年 5 月份，我开始负责学校的国际交流项目的相关工作，这是我在目前的人生阶段觉得自己想要去尝试并努力的事情，我想这跟我在美国的经历是有着必然联系的。

前几天，与詹姆斯敦很久没有联系过的老师纳尔逊沟通。我告诉他我现在的工作是在电子科技大学担任国际协调员，他很开心，也特别好奇。我们希望通过我目前的角色来开展一些交流活动。

这一切感觉很奇妙，因为这不仅仅是工作，更多的是我们的那些情怀。我想，也许就在不久的将来，我可以重返詹姆斯敦，去看看我们离开时种下的那棵树。

interested in English. After returning home, I participated in many activities, including various international conferences, international competitions, volunteering, and sometimes being invited to help host some international exchange activities. During my graduate study, I joined the student branch of the IEEE (Institute of Electrical and Electronics Engineers) and took an active part in its various events. In 2013, I received the Richard E. Merwin Student Scholarship from the IEEE Computer Society, which awards per year 16 student members who have performed outstandingly in academic and social activities worldwide, and I also became a student ambassador for IEEE Asia Pacific. In 2014, I graduated from the University of Electronic Science and Technology with a master's degree and won the title of Sichuan Excellent Graduate. After graduation, I chose to work in my school. From May of this year, I am in charge of work related to international exchanges, which is what I feel that I want to try and work hard at in the current stage of life. I think this is indispensable with my experience in the United States.

A few days ago, I regained communication with Nelson, a teacher of Jamestown, whom I hadn't contacted for a long time. When I told him that my current job was an international coordinator at the University of Electronic Science and Technology, he was very happy and very curious. We hope to promote more international exchange projects again with the aid of my current role.

All this was wonderful, because it was those feelings inside rather than the work only. I believe that I can go back to Jamestown in the near future to visit that tree we planted before we left.

## 感念

### My Gratitude

感谢中国留学基金委员会和SUNY在十年前合力促成了"CSC-SUNY 150奖学金项目"这么棒的项目，感谢所有背后付出的人们。我想"CSC-SUNY 150奖学金项目"中很多人的人生会因此而有了或多或少的改变。感谢詹姆斯敦社区大学，给了我难忘的生活和学习体验，并且有幸认识那么多善良、有趣的人们。

今后，我希望在国际交流工作中做更多有意义的事情，参与公益活动。希望未来某一天，我能够通过教育部驻外后备干部的选拔去到某个国家，换个角度和层次去实现自己的价值。我想，人生的价值不需要金钱和地位来衡量。在每一个当下我都做自己认为有意义的事情，对社会产生了一点点的益处，那便足矣。

Thanks to the China Scholarship Council and SUNY for contributing to such a great program CSC-SUNY 150 ten years ago, and thanks to everyone who has been working behind it. I believe that lives of many people in the CSC-SUNY 150 Program have changed more or less. Thanks to Jamestown Community College for giving me an unforgettable life and learning experience, and thanks for the luck of meeting so many good and interesting people.

For the future, I hope I can promote more meaningful projects in international exchanges, and participate more in public welfare affairs. I hope that one day, I may go to a certain country through the selection of the overseas reserve cadres of the Ministry of Education so as to achieve my value from a different angle and level. I don't think that life can be weighed by money and status. At every moment, I do what I think is meaningful and beneficial to the society, and that is enough.

# 美国之行，我人生轨迹的转折点

## The Trip to America, a Turning Point of My Life Path

杨永益 / 电子科技大学　纽约州立大学詹姆斯敦社区学院

Yang Yongyi / University of Electronic Science and Technology of China　SUNY Jamestown Community College

"CSC-SUNY 150奖学金项目"已经是十年前的事了。那一年中大多数片段恍如梦境，但认识的人、受到的感动却又那么真切。它们已是我生命中的一部分并将永远留在记忆中。

得知"CSC-SUNY 150奖学金项目"的消息，是在"5·12"汶川特大地震后的一个下午。彼时暑假刚刚开始，我正在老家都江堰的一个灾民安置点与父母的朋友一起做整理。虽经历了灾难，幸运的是除了房屋倒塌家人并没有受伤，看来那里在一个时期内会成为我们暂时的家了。

告诉我"CSC-SUNY 150奖学金项目"的是大学辅导员张老师。当然报名的人很多，要经过严格的选拔

It's been ten years since the CSC-SUNY 150 Program started up. Too many fragments in that year were just like dreams. However, the people we met, the touching feeling we felt were so real that they have become part of my life, which I will always cherish.

I got the information of the program in one afternoon of the summer vacation after the Wenchuan earthquake when I was cleaning up with my parents' friends in a temporary settlement in my hometown—Dujiangyan City. Although we just went through a disaster that had made houses collapsed, luckily nobody in my family got injured. It seemed that the settlement would be our temporary home for a while.

Mr. Zhang, my university counselor, told me about the program and he also mentioned that there would be a strict screening before I could make it. I don't remember clearly the details about the screening, but I still could feel the

才能够成行。现在已记不清一路选拔的细节，但当最后进入大名单时，还是觉得不可思议。"真的有这样的事情？"即使参加了接近两周的选拔，我到最后仍然还在问自己这个问题。对于在山区长大的我来说，飞机都还没坐过，如果获得一个机会去上海，我就会很高兴了。但如果突然告诉我是去美国，我会觉得这完全是个玩笑。

## 詹姆斯敦很小，却充满温情

就这样，带着疑惑、兴奋、憧憬以及第一次离开家乡的忐忑，我们踏上了美国的土地。我记得当时正值北京奥运会开幕之际，通过电视，很多普通美国民众也是第一次如此清晰地了解现在的中国，也因为北京奥运会，我们有了很好的机会尽快融入当地的生活。我们也是第一次在电视之外，接触到普通的美国人，走进美国人的生活。

excitement when I saw myself on the candidate list with other 149 people. "That was incredible!" I kept asking myself if this was true until the last minute, even though I had been in the screening process for nearly two weeks. I grew up in a remote mountainous area and had never traveled by plane. I guess I would have been very happy if somebody told me that I could go to Shanghai. But if he told me that I could go to the United States, I would think he must have been joking with me.

### The Small Town of Jamestown But Full of Warmth

With the feelings of suspicion, excitement, longing and anxiety, we left Sichuan for the US for the first time. It was during the Beijing Olympic Games then. Many American people got to know a modern China with a clearer picture through television for the first time. Thanks to the Beijing Olympic Games, we had got a precious opportunity to integrate ourselves into American life and to meet general American people.

I was assigned to go to the Jamestown Community College (JCC) with four other peers. The college was located in a beautiful town of Jamestown in northwest New York State. Unlike the prosperous and bustling big cities like New York City, Jamestown was full of warmth and kindness.

What impressed me a lot was that the second day after we arrived at Jamestown, we came across an old couple while walking in a park after dinner. As soon as they saw us with typical Asian faces, they greeted us in a very friendly way and asked us if we were the

我与其他四个同学被分配到位于纽约州西北部的詹姆斯敦的社区学院进行项目交流，这是一个非常美丽的小镇，它不像纽约等大城市那样繁华，但充满了温馨与人情。

令我印象很深的一件事是在我们到达詹姆斯敦的第二天，我们一行人吃过晚饭在住地旁的一个公园散步，迎面走来一对老年夫妇，见到我们几个东方面孔便立刻友好地向我们打招呼，问我们是不是那五个中国交换生。我感到很诧异，询问他们为什么知道此事，是不是学校的老师。原来他们与校长、教务主任等都会去同一个教堂，用他们的话说，詹姆斯敦很小，大家也都经常走动，有五个外国留学生那是可以上当地报纸的大新闻了。就这样，我们在詹姆斯敦的一年，除了平时上课，学校的老师、同学，包括当地认识的其他朋友总是把我们的周末安排得满满的，邀请我们参加他们的聚会，或者到当地名胜参观或到他们的家中拜访，我们过得相当充实。

这期间，詹姆斯敦的校方及老师们也给了我们无微不至的关照，我们到达时，副校长玛里琳·扎格拉及主任纳尔逊亲自来机场接我们到住地，并专门安排我们生活起居的方方面面，可以说尽最大可能让我们适应当

five exchange students from China. I felt quite surprised that they knew us, and asked why and wondered if they were teachers in the college after giving them a positive reply. They told us that they would go to the same church with the principal and provost, and Jamestown was so small that even five international students from China could dominate the headlines. Therefore, for the whole year in Jamestown, our weekends were all filled with various appointments with teachers and classmates from the college and friends we'd made in the town. We went to their parties, visited their houses or took sightseeing around some scenic spots. Life there had become substantial and fulfilling.

The managers and teachers from JCC also offered us thoughtful help during our stay. Ms. Marilyn Zagora, the vice-principal, and Mr. Nelson Garifi, the director of the college, picked us up at the airport and even arranged everything for our living. They tried their best to make us better adapted to the local life. For all that I can recall are just some fragmentary memories, those friends and teachers were definitely the most cherished treasure in my life in that wonderful and busy year.

When we were about to leave America, Marilyn even came all the way to New York City from Jamestown to see us off.

地的生活。虽然现在只能想起一些零星的片段，但是这些朋友与老师让我们度过了快乐而又充实的一年。

在我们即将离开美国的时候，玛里琳还专程从詹姆斯敦飞到纽约和我们道别。

## 从腼腆内向到为爱打拼

回看这些年的人生选择，受美国之行的影响较大。我从一个性格比较腼腆内向的大男孩变成了一个渴望国际化视野的"菜鸟"毕业生。

大学毕业后，我到专业较为对口的华为技术有限公司工作。由于有在国外学习的相关背景，在华为也负责对国外项目的投标，包括部分交付工作。这期间，我在德国、法国、荷兰等地都留下了战斗的足迹。当然，这些算不上什么成就，只能算是一种经历。通过与形形色色的项目、客户打交道，我也在积累经验，寻找真正可以为之奋斗一生的目标。

### A Shy Boy Turned into a Bold One

I can say that the life path of mine has been deeply influenced by the trip to the US. I grew up from an introverted and shy boy to a newbie graduate who was longing for an international view.

Hence, after graduation, I went to Huawei Technologies Co., Ltd., for the works in Huawei fitted with my major. Because of my overseas studying background, I was in charge of foreign project bidding as well as some delivery work. Because of this, I travelled to Germany, France, and Netherlands. However, I'd rather call it experience than achievements. Through communicating with numerous clients and accomplishing different projects, I kept improving myself and continued to seek for a goal that I would fight for in my whole life.

After travelling over the world for several years, I finally chose to go back to China, to my hometown—Sichuan, where all my families and friends are, and started my own career in Chengdu.

In the next decade, I will devote my most valuable time and energy in my hometown, where the CSC-SUNY 150 Program started. Ten years after the earthquake, my hometown now is full of vigor and vitality.

经过几年在世界各地的奔波，我选择回国内发展，回到了成都家人朋友的身边，在这里继续奋斗。

未来的十年，我将把人生中最精华的一段时间和精力用在四川，我的家乡。这里是我与"CSC-SUNY 150奖学金项目"结缘的地方，地震十年后，这里正焕发出勃勃的生机。

感谢"CSC-SUNY 150奖学金项目"，让我有机会开启了一段不平凡的经历，也在这个过程中获得了很多宝贵的经验。感谢远在詹姆斯敦的老师，虽然现在只能通过电子邮件跟他们联系，但我还是定下一个小目标，在不远的将来邀请他们到四川来看看，请他们看看这个他们曾经帮助和关照过的男孩儿深爱并将继续挥洒热血的地方。我深知，回报他们的最好方式，就是在这片土地上做出更大的贡献。

I would like to thank the CSC-SUNY 150 Program for providing me a chance to start a unique adventure, gaining tons of experiences and abilities. My great appreciation also goes to those teachers in Jamestown. Although we can only contact with each other via e-mails, I still make up my mind that someday in the near future I will invite all of them to visit Sichuan, for the boy they used to help and take care of has profound love for his hometown and will continue to fight for his career there. I truly believe that the best way to reward those helps and caring is to create my own value on this land.

# 难忘那一年

## That Unforgettable Year

钟灏／电子科技大学　纽约州立大学法明戴尔分校

Zhong Hao / University of Electronic Science and Technology of China　SUNY Farmingdale State College

我毕业于电子科技大学，在美学习期间就读于纽约州立大学法明戴尔分校。现就职于四川省绵阳市公安局交警支队。

岁月如梭，一眨眼十年过去了，经历了十年的成长，再次回忆过去的时光，真是感慨万千。

2008 年的那个夏天，刚刚从地震中缓过神来的我们接到了前往纽约学习一年的邀请。在两国政府和学校的大力支持下，在短短一个月的时间内便完成了培训、签证等准备工作，速度之快让我在踏上飞机的那一刻都还有一种在做梦的感觉。

直到飞机起飞，看着脚下的故土越来越远，我才慢慢梳理好那些兴奋、

I am from the UESTC (University of Electronic Science and Technology of China). I studied at the State University of New York at Farmingdale during my studies in the United States. Now I am working in the Traffic Police Detachment of the Public Security Bureau of Mianyang, Sichuan Province.

How time flies! A decade has passed in the blink of an eye. However, I always feel amazed at my growth of the ten years whenever I recall the past.

In the summer of 2008, when we were still in the shock of the earthquake, we received an invitation to study in New York. With the support of the governments and schools of both China and United States, we completed all the preparatory work such as training and visa within one month, so quickly that I felt as if I were in a dream even at the moment I stepped on the plane.

It wasn't until the plane took off, watching

憧憬、思念交织的情绪，准备开始一段全新的生活。

## 感恩遇见

在美国的一年，美国人民和在美华人等众多热心人士给予我们很多帮助和关爱，远离家乡的孤独感在他们友善的态度中慢慢消融。

记得刚到美国时，因为交流不畅，生活习惯不同，我倍感不适，但是有幸结实了美国的同班同学阿俊，在他的帮助下，我在美国的生活省去了不少麻烦。

阿俊是华裔移民，八九岁时便随母亲一起移民到了美国，可以说是地道的美国人了。留学期间，阿俊用他不太流畅的汉语帮我们做翻译，在他的帮助下，我们快速了解了美国的人情风俗、文化习惯。

私家车在美国很普遍，人们自己开车出行，乘坐公交的人很少，一小

the homeland under my feet getting farther and farther, that I gradually held down the emotions of excitement, vision, and thoughts, and started a brand new life.

### Grateful for the Encounter

The year at the United States witnessed help and care for us from the American people, overseas Chinese in the US and many enthusiasts. The sense of loneliness away from home was slowly melting in their kindness.

I can still recall that I was not suited to the difficult communication and different life style when I first arrived in the United States. However, I was fortunate enough to encounter a good American classmate, Ah Jun, whose help saved us tons of trouble in our life in the United States.

Ah Jun, a Chinese immigrant, who moved to the United States with his mother when he was eight or nine years old, is almost a native American. During our one-year overseas study, Ah Jun translated for us in his broken Chinese, and with his help, we were able to quickly understand the social custom and cultural habits of the United States.

Private cars were quite common in the United States, and almost all the Americans drove to a trip by themselves. Thus the bus ran hourly since few people took it, and this situation brought us much inconvenience in travel in the United States. Therefore, Ah Jun drove us to bookstores and shopping malls nearby to buy books and daily necessities on weekends.

The car was bought by Ah Jun himself, who had began working part-time to earn his tuition

时才一趟，这让我们在美国出行有些不方便。到了周末，阿俊便用他的车载我们去附近的书店、商场买书和生活用品。

车是阿俊自己赚钱买的，他从高中开始就自己打工赚学费，还要分担家里的生活开支，这让当时和他同龄的我们感到敬佩不已。不仅是阿俊，其实在美国，很多学生早早就开始勤工助学，自己养活自己，这一点和中国有很大不同。我感觉美国的教育确实更注重培养孩子独立、自主的能力。如今我的儿子已经一岁多了，因为在阿俊身上感受到了美国教育方式的优点，在教育孩子的过程中我也会更注重培养孩子独立自主的能力。

在美国学习期间，不知道是因为刚经历了一次灾难还是身处异国他乡，我变得敏感了许多，时常被来自陌生人的善意感动。

记得有一次我参加学校安排的体检，因为校医务室的冷气开得太足，导致我的血管收缩，再加上血管本身很纤细，给医务人员抽血增加了难度，已经头发花白的老校医耐心地尝试了很多次后，依然没有成功。我因为紧张晕针，差点当场倒下。当时为我抽血的老校医和在场的医护人员、同学都非常紧张，医生和护士赶紧为我做了一些急救措施。尽管我一再说我的

since high school and also shared the expenses of living at home, and this made us, his peers, admire him greatly. It is quite different from the Chinese education that not only Ah Jun but also many other students in the US take part-time jobs while studying to support themselves. I think that education in the US places more emphasis on cultivating children's independence and self-reliance. Now my son is over a year old; I will pay more attention to cultivating his ability of independence since I was impressed by the advantages of American education from Ah Jun.

During my stay in the States, I didn't know whether it was out of my recent experience of a disaster or of my living abroad that I became more sensitive and was touched by the kindness from strangers more often than before.

I can remember the situation in which I attended the medical examination arranged by the school. Because of my vasoconstriction under too much cold air of the school infirmary's cooler plus my born slender blood vessels, it became more difficult for the medical staff to draw blood. The grizzled old school doctor failed all his attempts to draw my blood though he tried patiently. It unnerved me so much that my needle sickness almost urged me to fall on the spot. Seeing this, everyone present including the old school doctor, medical staffs and my classmates also became worried, and the doctor and nurses immediately took some first-aid measures for me. Although I said repeatedly, "It's OK, I am fine," the school and the infirmary still arranged a car to send me to a larger hospital on the company of my classmates and medical staff. On the way to the hospital, the African-American classmate kept amusing me by telling jokes when he saw that I

身体已经没什么大碍了，校医院和学校还是联系了一辆车，并让同学和医护人员陪同，送我去更大的医院检查。在车上，陪同的非裔同学看我精神不济，便不停地讲笑话逗我开心，但我实在没有力气回应他一个微笑，如今想来还有些内疚。

阿俊、医护人员、讲笑话的同学以及很多我接触过的人，用温暖和善意的关怀消除了我在异国他乡的孤独感，让我的美国之行变得丰富多彩。

## 在美的学习生活

在美国，除了生活方式和国内不同，大学课堂也有些差异，我感受最深的便是他们开放、自由的课堂氛围。

美国课堂上，老师很重视和学生的互动，以此来培养学生的批判性思维。在课堂上，老师讲到某个知识点时，学生可以随时和老师讨论交流，不用举手示意或站起来。学生的发问就像我们课下聊天一样自由。而在国内的课堂上，通常是等老师发问，学生才会通过回答问题与老师有简短的交流。

美国师生之间较强的互动性可能得益于他们的小班教学模式，在我就读的美国学校，通常一个班只有十来个学生，极个别的大班也只有二十多

was muzzy, but I really didn't have any strength to squeeze a smile as a response. Now every thought of it always makes me feel ashamed and uneasy.

Ah Jun, the medical staff, the African-American classmate and many other Americans I had contacted drove away my loneness as an alien with their warmth and consideration and made my trip to the United States rich and colorful.

### School Life in the United States

In the United States, apart from some differences in life style, the university classrooms are also different from those in China. What has impressed me most is their open, and free classroom atmosphere.

In the American classroom, teachers value the interaction with students so as to cultivate students' critical thinking. In class, when the teacher came to a certain information, it is as natural and free as chatting after class for students to interrupt and discuss it or communicate it with the teacher at any time, without raising his hand or rising from his seat. However in our domestic classroom, it is more often for students to answer the questions and have a brief communication with the teacher only when they are asked.

The better interaction between teachers and students in the US may benefit from their small class model; for instance, there were only a dozen students in a class, or seldom about 20 students in a larger class in the school in which I studied in the US. In this case, each student has the opportunity to interact with the teacher because the small number of students guarantees that the classroom order will not be affected even in full interaction.

个学生。这种情况下，每个学生都有和老师互动的机会，因为人数较少，充分互动也不会影响课堂秩序。

因为我们是插班生，所以可以自由选择喜欢的课程。我选择了一些和国内学习有关联的课程。撇开语言障碍不谈，他们的课程内容整体要比国内浅显一些，不太注重理论教学，而是更注重培养学生的实践能力和合作能力，经常让我们以小组为单位完成相关课程训练。

美国学生课外生活都非常丰富，师生关系也很融洽。十年过去了，很多记忆都变得模糊了，但是我还清楚地记得一些情景：在校长家做中国大餐，去老师家开派对，和美国同学探讨学习；感恩节的游行、圣诞节的滑冰、NBA 的篮球赛、华盛顿的白宫、纽约的时代广场、奥兰多的迪士尼等等。数不清的画面涌上心头，很多地方都留下了我们和美国朋友们的足迹。它们记录了我们在美国的快乐时光，也见证了两国人民深深的友谊。

交通和互联网的快速发展，使得如今赴美留学已经变得非常容易和普遍，我们当年遇到的困难和留学感受，如今可能已经没有多少借鉴意义。但是如果选择了留学，掌握当地通用语言是一条不变的定律，是否能够熟练使用当地语言决定你能否听懂课堂上

Since we were transfer students, we could choose any course we liked. Thus I chose some courses related to my domestic study. Besides the language barriers, I found their course content to be generally simpler than domestic ones, and they laid more emphasis on cultivating students' practical and cooperative abilities rather than on theoretical teaching. Therefore, we were often required to complete the relevant courses in groups to achieve the teaching objectives.

American students have a rich extra curricular life, and the teacher-students relationship is also very harmonious. Ten years later, although many memories have become vague, some scenes are still vivid in my mind, such as cooking the Chinese dinner at the principal's home, having a party at a teacher's house, discussing with American students, the Thanksgiving parade, skating on Christmas, the NBA basketball game, the White House at Washington, the Times Square in New York, Disney at Orlando, etc., all of which are marked with the footprints of us and our American friends and now rise in my mind like innumerable vivid pictures. They are the records of our good time in the United States and the witness of the deep friendship between the peoples of both countries.

的知识，能否快速融入当地的生活。

## 回国后的日子

回国后，我时常想起在美国的那段岁月，它拓宽了我的眼界，增加了我的阅历，让我在现在的生活中能以更广的视野去观察生活、思考工作。虽然我现在在一个平凡的岗位上做着一份平凡的工作，但是当年学到的各种知识和锻炼的能力，依然让我在工作中做出了不错的成绩，获得了单位的认可。

我本科学的是软件工程专业，2010年毕业时班上很多同学都投身互联网行业。如果没有去美国学习一年，可能我也会和大多数同学一样找一份专业对口的工作，毕竟2010年正是互联网浪潮，人人都想做时代的弄潮儿。但是美国之行多少影响了我的择业观。在那里生活时，我充分感受到美国人民对中国学生的爱护和尊重，

Thanks to the rapid development of transportation and the Internet, it is now very easy and universal to study in the United States. The difficulties we encountered and the feelings we had while studying abroad may not be of any reference today, but if you choose to study abroad, it is a constant law that you should master the local language, the proficiency of which will determine whether you can understand the knowledge in the classroom and whether you can integrate into the local life quickly.

### Life after Returning to China

After I came back to China, I often recalled my study life in the United States, which has broadened my horizons, enriched my experience, and allowed me to observe the life and think about work with a higher view and a more comprehensive perspective. Although I am doing an ordinary job in an ordinary position, the various kinds of knowledge I learned in the US has still benefited me from the company's recognition for the job well done.

As an undergraduate, my major was software engineering. When I graduated in 2010, many of my classmates joined the Internet industry. Hadn't I studied in the US for one year, I might have found a job fit in with my major as most of my classmates did. After all, in 2010 everyone wanted to be a beach swimmer to ride on the wave of the Internet. However, after the end of the trip to the United States, it more or less affected my concept of career choice. When I lived there, I fully felt the love and respect of the American people for Chinese students, which greatly satisfied my national pride. I especially wanted to join in the construction of

增强了我的民族自尊心、民族自豪感，当时我就特别想毕业后投身祖国的建设中，为祖国的繁荣昌盛贡献自己的一分力量。

毕业时，家人建议我报考绵阳的事业单位，经过充分准备，我考进了绵阳交警支队车管所。如今我已经在这里工作了六个年头，我如愿成了一名公职人员。为人民服务，做好一颗小螺丝钉，我很满足。

十年过去了，我的生活发生了很大变化，我组建了自己的家庭，有了可爱的宝宝，与在美国的朋友因为时差和生活方式不同也渐渐失去了联系。十年前的美国之行已经变成尘封的记忆，鲜有机会去触碰。我们同去的 150 人，有的已经在美国工作、定居，有的在做跨国商务，从我目前的状态来看，美国的学习体验对我如今的工作影响不大，但它却深深影响了我的人生观、世界观和价值观。

如果说我现在看待事物更包容、更多元，我对待人生的态度变得更豁

the motherland after graduation, and contribute to the prosperity of the motherland.

Upon graduation, my family suggested that I apply for a position of the public institution in Mianyang. After thorough preparation, I was admitted to the vehicle management office of the Mianyang Traffic Police Detachment. Now I have been working here for six years. I have fulfilled my wish to be a civil servant. Just as a small screw, I am still satisfied with doing my part by serving the people.

My life has changed greatly for the ten years. I have my own family and a lovely baby now, and gradually lost contact with my friends in the States due to the jet lag and different lifestyle. The trip to the United States ten years ago has almost become dust-filled memories which are rarely to be touched. Among the 150 people I went with, some have worked and settled in the United States, and some are doing multinational business. In the light of my current state, my American learning experience affects little on my current work, but it has imprinted my outlook on life, worldview and values.

It must be inseparable from the trip to the United States in 2008 that I become more inclusive, treating things from diversified perspectives, and more open-minded to deal with life. While living in the States, we were exposed to vivid and lively individuals with distinct personalities, who, just like ordinary people in our country, treated people friendly and loved their country. At the same time, because I have contacted different cultures and experienced different lifestyles, my vision and pattern have been improved. Thus I have learned not to be entangled with trivial things in my life, and adjust

达，那一定离不开 2008 年的美国之行。在美国的那一年，我们接触的是一个个生动立体、性格鲜明的普通人。他们和我们国家的普通百姓一样，待人友善，热爱自己的国家。同时，因为接触了不同的文化，感受了不同的生活方式，我的视野开阔了。我不再纠结于生活中一些鸡毛蒜皮的小事，生活中遇到难过的事也会快速调节自己的情绪。这种积极的处世方式，是美国之行馈赠给我最大的礼物。

未来的某一天，我希望带着我的家人和孩子重新回我生活学习过的地方，带他们看看世界的辽阔，给他们讲讲我在美国的故事。

如今，国家鼓励年轻人外出交流学习，通过"走出去"和"引进来"，提升青年的眼界和格局，以更加开放和包容的姿态来面对世界的竞争和挑战。很多高校也开展了

my mood quickly when I come across something sad. Such kind of positive attitude toward life is the greatest reward to me by the trip to the United States.

One day in the future, I will take my family and children back to the places I once lived and studied in, and take them to see the vastness of the world, to feel the friendship of the American people, and to tell them my old stories in the United States. I also hope that in the next ten years, I will have the opportunity to meet more American friends and have the opportunity to make greater contributions to consolidate the Sino-US friendship.

Nowadays, the state encourages young people to go abroad for exchange and study. Through continuous implemenation of "going global" and "bringing in" strategy, the vision and pattern of the youth will be improved so

对外交流学习项目，与当时的我们相比，现在的学生有更多机会走出国门看看，这是中国教育非常大的进步。

as to meet the world competition and challenges in a more open and inclusive manner. Now since many colleges and universities in China have also set up exchange programs for foreign exchanges, students have more opportunities to go abroad as compared with us at that time, and this is a huge step forward in Chinese education.

# 十年回首，枝繁叶茂

## Ten Years Has Witnessed the Flourish of My life

张锐 / 电子科技大学　纽约州立大学法明戴尔分校

Zhang Rui / University of Electronic Science and Technology of China　SUNY Farmingdale State College

2018 年，从年初到现在，我已为 "CSC-SUNY 150 奖学金项目" 十周年做了很多准备，且早已开始回忆这十年来的点点滴滴，虽不至感慨万千，心底却也有话可说。

数次，我们在不同场合提到了这个项目的特殊性。美方的慷慨开放，中方的竭尽全力，最终促成了中美交流史上一次特殊的案例，而懵懵懂懂的我有幸成为其中一员。

### 过去的人和 事永留心底

在美国的一年，我们经历了太多令人感动的人和事。在法明戴尔这个纽约长岛小小的分校里，我们 19 名学生成了最特殊的群体，学校的老师、

From the beginning of 2018 till now, I have been busy on the preparation work of the 10th Anniversary of CSC-SUNY 150 Program, I have picked up countless memories in the past ten years, which, though not bringing up all sorts of feelings well up in my mind, are worth to mention.

We have mentioned the peculiarity of this program in different occasions for multiple times. With generosity and openness by the American side and full support by the Chinese side, we finally made this special case in China-US cultural exchange history. As a participant of it, I was extremely lucky even if with a bit confusion then.

### All of Those People and Experiences Imprinted on My Mind

During the year in America, I met too many

管理团队、同学向我们展示了主人的热情和慷慨。

除了校方，当地的华人也十分照顾我们。他们会在节日里邀请我们到家里做客，感受家人们团聚的氛围；在周末带我们去海滩游玩儿，帮助我们放松，减轻压力。同样，他们也希望我们能尽量多了解、多学习，回国后为祖国贡献自己的力量。

吉姆是一位和蔼的老者，其实他并不是我们任何人的专业课程老师，但他主动帮助我们提高英语能力，了解美国文化和历史。他每周抽出一个晚上，邀请我们围坐在一起，就某个特定的主题和材料，朗读、解释、讨论，提高我们的英文表达能力，了解我们过去未曾关注的美国选举、时政新闻、哲学等。渐渐地，大家成了跨越年龄差距的好朋友，而我们所呈现出来的中国青年人的特质，也让他感受到了中国文化和教育的不同，为他之后到中国教学埋下了种子。

苏伊是一位热心的台湾老师，

things and people that stirred my thoughts and feelings. In Farmingdale, a small campus of State University of New York (SUNY) on Long Island, I and the other 18 students formed a very special group in the school, where teachers, faculties, students and other working staff had impressed us with their great hospitality and generosity.

Besides the school, the local Chinese also cared for us a lot. We were invited to visit their families during holidays and they made us feel like home. On weekends, we would be going to beaches together with them for some relaxation. Meanwhile we were expected to learn more about everything there so that we would be able to serve our country better after returning to China.

Jim, a kind and mild elderly man, who was actually not our teacher any way, had always invited 19 of us to gather with him one evening every week to read, explain, and discuss some certain kinds of topics and materials just with the aim of improving our English level and enhancing our understanding of American culture and history, thus bringing us better competence and confidence in English expression. We, thus, got to learn more knowledge that we had not known well before, such as the US presidential election, political hotspot issues, and western philosophies. Gradually, we had built very good

从感恩节邀请我们几位学生到家做客起，我们与她的家人们在一年里数次相聚，他们会毫无保留地讲述自己的近况，分享心得和工作经验。还会在我们遇到困难时为我们排忧解难，设身处地地为我们提建议，特别是关于和美国当地同学、舍友的相处方式。十年来，我们也一直保持联系，甚至工作方面也有过交集，不禁让人感叹人生的幸运和有趣。

在朋友、老师、华人同胞的安排下我们第一次现场观看 NBA 比赛，还兴奋地打电话吵醒了国内的好友；第一次挑战自己去给美国大学生做数学辅导员，感叹国内数学基础教育的强大；第一次做志愿者引领新生游览校园，感受到自己外向的一面；第一次为了完成毕业课题开了网店，在美国倒腾电子产品，积累了大量素材；第一次勇敢地去找银行面试实习工

friendship despite the age difference. And as young people from China, we showed typical features and ways of expression, which also amazed him in the perspective of Chinese culture and education, and become his motive power to go to teach in China in the following years.

Suiv, a warmhearted teacher from Taiwan, arranged gatherings with us for several times within the year ever since she invited some of us to hers to celebrate the Thanksgiving Day. She and her family were candid about their recent condition, sharing their own ideas and work experiences with us, comforting and supporting us whenever we had difficulties. They would always provide good suggestions to us, which were especially about how to get along with the American students and our roommates. In the past 10 years, we've kept in contact with each other and even been closely related in terms of our jobs, and this has made me feel marveled at my fortunate and interesting life.

We experienced too many special things because of our friends, teachers, and local Chinese in Farmingdale. Within the year in America, it was the first time for me to watch

作，发现自己其实具备自己不曾注意的沟通能力……太多的经历让我永生难忘。

## 追梦的脚步从不停止

回国以后，回到了熟悉又陌生的环境。我调整规划，毕业后很快投入了工作。无论工作多么繁忙，我们法明戴尔的 19 名同学联系紧密，一起聚会，一起见证人生大事，一起回味那难忘的一年。

我一直相信"CSC-SUNY 150 奖学金项目"设立的初衷是让我们更为深刻地认识自己、思考人生、发挥自己的作用。2016 年，或许是受美国青年身上的自由和追求梦想的特质影响，我在从事金融工作 6 年后，决心改变职业，跳出舒适区，找到自己真正想要从事的工作。因此，我加入了正在复兴道路上的四川足球，在四川安纳普尔那足球俱乐部工作。两年的努力和坚持使我们在 2018 年 10 月 27 日实现了四川足球时隔十年重返中

the NBA game on the spot. I was so excited that I even made the midnight call to my best friend back in China. I took my first challenge to become a math instructor, which made me feel assured of the solid but cruel math education in China. I took the first opportunity to become the guide to help with the orientation work for the freshmen, which made me realize the other side of myself. To finish my project, I opened an online store selling American electronic products for the first time, which won me a bunch of project materials. And also for the very first time, I took the bank interview for the internship and later realized that I still had a long way to go in communication. All these wonderful experiences have been imprinted on my mind.

### Nothing Will Hold Back My Steps to My Dreams

After returning to China, to the familiar as well as unfamiliar place, I quickly adjusted myself to the environment, and very soon I found my job after graduation. No matter how busy we are, the 19 of us from Farmingdale have built very close ties. We often get together, witness each other's significant moments, and also recall our wonderful year in America.

I always believe that the original intention of establishing CSC-SUNY150 Program was to let us know ourselves better, to raise deeper thoughts about life, and to maximize our value. In 2016, maybe driven by the spirit of freedom and chasing after dreams from my American peers, I made up my mind to quit my 6-year long financial job, to get out of comfort zone, and to find what I was really aspiring to do. I became

甲联赛的梦想。我很自豪自己能作为一分子并有所贡献，参与到四川足球的发展和改革中，并向着川足重返顶级联赛的宏大目标继续前进。

在这两年的工作中，受益于这个项目，我凭借语言优势和国外俱乐部探讨、沟通。因为那段特殊经历，我特别关注美国职业足球的发展和动态，不久的将来，我相信我会促成俱乐部和美国同行的交流合作，参与两国足球事业的共同发展。

十年的故事，无须赘述，但所有的过往和心路进程，都或多或少受当年特殊经历的影响。太多的人和事，早已是我人生的一部分。

十年回首，早已枝繁叶茂。

a member on the revival course of Sichuan football. I joined Sichuan Annapurna Football Club. With two years' perseverance and hard work, we finally witnessed the realization of the 10-year dream of returning to Chinese Football Association China League (CFACL) on October 27th, 2018. I am proud to strive for the dream, and as a part of the great course, I have participated in the development and reform of football course in Sichuan. We will continue to fight until we go back to the Super League.

Looking back on the past two years, I have been greatly benefited by what the program has brought to me, which enhanced my capability and higher quality. With the language advantage, I've been capable of communicating and exploring further cooperation with foreign football clubs. Thanks to my American journey, I've paid special attentions to the development and trends of American professional soccer games. I believe that, in the near future, the cooperation between our club and American counterpart will be materialized and I will definitely be involved in the football development between the two nations.

There's no need to go into details of past ten years. But all the memories and experiences have more or less been related to my special journey. Those people and experiences have become part of my life.

Time of ten years has witnessed the flourish of my life.

乐山师范
学院

Leshan Normal University

行
如
楼

# 怀揣感恩 不忘初心

## Keep My Original Intention with Gratitude in Heart

邓霞 / 乐山师范学院　纽约州立大学布法罗分校

Deng Xia / Leshan Normal University　SUNY at Buffalo

"CSC-SUNY 150奖学金项目"的面试之夜，面试老师问我去美国学习的目的是什么，我当时的回答是：在美国将英语学习得更好，并学习美国优秀的师范技巧，然后回到中国，为自己的家乡建设尽自己的绵薄之力。

"5·12"汶川特大地震带走了千千万万的生命，带走了我儿时的玩伴、高中的同学，带走了邻居家的小弟弟，还带走了我的亲人。

幸运的是，灾难后我们看到人与人之间的互助、陌生人之间的真诚和两个大国之间的友好，而我幸运地成

In the evening during my CSC-SUNY 150 Program interview, when the interviewer asked me about my purpose for my study abroad in the US, I answered that in the US, I could have a better commanding of English and learn the most advanced teaching pedagogy, and then come back home to make little contributions to the reconstruction of my hometown.

Unluckily, the natural disaster—the Wenchuan Earthquake—took away thousands and thousands of people's lives, including my friends in my childhood, my high school classmates, a little boy of my neighbor and even some of my family members and relatives.

Luckily, this earthquake witnessed the mutual help between people, the sincerity from strangers and the friendship between China and the USA. And I was lucky enough to be a

了两国之间的小小使者。作为英语专业的学生，在这一年的努力学习中，我很好地掌握了这门语言，较深入地了解了这门语言背后的文化。

在美国的学习让我决心做一个有爱心的人。我深深地感受到普通美国人、美国学校以及在美华人对我们的关心和帮助。善良和感恩是一个人最重要的品质，拥有这两点，他就会感到社会的温暖，对物质的追求也没有那么狂热。

原则也非常重要。在美国，每个条款、条约、规定都非常详细。老师会将给我们布置的任务发到我们的邮箱，罗列出所有的细节，比如应该用哪样东西去完成这个任务。受此启发，我以后做事情讲究原则性和贯彻性。

此外，我觉得一定要有自己的思想，做一个独立的人。其实在过去我未曾思考过我想做什么样的人，或者是我应该做什么样的事情。但是这个项目让我从另一个角度看到了很多不同的东西。我深刻地感受到独立思考，自己去行动、实践的重要性。只有自己去尝试了，才知道这件事情是否可行，不能人云亦云，更不能相信谣言。

不管是在美国的大学课堂，还是在母校的课堂，师生关系都非常融洽。我印象比较深的一节课就是，我们有一个老师大大咧咧的，他推着婴儿车

"missionary" between these two countries. As an English major, I studied industriously in the only year there, having a better commanding of the language and also a deeper insight of the culture behind it.

During my study in the US, I felt that I should be a person with a loving heart. We came to the US because of the earthquake. So I was imbued with my appreciation for help and caring from Americans, American schools and overseas Chinese in the United States. Being kind and being grateful are the most essential qualities for a human being. Once with them, one can enjoy the warmth from the society without being too materialistic.

In addition, the principle counts a lot in the US, where every provision, treaty and rule is all as detailed as possible. For example, if a teacher assigned us a task bye-mail, all the details would be listed in it, such as what we needed to finish this task. This has enlightened me in my future work, teaching me the significance of the principle and the continuity. No matter what one does, one has to be persistent.

Furthermore, I feel that one has to be an independent individual with his or her own opinion. Actually, in the past, I had never thought about what I wanted to be, or what I should do, or what I should become. However, after I arrived in the US, I began to look at various ideas from different perspectives and understand the significance of independent thinking, and at the same time, it was equally important to put my idea into action, and solve any problem in practice. Only when I have tried by myself, can I know whether I could achieve success or not. What others tell you may not be true. Don't go

来给我们上课。他说家里人很忙，没有时间带小孩，所以他今天把小孩推着一起来上课。当时我们都觉得特别好笑，现在回想起来都还会笑出声。在国内，我们有很强的班级概念，但是在美国完全没有班级的概念，每个班的课不一样，同学就不一样。同学年龄跨度也很大，当时法语课上就有一个看起来五十多岁的同学。在课堂上，学生充分交流、表达，最后老师来总结，并尊重学生探索出来的知识。

在我大学毕业的那一年，房地产行业在中国蓬勃发展，很多人因好找工作而选择这个行业，但去美国之后，我知道工作一定要选自己真正热爱的。我在美国见到很多人，他们都是选择自己喜欢的工作，过上比较快乐的生活，而并不是一味地去选择赚钱快或者赚钱多的行业。在美国，大家在读大学的过程中就不断去尝试各种行业，寻找自己最喜欢的行业和领域。而我和大部分同学在大学期间只是停留在已有的知识范围和工作内容上，缺少不断尝试的勇气。

大学毕业之后，也正是这段学习经历让我顺利找到了自己喜欢的工作。也正是这段经历让我在工作中能够更好地发挥英语特长。在我近八年的工作中，我一直扮演着中美商务高尔夫平台上的桥梁和使者的角色。

with the flow and never trust gossips.

The teacher-student relationship is always good in class either in China or in the US. One class impressed me most because in that class, our teacher, an easy and casual man began the class, leaving his baby in a baby carriage somewhere in the classroom. When he told us that his family members were all busy that day without time to take care of the baby and he had to take the baby to class, we all laughed. Now, in retrospect, I still could not help laughing. In China, the class is like a fixed concept for everyone. However, in the US, it seems that both teachers and students have no idea about what "class" is. Students from different majors would sit in the same classroom for their selected course, and there is always a wide age gap between them. In my French class, there sat a student looking like he was in his fifties. In class, students always had fierce debate and discussion and expressed their ideas. In the end, the teacher would wrap up and show his or her recognition of the new idea from students' exploration in their study.

In the year when I graduated, the industry of real estate thrived in China. Many people felt that it was comparatively easier to find a job in this field. However, my one-year stay in the US taught me that I really needed to do what I really loved. In the US, I met a lot of people doing the job that they were really interested in instead of working just for making fast money in the most profitable industries. In this way, they lived a relatively happier life. Americans in the US tried different jobs in their college life, so they would find their favorite job and industry. However, lacking the courage to try new things, most of my Chinese counterparts and I only studied academic knowledge and had very superficial idea about

2016 年，我们带着家长的期许和中国高尔夫行业的需要，走向美国的高尔夫协会；带着孩子的需要，到美国高尔夫博览盛会上寻找机会。在成都，我和我的美国同事成立了成都高尔夫咨询公司，致力高尔夫文化的传播以及青少年高尔夫人才的培养。

2017 年，为了更好地促进中国青少年高尔夫球手的培养和高尔夫文化的推广，我和投资人以及美国的同事在美国建立了"圣地亚哥 PGA"学校，把渴望学球的中国孩子送到美国，享受更多的教育资源。

而立之年，我自己内心小小的梦想终于实现了。2017 年下半年，在朋友的支持下，我的 EG 英语学校正式开课。还记得当初自己在学习英语时遇到的困惑：外教资源的稀缺、英

work.

After my graduation, thanks to my study abroad in the US, I soon found a job that I really liked. It was the study experience abroad that granted me the opportunity to make better use of my English in my work. In my almost 8-year-long work, I served as a "bridge" and a "missionary" in the field of golf business between China and the US.

In 2016, with the expectation of Chinese parents and in consideration of the need of the golf business in China, we went to the United States and built up the relationship with the US Golf Association. With the children's needs, we searched for opportunities in the US Golf Exhibition. In Chengdu, my American colleagues and I established a golf consulting company based on the spread of golf culture and the cultivation of the young golf talents.

In 2017, for the perfection of the system to cultivate young Chinese golf players and also the promotion of the golf culture, my investors, my American colleagues and I established a PGA school at San Diego in the US, making it possible for me, the contact person in China, to send more children from China to the US, where they could have access to more education resources.

When I am in my thirties, my humble dream has finally come true. In the second half of 2017, with the help of my friends, my EG English Training School finally opened. I still remembered all the problems and confusion I had encountered in my English learning, including the insufficient foreign teachers, difficulties in English speaking and listening, etc. My exploration of these problems helped me find a good set of English teaching and learning

语听说水平的突破等，这个过程让我找到了一套不错的学习和讲授英语的方法。我希望通过自己的努力，让更多的学生轻松地学习和运用英语，不再为学习英语而头疼。

大地震之后，大家更加珍视自己的生命，注重生活质量和身体健康。如果没有当时在美国那一年的经历，我可能不会选择从事高尔夫行业的工作，我也不可能用自己的财力、人力、物力去实现自己的梦想。

感谢"CSC-SUNY 150 奖学金项目"给予我生命的转机，这个项目让我变得更加感恩和坚强。在这个项目中，我感受到了社会各个行业、各个团体给予我们的关心和帮助，明白在工作和生活中一定要用感恩的心去面对人和事。在这个项目中，我体会到无论在世界哪个角落，人们每天都在坚强地面对生活。我们也需要用勇敢的心去征服生活的高峰。

现在赴美留学确实越来越普遍了，我觉得在留学过程中有些方面一定要注意。首先，诚实非常关键，在美国，诚实是很重要的品质；其次，在留学过程中有一定扎实的英文基础非常重要，英文越扎实，在整个生活学习的过程中和他人交流学习的效果就越好；第三，多向有留学经验的老

methods. I really hope that through my hard working, students may learn English in a more relaxing and happier way without feeling painful in their future English learning.

After the earthquake, everyone has begun to pay attention to the quality of life and living, especially of his or her physical health. Without my study in the US, neither would I choose to work in the golf industry, nor would it be possible for me to fulfill my dream with my own money and human resource. If one does not have adequate food and clothing, how could he or she make his or her dreams come true eventually?

I really appreciate the CSC-SUNY 150 Program, which has provided me with a turning point in my life and made me become stronger and more grateful. In the whole project, I received help and care from all the lines and organizations of society. I understand that I should show my gratitude to everything and everyone in both my work and my daily life. From this program, I have realized that wherever people live, even in developed countries, they should struggle to live every day with confidence and bravery. For us, we all need to conquer all the "peaks" in our life with a brave heart, too.

Now, there is an increasing number of students pursuing their study in the US. Here are some tips for them. First, being honest is a key. In the US, honesty is at the very top level. Second, a good commanding of English is necessary in overseas study. The more fluent your English is, the easier it is for you to communicate with others in your study. Therefore, all students determined to go to study abroad must learn English well. Third, frequently learn from experienced teachers and students. Once living in a foreign country,

师、同学取经。一个人去异国他乡生活的时候，应主动拓展一个比较健康的社交环境。

students must actively expand a healthier social environment.

# 蜕变

## The Great Change

冯叶婷 / 乐山师范学院　纽约州立大学杰纳西社区学院

Feng Yeting / Leshan Normal University　SUNY Genesee Community College

十年了，心底有很多想说的话，提起笔，却又不知从何说起。

When I was asked to say something about my stay in the US in the previous decade, I just felt a little bit speechless.

### 启程

### The Start

我还清晰地记得，2008 年，我在家接到乐山师范学院外事办廖老师的电话，他说我通过了所有的面试。于是我收拾东西回学校，准备去参加出国前的培训。当时我的母亲就坐在我旁边，我挂了电话，告诉她学校老师通知我可以去美国读书了，她高兴极了，紧紧地抱着我，然后给父亲打了电话，这就是这件事的开始。

父母送我去四川大学集合的那天中午，母亲为我和父亲在附近公园照

I can clearly remember that day in 2008 when I received a phone call from Mr. Liao from the foreign affairs office, telling me that I had passed all the interviews and asking me to pack my suitcase and be ready to go back to school for the training for my future study in the US. The minute I hung up the phone and told my mother that I would go to the US, she, sitting next to me, felt pretty happy and excited. She hugged me tightly and then called my father. The whole story began at that moment.

The noon when my parents sent me to get together with other students, my mother took a picture of me and my father at the park nearby,

了相，到现在它还挂在家里客厅的墙上。那天我们笑得特别开心，那个时候还没有自拍，所以母亲不在合照里，后来我就跟着同学们一起出发去美国了。

到了美国纽约州立大学，我得知我将就读的校区是杰纳西社区学院。这个学校不是很大，学校周围环境安静，我们可以静下心来认真学习。在留学期间，我们去了很多地方，也许是这辈子只会去一次的地方；也见到了很多人，也许是这辈子见过的最厉害的人，他们在我的记忆中留下了很深的印象。

## 那些人

我印象最深的是当时的社会学课程老师。我第一学期就选了社会学这门课，当时的任课老师听说我是来自中国的留学生，对我非常感兴趣。她告诉我，她去过福建旅游，还带回了很多当地的特色旅游产品，后来她还专门在学校举办了一个中国文化展来展示这些物品。虽然展出的物品都是福建的，而我们是从四川去的学生，但是我们仍然很感激她对中国文化的推广。毕竟在上地理课的时候，有的学生甚至连中国在哪里都不知道。

在她的帮助下，我们还办起了中

which is still hanged on the wall of my living room. That day, we all laughed happily. Selfies were not popular at that time, so my mother was not in that picture. However, her smile still remained in my memory. Then, I started my study in the US with other students.

Arriving at the State University of New York, I was sent to the Genesee Community College, not very big but with a quiet neighborhood, where we could concentrate on our study without any distraction. During my overseas study, I went to many different places, some of which I might have no opportunity to visit again in the rest of my life. In addition, I met a lot of people, who might be the most excellent ones I encountered in my life. Although a long period of time has passed, I have been out of touch with many of them, and even am unable to remember some of their names; they have still left everlasting impressions in my mind.

### Those People

Among them, the one impresses me most is my teacher of sociology. In the first term, I selected the course related to sociology. When the teacher learned that I was from China, she showed much interest in me. She told me that she once travelled to Fujian and took back many tourism products of Fujian characteristics, for which she held an exhibition about Chinese culture on campus. Although these products were from Fujian Province and we were students from Sichuan Province, we still appreciated her promotion of Chinese culture. After all, in geography class, some American students had no idea about where China is located.

With her help, we organized Chinese class

文班并举办了中国新年的活动。我们自己做了团圆饭，所有的同学以及从西班牙过来的华人也和我们一起过了春节。学校的很多同学和老师也渐渐知道我们是来自中国的留学生。我的这位社会学老师很和蔼，也很喜欢和我们交流，她曾经请我们所有的同学去她家吃饭。她家的猫好胖，那是我第一次见到胖到走不动路的橘猫。

## 那些事

除了这些让人印象深刻的老师，在美国期间还发生了一些让人感动的事，直至今日我仍记忆犹新。其中一件是关于我的西班牙语老师的。有一次我把上课时间记错了，错过了一节西班牙语课。后来老师给我发邮件，让我找时间去见她，她把那节没上的课的内容全部给我讲了一遍，这是我一直坚持学西班牙语的一个重要原因。是她让我喜欢上了西班牙语，直到现在我家里还保存着当时的西班牙语课本。

另一件事是关于博伊茨夫人的。他们夫妇带我们去逛商场，给我们讲美国文化。博伊茨先生是一位头发稀疏的老者，他讲话的时候特别温柔。我们临走时去他家吃饭，他告诉我们，要是以后去美国读研的话，没地方住

and activities to celebrate Chinese Lunar New Year. We made the family reunion dinner, and all the students and overseas Chinese from Spain joined us to celebrate the New Year together. Many students and teachers gradually knew that we were overseas students from China. I still remember that at the beginning of a new term, the school held a BBQ party when a female teacher greeted us in Japanese. To be honest, we were very upset at that time, but the misunderstanding was gone later through the explanation of other students. This sociology teacher is very kind, always willing to get along with us. She once invited all of us Chinese students to dinner at her home. The cat at her home was pretty fat. It was also the first time I saw a hosico cat too fat to move.

### Those Things

Besides teachers who impressed us a lot, a variety of touching incidents also took place in the US that I still remember now. One of them was about our Spanish teacher. Once, I was absent from one Spanish class because I confused the time. Later, our Spanish teacher sent me an e-mail, asking me to go to her office when I was available so as to teach me everything I missed that day. This is why I still keep learning Spanish. It was she who made me love Spanish. Till now, I still keep the Spanish textbook at home.

Another thing was about Mrs. Boyds. Mrs. Boyds and Mr. Boyds took us to the supermarket, teaching us American culture. Mr. Boyd was a senior with white hair, and pretty gentle while speaking. Before we left the US, he told us that if we furthered our study later as a postgraduate in the US and had no place to live, he could accommodate us, because his children all had

可以在他家住,他的孩子们都工作了,家里有房子可以住。虽然我最终没有去美国读研,但是我还是很感激他。

这些温柔和蔼的老师带给我不少温暖,也给予我很多启发。我们从小所受的教育是尊师重教,我想老师们喜欢我们这些从中国去的学生,很大程度上是因为我们尊敬他们。

## 体悟

到了美国以后,我也渐渐发现中美大学的课堂是很不一样的,包括授课方式、学习方式、教学观念、师生互动、课外实践等。其中让我感触最深的一点就是我在美国学习的时候,论文写作里面通常会有"我认为""我想"这类词,但是美国的老师告诉我:"这篇文章是你写的,上面的观点都是你自己的,你不需要写'我认为'这类词。"后来我回乐山师院写毕业论文的时候,就没有写这样的词,我的导师拿着我的论文初稿问我:"你这篇论文里面怎么没有你自己的观点,我没看到你的观点。"

这件事一度让我很矛盾:到底怎样才算这篇文章是我自己写的,有我自己的观点?在这件事上,我似乎明白了一个道理:并不是谁对谁错,而是思维方式的不同。

their own work. Although I did not go to the US for my Master's degree, I still appreciated his offer. After all, no one wants to accommodate people whom they are not quite familiar with.

These gentle and kind teachers warmed us a lot during our days in the US and also enlightened us a lot. What they did made us understand that the relationship of people between China and the US could be kept to a higher level, which is not directly related to economy but influenced by culture. The education that we received from our childhood has always valued the respect for teachers, education and the elderly. I believe that our teachers liked us students from China, just because we really respected them as our teachers and the elderly. Since the Confucian culture may have the power to influence the world, we are supposed to strengthen the influence of Chinese culture and language in the world.

### Learn from Experience

When I arrived in the US, I increasingly found that the class in the US was quite different from that in China in many aspects, including the pedagogical method, the learning method, the teaching concept, the interaction between teachers and students, the extracurricular practice, etc. And one thing in my study deeply impressed me. In my thesis, I always used "I think", "I believe", etc.; however, my American teacher told me, "You write down your own opinions in your essay, so you needn't use such expressions like "I think." When I came back for my graduation thesis in my school, Leshan Normal University, I tried to avoid these words. But when my tutor asked me why she could not see any of my ideas

对这件事的体悟让我在后来的工作中学会了从不同的角度看问题。这样我能明白别人做事的初衷，也能更好地理解别人，与同事的相处也更融洽。

大学毕业后我就参加工作了。这和我最初上大学时的想法有些不太一样，那时候以为自己会直接读研，然后找一份稳定的工作。事实是，我去了一家私企做翻译。刚开始，我遇到了不少的困难和挑战，尤其是在和外国专家沟通的时候。但是在国外学习的经历给我不少帮助，比如让我了解了与外国人相处的方式，每次遇到问题的时候都能很好地解决问题，后来也和大家成了好朋友。也是在这份工作中，我看清了自身的弱点——不够勇敢，不够大胆，在机会前喜欢逃避。当我逐渐明白我的弱点时，我却没有很好的方法去调整自己，就这样一直过了几年。

我一直在反复思考应当如何调整自己，我的人生是不是就这样定格了？直到2013年的一天，一位老师打电话问我的近况，我才不禁又想起我曾在17岁的时候远离家乡，到地球的另一边学习的情景。我没有因为离开而感到悲伤，也没有因离开时包里只有家里给的4000元钱而自卑，而是自信地去一个陌生的国家，度过

because I did not use "I think" and words like that, I felt quite confused, not knowing whether I should use "I think" or not to show to others that I completed the thesis by myself and anything presented in thesis was from me. However, I seemed to understand from this incident that it was not the question of whether the teachers were wrong or right but of their different thinking modes. Teachers from different countries have different perspectives.

Thanks to my understanding of this, I have learned how to look at problems from another angle in my future work. Only in this way, can I understand the others better by knowing their original intention and can I know more about how to get along well with my colleagues.

After my graduation, I obtained a job, which was quite different from my original intention during my college days, when I thought I would study for my Master's degree and then find a stable job. Actually, I became a translator in a private company, where I met many challenges and difficulties, especially when I communicated with foreign experts. However, my study experience in the US helped a lot in my work. For example, such an experience taught me the way of how to get along with foreigners; so whenever I met problems, I could deal with them successfully and even made good friends with them later. Also from my work, I found my weakness that I was not brave and ambitious enough to grasp any chance in front of me. This was my most obvious weakness in both my life and work. Although I came to understand the causes of my weakness, I could not find any way to adjust myself, and my life went as usual without any change in the following several years.

了一段精彩的时光。我记起独自一人和不同肤色的同学一起上课，记起和同学们一起走路去杰纳西小镇又走路回学校，记起独自一人去小镇上和老师一起吃午餐……我曾经也勇敢过！所以，无论以前是什么原因让我胆怯，我都不再去想。现在的我，应当像17岁时的自己那样勇敢而自信！

每每看到律政剧中刚直不阿的法官和自信满满的律师，我都希望自己能像他们一样，无论在什么困难面前都能镇定自若、冷静思考。于是，我辞去了工作并成功考取了法学专业的研究生，毕业后考进西部地区一个基层法院，现在是一名法官助理。在美国的学习和生活，让我知道了独立的重要性，也让我明白认识自己有多么重要，而更重要的是要做一个有梦想的人。

## 尾声

十年的时间，看似很长，却过得好快。我曾以为我走了很多弯路，现在看来这些都很值得。这十年的时间我做过翻译，做过老师，读了研究生，最后考了公务员。这十年的生活和工作让我遇见很多人，让我更加了解自己，也更加明白自己的人生目标。现在站在人生新的起点，或许比其他同

I kept thinking about whether I could change my character and whether the rest of my life would be lived in the same way. One day in 2013, when a teacher called me, asking about the current developments of the CSC-SUNY 150 Program, all the memories about my departure from my hometown to the US when I was seventeen came back to my mind. I did not feed sad at my departure nor did I feel inferior for my departure with the whole and only RMB 4000 yuan my family could give me; instead, I went to another strange country confidently, where I had the most wonderful period of time in my life. I still remember that I went to class with students of different ethnicities; that I went to Genesee Town with my classmates on feet and then walked all the way back to the school; that I walked alone to the small town to have lunch together with my teacher … I endeavored to be brave! Therefore, no matter what caused my timidity, I do not want to think about it any more. I just want to be as brave and confident as I was when I was 17 years old.

Whenever I saw upright and outspoken judges and confident lawyers in TV law shows, I hoped that I would be like them, being calm in thinking in front of all difficulties. Therefore, I quit my job and became a postgraduate majoring in Law. After my graduation, I passed the exam and worked in a grass-roots court. Now I am a judge assistant. My life and study in the US enabled me to understand the significance of independence and self-knowledge, and it is more important to be a person with dreams.

## The Epilogue

A decade seems pretty long but passes very

学都起步得晚，但是我却更加了解自己。

现在的我每天都充满自信，我不再去思考那些曾经让我胆怯的原因。我相信17岁是我人生的一个重要转折，而现在的我开始了新的人生。这是一个新的开始，但是我决心不去想未来会怎样，我要像十年前的我一样自信而勇敢，因为没人知道机会什么时候到来，正如十年前廖老师的那通电话一样。

quickly. Once I thought I had taken many detours, but now in retrospect, I feel that everything I have done is worth doing. In the past decade, I have worked as a translator and a teacher, studied for my Master's degree and finally become a civil servant. I have met a lot of people in both my life and study, through whom I have gotten a better understanding of myself and become more certain about my life goal. Now I am at the beginning of a new life. Maybe I have a late start, but I have a better understanding of myself. At least, I trust my choice.

Now, I am full of confidence every day, without any desire to think about what made me timid in the past. I believe that my seventeenth birthday was a crucial turning point in my life. Now, I have begun a new life, a brand new one. I have made up my mind not to think about what the future will be. I want to be as brave and confident as I was ten years ago, for no one knows when opportunities will come, just like the phone made by Mr. Liao ten years ago.

# 那年时光，别样人生

## That Year Makes a Different Life

黄清华 / 乐山师范学院　纽约州立大学林基默县社区学院

Huang Qinghua / Leshan Normal University　SUNY Herkimer County Community College

从脆弱、没有依靠，到坚强、感恩、上进，"CSC-SUNY 150奖学金项目"开启了我不一样的人生。

从成都到北京，从纽约到林基默县，挥别故土踏上异乡，一切像做梦一样，发生得太快。还来不及伤感，美国，曾经遥远的地方，已真真切切地展现在了我们眼前。

在一个阳光灿烂的午后，我们到达了林基默县，一个美丽、宁静的小镇。迎接我们的是一群可爱的美国人。他们为我们精心准备了生活必需品：宽敞整洁的房间里，大到床垫被褥，小到毛巾牙刷，一应俱全。为了照顾我们的饮食习惯，他们还同时准备了中式、西式两种厨具、餐具，包括专

The CSC-SUNY 150 Program has made a huge difference in my life in these ten years. I have grown up from a delicate girl with no dependence to a more tough, ambitious person with gratitude.

From Chengdu to Beijing, then from New York to Herkimer, stepping on the foreign land was like a dream, happening too soon for me to feel any sadness due to my departure from my home. The US, once a strange name, did stand in front of me so vividly.

In a sunny afternoon, no sooner had we arrived at Herkimer, a tranquil and beautiful small town than a group of Americans showed up welcoming us. They provided us with all the necessities we needed there with considerate preparation, including spacious and tidy rooms, mattress, quilts, toothbrushes, towels and so on. In order to cater to our eating habits, they prepared both Chinese and American tableware

四海之纽
Taking the World as a
Link to Study in USA  川山自纽

门添置的电饭煲，便于我们做中餐。

一切都是新的，一切都令人兴奋。

## 全新的学习生活

我所在的校区是纽约州立大学林基默县社区学院（简称 HCCC），我们有 11 名同学在这所大学。学校占地面积不大，学生人数也不多，但是设施齐备，无论是学习还是生活，都非常便捷舒适。

这里的学习相对于在中国来说轻松一些，学习任务不是很重。虽然也有频繁的考试和测验，但难度适中，而且不失趣味性。刚去的时候，我对全英文教学不太适应，不到两个月，我已经完全适应了他们的教学模式。

美国大学的教学大多以播放电视视频、录像，然后学生自由讨论、老师指导答疑的方式进行。很少有老师按照课本的固定顺序来安排讲课。所有教授和讲师的课都向学生开放，学生可以根据自己的专业来选择感兴趣的内容，自己安排自己的课程表，没有年级大小之分，没有成绩高低之分。

在期末考试前的一个月，不论哪门课程，只要你估计不能考过，都可以选择自主退课，这样就不会影响你的绩点。期末考试和平时考试的成绩占比一般是 1:3，这样学生就不会因

and kitchenware, including an electric rice cooker they bought for us in case we wanted to cook Chinese food.

Everything was brand new; everything was exciting.

## A Brand-new Study Life

10 other students and I studied at HCCC in New York, a community college with a small number of students and a small area but complicated equipment and devices. Therefore, it was convenient and comfortable for students to both live and study here.

For Chinese, the study here was comparatively easier because of fewer assignments. Although there were frequent tests and examinations, they were neither too difficult nor too easy and with much fun. At the very beginning, I did not quite adapt to the teaching with only English. Nevertheless, within two months, I could completely acclimatize myself to the teaching mode there.

In most of the classes, teachers showed students videos from TV or recordings first and then asked students to have a free discussion based on what they had watched. Teachers answered students' questions and provided guidance. Seldom did the teachers all teach totally based on the sequences of textbooks. All the classes of both professors and lecturers were open to all the students, who could select the courses they were interested in and make their own schedules based on their majors, with no limits on their grades or scores.

If you thought that you could not pass the examination of any of the courses you had chosen, you could choose to drop it one month

期末考试发挥不好而挂科。在纽约州立大学林基默县社区学院里面，几乎所有的学生绩点都在3.8分以上，甚至很多人达到了4.0分的满分。

学校留学处的老师们对我们照顾得细致入微，想尽办法为我们解决一切困难。不管是课程学习，还是日常生活，都安排得井井有条。

那时，家人虽不在身边，我却并不觉得孤单。每逢西方节日，老师们总会为我们举办热闹的派对。而我们也在中国节日为老师们举办有"中国特色"的派对，为他们烹饪美味的中国食物，准备小礼物，介绍中国的传统文化。

每到假期，老师们会轮流带我们参加各种集市、聚会，帮助我们融入当地的文化和生活。如果假期时间充裕，我们还会四处旅行，纽约、华盛顿、阿尔巴尼、克林顿、尼亚加拉大瀑布都留下了我们的轻快脚步和欢声笑语。

## 三位人生导师

在这一年中，有三位老师给我留下了深刻的印象。

一位是萨莉·德基，我们中国的这群孩子都亲切地叫她"德基妈妈"，她就像妈妈一样关心爱护我们。

before the final test in order to not influence your GPA. The final examination usually accounted for about 25% and the scores for tests in daily study made up the other 75%. In this way, students would not be failed due to their bad performance in their final examinations. In HCCC, almost all the students' GPA were over 3.8, some of which might have reached the highest 4.0.

The faculty in the Foreign Affairs Office gave us much caring, trying their best to deal with all the problems for us. Our study and daily life were arranged in perfect order.

During that period of time, although my parents were not with me, I did not feel lonely at all. Teachers held very warm and exciting parties for us every single western holiday. In return, we, the 11 Chinese students, also held parties with "Chinese characteristics" for them every single Chinese holiday, cooking them delicious Chinese cuisines, distributing gifts and introducing traditional Chinese culture.

During vacations, teachers would take turns taking us to various market affairs and parties so as to help us become integrated into the local culture and life. If time allowed for vacation, we usually traveled to different places, like New York, Washington, Albania, Clinton, Niagara Waterfall, leaving our delightful footsteps and happy laughs and cheerful voices all the way.

### The Three Mentors

During the only year studying in the US, three teachers impressed me most.

Sally Durkee was one of them. We Chinese all called her Mom Durkee, because she took good care of and protected us like our own mom.

记得圣诞节的早上，雪很大，我打开门，她就站在门外，提着满满一袋礼物，一看见我就大声喊道："圣诞快乐！"她的碧眼满含柔情，那时，我真的感觉，她就是我们所有人的妈妈。

我们都很喜欢她讲授的公共演讲课程，她的讲解生动形象、深入浅出。理论讲解总是伴随着丰富翔实的例证分析，具有很强的实用性和操作性。

还记得离别前的一个下午，阳光正好，大家围坐在她家的小院子里，玩耍、吃东西、聊天、游戏、吹泡泡，大家都特别开心，离别的伤感和哀愁冲淡了。那一张张笑脸，灿烂了我的人生。

另外一位是阿尔老师，他温柔慈爱，就像圣诞老爷爷。课余，他开车载着我们到处旅游，让我们体验当地的风土人情。他家养了三只从救助站

On Christmas morning, it was snowing heavily outside. The minute I opened my door, I saw her standing outside with a full bag of gifts. She raised her voice, saying "Merry Christmas" with all the gentleness in her eyes. At that moment, I really felt that she was the mom for all of us.

We all liked her course of Public Speaking, which was practical and operational. Her demonstration was pretty vivid with adequate examples and analyses. She explained abstruse knowledge in a simple and easy-to-understand way.

In a sunny afternoon before we left for China, we sat in her small yard, chatting with each other, playing games, having snacks and making bubbles. We had too much fun to feel the sadness and depression caused by our departure. All the smiling faces brightened my life.

领养的流浪狗。其中有一只叫大黑，活泼帅气。阿尔说他刚捡到大黑时，它被人打伤了腿，非常可怜。每个周末，阿尔都会到社区医院做义务护工，照顾那些请不起护工的病人，还时不时掏钱资助他们。整天都乐呵呵的阿尔，用快乐感染着周围的人。从他身上，我感受到了善良、纯真的力量。

还有一位是蔡·德克·西姆老师。在第二学期开始选课的时候，我们几个同学发现房间里网速较慢，大家都很担心会影响下学期的选课，影响最后的学分和绩点。学校负责我们事的蔡·德克·西姆老师知道后，立即在学校外面的酒店给我们订了一个房间，一直陪我们等到当天晚上 12 点选课系统开放。一起等待时光静静流过，异国他乡的夜晚静谧美好。系统开放后，蔡·德克·西姆老师又指导我们选课。最终，大家都选到了心仪的课程。

## 因为你们，我们的世界变得不一样

一年届满，离别如期而至。回国之后，读完大学，我继续攻读研究生，取得了商务英语硕士学位。目前在政府机关单位工作。不论是读书、就业，还是组建家庭，我人生道路上的重要选择，冥冥之中，都有那一年、那些

Another one was Al, gentle and kind, as cute as the Santa Clause. In the spare time, he liked driving us to different places, providing us opportunities to experience local customs and traditions. He raised three stray dogs adopted from the animal shelter. One of the dogs was named "Da Hei," who was pretty handsome and active. Al told us that when he found "Da Hei," he was a poor dog with the legs beaten by someone. Besides, Al went to the community hospital every weekend, working as a nursing worker to take care of those who could not afford nursing workers. From time to time, he gave money to these patients in need. He was a cheerful guy, and the happiness from him was contagious. From him, I saw the power of kindness and sincerity.

The third teacher was Tze Teck Sim. In the beginning of the second term, several classmates and I found that the Internet speed in our dorm was pretty slow. All of us were worried that this might influence us selecting the courses and then might have negative effects on our final credits and GPA. When Tze Teck Sim heard about this, he booked us a hotel room outside of the campus, staying with us until the course selection system was open at midnight that day. We sat together, watching the time passing by at the night so quiet and beautiful in a foreign country. When the system was open, Tze Teck Sim taught us how to select courses. Consequently, we had all chosen the course that we really liked.

### Because of You, Our World is Totally Different

One year passed very quickly and the time to say goodbye finally drew nearer. When I returned

人的指引。

　　而今，每每回忆起那时走过的路、吹过的风、淋过的雨、玩过的雪，还有最可爱的同学和老师，感动的热流仍在心间流淌。那些笑容都在我的记忆里一如昨日，暖意融融。晨间上学时朝阳下拉长的校车影子，傍晚归家时美丽绚烂的晚霞和同伴们三三两两的身影，还有路边那一片片青色的草地和堆积的金黄落叶，都是那样光亮鲜活。那年青春年少，那年岁月正好，那年我们的生命荡起涟漪。

　　心中珍藏的那年时光和情感为我的人生注入力量，激励我不断前行。感谢每一位为"CSC-SUNY 150 奖学金项目"辛勤付出的老师，因为你们，我们的世界变得不一样；因为你们，我们更明了爱与被爱的价值与意义；因为你们，我们立志做一个心中有爱、感恩上进的人。

to China, I first finished my undergraduate study and then furthered my study as a postgraduate majoring in Business English. Now, I am a government official of the middle level. When I was at the intersection of my life, having no idea about which way to choose, it seemed that my experience of that year and the people I met in the US guided me in my study, my work and even the establishment of my family.

Now, in retrospect of the roads we once walked along, the wind blowing in our face, the rain that we were caught in, the snow we played with and all the cute students and teachers, I still feel pretty touched. All the smiles are still in my mind, so fresh and warm to me. The shadow of the school bus in the morning sunrise, the shadow of our figures in the sunset at dusk, the green grasslands with piles of golden yellow leaves are still all this bright. That year, we were quite young, the days in the US were so wonderful, and our life was so exciting.

That time and my feelings buried deep in my heart energize my life and encourage me to make more progress. I really want to show my gratitude to all the teachers working day in and day out for the CSC-SUNY 150 Program. Because of you, our world is totally different; because of you, we better understand the meaning and value of love and being loved; because of you, we are determined to be ambitious people with love and gratitude.

# 写在 "CSC–SUNY 150" 项目十年之后

## A Decade after the CSC-SUNY 150 Program

何文／乐山师范学院　　纽约州立大学法明戴尔分校

He Wen / Leshan Normal University　SUNY Farmingdale State College

　　弹指间，十年已过，我经历了 "5·12" 汶川特大地震，度过了美好的留学时光，步入了社会，组建了家庭，已从当初那个青涩的学生蜕变为一个为家庭和理想而不断奔波的青年。这十年中，最能温暖我心的便是参加 "CSC–SUNY 150 奖学金项目" 那一年。

In such a short period of time, a decade has just passed, in which I survived the Wenchuan Earthquake, enjoyed my amazing overseas study in the US, stepped into the society and established my family. I have changed from an immature and innocent student into a middle-aged man busy with my work for not only my dream but also my family. However, during these ten years, the year when I joined in the CSC-SUNY 150 Program has impressed me most with much warmth.

### 无微不至的安娜

### The Considerate Anna

　　那一年，我深切地体会到人情的温暖。安娜的出现，让初次迈出国门的我，在异国他乡感受到了家人般的关怀。整理这十年，最先浮现出来的，依然是这一段浓烈的如亲情般的

It was the first time that I went abroad in 2008, and immediately I deeply felt the warmth and hospitality from other people, especially from Anna, whose loving care made my stay in the US like the one in China. In this decade, what firstly comes into my mind is still a strong family affection-like friendship between Anna and me.

友谊。

记得刚刚到美国的时候，美国老师安娜带领华人朋友们一起去长岛游玩。从小生活在祖国内陆小城的我，从来没有见过大海。那天碧海蓝天，海面在太阳的辉映下波光粼粼，显得极为壮观。我顿时就被眼前的美景吸引住了，激动得纵身一跃，一个猛子扎进凉凉的海水里。当那股透心凉的感觉传来，浑身一阵舒爽之后，才突然意识到我的钥匙还装在裤兜里。伸手一摸裤兜，空空如也，钥匙掉到海里去了。当时心里暗叫一声："不好！"

果然，回到宿舍后，立刻去学校的后勤管理部门报告并陈述事情的经过。但当时学校的规定是：一个学生的钥匙丢了，为了避免安全隐患，需要将整个宿舍的学生钥匙全部更换。当时我们的宿舍是一个大门进去，有两个房间。因此，按规定我必须赔偿150美元，按照当时的汇率，我大概需要赔偿人民币1000元，这对于一个普通学生而言，已经是国内两个月的生活费。在国内，换个大门锁最多需要人民币50元，消费层面的地域差异让那个年龄段的我一时间感到气愤难平。于是我找到安娜，向她讲述了这件事，并表达了我的观点。原本以为安娜会和从电影里看来的美式风

I still remember the minute we stepped onto the land of the US, our American teacher Anna took all of us Chinese to the Long Island. Growing up and living in an inland city in China, I had never seen an ocean so magnificent under the blue sky and glittering in the sunshine. The splendid scenery suddenly attracted me, and I dived into the cold ocean excitedly. With a sudden coldness spreading across my whole body, I felt so good until I realized that the key was still in the pocket of my pants. Then, I fumbled in the pocket, but found nothing. The key had vanished into the deep ocean. "That's too bad," I murmured to myself.

Undoubtedly, hardly did I return to my dormitory when I went to the logistics department, reporting this incident and giving more detailed information. The rule of the school then stipulated that if a student lost the key, all the keys of the dormitory were supposed to be changed. It was worth noting that there were two rooms in my dormitory but with a single entrance gate.

格一样，对于事实的坚持会超越人情。但安娜的反应大大出乎我的意料，她也认为处罚过重，对于刚刚到美国的学生而言确实是很大的负担。安娜立刻主动与后勤管理部门进行沟通，从人文关怀的角度进行说服，最终帮我度过了这一难关。

安娜对这件事情的处理方式，让我从心底感到温暖：在异国他乡遇见一位能如此设身处地为我们这群中国留学生着想的老师，像家长一样保护我们。这份安全感，使我在美国继续学习的动力更足了。

另一件关于安娜的事也让我备感温暖。担心寒假期间我们在校园里没饭吃，她亲自做了好多意大利通心粉和馅饼。看着食物塞满我们宿舍的冰箱，安娜开心地大笑："这样就不担心你们饿肚子了。"当安娜转身离开的时候，我眼含泪水。年纪不大的安娜对我们无微不至的照顾，像极了妈妈。

## 宝贵的人生财富

有人说过，你如今的样子，很大部分取决于你青春期即将结束之时遇见了谁。而我，很幸运地遇见了这样一群人，他们给了我温暖感动，让我学会了坚持，催我奋发向上。

Thus, based on the rule, I had to pay for the new keys 150 US dollars, or RMB 1000 yuan at the exchange rate then, equally two months' living expenses for a common student in China. By contrast, in China, changing the key of the entrance door costs RMB 50 yuan at most. Such huge gap caused by geographical differences made me so upset at that age. Therefore, I went to Anna, telling her the whole story and my opinion about it. I had thought that Anna would stick to principles rather than human relationship in the same manner as the people in American movies did. However, Anna's response was quite out of my expectation. She thought that this punishment was too severe and would be a heavy burden for a student just arriving in the US. She immediately contacted the faculty of the logistics department, convincing them to make some changes from the angle of humanistic care. This problem was eventually settled with Anna's help.

Anna's way to address this problem warmed me from the deep of my heart. She gave me a sense of safety and motivation to continue my study in the US, protecting us like our parents as well as caring us by putting herself into our shoes.

I was moved tremendously by another incident. Thinking that we might not have enough food to eat during the winter holiday, Anna made us a lot of spaghetti and pies by herself. Seeing our refrigerator became full, she laughed, saying, "I will not be worried that you will be starved." When Anna left, my eyes were full of tears. Young as she was, she took good care of us like our mom.

## Precious Life Treasures

Someone once said that one's current

吉姆和凯西·科利的出现，让我深深地感受到美国人的热情。当一群来自中国地震灾区的孩子初到美国，还不能和当地人顺畅交流时，吉姆主动提出每周三晚上下班后，在学校的小会议室陪我们练习口语。这一练就是几个月，直到我们大多数人都能说一口流利的美式英语。凯西·科利为了让我们感受纯正的万圣节，一个人在家不辞辛劳地布置，还为我们每个人准备了不一样的服饰。

丹尼教会了我人生是可以自由选择的。丹尼是学校的生物实验老师，在学校名气很大。他爱他那美丽贤惠的妻子和帅气的儿子，他也热爱自己的工作，工作和家庭他兼顾得非常完美。但这一切都不影响他追求自己的爱好——戏剧创作，并且将戏剧创作做到了极致，他的作品还曾在上海歌剧院演出过。

基恩博士用行动让我学会了坚

situation, to a large extent, depends on whom he met during his late puberty. And luckily enough, I met such a group of wonderful people, who brought me warmth, moved me, taught me how to persevere and excel myself.

From Jim and Kathy Coley, I felt the hospitality of the Americans again. When a group of children from the earthquake-stricken area of China came to the US, they could not communicate well with the locals there fluently. Jim proposed that he could help us with oral English in the small meeting room in our school every Wednesday night after his work. The practice lasted for several months until most of us could speak comparatively fluent American English. Kathy Coley, in order to introduce an authentic Halloween to us, decorated her house all by herself and prepared a unique costume for each of us.

Danny taught me that I had a bunch of choices to make in my life. He was pretty famous as a teacher teaching biology experiments in our school. He loved his gorgeous and virtuous wife and his handsome son, and he loved his work, too. He was busy at school but still spent much time being together with his family. However, neither his family nor his work could stop his

毅。基恩博士是法明戴尔州立大学的校长，我们回国后不久才得知他唯一的儿子去世了，而这一切我们在校期间完全不知道。儿子的去世，对两个白发苍苍的老人打击一定很大，我们很心痛，非常担心。可让我们惊讶的是，年近花甲的他，勇敢坚强地面对现实，并且以更加饱满的热情投入工作。

瓦伦蒂诺也让我感动。当得知我们学期结束即将归国时，他居然一个人追到机场来与我们道别，祝福我们。那一个紧紧的美国式拥抱，我至今都难以忘怀。

这些故事，我把它深藏在记忆里，十年后再次翻出仍是如数家珍。它们出现在我的人生观、价值观即将定型之际，深深地影响了我此后的整个人生，是我人生最宝贵的财富。

## 言有尽而意无穷

"CSC-SUNY 150奖学金项目"

pursuit of his hobby of drama creation. He did almost reach the acme of drama. His play was once performed in an opera theater in Shanghai.

Dr. Keen, President of Farmingdale State College, taught me how to be persistent with his own deeds. The minute we returned to China, the news spread that his only son died. However, we had no idea about this when we were in school. His son's death was a heavy blow for these two old persons, and also saddened us. All the students were worried about them. However, to our surprise, he, an old man of almost sixty years of age, chose to face the reality with such a brave and tough heart. He soon got engaged into his work with more vigor and enthusiasm.

Kathy Valentino, my bro in the US moved me to tears. When he knew that we were about to leave at the end of that term, he hurried to the airport to say goodbye to us, sending his best wishes to us, like living a healthy life after back to China, etc. That tight and powerful American hug left me an unforgettable impression.

I have kept all of these stories in my deep mind for a decade. With the ten years passing in the blink of an eye, I can still retell all of them one by one with great familiarity. As they happened at the moment when my life views and values were to be shaped, they have changed my value and influenced me on my later development. They are really my dearest treasures in the whole life.

### Endless Meaning But Limited Words

The CSC-SUNY 150 Program was finished ten years ago. When asked what this program has left me, I would say that it has not only left me

结束快十年了，如果说这个项目留给我的，绝不仅仅是口语更加流利，知识更加渊博。我想更多的应该是教会了我如何用真心和热情去温暖身边的人，如何以乐观的态度去做好工作、过好生活，去追求自己的爱好，坚强地面对生活中的一切挫折。美国人的家庭观念我非常认同。中文有个俗语叫成家立业，意思是先有家，再有事业。我认为应该把更多时间用来陪伴家人，人的生活重心先是家庭才是工作。回国这十年，我一直坚持每个周末都推掉所有工作和应酬待在家里。现在我有了两个女儿，依然保持这个习惯。周末在家可能会给工作带来一些小损失，但每当看着孩子们对自己的依赖，看着她们天真烂漫的笑容，就会感觉一切都是值得的。

美国之行也改变了我的人生格局，对我的事业产生了很大的影响。去美国之前我从来没想过要考研，原计划读到大三就开始准备考公务员。到美国之后，我发现美国的小学、初中老师都需要有研究生学历，当时就觉得我们国家也在飞速发展，今后对高学历的需求会越来越大，因此我毅然决定考研。在老师、家长的支持下，经过努力，我考上了浙江大学的研究

fluent oral English and more profound knowledge but also taught me how to warm people around me with sincerity, how to be devoted into my work, and live my life with conscience and positive attitudes, how to pursue my hobby, and how to face all the obstacles in my life with bravery.

Most important of all, I really appreciate Americans' attitudes towards their family. In the US, every one values his or her family. I totally appreciate this value, which has influenced me very deeply. There is an old saying in China, "get married and start one's career." The family goes first and then comes the career. I think that most of the time should be spent being with our family. The focus of one's life should be given to his or her family. In these ten years after coming back, I have gotten rid of all work and refused all the appointments on weekends, enjoying happiness with my family. Now I have two daughters, but this habit has never changed. In this way, I might lose something in my work, but whenever I see my daughters' dependence on me, their innocent smiles, I feel what I do is worth doing.

My study in the US has also changed my life pattern, exerting profound influence on my career. Before going to the US, I had never thought that I would further my study as a postgraduate. I planned to take the Civil Servant Examination in the third year. When I came to the US, seeing that the basic requirement for even primary and middle school teachers was a Master's degree, I realized that there would be greater demands for people of higher educational background in China with her fast development. Thus, I made up my mind to take the postgraduate examination. With the help and support of both

生。在浙江大学两年半的学习中，我拓宽了眼界，择业时有了更大的优势和更多的机会。

十年间，我考上了研究生，也工作了近七年。作为优秀引进人才，去过北京锻炼，又回到基层工作，得到领导和同事的认可，自己也比较满意。记得毕业实习时有一位老师给我讲过一段话："当一个官员一心为民并做到一定层次后，就可以创新立功，切切实实为老百姓做一些事，用实际行动去为一方百姓带来一些福利。"这其实也是我的理想，在公务员这个平台上，用自己的努力和勤奋为更多人带来福利。

人首先要进行自我评估，找到适合自己的舞台。如果自己的理想、才华与工作内容刚好契合，那是最幸运的了。末了，我想对即将去美国留学的学弟学妹们说：本科出去留学的话，建议多走、多看、多了解风土人情，多了解美国人分析问题、解决问

my teachers and parents and with my own hard working, I became a graduate student in Zhejiang University. During my two-year-and-a-half study there, I broadened my horizon, escalated my pattern and was faced up with more opportunities and advantages while choosing my future job.

In these ten years, I became a postgraduate in Zhejiang University and have worked for almost seven years. As an introduced talent, I once worked in Beijing to make a better me. Then I came back to work in grass-roots units, being recognized by my boss and my colleagues. I am satisfied with my current state. I still remember during the time when I started my internship, one teacher told me, "As an official, as long as you wholeheartedly work for the citizens well enough, you will definitely achieve new success. You must be down to earth to serve for citizens and be sure that what you do can benefit them." This is, in fact, my own dream. As an official, I desire to bring more benefits to more people through my hard work and efforts.

Self-assessment is a priority for us to find our own position on the stage. If your dream, talent and work accord with each other, you are the chosen one. In the very end, I want to tell the students who will go to study in the US that if you study abroad as a undergraduate, you

题的思维方式，以及他们的人生观、价值观。硕士研究生出去的话，应该把精力放在学术钻研上。美国在生命科学、计算机互联网方面比我们先进很多，我们应该把更多时间用于学习他们的先进技术和理念上，学成归来报效祖国。

should visit more places, experience various customs, and know more about the way in which Americans analyze and address problems and their values. If you go abroad as a postgraduate, you should be more focused on your academic study. The US does surpass China in fields like Life Science, Computers and the Internet. Therefore, we should spend more time learning their advanced technology and concepts so as to make contributions to our own country after graduation.

1896

四川
大学

Sichuan University

# 心存感恩，我们希望可以做得更多

## Hoping to Do More with Constant Gratitude

陈晨／四川大学　纽约州立大学科布尔斯基分校

Chen Chen / Sichuan University　SUNY at Cobleskill

"SUNY 最小的分校之一科布尔斯基拥有项目学生最多。" 我时常想起 "爷爷" 的这句话。2008年 "5·12" 汶川特大地震后参加 "CSC-SUNY 150 奖学金项目" 的时候，科布尔斯基作为纽约州立大学中较小的分校之一，共接纳了包括我在内的 18 名中国学生，这是一次特别的学旅之行，影响我们的一生。

"CSC-SUNY 150 奖学金项目" 从 "5·12" 汶川特大地震之后开始筹备，在不到两个月的时间内便完成了的前期准备工作，然后又仅用一个月的时间完成了对四川众多高校数千名学生进行招考、评定以及签证办理和与校方沟通确认等方面的工作。

I often think of Grandpa's words, "We Cobleskill, as one of the smallest campuses of SUNY, now have the biggest group of the CSC-SUNY 150 Program." When I was taken into the CSC-SUNY 150 Program after the 2008 earthquake, Cobleskill, as the smaller branch school in SUNY, accepted 18 Chinese students including me. This was a special study tour, an experience that would influence our whole lives.

Preparations for the CSC-SUNY 150 Program began immediately after the Earthquake and all the preliminary work was completed in less than two months. Then it took only one month to finish the admission by examination on and assessment of thousands of students from various universities in Sichuan, visa processing, communication and confirmation with schools in the United States. On the 15th of August 2008, 150 college students from Sichuan boarded a plane to New York. This incredible speed and

2008 年 8 月 15 日，150 名四川大学生登上了飞往纽约的飞机。这令人难以置信的速度与效率背后，无疑离不开两国政府、社会各界以及学校各方的重视、关怀与帮助。一路走来，我们需要感谢与铭记的那些人、那些事，真的太多太多。

我记得在接我们到学校的大巴上，学长鲍勃纠正我说黑人的称谓不是"black people"，而应该是"African American"。

我记得我的非裔美国人室友 E，我们从一开始无话可说，到后来变得无话不说，甚至有一次在食堂他为了顾及我的感受，特意从他朋友那桌抽身过来陪我。

我记得学校食堂的厨房每周末为我们 18 名中国学生开放一天，我们可以自己买菜做饭，做川菜，吃火锅！

我记得"爷爷""奶奶"冬天带我们去沃尔玛，给我们所有人都买了暖和的羽绒服；夏天带我们去佛罗里达，去迪士尼，去海边；我们几乎每个周末都会跑去"爷爷""奶奶"家，吃烧烤、看影碟。

我记得学校"留学生协会"的老师带我们去博物馆、国家公园，去波士顿，游哈佛、麻省理工学院。

我记得我们一群人在零下十几度的寒冬登上帝国大厦，俯瞰整个纽约，

efficiency were undoubtedly the result of mutual attention, care and help of the governments of the two countries, all the social sectors and all the school parties concerned. Throughout the whole process, there were too many people and things we need to thank and remember respectively.

I can remember the first time when I arrived in the US and was on the bus to the school, Senior Bob corrected me that I should address those people "African Americans" instead of "black people."

Still I can remember my African American roommate E. In the beginning, we had nothing to say, but afterwards, we had everything to talk with each other. Once in the cafeteria, he even deliberately walked over from his friend's table to sit with me to show his concern about my feelings.

I also remember that the kitchen in the school cafeteria was open to us 18 Chinese students every weekend, when we could cook Sichuan cuisine and enjoy hot pots with food and vegetables we bought outside!

I can remember that in the winter, the grandparents took us to Walmart and bought warm down jackets for all of us; in the summer, he took us to Florida, Disneyland, and the beach; we spent almost every weekend at the grandparents' home, doing BBQs and watching DVDs.

心中热血澎湃。

我记得我们特意跑到联合国，把盖有联合国标记的明信片寄给我们思念的人。

我记得我的英语老师当着全班同学的面，表扬我的期末论文比很多美国同学都写得好，并且会将我的论文作为范例在今后的课堂上进行讲解。

我记得我的专业课老师戴利说他很喜欢中国，并且邀请我去他家里过感恩节，还送我小礼物"Dream Catcher"，我珍藏至今。

我记得我们经常跟一群日本、美国同学打羽毛球、打篮球，他们还邀请我们去参加他们的派对。

我记得SUNY和留学基金委专门带我们150个人到新泽西去看NBA比赛，火箭（姚明）VS网队（易建联），当时我们就像小时候第一次吃到美味的蛋糕一样兴奋。

我记得结业典礼是在纽约河畔的一个公园举行的，里面有一个大大的

I remember that the teachers of the International Student Association took us to visit museums, national parks, Boston, Harvard and MIT.

I can remember that we felt very excited and shocked when several of us climbed up to the top of the Empire State Building in the winter below −10℃ and overlooked the whole of New York.

I can remember that we went to Headquarters of the United Nations for the purpose of sending postcards with the special postmark to the people we missed.

I can still remember that my English teacher praised me in class by saying that my final paper was better than many American students' and would take my thesis as an example in future classes.

I can remember that Daly, one of my major course teachers, said that he liked China very much, invited me to go to his home for Thanksgiving and gave me a small gift—Dream Catcher—which I have always treasured.

I can also remember that we often played badminton and basketball games with a group of Japanese and American students. They also

舞台，就是电影中蜘蛛侠女朋友毕业典礼举行的地方。当天太阳很大，晒得很多人不住地揉眼。

我当然还记得纽约大使馆胡思源叔叔多次邀请我们参加活动，并请我们吃了可口的粤菜；记得纽约州州长夫人邀请我们到她的府邸做客，并种下了"中美友谊长青之树"；甚至国务委员刘延东女士也惦记着我们，并亲自到学校米看望，带来了来自祖国的关怀与期望。

## 远在大洋彼岸的"爷爷"

我前面说的"爷爷"，其实是我们所在分校的招生办主任。从第一天笑着迎接我们，到最后一天哭着与我们分别，这期间美妙而充满爱的经历让我们与他成了真正的亲人，所以还在学校的时候，我们便已在私下开始叫他"爷爷"。项目结束后，"爷爷"带着"奶奶"两次到中国看我们，而我们当中的一些同学，也很幸运地有

invited us to attend their parties.

I can still remember that SUNY and the CSC took us 150 Chinese students to New Jersey to watch the NBA game of the Rockets (Yao Ming) vs. Nets (Yi Jianlian), and my feeling then was so sweet as I had a delicious cake for the first time when I was a child.

I can remember that our graduation ceremony was held at a big stage in a park on the bank of the New York River, the same place as where the graduation ceremony of Spiderman's girlfriend took place in the movie. The sunshine was so strong that day that many people could not blink.

Of course, I also remember that Uncle Hu Siyuan of the New York Embassy invited us to participate in the event and offered us delicious Cantonese food. I can remember the New York Governor's wife, who invited us to visit her house and planted there "The Tree of Everlasting Friendship between China and the United States"; even the State Councilor Ms. Liu Yandong also came to visit us at the school to show the care and expectations from the motherland.

### "Ye Ye" on the Other Side of the Ocean

In fact, Grandpa was "Dean of the Enrollment" of our branch school. The wonderful and loving experience of this period from greeting us with smiles on the first day to separating from us with

机会回到美国去看望他们。这绵延的情意是思念，是感恩，是爱。这一年中，印象最深刻的人当然是"爷爷"，我想应该大部分科布尔斯基的同学也都这么觉得。

## 诚信是道德，自律是文化

初到美国，我们几个中国学生去沃尔玛买东西常借身边的人的会员卡，这样我们可以得到一定的折扣，他们也会增加一部分积分。所以很多人出于意愿或者礼貌，都会答应。直到遇见一个人，当他说出"我为什么要借你？"时，我没敢看他的眼睛，羞愧不已。

其实，类似这种的小脑筋大家都会动，但美国人却很少有人拿来钻空子，没有就是没有，这是最起码的诚信问题。所以从那儿以后，我再也没有借过别人的会员卡，也深深受这种自律文化的影响。

tears on the last day made him seem like one of our family members. So when we were still at school, we started to call him Ye Ye (Grandpa) in private. Even after the program ended, Grandpa and Grandmother also came to China to see us twice, and some of our classmates were fortunate enough to have the opportunity to return to the United States to visit them. This long-lasting affection comes from our gratitude to, missing and love of him.

Of course, the most impressive person of the year was Ye Ye, and I think most of Cobleskill students would think so.

**Honesty & Self-discipline**

When we several Chinese students went shopping at Walmart, we would like to ask people around to borrow their membership cards, and many people are willing to do so either from intention or courtesy so that we could get a certain discount and they would also increase some points. Until I met that person, I felt no shame; I even didn't dare to look at his eyes when he said "Why would I lend it to you?"

In fact, most people like to try some simpler tricks of this kind, but few Americans take advantage of them. If you are not entitled to something, you'd never claim it because this

## 课堂上学到的工作基本素质

我相信很多同学跟我有同样的感受，与中国课堂最大的不同是美国课堂上一个接一个的"presentation"。从开始的分组、选择主题、讨论、分工、制订计划与时间表，各自完成以及充分沟通，到最后的成型和课堂呈现，这确实是一种个人价值与团队协作都能得到充分发挥的学习方式。而这期间反复学习和锻炼的，其实就是工作当中所需要具备的基本素质和能力，如团队搭建能力、沟通与表达能力、深度思考能力、时间管理能力、逻辑思维能力、公众场合演讲能力等。

is the minimum issue of integrity. So since then, I have never borrowed the membership card from someone else and understood the discipline culture better.

### Basic Quality of Work Learnt in Class

I believe that many of my classmates have the same feelings as mine that the biggest difference is the "presentation" one after another in the American classroom. This is indeed a learning style giving full play of personal value and teamwork from the grouping, selection of topics, discussion, division of work, making plans and the timetable in the beginning, further to the completion of individual task and full communication during the process, and to the draft finalization and classroom presentation at the end. During this process, what you repeat in learning and training is actually the basic

## 学会爱，保持初心

一年很长，长到我们所经历的一切可以让我们讲述和回忆，直到永远。一年也很短，短到不够，短到不舍。再回首，十年更是匆匆。我现在有一个非常幸福的家庭。我和我妻子是初中同桌，我们保持初心，彼此深爱对方；我们有一个可爱的女儿，长得像我，也像她。在工作方面，因为有留学的背景，我的第一份工作便是赴公司美国办事处工作，后来由于某些私人原因没能实现；第二份工作我抓住机会，常驻香港，负责公司部分进出口方面的业务。而现在，我在一家自己比较满意的单位工作，领导关怀我，同事支持我，同时我也能很好地照顾到家庭。

一年的留美学习与生活，让我更加自信，各方面能力有所提升，同时我学会了分享，学会了保持初心。更重要的是我有了一颗感恩的心、一颗有爱的心。这些都让我的生活更有温度。

## 爱与包容是我们共同的追求

我时常在想："CSC-SUNY 150奖学金项目"到底给我们留下了什么？是更开放、自信的心态，是同情

qualities and abilities that you'll need to have in your work, such as team building ability, communication and expression skills, deep thinking ability, time management ability, logical thinking ability, public speaking ability, etc.

### Learn to Love Others & Follow My Heart

A year is so long that everything we experienced there has become an endless story for us to tell and remember forever. A year is also short, too short for us to taste all and say goodbye to it. Now when we are looking back, a decade has gone by in a hurry.

I have a very happy family now. My wife and I were the classmates of a junior high school. We have loved each other deeply from the very beginning and have a lovely daughter, who looks like me and like her. In terms of work, I got my first job offer to work in the US office of a company because of my background of studying abroad; unfortunately, I had to give it up later for some personal reasons. However, I caught the opportunity in the second job offer and worked as the permanent representative responsible for part of the company's import and export business in Hong Kong. Now, I am working in a unit, where I am satisfied with leaders' care and colleagues' support, and at the same time I can take good care of my family.

One year of study and life in the United States has made me more confident and improved in all aspects. At the same time, I have learned how to share ideas with others and how to follow my heart. What is more important is that I have gotten a heart with gratitude to and love of others, which, in turn, has made me feel more warm in life.

心、同理心、包容心，是更辩证的世界观与人生观，是感恩的心，是爱。无论在生活还是工作中，每当遇到急切焦灼的情况，我都会想起我们刚到科布尔斯基时，那位帮我们选课的老师，他是那样耐心地根据我们每一个人的专业和意愿来进行筛选，即使由于我们自己不确定的原因，前前后后调整修改了无数次；每当身边有人非常极端地看待中日关系或中美关系时，我都会心平气和、不遗余力地给他们讲我自己的亲身感受，告诉他们其实两国绝大多数民众都有着和平与和谐的共同愿望；每当自己能够尽自己的能力帮助他人的时候，我都会毫不犹豫，从无偿献血，到儿童基金会，再到无国界医生……

我还记得，在一次活动中，"CSC-SUNY 150奖学金项目"中的一位同学发言说："我们都觉得美国的天气预报非常精确，说2点刮风就2点刮风，说3点下雨就3点下雨，我希望我们也能够有更多的人可以学习和钻研气象领域的知识，把这种能力和技术带回中国！"果然，现在我们的天气预报也能够做到精确播报。我想，这一定是很多有心人共同努力结果。现在，也有越来越多的美国以及其他国家的朋友来中国学习和生活，我们高兴地发现，他们对于中

## Our Common Goal—Love & Inclusiveness

I often wonder what the CSC-SUNY 150 Program has left for us. In my opinion, it gives us a grateful heart of love with more open and confident mentality, compassion, empathy, tolerance, and a more dialectical view of the world and life as well. Whenever I encounter anxious situations either in life or at work, I would remember the teacher who helped us choose the course when we 18 students came to Cobleskill. He was so patient in helping us select courses in accordance with the specialty and will of each of us, irrespective of adjustments and revisions for many times just because of our own uncertainties. What's more, whenever I find someone around us gives a very extreme view on China-Japan relations or Sino-US relations, I will spare no effort to placidly tell him through my personal experience that in fact the vast majority of the people of both countries have the common aspirations of peace and harmony. And whenever I can do my best to help others, I will be wholeheartedly ready to do so without hesitation, such as voluntary blood donation, contributions to children funds and becoming a member of MSF...

I still remember that during an event, one of the 150 students said, "We all agree that the weather forecast in the United States is very accurate. If it forecasts there will be the wind at 2 o'clock, it will really blow at that hour, and if it forecasts a rain at 3 o'clock, it will be rainy punctually. I hope that there will be more people to learn and delve into the knowledge of meteorology, and bring this ability and technology back to China!" As expected, now our weather

四海之纽
Taking the World as a
Link to Study in USA 川山首绿

国也有了全新的认识和理解，并且有意愿去影响身边甚至更多的人，希望他们能够看到一个更先进、更有包容心、更有爱的中国。

我想，这就是文化交流的意义。

有一次，戴利带我和余海涛去参观石堡博物馆。我们在博物馆的心愿墙上用羽毛笔写下了我们的愿望。我还清晰地记得，托比写的是"上帝保佑美国"，我写的是"世界和平"，这都是我们的真心话。

十年，又是一个新的开始。我们一直心存感恩，希望可以做得更多。

forecast can be very accurate and great. I think this must be due to the joint efforts of many people of intention. Now, with more and more friends from the United States and other countries who come to study and live in China, we will be very happy to discover that with a brand-new perspective and understanding of China, they are very willing to influence the people around and even more others, hoping that they can see a more advanced and more inclusive new China with love.

I think this is the meaning of cultural exchange.

Once, Daly took Toby (Yu Haitao) and me to a nearby museum, Stone Fort Museum. We wrote our wishes with a quill-pen on the wish wall of the museum. I also clearly remember that Toby wrote down "God bless America" while I wrote down "World Peace". And I think we were sincere from our inner heart.

Ten years is another new beginning. We have always been grateful and hope to do more.

# 属于我们的 2008

## Our 2008

姜藜藜／四川大学　纽约州立大学奥斯威戈分校

Jiang LiLi / Sichuan University　SUNY at Oswego

记得 2004 年上高中的时候，大街小巷和 KTV 里经常听到那首《十年》。我不会唱歌，但是总能跟着哼出"十年之前，我不认识你，你不属于我"。那个时候的我 16 岁，觉得这怀念十年的歌词离我好遥远。但是没想到，光阴如梭，我已经开始怀念属于我自己的十年。

这个十年，开始于 2008，是一个最好的时代，她带给"85 后"的年轻人最大的灾难，却也赋予他们宝贵的精神财富。2008 到 2018，也是属于我们"CSC-SUNY150 奖学金项目"每一位同龄人的十年。

I could still remember when I was a high school student in 2004, the song called "Ten Years" spread far and wide throughout the city and of course in the KTVs. I couldn't sing it completely but could hum the part of it: "Ten years ago, I didn't know who you were, and you were not mine." I was 16 at that time, feeling myself far away from the meaning of the lyrics. Unexpectedly, however, I have begun to cherish the memory of the decade that especially belonged to me.

The decade started in 2008, and was the best time for me. Although it brought the greatest disaster to the young generation born after 1985, it gave them the most valuable spiritual wealth. The decade between 2008 and 2018 has been the most special period of time for every peer of mine in the CSC-SUNY 150 Program.

## 生活在美国电影里的一年

2008 那年我刚好 20 岁，离开家的第二年，在大学校园里懵懵懂懂地探索自己的生命方向。突然，5 月下午的那场大地震，冥冥之中将我的人生引向了另一个方向。

那场地震让我第一次感受到大自然的力量，却也让我懂得人情的温暖和生命的可贵。当然，直接受益的是我们 150 名四川大学生，我们有机会来到万里之外的纽约校园。

还记得第一次坐飞机的兴奋和刚到纽约的不真实感。直到几经辗转到达雪城机场，校方老师送给我大大的拥抱，我才真实地感受到，我已经进入另外一个文化环境。第二天早上从梦中醒来，听到楼下路人用英语聊天，我还一度以为自己置身于美国电影中。

就这样，我开始了我的新生活，认识了新朋友、新老师。我开始发现，美国人不是好莱坞电影里千篇一律的固定造型，而是一个个与众不同的有温度的个体。

## 那些人，那些第一次

最早接待我们的朱利亚和珍尼是传媒系的老师，他们带着一台摄影机说是要记录我们的故事。朱利亚是

## A Year in the US Movies

It was the second year after I left home for study in Chengdu. I was just 20 years old in 2008, exploring my life path on campus in a confused way. Imperceptibly but inexorably, my life was led to another direction after the big earthquake occurred abruptly in one afternoon of May.

The earthquake scared me with the terrible power of nature for the first time, but also made me realize the warmth of human sympathy and the true value of life. Of course, the most direct beneficiaries are the 150 students of us from different universities in Sichuan. The 150 of us had finally got the chance to stay on the campus of universities in New York, thousands of miles away from our motherland.

I still have a fresh memory of the excitement of taking an airplane and the sense of unreality as I just arrived in New York. After a tiring tour, we finally reached Syracuse Airport. When teachers from Oswego greeted us with a big hug, I could realize that I had been in a totally different culture. I felt as if I had been in the dream of an American movie until I heard people downstairs talking in English the next morning.

I started my new life here, making new friends, and meeting new teachers. I began to realize that the real Americans were not always like the ones in Hollywood movies but a group of people with specific uniqueness.

## Those People, Those First Times

Julia and Jane were the first to receive us in Department of Media. They told us that they'd carried a camera to record our story. Julia was

德国裔，到美国的那个寒假我们去参加活动，她俩作为摄影师跟我们一起旅行。现在回想起来，我人生中说出的第一个德语短语"Gute Nacht"，竟然是她在途中教会我的。朱利亚喜欢马和狗，我第一次知道，原来在美国，一个人可以拥有一匹属于自己的马，哪怕你不住在农场。

校长助理霍华德是我们认识比较早的男老师，也是我认识的第一位黑人老师。他戴着一副眼镜，脑袋圆圆的，总是穿着笔挺的西装。我记得他第一次见面安顿好我们，轻轻地告诉我他也是作家和诗人。我现在都记得他讲到他如何在繁忙重复的公务中每天抽出一个小时的时间，安静地坐在书桌前，写完一本本属于他的故事和诗歌时的满脸自豪。后来我看到他的故事和诗歌，都是与非裔身份有关。这是我第一次发现，原来一个人可以有一份职业，但是也可以拥有不同的身份。

第一位英语老师兼国际学生顾问戈蒂普在马来西亚出生，她小小的个子充满能量。记得第一学期我选了所有给国际生的英语课，戈蒂普是我最喜欢的老师，她耐心细致，大方幽默。我还清楚记得她盘腿坐在讲台上陪我们用 NPR 的广播练习听力的情景。还记得她在那堂听力课上给我们播放

a German American. They traveled with us as photographers in the CSC-SUNY150 Program during our first winter vacation in the US. Looking back now, the first German phrase of "Gute Nacht" I learned in my life was taught by her on our journey. Julia liked horses and dogs, and I was surprised that in the US, a person could own a horse of his own, even if he didn't live on the farm.

Howard, an assistant to the principal, was a male teacher whom we'd known earlier, and also the first black teacher I met. He had a round head, wearing a pair of glasses and a handsome suit. I remember that he told me that he was also a writer and poet after he settled us down during the first meeting. And I also remember his proud and satisfied face when he talked about how he took an hour off every day from his busy schedule to write bunches of stories and poems at his desk. Later, when I read his works, I noticed that all he had written was related to the African identity. For the first time, I saw that a man could have his special job while he could boast various identities.

Gurdeep, my first English teacher and international student consultant, was a small Malaysian lady with great vitality. In the first semester, I selected all the English courses for international students. Gurdeep had become my utmost favorite teacher for she was patient, meticulous, generous and humorous. I also remember clearly that she sat cross-legged on the podium, playing the NPR broadcast for us to practice our listening skills. In that listening class, she also played us the movie "The Joy Luck Club," which was the first time that I heard about the female stories of different generations under

《喜福会》，这是我第一次听中美文化冲突下不同代际的女性故事，开始对之甚感兴趣，这也是我第一次知道作家谭恩美。我21岁生日那天刚下了雪，上完戈蒂普的英语演讲辩论课，她得知当天是我的生日，就赶去学校纪念品店，回来送给我一枚印着学校标志的徽章，神秘地笑着说"祝你生日快乐"。这是我第一次，估计也是唯一一次收到老师送的生日礼物。我还记得那天白雪茫茫，配着那枚绿字黄底的学校名奥斯维戈的校徽分外好看。

玛丽·安和安迪是一对退休的重组家庭夫妻，也是我们认识的第一对校外的朋友。老两口曾经是大学职员，退休后把时间奉献给了国际生。玛丽·安一头银丝，安迪总是笑容可掬，他们为国际学生提供无偿的英语辅导。我还清楚记得玛丽来到我们的英语课堂，把自己手工剪裁的名片一张一张发给大家的情景。之后，我不仅经常用半生不熟的英语作业"骚扰"玛丽·安，还经常被她邀请到家里去做客。那是我第一次看到温暖的壁炉，靠着沙发坐在地上，听老人家给我们讲过去的故事。老人厨房里的冰箱上不是各地旅游搜集来的冰箱贴，而是全球各地来奥斯威戈求学和他们度过美好时光的年轻人的照片。我也被荣

the conflicts between Chinese and American cultures. And I got to know the writer Amy Tan and started to becoming interested in the story. It snowed on my 21st birthday. She heard about it when we just finished her English speech debate class. Then she rushed to the school's souvenir shop and returned with a badge of university logo as a birthday gift for me. She smiled mysteriously and said, "Happy birthday". That was the first time and might be the only time for me to receive a birthday present from my teacher. The badge carved in green words of "Oswego" on the yellow background looked pretty nice on the snowy day.

Mary Anne and Andy were the retired couple in their reconstituted family. They were the first friends or even family to us outside of the school. The couple used to be university staff, and dedicated their time to international students work after retirement. Mary had gray hair, and Andy was always smiling kindly. They provided free English tutoring for international students. I still remember the situation when Mary came to our English class and handed out her hand-made business cards to us one by one. After that, I often troubled Mary Anne with my unskilled English homework, while she always helped me patiently. She often invited me to visit her home. It was the first time I saw a warm fireplace. I sat on the floor leaning against the sofa, listening to them telling the stories about the past. The surface of refrigerator in the kitchen was not covered by magnets collected from various places, but pictures of young people who spent good time with them. And my picture was also pasted on the refrigerator later on. The couple then went to China to visit those students who had studied in Oswego. They treated these Chinese students as

幸贴在了他家的冰箱上。后来老人来到了中国，探望曾经在奥斯威戈学习的学生们，就像探望自己出远门未归的孩子。为了方便联系，现在他们也跟上时代，用上了微信。

萧老师，是我认识的第一位中国台湾老师，也是第一位在海外教汉语的老师。萧老师跟随她的先生，20年前从台北来到纽约，一直在大学里教汉语。我在本科学习对外汉语专业，但在国内一直苦于没有机会实习，到了奥斯维戈，理论知识有了用武之地。我第一次成为一名汉语辅导员，还在萧老师的鼓励下，帮助老师搜集资料做研究。那个时候我没有写过一篇研究文章，也没有做过科研调查，连基本的引用格式都完全不清楚。她温和耐心，她的支持第一次让我感受到做研究最快乐的不是结果而是学习的过程。

## 生命中温柔的力量

这些点点滴滴的第一次，一直伴随着我这十年的成长。十年后的现在，坐在德国纽伦堡城北家里的电脑前，我依然能够感受他们的力量。十年后的我痛并快乐地写着我关于中国留学生在海外的身份认同和归属感变化的博士论文。我发现，当年在纽约幸运

their own children. For better convenience, they have caught up with the trend and started to use Wechat for communication.

Ms. Xiao was the first teacher I met in the university from Taiwan. She was also the first teacher who taught Chinese overseas. Ms. Xiao went with her husband to New York from Taipei 20 years ago and had been teaching Chinese in the university. My major was TCFL when I was an undergraduate, but I had not got a chance to get an internship when I was in China. After I came to Oswego, I had a chance to put my theoretical knowledge into practice. Then I became a Chinese instructor for the first time, and began to help teachers collect materials for research under the encouragement from Ms. Xiao. I had not done any dissertation yet at that moment, nor did any scientific research. I was even completely unfamiliar with the basic format. With her gentle patience and support, I understood that the happiest thing of doing research was not the conclusion I'd made, but the whole process.

### The Gentle Power in My Life

All these first times have witnessed the growth of mine in the past decade. Ten years later, sitting in front of my computer in the north of Nuremberg in Germany, I still can truly feel the strength. Ten years later, painfully but also joyfully, I am writing my doctoral thesis of "Changes on the Chinese Overseas Students' Sense of Identity and Belongingness." I have found that those people and things that I fortunately met in New York have become not only the origin and motivation of my academic

遇见的这些人与事不仅成了我学术兴趣的起点和动力，更让我感受到生命中温柔的力量。这份温柔可能在外人看来微不足道，可是在我心里，她强大到足以击败自然的冷漠无情和文化语言的重重障碍。

十年之前，我不认识你，你不属于我。十年之后，我们存在于彼此的生命里。

interest, but also made me feel the gentle power in life. The gentleness may seem to be trifle for others, while, in my mind, it's strong enough to defeat the apathy of nature and all the obstacles of language and culture.

Ten years ago, I didn't know who you were, and you were not mine. And ten years later, we are part of each other's life.

四川农业大学

Sichuan Agricultural University

四川農業大學

SICHUAN AGRICULTURAL UNIVERSITY

# 致敬十年，与爱同在

## Salute the Ten Years with Constant Love

何世鸣 / 四川农业大学　纽约州立大学海事学院

He Shiming / Sichuan Agricultural University　SUNY Maritime College

一眼十年，时间已渐渐让我们的创伤愈合。国之殇，川之伤；人之恸，民之哀。经历如此大灾，我们很幸运，仍能得到命运的垂青，得到全额奖学金赴美留学的机会。留美学习一年，对 150 名还是孩子的我们的一生都有重大影响。

As ten years flashes by, time has gradually healed our deep wounds, despite of the huge destruction of the country and hometown in the 5·12 Wenchuan Earthquake, leaving great mourning and grief to the people. However, we were lucky to be able to get the chance to study in the US with a full scholarship after such a great disaster. For the 150 people of us who once were so young, the one-year study in the US has changed our whole lives.

### 2008，搭起友谊的桥梁

### 2008, the Bridge of Friendship

我永远记得魏老师（我们后来一直叫她琳姐），"CSC-SUNY 150 奖学金项目"在纽约州立大学的项目负责人，她时刻操心着我们在美国的一切事宜。当然，我们后来才得知，我们赴美的前前后后，有着多少个琳

I always remember Ms. Wei (whom we later called "Sister Lin"), the CSC-SUNY 150 Program's director at the State University of New York (SUNY), always took care of everything for us in the United States. Of course, we learned later that before and after our trip to the United States, there were many teachers like "Sister Lin" who

姐为我们付出心力。

　　地震三个月后的盛夏，北京奥运会刚刚开始，18岁的我们便要启程前往美国学习。我们中大部分人满怀憧憬，也忐忑不安，那种地动山摇的恐惧始终挥之不去。而琳姐一句"Be happy, be always happy"，时至今日，仍然"护"着我——没有什么是挺不过去的。

　　一年的留学生活，给我们留下很多精彩的瞬间，至今难以忘怀。我被分配到纽约州立大学位于布朗克斯郡（纽约市五大区之一）的海事学院，也是我们150名同学被分到的23所州立大学分校里唯一一个在纽约市市区的校区，到曼哈顿地铁即达，海景学区。我们也承担着"市区"联络员的任务，其他同学要来市区参观学习，都可以到我们这儿借宿。

　　无课休假时，我们就奔曼哈顿，去上东区的大都会博物馆看遗落海外的敦煌壁画，去中城现代艺术博物馆看我的最爱——莫奈的睡莲，去地标

had devoted their efforts to us.

Only 3 months after the earthquake, in the middle of summer, the Beijing Olympic Games began. And we, at the age of 18, also began our journey to study in the most developed country in the world. There is no denying that most of us were excited and full of longing. Meanwhile, we were all actually in a state of anxiety, as the fear of the earthquake never diminished. But Sister Lin's words of "be happy, be always happy" still "protected" me—I could get through everything.

The year of studying abroad has left us a lot of wonderful and unforgettable moments. And I was fortunately assigned to the Maritime campus of SUNY in Bronx (one of the five districts of New York City), which was the only campus in downtown New York City of all the 23 SUNY campuses for 150 of us students. It was said that there was the direct subway connection between our campus and Manhattan, and all the dormitories boasted beautiful seascapes. So we also played the role of "downtown" liaison men, providing accommodation for our fellow students coming from other campuses.

We often went to Manhattan when there was no class, going to the Metropolitan Museum in the Upper East to appreciate the Dunhuang frescoes that were left overseas, rushing to MOMA in Midtown to enjoy my favorite Water Lilies by Monet, walking on the Brooklyn Bridge, a landmark of the city, to see the skyline of Manhattan, and strolling in the Central Park to watch the artistic performances by various ethnic groups. My utmost favorite place was Greenwich Village, where I made a wish under the purple school banner with a torch in the middle that I would come back here again to continue to study after the one-year program.

布鲁克林大桥看曼哈顿的城际线，去中央公园看各族群的艺术表演。最爱的，还是去格林威治村，在一面紫色的有着火炬的校旗下，许下一个愿望：希望我们短暂的一年求学之后，我还能够来这里，来纽约大学继续求学。

2008年的留学经历，是疗伤之旅，是领导力塑造之旅，更是文化传递、信息交流、纽带建立之旅。

## 2012 年，追梦第二旅

与 2008 年的那一次短暂的学习相比，这次来纽约，兴奋中带着更多的自我期待。

硕士阶段的求学经历，没有 149 位同学，没有时刻关注我们的老师，一切是靠着自己，重新去适应纽约这个大熔炉。幸运的是，纽约于我依然是那么熟悉，从着陆肯尼迪机场到"家"，我没有新留学生那样的"艰辛"——推着几个巨大的行李箱，耐着饥寒四处寻觅住宿的经历。

2008 年，我结识了一个很好的朋友，克里斯多夫·麦克米兰，其实也是我们英语课教授。他是一个非常酷的老男孩，六十岁左右，教英语也酷炫地穿着嬉皮的皮衣皮裤、驾着他的哈雷摩托。克里斯多夫的两个小孩都成年了，小儿子刚刚念大学，他就

The 2008 US journey was not only a journey of healing, but a journey of leadership cultivation, and the one of even significant missions—building the bridge of friendship between our two countries, transmitting cultures, exchanging ideas, and establishing the ties.

### 2012, the Second Journey of Dream

Compared with the one-year study in 2008, the second time that I flied to New York City was of excitement with more self-expectations.

For the master's education, away from my 149 peers and teachers who always cared about, and in the big melting pot of New York City, I had to depend on myself. Fortunately, I was still so familiar with the city that all the way from landing JFK (John F. Kennedy International Airport) to "home," I even didn't have any discomfort—pushing a few huge luggage, enduring hunger and cold, and looking for the accommodation, which most freshmen might experience.

In 2008, I met Christopher McMillan, a very good friend of mine, and also a literature professor of our English course. He was a cool old boy in his sixties, who taught English but

把家里的房间腾出一间来租给我，其实也是补贴小儿子的私立大学学费。对于这位哥大毕业的教书 30 年的教授，美国中产阶级的典型代表，私立大学的学费仍是一笔不小的开支。

作为一个大龄室友，我最喜欢他的一点，当然是每天早上六点，总是多给我煮一份热腾腾的、微甜的咖啡，然后他一边喝咖啡一边看 Pepper 猫在隔壁阳台晒太阳。

哦，差点忘记提，我们住在曼哈顿老人养护区——罗斯福岛，一片安静祥和之地，与世隔绝般存在于繁忙的曼哈顿和稍微复杂的皇后区之间。

当然，英语老师当室友，口语总是"莫名其妙"地有些提升，虽然他一早就去上班了，晚上归家后竟然一副要给我开小灶的感觉。最让我头疼的是四川人的特色口音了——他总是纠结于我有没有准确地发出 /l/ 和 /n/ 的音，害得我总是耍赖地说："我是南方人，我的南方口音没法改了！"（意思是跟美国一样，美国南部也有着很强的南方口音，经常被美国东北部早期发达的区域嘲笑。）

我经常忘记带钥匙，他干脆让我写个中文"钥匙"贴在门上，以防我上学出门的时候忘记带钥匙。

作为"美国好室友"，他还帮我准备实习面试，让我学会了系领带。

was keen on wearing Hippie leather pants and driving his Harley Davidson motorcycle. Both of Chris's children had come of age. The youngest son just went to college, so he rented one of his rooms to me. In fact, this also could cover part of his youngest son's tuition in a private university. But for him, a Columbia University alumnus, a typical American mid-class representative, who had been teaching for 30 years, tuition fees in private universities was still a big burden.

As an older roommate, the thing I liked about him was, of course, that he always prepared for me a cup of hot and slightly sweet coffee at six o'clock every morning before he drank his while watching Pepper, a pet cat, basking itself on the balcony of the next door.

Oh, I forget to mention that we lived in the Old Manhattan Conservation Area of Roosevelt Island, a quiet and peaceful place located between the busy Manhattan and the slightly complicated Queens.

Of course, your spoken English would always somewhat improve when your roommate is an English teacher. Although he went to work very early in the morning, he still felt like giving me extra lessons when he returned home at night. What annoyed me the most was my Sichuan accent—he always wondered if I could pronounce /l/ and /n/ accurately. So I always had to say, "I'm a southern country boy with a strong southern accent, I just can't help!" (People in the southern part of America have a strong southern accent, which is often ridiculed by those who live in the developed regions of the northeastern America.)

I often forgot to take the key, so he told me to write a Chinese word of "key" and pasted on the door, in case I forgot to take the key when I went out for class.

每一次提到人生中的第一次，都意味着成长，成长就意味着快离家了。和"美国好室友"快乐的时光不到一年，我就搬出去了，但是，不可否认，那是我硕士两年最开心的时光。

研究生两年时间过得很快，和其他留学生一样，纽约大学的学习压力着实不小，大家铆足劲儿学习，日历上密密麻麻地标记着要去参加的"Bootcamp"以及"Career Center"举办的校招（OCR, On-Campus Recruitment）活动、全网（学校的"CareerNet"上会列出所有按门类的招聘信息）投简历获取实习机会，等等。

在此，我不得不提一下纽约大学最具实力和特色的就业服务中心，纽约所有的公司如果校园招聘，岗位信息要么放到瓦瑟曼就业服务中心，要么是哥伦比亚大学的CCE就业服务中心（大多数时候是两个同时放）。

诚然，美国的大学和研究生教育

As "the best roommate ever in America", he also helped me to suit up for internship interviews. For the first time in my life, I learned to tie my necktie.

Every time I mention the first times in life, it means growth, and growth means leaving home. I moved out after less than a year of sharing happiness with my American roommate. However, it was undeniable that it had been the happiest time of my two-year graduate study journey in America.

The two-year graduate study passed quickly. Like other international students, I had gotten a lot of pressure from SUNY, and everyone there was studying so hard that his or her schedules were dotted with event notices, such as OCR (On-Campus Recruitment) and CareerNet (where the university would list all the recruitment information by different categories) organized by Bootcamp and Career Center, to help students get the chances of internship.

I have to make a special mark of the most competitive and outstanding organization of NYU—Wasserman Career Center (a career service center); all the job information from companies in New York City would be released

体系，对于学生而言，是职业发展和薪酬提升的重要途径，更是一笔不菲的投资。对于我而言，衡量一个学校最直观的尺度是，它有没有强大的就业服务体系：集合顶级公司的校招资源的平台、顶级公司高频率地来校路演展示以及与学生互动的机会、学生的职业规划和简历打造，等等。

## 2014，回国回家回四川

得益于学校良好的教学和实践资源，我有幸最终在纽约的一家世界五百强金融服务领域的公司工作，公司位于大家熟知的华尔街。

每日地铁 F 线通勤于罗斯福岛和中城之间，出站便是第六大道 55 街的街口，路过"Radio City"、洛克菲勒中心，直奔位于 56 街的办公室。自己似乎已经忘却 2008 年才去纽约的激动心情，仰望鳞次栉比的摩天大楼，看西装笔挺的纽约人快速大步穿梭于楼宇之间，以及永远有人在挥向永远打不到的纽约出租车，满满的工作负荷让自己有些迷失。

直到 2014 年的秋天，毕业后工作不到半年，一位叔叔远渡重洋赴美治疗，已是肺癌晚期的他，抱着最后一丝希望，来到纽约的"MSKCC（Memorial Sloan Kettering Cancer

on either Wasserman or CCE Employment Service Center of Columbia University.

To be honest, the University and graduate education system in the US have been an important channel for students to get better career development and salary promotion. It is also a great investment of the students. Therefore, the most intuitive criteria for me to evaluate a university is whether it has a competent employment service system: a platform of integrating campus recruitment resources of all top companies, frequent road shows by top companies, the interaction between top companies and students, and career planning and resume development by students.

**2014, My Decision to Go Home**

Thanks to the school's excellent teaching and practical resources, I was finally fortunate to work for a company in New York City, one of the top 500 financial services companies in the world. Wall Street is a famous landmark in New York City and has taken its root in the global financial center.

The F line of the subway brought me directly from Roosevelt Island to Midtown, where I could reach the junction of the $55^{th}$ Street on the $6^{th}$ Avenue. Passing through the Radio

Center）"治疗。这是美国排名第二的癌症治疗中心。

那一年家里有太多的变故，最后只有只会一点英文的姑姑来美国陪他在医院治疗，我也只能白天抽时间去医院，晚上才能回家照顾他。

难以想象，姑姑和一直抱有希望的叔叔，白天在医院里，没有我的帮助，他们是怎么度过的：专业的医疗词汇、复杂的治疗方案，医生讲着他们听不懂的英文。对此，我至今心怀愧疚。但是，我们还是感受到了美国人性化的医疗服务和对病人无微不至的关怀。

美国的天总是很蓝，在叔叔最后的时光里，我们陪他去短途旅行，去长岛看海，感受纽约最美的秋天，或者在罗斯福岛静静地看东河对面的曼哈顿……

时间，和疾病一样，是最无情的"杀手"。不到两个月，我看着叔叔每况愈下的身体，医院也没有更好的治疗方案，我不敢在他面前提"放弃"——他的身体已经支撑不住了。我只能安慰他，要不再回国试试中医治疗，听说很多中医治疗是很有效果的。

那一年，纽约、成都还没有直飞，我们决定告别医院，回家！可是，叔叔没撑住，在旧金山转机的时候，最

City and Rockefeller Center, I would arrive at my office on the 56th Street. It seemed that excitement I had when I just arrived in New York City in 2008 had been forgotten. Looking up at the countless skyscrapers, and watching New Yorkers moving swiftly among buildings and some of them waving their hands to the yellow cabs that seemed would never stop, I, suffocated by the full workload, was kind of losing myself.

In the fall of 2014, less than half a year after my graduation, my uncle visited me from China for his cancer treatment. He had already been diagnosed the terminal stage of lung cancer, and with the last glimmer of hope, he went to MSKCC (Memorial Sloan Kettering Cancer Center), the second largest cancer treatment center in the US, to take his treatment.

Too many sudden events happened at home that year. My aunt, who could spoke little English, flied to the US to accompany my uncle in the hospital. I could only go to the hospital from my office in the daytime when I got some time off, and took care of him in the evening after getting off work.

I could imagine how helpless my aunt and uncle, who was always with hope, would be in the hospitals without my help in the daytime: medical terms, complex therapeutic regimen, and doctors' orders and advices in English that they could not understand. I'm still feeling guilty about them. However, we have still experienced the humanized medical services and considerate care for the patients in the US.

The skies there were always blue. We had accompanied my uncle to take some excursions in his final days. We went to the sea along Long Island, enjoyed the most beautiful fall in New

强的止痛药已经不起作用了。我第一次听到他痛得叫出声音来，甚至从轮椅上瘫倒下来——坚强的他在化疗的时候都从来不吭声。我们没能赶上回家的飞机。

人生最艰难的时刻，便是看亲人离去，无所依靠。在完全陌生的城市——旧金山，我和姑姑处理了叔叔的后事——因为我们不能带他的遗体回国。

那时，我总是不断地想起琳姐的话，"Be happy, be always happy！"但我更觉得，"Be Happy, be always happy with the beloved！"至亲至爱更重要！

于是，我辞掉了纽约的工作，回国，回家，回四川。

因为他们都在！

York City, and even simply stayed in Roosevelt Island to watch Manhattan across the East River.

Time, just like illness, is the most ruthless killer. Within no more than two months, my uncle had gotten worse, and we could not get any better treatments from the hospital. I dared not to say, "Give up" in front of him for he had already being unable to support his body. I could do nothing but comfort him that we could go back to China to try the TCM (Traditional Chinese Medicine) treatment. "I heard that many TCM treatments are extremely effective..." I said.

There was no direct flight from New York City to Chengdu that year, but we still decided to leave the hospital and go home. However, my uncle didn't make it. On the transfer in San Francisco, the strongest painkillers were no longer effective on him. For the first time, he screamed out in pain and even collapsed from his wheelchair—my uncle, who never gave up in his radiotherapy and chemotherapy—and we failed to catch the plane back home.

The hardest time in life is seeing one's relatives pass away without family support. In San Francisco, a completely unfamiliar city, I dealt with my uncle's funeral along with my aunt, for we couldn't take his body back.

In those days, I always thought of those words of Sister Lin, "Be happy, be always happy！" But I still preferred "Be Happy, be always happy with the beloved！" Those beloved ones in my family are more important than anything else!

So I quit my job in New York City, returned to China, and went back to Sichuan, my hometown.

Because that's where my beloved ones are!

# 一百五十分之一的我，足够幸运

## Lucky Enough to Be One of the 150

李锦 / 四川农业大学　纽约州立大学科布尔斯基农业与技术学院

Li Jin / Sichuan Agricultural University　SUNY at Cobleskill

十年前，我在四川农业大学就读水产养殖（鱼病与渔药）专业，听说"CSC-SUNY 150 奖学金项目"之后，我毅然报名。幸运的是，作为项目的一员，我去了纽约州立大学科布尔斯基农业与技术学院继续攻读水产养殖（鱼病与渔药）专业。

在美国留学的一年中，我遇到了许多难忘的老师和同学，其中有三个人对我来说特别重要，他们就是约翰·莫雷尔、马克·康韦尔和凯文·伯纳。同去的人中对约翰·莫雷尔做了非常多的描述，也包括我对他的敬意和感激。在《纽约，我心飞扬》一书里，我向大家介绍了马克老师。这一次，我想给大家说说我的另外一位

Ten years ago, I was majoring in Aquaculture (fish disease and fishery medicine) at Sichuan Agricultural University. After knowing the CSC-SUNY 150 Program, I signed up for it right away. Luckily, I was selected as the candidate of the program and was assigned to go to State University of New York (SUNY) to study Aquaculture (Fish disease and fishery medicine).

I met many wonderful and unforgettable teachers and students during the one-year study in the US. Three of them were special to me. They were John Morell, Mark Cornwell and Kevin Berner. My peers have done a lot of description of John Morell, to show our respect and gratitude for him. In the book *New York, Let Our Dreams Fly,* I have already introduced Mark, my teacher. This time, I would like talk about another teacher, Kevin Berner.

老师，凯文·伯纳。

第一次见到凯文老师的时候，是我最窘迫的时候。因为记错了上课时间，我到地下室教室的时候，马克老师和同学们都已经去野外了。我失落地坐在空荡荡的教室里，等着老师和同学们从野外回来向他们解释。

不知道等了多长时间后，门"吱呀"一声开了，我以为老师回来了。然而，从门后探出一张陌生的面孔，我们面面相觑。回过神来，凯文和我都介绍了自己。

凯文的办公室在教室的尽头，他教博物学、鸟类学等课程。我向他讲述了自己错过上课时间的过程，他耐心而安静地倾听，随后又询问我在这里上学的感受、遇到的困难。我们"吐槽"各自背诵鱼类拉丁文名的烦恼，他安慰我说即使本地的学生也感觉这门课程很难，建议我去图书馆请导师帮忙。

那天和他交谈后，我从孤独、自责和恐惧中走了出来。第一次见面，我就觉得他是一个非常温暖的人。

后来，我选择了凯文老师的博物学课程，成了众多喜欢他的学生之一。他的课堂生动幽默。有一次，他站在讲台上，煞有介事地说，今天他要为我们介绍一种我们从来都没有见过的鱼类。这条鱼现在坐在他的办公

I was in an embarrassing state when I first met Mr. Kevin. As I got a lapse of memory of the time for class, by the moment I arrived at the classroom in the basement of Alumi Hall, Professor Cornwell had left with the other students. I had to wait in the empty room, ready to apologize and explain my being late.

Without being aware of how long it had been, I heard the door opened. The professor must be back! My heart almost jumped out to my throat. However, it turned out to be a man with an unfamiliar but surprised face. After a short while, we introduced ourselves to each other.

Kevin's office was at the end of the classroom; he was a professor teaching natural science, ornithology and so on. I told him my awkward experience of missing the class while he listened to it in a quiet way. Then he asked me how I felt about the study here and also about difficulties that I met here. I roasted the difficulty of reciting the Latin names of fishes. He comforted me that even the local students have trouble learning this course, and also advised me to go to the library and ask for help from the tutor.

Our conversation did relieve me from isolation, self-blame and fear. It was a truly unforgettable meeting. He was found to be a very warmhearted person even if we just met each other for the first time.

室，请容他进去把这位"鱼大爷"请出来。结果，这条"鱼大爷"是用一根香蕉当鱼身，在中间插上两个三角板当鱼鳍做成的！他还给它取了一个拉丁名。"太有才了！"教室里爆发出一阵掌声和笑声。还有一次，讲到哺乳动物章节时，凯文为了强调雄性动物也有乳房，让全班男生跟着他走到教室外面，站在台阶上，对着过往的人群，大声宣布："我有乳房，我骄傲！"他真是一个非常有趣的人。

2009年感恩节，凯文邀请了在科布尔斯基农业与技术学院学习的"CSC-SUNY 150奖学金项目"的同学去他家体验他们的文化。凯文开车来接我们，作为土生土长的科布尔斯基农业与技术学院人，途中，他向我们介绍了学院的历史、文化，带我们参观了本地一家酿造枫糖浆的作坊。

在无限的期许和欢歌笑语中，我们来到了他的家中，他热情好客的妻子南希和俊朗腼腆的儿子亚历克斯出门迎接我们。我们参观了他的家，一栋距今已有一百多年历史的两层木制楼房，二楼是对窗而立的天文望远镜，放满唱片、吉他、贝斯和钢琴的玻璃娱乐房以及高大的壁炉；两层木制楼房前是一片广阔的草地，三分之一的土地开垦出来作为菜园。远处的一棵大树上，还有他为儿子建造的一间树

Later, I selected the natural science by Kevin, becoming one of his fans in the class. His class was very interesting. One day, he stood on the podium and told us seriously that he would introduce us to a kind of fish that none of us had seen before. The fish was now sitting in his office and everyone should be waiting for him to let the Mr. Fish come in. With a banana as the body, two set squares inserted as the fins, here came the Mr. Fish. It even had got a Latin name from Kevin. "Bravo!" The classroom burst into thunderous cheers, applause, and laughter. On the other day, in the class of introducing mammals, he tried to stress that all male mammals have boobs by inviting all his male students to go out of the classroom with him, standing on the steps, and crying out to all the passersby, "I have boobs! I'm proud of them!" What an amazing class! I began to realize that he was an extraordinarily funny person.

On Thanksgiving Day in 2009, Kevin invited the CSC-SUNY 150 Progam students in Cobleskill School to his house to experience real American culture. He drove us to his house. He was an alumnus of Cobleskill School. On the way to his house, he introduced us the history and culture of the school, and also brought us to a maple syrup workshop.

屋。他的家，满足了我对美国乡村田园的憧憬和想象。

让我印象深刻的还有他们对儿子亚历克斯的教育。玻璃房中的乐器都是亚历克斯的自学设备，他没有参加辅导班，只是一家人一起玩音乐。上初中的亚历克斯每天 6 点起床，周末也雷打不动。当同行的一位小伙伴问他为什么不睡懒觉时，亚历克斯说想把时间留给自己喜欢的东西。现在，亚历克斯已经从一所著名的音乐学院毕业，从事音乐制作方面的工作。凯文每每说起儿子，脸上总是骄傲和欣喜的神情。

在某种程度上，凯文一家人已经成为我追求美好生活的一个可以触摸的活生生的样本。他的言谈、他的学识、他待人的热情周到，深深地烙在了我的心里。

2016 年，在我读博期间，我们实验室的一位合作教授布雷思·墨菲到访中国。言谈中，我惊喜地发现，墨菲知道纽约州立大学科布尔斯基农业与技术学院，知道马克。我曾经学过的一门鱼类技术课程，马克使用的正是他主编的书。原来缘分早已注定。这位老教授特别喜欢观鸟，凯文在博物学课堂上教授我们的鸟类学知识，让我和墨菲教授总有聊不完的话题。墨菲教授和他的妻子

With so many expectations and laughter, we arrived at his house. Nancy, Kevin's wife, was of gracious hospitality. And Alex, Kevin's son, was a handsome but shy boy. They came out to welcome us. We were guided in his house, a wooden two-floor building with a history of over 100 years. An astronomical telescope was standing to the window of a glass entertainment room on the second floor, filled by records, guitars, basses, a piano, and a tall fireplace. In front of the wooden house, there was a vast lawn, one third of which was occupied by green vegetables. Kevin even built a tree house for his son on a big tree at the end of the yard. His house exactly matched my imagination of the countryside life in the US.

What also impressed me a lot was the education they'd given to Alex. Without attending any special class, Alex learned every instrument in the glass room all by himself. He played music together with his parents. As a student in junior high school, Alex got up at 6 o'clock every morning even on weekends. One of my fellows asked him why he got up so early, and he said he wanted to save more time for the things he was keen on. Currently, Alex has graduated from a famous conservatory of music and he has been working on music production. He'd be full of pride and joy every time when we talked about music.

邀请我作为他们为期近二十天的访问陪同人员，我们由此结下了深厚的友谊。

如今，十年过去，我已 29 岁，刚刚完成自己的博士学业，即将成为一名大学教师。在美国留学一年中所学到的，像火种一样，引燃了我的热情。我仍然从事着与水和生物相关的工作，仍然热爱着乡村、动物和滋养我们的大自然。

回想十年前，家里的经济作物因为地震遭受很大的损失，我以为自己可能上不了学了。没想到，自己能够幸运地成为"CSC-SUNY 150 奖学金项目"的一员，不仅完成了学业，还能够去往另外一个国家，开启自己不一样的人生。

现在赴美留学的机会更多了，去国外追寻自己梦想的人也越来越多。无论贫寒富裕，走出国门，才会更加懂得和珍惜自己中国人的身份。带着对祖国文化的认同走出国门，用比较

In some way, the Berners have set a vivid example for me to chase after my dream life. The way Kevin talked, the great knowledge he had, and the warm hospitality he had shown have been engraved in my heart.

During my Ph.D. study in 2016, Mr. Brian Murphy, one of the cooperation professors, visited our lab in China. In our talk, it turned out that Mr. Murphy knew the Cobleskill School of Agriculture and Technology of SUNY; also, he knew Mark. One of the textbooks that Mark was using in his course of fish technology was edited by Mr. Murphy. What a wonderful destiny! This senior professor liked bird watching. Kevin used to teach us knowledge about birds in his natural science class, so this coincidence ignited sparks of various topics between Professor Murphy and me. I was then invited to keep company with him and his wife for a 20-day-tour, which has laid the root for our strong friendship.

It's been 10 years since I first arrived in America. I'm now 29 years old and have just completed my Ph.D. I will become a teacher in a university. The one-year journey in the US is just like a fire that can ignite my passion. I'm still engaging in the work related to water and biology, and I'm still enthusiastic about the countryside, animals, and our mother nature.

Looking back on 10 years ago, the commercial crops of my family suffered serious reduction due to the earthquake. I thought I had to drop out of school. It was definitely beyond my expectation that I was lucky enough to be selected as one of the participants in the CSC-SUNY 150 Program and go to another country to continue my study and usher in a whole new life.

There are more and more opportunities for students to go aboard nowadays, and thus more

的眼光来观察中外文化，才能更清楚地看清中国文化的轮廓，我们的勤勉、友善、仁义，我们悠久的历史中蕴含的内敛和包容，才更能保持一颗热爱祖国、团结同胞的初心。

我相信，交流会培养出更多的优秀人才，为祖国的建设增加新动力。目前，我最大的愿望就是为乡村振兴尽一份自己的力量，努力提高农民的生活水平。同时，让更多的农民子弟成为像我一样的幸运儿，走出国门进行文化交流，为祖国的发展添砖加瓦。

and more of them rush to foreign countries to pursue their dreams. No matter how poor or rich you are, you'll truly recognize how important it is to cherish your identity as a Chinese once going abroad. When we go out with a high recognition of cultural identity, observing the differences between China and the rest of the world in a comparative perspective, we'll get a crystal clear picture of our own culture. That is diligence, friendship, benevolence and righteousness, as well as introverted and inclusive quality that evolved from the profound history. Only with the excellent quality can we stay true to our original mind of patriotism and solidarity.

I believe that more excellent people will be cultivated by means of exchanges, which will impart momentum to the construction of the country. Currently, my greatest hope is to strive for the revitalization of rural areas in China, improving living standards and cultivation for farmers, helping more farmers' children like me to go out of the country for cultural exchange so that they will better contribute to the development of our country.

重德 博學

務實 尚美

四川師範大學

# 四川师范大学

Sichuan Normal University

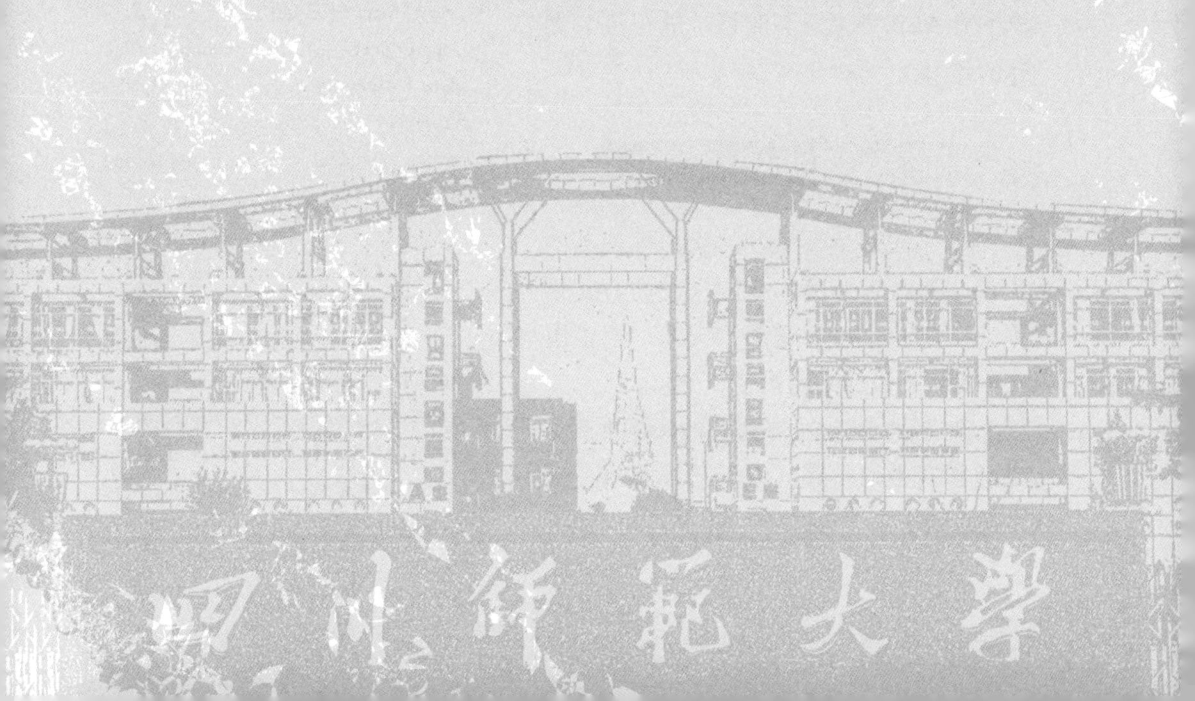

四海之纽
*Taking the World as a
Link to Study in USA* 川山首经

# 做好自己，在未来创造新的可能

## Be Yourself, and Create New Possibilities in the Future

陈韵旭 / 四川师范大学　纽约州立大学奥尔巴尼分校

Chen Yunxu / Sichuan Normal University　SUNY at Albany

我叫陈韵旭，来自四川师范大学狮子山校区文学院中文系。经过遴选，我终于进入到"CSC-SUNY 150 奖学金项目"这个温暖的大家庭。2008 至 2009 学年度，我被选拔到美国纽约州立大学奥尔巴尼校区（SUNY-ALBANY）东亚系，进行了为期一年的学习。

### 在美国，我们获得很多成长的机会

2008 年的那个夏天，一次山摇地动的大灾难，把四川人民和全国人民的心紧紧联系在了一起。也正是那次灾难，把中国人民和美国人民的心连接在了一起。

大地震后，我过了半个月的帐篷生活。与老师和同学们一起，天天熬夜背书，迎接考试。

I am Chen Yunxu, a student from the Chinese Department of the Faculty of Arts, Shizishan Campus, Sichuan Normal University. After the program selection, I became one member of the CSC-SUNY 150 Program. In the 2008-2009 academic year, I was selected to the East Asia Department of the Albany Campus of the State University of New York (SUNY-ALBANY) for a one-year study as an exchange student studying in the United States.

### An Opportunity in the US

In the summer of 2008, a turbulent movement and a disaster connected Sichuan people with all the Chinese people. Because of that disaster, some Chinese people and the Americans were connected.

这时，我经过层层选拔，和另外 149 名伙伴成了幸运儿。推着两个大大的行李箱，我来到纽约，开始了为期一学年（9 个月）的留学交换生学习生活。

"年轻""开放""自由""轻松""友好""Friendly and happy""激动"，这些词足以概括我们的美国生活。什么可能性都存在，什么事情都有可能发生。

最有意思的还是学习生活。在这里，我们的每一天都很难忘。美国老师的风趣、同学们的友善、学习制度的自由与严格并存，以及对自律性的要求，都让我们中国学生感慨不已。

在国内，我们疲于应付学习，应付背书、应付考试。而在美国，我们被要求不要模仿，不要拖延，不要忘记和偏离自己学习的初衷。如此强调"Individual"的社会价值观，和中国的十年前的教育理念是不同的。当然，在这过去的十年里，我们回国后，发现大家的心态也逐渐开放起来，甚至有时候优于美国。正是因为美国人强调个性化和自由，对于集体感稍有欠缺，也为很多事情带来了不便。

在美国一年的学习生活中，我们认识了很多美国当地人，当然，也认识了一些了从中国来到美国奋斗的华侨华裔。他们中，有的不乏新思维，有的依旧保留着中国传统的文化和思想，对子女的教育理念也存在各种差异，并由此产生了各种不适和文化挣扎。

After the earthquake, I lived in a tent for half a month. Together with the teachers and classmates, I worked day and night to prepare for the exam.

At the same time, with the other 149 students, I was selected and became one of the lucky dogs. Taking two big suitcases, I came to New York City and started a one-year (9 months) study tour as an exchange student studying in the United States.

"Young", "open", "free", "relax", "friendly", "happy" and "excited" are words to summarize our American life. But there may be any possibilities and anything may happen.

The most interesting thing in the US was the academic life and it was an unforgettable experience. The humor of American teachers, the friendliness of the students, coexistence of freedom and rule, and the requirements for self-discipline impressed us very much.

作为一群特殊的到访者，我们应邀到纽约州府邸和驻美国纽约中国大使馆参观，甚至去了华盛顿、费城。我们甚至还获得了和高级官员一起聚餐、唱歌、聊天的机会，交换各自的思想和经历，这是非常宝贵的经验。

我们感受到，他们的心态更加开放，不会拘泥于各种文化的不同，而是心态更加包容，也不会因当时美国面临的经济危机而对美国的工作生活产生消极的看法。华人在哪里都能找到集体和共性，都能一起解决问题。大地震之后，美国华裔第一时间得到消息，并为四川捐出一笔又一笔善款。这些善款，并不是来自某一位富豪，而是来自那些对祖国有着特殊情感的爱心人士。一笔笔善款，聚少成多，汇总后寄到中国的慈善机构，再发放到需要支持的地区。

2008年8月，我们到达纽约华人中心后，收到了带着满满爱意的礼物。我们的项目也建立了自己的小小基金会，由负责老师保管。我们希望这个基金以后继续壮大，帮助到更多需要帮助的人。

In the one-year study in the United States, we knew many local people in the United States, besides teachers and classmates, and I met a variety of Chinese who moved to the United States. Among them, some had new ideas, while some still retained Chinese traditional thoughts, and had various differences in their educational concepts for their children, resulting in various discomforts and cultural conflicts.

As a special group of visitors, we were invited to visit the New York State House and the Chinese Embassy in New York, USA, and took a trip to Washington and Philadelphia. It was not just a visit but also an opportunity to participate. It was an invaluable experience to gather, sing, chat, and exchange ideas and experiences with the senior officials.

We felt that Americans' mentality was more open. They would not be constrained by different cultures, but wonld accept them with a more inclusive attitude, and they would not have a negative view of their work and life even in the economic crisis facing the United States at that time. The Chinese pay more attention to the collective and commonalities everywhere, and can solve problems together. After the earthquake, when Chinese Americans got the news for the first time, they donated a lot of money for Sichuan. These donations were not from one person, but from those who were patriotic. A small

## 纠结：考研还是工作？

2009 年 5 月，我们正式完成了在纽约州立大学为期一年的学习，回到了中国。由于出国前我是即将大三的学生，回国后就面临最后一年大四的学习以及毕业的问题。除了要补上大三赴美后落下的国内课程，我们必须向学校申请重新考试，完成大三的课程补考。然后，顺利进行大四期间的课程以及毕业论文。

2009 至 2010 年，应该是我最忙的一年。既要补上大三的十多门考试，又要积极参加大四的实习准备，还不能落下大四的课程。

再次出国，选择赴美读研究生，也是一条路。看着大家都在积极准备 GRE 和托福，我也并没有停下脚步。可我也知道，没有"CSC-SUNY 150 奖学金项目"的支持，作为一名文科生再次申请奖学金，难度是非常大的。所以，我当初没有选择马上申请，而是准备先考国内的研究生，以这一次的试验作为间歇的休息。可没想到，国内的研究生准备课程，压力并不低于出国考试的课业量。专业课之外，还加上了政治课和数学课，我只能抽出周末和假期的时间复习。当时我绝望地想，要考上几乎是不可能完成的任务。

2010 年春天那次研究生初试，我败在了政治科和专业课上。这也在意料之中，毕竟时间太短。出国那一年的经历，其实已经给我们带来了太大的影响，尤其是心

sum of money was gathered together and sent to a charity in China, then distributed to the areas where supports were needed.

In August 2008, after we arrived at the New York Chinese Center, we received some donations. Our program has also established its own small foundation, which is kept running by our staff. We hope that this fund will continue to grow in the future and will help more people in need.

### Postgraduate Study or Work？

It would be a good choice for a graduate student to go to study in the United States. Seeing everyone actively preparing for GRE and TOEFL, I had to do something to catch up with my peers. However, I knew that without the scholarship from the CSC-SUNY150 program, it is too hard for a liberal arts student to apply for a scholarship. Therefore, I did not choose to apply immediately, but to prepare myself to take the domestic postgraduate exam, and take the exam as an intermittent break. Unexpectedly, the pressure from the domestic postgraduate exam preparation courses was still overwhelming. Because of the major courses, plus political science and math classes, I could only prepare during weekends and holidays. At that time, I was desperate to think that it was almost impossible to complete the task.

In the spring of 2010, I failed in the

态和思想上的转变。我父母也并没有因为这次考试失利而责怪我。他们反而鼓励我，要不要考考托福，准备一下 GRE，再次申请美国研究生。

可是我知道，大四剩下半年不到的时间，而美国研究生是要提前半年申请的。那时，已经过了春季招生申请时间，只能申请夏季，可我连一科考试都没有准备过。我只能和其他同学一样，继续准备毕业、找工作等。这期间，我们的"CSC-SUNY 150 奖学金项目"又举行过几次活动，美国的老师居然来中国看望我们。他们非常欢迎我们继续考取美国研究生，回到美国一起学习，这让我们非常感动。

## 实习与工作

毕业那年，遴选到最后，有两家很好的单位给我打了复试电话。一个是成都电视台，当时的经济栏目开了一个新的专题节目，邀请我们 6 位毕业生（其中 3 名四川大学研究生，3 名四川师范大学本科生）去参加为期两个月的毕业实习。二是新东方教育集团成都分校，英文教师和中文教师的实习训练。

我当然更倾向于第一个机会，毕竟能进入电视台实习，是大部分中文系同学的梦想。在此之前，我已经有

political science and major exams. I had expected the result before hand. After all, the preparing time was too short and I was overloaded. The one-year experience of going abroad had influenced me greatly, especially the mentality and ideological changes. My parents did not blame me for failing the exam. Instead, they encouraged me to take TOEFL, prepare for GRE, and consider re-applying for US postgraduate program.

However, I knew that there was less than half a year left in senior year, and the US postgraduate program required applicants to apply half a year in advance. At that time, I had already missed the application for enrollment in the spring, and I could only apply for the summer, but I hadn't gotten myself well prepared. Therefore, I could only continue to prepare for graduation and job hunting, just as other students did. During that period, the CSC-SUNY 150 Program held several events, and American teachers actually came to China to visit us. It moved me very much when they said that we would be welcomed to return to study in American postgraduate programs.

**Internship and Job**

At the end of the graduation year, two very good companies gave me a retest call. One of them was the Chengdu TV Station. At that time,

过一个多月的新闻网编辑经验。虽然时间很短，但我对传媒人的工作性质有了一些了解……

接下来，我到新东方工作了一年。离开了新东方后，我选择为自己而活。

## 突然之间，感到自己好像被遗弃了

两年左右的时间，我在家做我自己喜欢的事情，同时也报了一些班，提升英文的同时，发展一些别的兴趣爱好。一边学习，一边生活；一边抱怨，又一边享受着。我的父母并没有对我有太多要求，也没给予太大的工作期望。

2016年春夏，我去了一趟北京，看望在北京读书的同学。这次旅行很短暂，和即将毕业的同学短暂相聚后，她们很快落实了工作，有的去了沿海城市，有的留下了。我对自己一个人在这里要重新打拼并没有信心，更多的还是陌生感。这和当年出国的心情，大大不同。

正好，随后就收到了"CSC-SUNY 150奖学金项目"魏琳老师的邮件。魏琳老师提醒大家，我们要正视自己的年龄了，要开始用新的眼光和心态看待自己和未来了。十年之约很快就要到来了。

时间就是过得这么快。我也断断

the economic column developed a new program, offering our six graduates (three from Sichuan University and the rest from Sichuan Normal University) an opportunity for a two-month graduation internship. The other was the New Oriental Education Group Chengdu Branch for the internship training as an English teacher or Chinese teacher.

I was more inclined to the first opportunity. After all, it was the dream of most Chinese majors to work in the TV station. Prior to this, I had had more than a month of news network editing experience. Although it was too short, I had gotten some understanding of the nature of the media work…

Then, I only stayed in New Oriental for one year. After leaving New Oriental, I chose to live for myself.

### Suddenly, I Felt that I was Abandoned

In about 2 years, I did what I liked at home, and I had also taken some classes to improve my English while developing other hobbies. My parents didn't have too many requests for me, nor give too many expectations on my job.

In the spring and summer of 2016, I went to Beijing to visit my classmates. It was a short

续续有过别的工作尝试，但如果一份工作只是为了养活自己，满足基本的生活费用需求，那就太枯燥和没有意义了。我们会因此感到迷茫和无奈，甚至会消极对待周围的人和事。

幸好，"CSC-SUNY 150 奖学金项目"一直是一个温暖的大家庭，我们有自己的微信群，也常常给美国老师写邮件，交换新的情况，写下新年祝福。不管什么时候，只要大家在，有人发言，微信群里必然是一条一条留言不断。

虽然，现在大家各奔东西，我们很难再相聚。相信这一次组稿，也能将大家的近况用比较好的方式呈现出来。我相信很多同学过得很精彩，这是需要有好的机会和经济实力的。

未来十年，我希望自己有更好的心态去面对，不管待在四川继续做自己也好，到四川以外的城市也好，在开阔眼界的同时交到更多的朋友，为未来创造一些新的可能。

trip. After a short meeting with the classmates who were about to graduate, they quickly had their jobs; some went to the coastal cities. I had no confidence to live alone in Beijing, for it still gave me a strange feeling. But this was very different from the mood of going abroad in the past.

Just now, I received an email from Ms. Wei Lin, a teacher of the CSC-SUNY 150 Program. She reminded everyone that we had to face up to our age and start to look at ourselves and the future with a new vision and attitude. The 10-year appointment was coming soon.

Time flies. I have had other work attempts on and off, but if a job is just to support myself and meet the basic cost of living, it is too boring and meaningless. We will feel confused and helpless, and even treat people around us negatively.

Fortunately, the CSC-SUNY 150 Program has always been a warm family. We have our own WeChat group. We often get a chance to send emails to American teachers, to exchange new information, and to write New Year's greetings.

However, now that we are doing different jobs and living at different places, it is hard for us to get together again. I believe that through this collection of chapters, the current situations of everyone can be presented in a better way. I believe that many of my classmates have a wonderful life, even if it requires good opportunities and economic strength.

In the next 10 years, I hope that I can have a better attitude, and whether I want to continue to stay in Sichuan, or to go to cities outside Sichuan, I want to make more friends in the future. There may be any possibility in the future.

# 在美国，开启我全新的人生

## A New Start at the United States

杜畅／四川师范大学　纽约州立大学克林顿社区大学

Du Chang / Sichuan Normal University　SUNY Clinton Community College

　　我出生在四川汉旺镇，爷爷、奶奶跟随三线建设的大部队从哈尔滨迁徙到了四川。他们都在东方汽轮机厂工作，这个工厂隶属于全国电力系统最大的东方电气集团。这个庞大的重工业厂区把小镇变成一个乌托邦式的封闭社区，里面有说着标准普通话的叔叔阿姨，有配套的学校、医院、体育场和超市。

　　如果没有那场地震，或许我会从四川师范大学心理系毕业，当一位老师或医生，又或者回到我的故乡汉旺镇，待在爸妈身边，在企业里做一名文员。然而没有"如果"，2008 年的地震改变了千千万万像我一样的普通人的命运。

I was born in Hanwang Town, Sichuan Province. My grandparents came from Harbin to Sichuan with the army for the Third-line Construction. They all worked in the East Turbine Plant, which is a subordinate factory to the largest East Electric Group in the national power system. This huge factory of heavy industry turned the town into a kind of utopian community with its own schools, hospitals, stadiums and supermarkets where people speak Mandarin in a Northern accent.

Under normal conditions, after graduating from the Department of Psychology in Sichuan Normal University, I would become a teacher or a doctor, or go back to my hometown to be around with my parents and be a clerk in the plant. The tragic coming of the Wenchuan Earthquake changed the fate of thousands of common people, and I was one of them.

## 那一年，我踏上去美国的征程

2008 年，我 19 岁。地震后的夏天莫名烦躁闷热，我的人生第一次充斥着离别、噩耗和劫后余生的坚强。在生活的一团乱麻中，我经过 3 轮面试，成为"CSC-SUNY 150 奖学金项目"的一员。

刚刚分到克林顿社区大学，其实是有些失望的。尽管学校风景优美，但学校是两年制社区大学，没有名校光环总是让人有些失落。转念一想，权且把这一年当作疗养吧。

或许正是有了开放的心态，我和同学们不再把自己拘泥于教室和图书馆之中，而是全身心地体会当地文化。骑着自行车四处转悠，被纽约上州的枫叶惊艳，去流浪动物救助站志愿遛狗，"怂恿"老师开车 8 小时带我们去观看 NBA 姚明和易建联的强强对决，跟着老师参加圣诞节聚会，自己策划了第一次旅行，去加拿大法语区蒙特利尔，在夜色黄昏中远观古堡……

回想这一年，学业上的东西大都不记得了，但是我明白了青春不只是学业，应该把自己的眼界放开阔些。非常感激在人生最有活力与激情的 20 岁，能遇见一群同样出色的年轻人，在一个几乎与世隔绝的小镇，开开心

### Leaving for the United States

In 2008, I was 19 years old. In that summer, I felt inexplicably restless and agitated. I witnessed life and death, got to know the true meaning of being separated by death and learnt to be strong. Busy with the troubled life and the preparation for the program, finally I became a member of the CSC-SUNY 150 Program after 3 rounds of interviews.

When I first arrived at Clinton Community College, I was kind of disappointed. Indeed, the campus was so beautiful, but I really couldn't overlook the fact it was a community college with two-year programs and enjoyed no place in the top universities list. On second thought, I told myself that I could just take my stay here as an opportunity to get my mind off the Earthquake.

With a different attitude, the fellow students and I no longer confined ourselves to classrooms and libraries. Instead, we began to immerse ourselves in the local culture. We cycled around and really enjoyed the beauty of maple trees at the upper side of New York. We also volunteered to walk dogs at a stray animal rescue station. Our teacher was so nice that he drove 8 hours to take us to watch the game between Yao Ming and Yi Jianlian, and invited us to his house for Christmas. I planned the first trip to Montreal. In the French-speaking Canadian area, we watched the castles in the twilight…

When I take a look back at that year, I realize it's an important turning point in my life. I have got to know that apart from the education we get from schools, there are always more things waiting for exploration. I am grateful that in the height of my youth I could have the

心地度过了最丰富有趣的大学生活。

尽管没有名校光环，但是老师和校长都特别认真负责，我们算得上是学校第一批国际学生了。短暂的一年之后，校长和老师给我们写了充满赞誉之词的推荐信，凭借推荐信，我很幸运地转到了纽约州立大学普拉茨堡继续我的学业。

## 那一年，我收获了满满的感动

在那一年交换留学的经历中，让我最感动的是和我的政治学老师克里斯多夫·德雷南的师生情谊。克里斯多夫是加拿大魁北克省蒙特利尔市人。在放寒假的时候，学校国际学生处带着我们去蒙特利尔市旅游，其中一个景点就是麦吉尔大学。麦吉尔大学是加拿大最古老的高等学府，百年来在国际上享有盛誉，被视为"北方哈佛"或"加拿大哈佛"。

回来以后，我和同学开玩笑说，习惯了寒冷的天气，真的很想申请去麦吉尔大学读研究生呢。不过对于当时的我来说，这像是一个随口说出的玩笑话。作为加拿大最难申请的大学，麦吉尔大学入学标准相当高，挑选的都是顶尖学生，以居高不下的新生入学平均分（90分以上）闻名北美，其平均录取分数居全国所有大学之首，

opportunity to broaden my horizon and meet a group of excellent young people. That was one of the happiest periods of my university time.

The faculty members there were very nice. There had been no international students before our arrival. The one-year stay was really short. Before we left, the president and the teachers wrote letters of recommendation for us. With these letters of recommendation, I was lucky to get an opportunity to continue my study in the State University of New York at Plattsburgh.

## A Year Filled with Touching Memories

The one-year stay there left me with a lot of touching memories, and the one I treasure most is that with Christopher Drennan, my political science professor. Chris is from Montreal, Quebec, Canada. During the winter vacation, the International Student Office took us to Montreal for a tour. We visited McGill University, the oldest institution of higher learning in Canada. It is renowned around the world as "Harvard of the North" or "Harvard of Canada".

After I came back from the tour in Canada, I joked with my classmates that I came to like the cold weather there and really wanted to go to McGill University for my master's degree. It was

也就是说麦吉尔大学是加拿大最难进的大学。

不知道克里斯多夫教授怎么听说了这件事，他郑重其事地对我说："好好努力，我觉得你一定能进入麦吉尔大学。"在每次的邮件交换中，克里斯多夫都鼓励、提醒我："麦吉尔大学有最好的心理学系，畅，你这样杰出的学生应该去最好的心理学系学习。"

很可惜，我没有成为麦吉尔大学的一员，我换了专业。每一次想到克里斯多夫老师对我毫无保留的信任和赞美，我都感动万分。人生道路上不可能轻松地心想事成，我感到非常温暖，在有梦想的年纪，一位有爱的老师呵护过我的梦想。

有一年，我收到了克里斯多夫的回信，他在信中说："我把你们的合照挂在我办公室的墙壁上，这是我放在办公室的第一张照片，我不能想象出还有比这更美好的事情。我称这张照片为'长城'，代表着你们这群小伙伴。"我感动万分，最真挚的感情在彼此的人生中留下深深的印记。

毕业快8年了，最近决定重新入校充电。美国大学制度对于全职工作者来说非常友好，有很多夜间课程可选，从申请到选课，每一个流程在网站上都标注清晰，也随时可以查询进

more like a fantasy to me at that time. It is highly competitive to apply for McGill University, which only admits to the very best applicants. The average score for admission is over 90 and tops all the other universities.

I kind of took it as a joke. When Professor Chris heard about it, he didn't take it as a joke. He said to me: "Just try your best. I believe you can win a place at McGill University." In every email he wrote to me, he would encourage me a lot, "McGill University has the best psychology program. Chang, you are one of the best, and you should fight for a place there."

However, I failed in the efforts to become a McGill University student because I changed my major. Whenever I think of Chris giving me his unreserved trust and praise, I am deeply touched. When I dreamed big, I was so lucky to have one professor to cheer me up.

Chris once wrote in a letter to me, "I have a picture wall in my office. You guys' photo is the very first one to go there. I call it 'The Great Wall' because that is what you guys are." I was touched. True bonding can really leave unforgettable memories.

Nearly 8 years after graduation, I recently decided to go back to university. The American

度，公立大学学费对于纳税人也有减税优惠。

## 那一年，成就了我的美满姻缘

一年的交换留学生涯让我得到在美国学习生活的机会，目前我在休斯敦一家石油公司的财务部门工作，这也促成了我和丈夫的缘分。我的丈夫亚历克斯来自福建，高中时移民到了美国，我们相识相爱于 SUNY 学校。

2015 年，我们举行了婚礼。双方家人在纽约唐人街一家酒店聚餐时，我对亚历克斯说，2008 年，我和同学们到达纽约后，福建华侨同乡会在此宴请过我们。在异国他乡，很多叔叔阿姨热情地招待我们，离家千万里，突然吃到了可口的故乡食物，让我们特别感动。

听到此，我的公公非常惊讶地说："原来就是你们这群孩子！"他说，在 2008 年地震发生后，华侨社区对国内灾区情况特别关心。当了解到有一群从四川灾区来美国访问学习的大学生后，福建同乡会的成员们都不约而同地捐款，想要为我们做些什么。

我和亚历克斯觉得缘分是如此奇妙。我的公公却说，2008 年许许多多在美国生活的华裔、华侨，都向灾

universities are very friendly to people who have full-time jobs. There are many night programs available which you can apply and select on the website of the university. Taxpayers can get cutbacks on tuition from the public universities.

### Meeting My Mr. Right in US

Because of the CSC-SUNY 150 Program, I had the opportunity to stay in the United States to study and work. Presently, I work in the financial department of a Houston Oil Company. My husband, Alex, came from Fujian and moved to the United States when he was a high school student. We met and fell in love at SUNY.

In 2015, we had our wedding. Our families had a gathering at a hotel in New York's Chinatown. I told Alex that when we first arrived in New York in 2008, Fujian Overseas Chinese Association threw a welcome party for us here. At that time, so far away from China, with the delicious Chinese food on the table, we were deeply touched by the hospitality from overseas Chinese.

Hearing this, my father-in-law was very surprised and said, "You were one of the kids!" He said that after the 2008 earthquake, the overseas Chinese community was deeply

区献出了爱心。他说，2008年中国城的捐款箱装满了捐款，每个省市的同乡会都支援过物资。

越是在异乡，越能体会同胞的爱国之心。我们太幸运了，相遇相爱的小故事，也都源自大爱背景。幸运的是，去年我们迎来了我们的小宝宝。

因为工作原因，我们迁居休斯敦，工作地点附近就是美国有名的安德森癌症医疗中心。在这里，我接触了很多从中国来求医的同胞，遇见了许多帮助国内病人和家属的公益组织志愿者，也尽自己所能去帮助那些需要帮助的人。因为曾经的我也接受过很多的爱和帮助，尽管力量微不足道，也

concerned about the situation in earthquake-stricken areas in China. When Fujian Overseas Chinese Association learned about a group of college students from Sichuan coming to the United States to study, they all wanted to do something for the group of students and donated money for the welcome party.

Alex and I thought it's the magic of destiny. But my father-in-law would not think that way. In his understanding, there was nothing accidental. In the year of 2008, many Chinese and overseas Chinese in the United States donated money for the earthquake victims. Every overseas Chinese association organized charity activities to collect money for the stricken areas. A lot of common people stood up against the anti-Chinese groups on the street.

The longer I stay in a foreign country, the more I understand the patriotic feelings of the

希望尽力把爱传递下去。

十年来，我保持一颗继续学习、上进奋斗的心。在那一年的留学生涯中，我最大的体会就是要勇于打破自己的舒适区，勇于交流，敢于经历。既然选择了历险（我认为留学就是一场历险），那就勇敢挑战自己。

overseas Chinese. Alex and I are so lucky to have met each other. If there had not been the natural bonding among Chinese people around the world, there would not have been us as a married couple, and there would not have been our little baby born last year.

Due to work, we moved to Houston. Near to the place where we work, there is the famous Anderson Cancer Medical Center. I got into contact with many Chinese who came from China to seek medical treatment. I also have met many volunteers from charity groups who offer help to patients and their family members. I am also trying my best to help people because I have gotten love and help from others. What I can do is very limited, but I want to pass the love on to others.

For the past ten years, I have been learning all the time and always on the way to work for a better self and a better future, which is my greatest achievement so far. During my first year in the United States, I learned it's important to break your comfort zone and to try something new. If you have chosen a path you know nothing about, then just move on and enjoy the adventure.

# 我在美国快速成长并邂逅爱情

## The Year for Personal Growth and Unexpected Love in the United States

秦誉心／四川师范大学　纽约州立大学詹姆斯敦社区学院

Qin Yuxin / Sichuan Normal University　SUNY Jamestown Community College

我叫秦誉心，是四川师范大学 2008 级英语教育专业的学生，现在是成都实验外国语学校的一名高中英语教师。四年前，我和丈夫王磊结束六年爱情长跑，走进婚姻殿堂；三年前，女儿索菲亚诞生，让我们感受到为人父母的喜悦。如今，我的生活平淡而幸福。

这一切都让我非常感恩 "CSC-SUNY 150 奖学金项目"，那一年的赴美留学对我的学习、生活甚至人生都产生了重大的影响。

2008 年对我来说是一个悲喜交加的一年。5 月，我还沉浸在地震摧毁家园、带走亲人的悲痛之中；8 月，我已身处高楼林立、令我目不暇接的纽约。

场景转换如此之快，仿佛这一切都是

My name is Qin Yuxin. I was an English major student in the Class of 2012 at Sichuan Normal University. Now I am a senior high school teacher of English in Chengdu Experimental Foreign Language School. Four years ago, after six years of committed relationship, Wang Lei and I got married. Three years ago, our daughter Sophia was born and we felt the joy of being parents. Now, I live a simple and happy life.

I am very grateful for the CSC-SUNY 150 Program. The one-year stay in the United States has had a great impact on my study, my life and even my ways of understanding the world.

2008 was a year of mixed feelings for me. In May, the earthquake destroyed my hometown, took away the lives of my relatives, and left me in deep grief. In the

梦境。我被拉进了一个全新的世界，就像爱丽丝一不小心掉进了那个兔子洞一样，开始了一段奇幻冒险。沿途的风景时而美不胜收，时而光怪陆离，让我忙于应对，无暇顾及伤痛。

## 我在美国快速成长

刚到美国时，我 17 岁，第一次离父母、朋友这么远，高兴之余，担心和害怕也是常有的情绪。

我被分配到位于詹姆斯敦的社区大学。这里本地人居多，外国人特别少。在一群金发碧眼的本地人中，我们 5 个来自中国的学生便特别醒目，这多少让我们感觉到不自在。为了让我们尽快熟悉同学、适应这里的生活，校方将我们 5 个人分在不同的寝室。住在寝室的第一晚，因为时差和陌生感，我久久不能入睡。

在选修课程时，由于专业不同，我没法和同行的国内同学选择相同的课程，于是，我们经常各自去上课。刚开始的生活总是有些害怕，每次踏进教室前，我都要给自己来几次深呼吸，然后头皮发麻地走进教室。在和同学、老师似懂非懂的交流中，艰难度过了我在美国的第一个月。所幸从第二个月起，一切都变得顺利起来。我们积极参与同学间的聚会和社团活动，结交了一些美国朋友，并逐渐克服了交流障碍，跟上老师的上课节奏，我们"被迫"并且顺利地融入

stricken areas, no matter where I went, what I saw was a scene of devastation. In August, I was in New York, and what greeted my eye was a dazzling city of tall buildings.

The sudden change of scenes made it almost unreal. I was dragged into a completely different world, just as Alice accidentally fell into that rabbit hole and started a fantastic adventure. The scenery along the way was so beautiful and sometimes even bizarre to my eye. I was busy digesting everything that leaped into my sight, and the sorrow was taken off my mind for the time being.

### My Rapid Growth in USA

When I arrived in the United States, I was 17 years old. For the first time, I was so far away from my parents and friends. I was happy to get the opportunity, but also frequented by emotions of worry and fear.

I was assigned to a community college in Jamestown. Foreigners were scarce there. We, the five Chinese students, kind of stood out among the locals, and this made us less at ease. The school wanted to give us more contacts with the local culture and arranged us to live in five different dorm rooms. Positioned in totally unfamiliar surroundings, I stayed awake for the first night in the dormitory. Jet lag was also one factor that contributed to my sleepless night.

了美国同学的学习和生活中。

完全陌生的环境，完全不同的生活、学习方式，在美国的这一年，我不断迎接来自生活和学习中的各种挑战，感觉自己是以成倍的速度在成长。

学校里，师生之间朋友般的相处方式常常让我惊讶和感动。

副校长玛丽琳和她的丈夫鲍勃经常邀请我们到她家聚餐、开派对。他们的善意和温暖让我们宾至如归，忘记了身处异乡的孤寂与不适。

记得有一次聚会是在圣诞节来临之际，玛丽琳和鲍勃各自开车载着我们5个同学去他们家提前过节日。12月的詹姆斯敦路面全是积雪，我们遇到了一个小坡，鲍勃的小轿车没法发力，车轮一直在原地打转，最后我们大家一起喊"加油，丰田"。在欢声笑语中，车子终于翻越了小坡。这个小插曲非但没有影响我们过节的心情，还活跃了气氛。

I would like to go to classes with the other four students, but we had different majors; therefore, we chose different courses. As a consequence, I had to go to my class alone. At the beginning, the school life was a bit scary. I had to breathe deeply before I stepped into the classroom and felt a sickness in my stomach. The first month was difficult for me. I had troubles in understanding the teachers and classmates. Fortunately, from the second month on, everything began to get better. We made an active participation in the activities held by the students and a variety of groups. We made some American friends, and gradually overcame the communication barriers and were able to follow the teaching in class. We did have pressure in our life and study, but with it, we finally mingled into the life there.

Almost everything there was different from what I had been used to at home, and I faced challenges from all aspects of life and learning, feeling that I was growing up at a double speed.

I was also amazed at the ways how the teachers and the students got along with each other, and I was deeply impressed.

Vice President Marilyn and her husband Bob often invited us to her home for dinners and parties. Their kindness and warmth made us feel at home and we were able to put the loneliness and inconveniences in a foreign land aside.

When Christmas was coming, Marilyn and Bob invited us to their home

到家后，我们看到了玛丽琳提前给我们备好的丰盛菜肴，第一次看到用锯子锯开一整块牛排，第一次吃到有牛油果的蔬菜沙拉……晚餐是伴着音乐进行的，让我感到惊喜的是播放的是碧昂丝的音乐。之前，我向鲍勃提到过我英语名字来源于碧昂丝之前所在的组合天命真女，他一定是把这么一件小事放了心上，特地去买了一张碧昂丝的CD放给我听，真的好贴心。

这次聚会让我深切地感受到，真诚的爱是可以跨越国界和种族的，人与人之间纯粹情感的流动是最动人的。因此，我更加坚定了自己择友、择偶以及选择事业的原则，那就是直面自己真实、纯粹的初心。

## 邂逅爱情、拥抱生活

美国一年之行结束后，我对自己也有了更清醒的认识，客观分析自身的情况之后，毕业时没有投身考研大军而是选择工作。本身是学的英语教育专业又有出国的经历，这让我的求职之路顺利了许多。择业的过程也是个和自己三观契合的过程。在选择工作的时候，我更看重团队的工作思维和方式是否是在不断更新和创新，而不是把待遇放在首位来考虑。所以，

to celebrate the holiday. They came to pick us up. In December, the roads were covered with snow. There was a slope, and with the wheels spinning in the snow, the car just couldn't move forward. We all shouted "come on! Toyota!" We all laughed. The car finally moved and we drove on. This was a happy episode on the way to Marilyn's house.

A big dinner was waiting for us in the house. For the first time, we saw a big steak sawn into pieces by a saw. For the first time, we had a vegetable salad with avocado in it. There was background music. To my surprise, it was Beyoncé. I once told Bob that my English name came from the singing group "Destiny's Child" and Beyoncé was once a member in this group. It's really sweet of him to keep it in mind.

I realized that genuine feelings really did not observe the boundaries of nations and races. I had a stronger confidence in my principles concerning friendship, love and career. I would always be true to myself.

四海之纽
Taking the World as a
Link to Study in USA 川山有约

我选择做一名英语教师。

在教学时，我也会用到我在美国学习时的经验，培养学生的实际应用能力和辩证思维能力。注重培养学生的辩证思维是我在美国上学期间汲取的教育理念。

每当看到我的学生在全国性英语竞赛上获奖时，我都无比骄傲，这种骄傲的心情就像 2008 年得知我被选中参与"CSC-SUNY 150奖学金项目"时一样。

最近两天我女儿出现发烧症状，情况有点严重，照顾女儿让我忙得焦头烂额，但是在接到"CSC-SUNY 150 奖学金项目"十周年纪念活动需要我对十年前赴美学习经历做一些回顾的通知时，我还是义无反顾地答应了编辑的采访要求。在照顾完女儿后，我熬夜写出了当年赴美之行给我人生带来的影响。那一年实在是让我收获太多，比如现在陪伴在我身边的丈夫和女儿。

我的先生王磊是"CSC-SUNY 150 奖学金项目"送给我最好的礼物。在美国的春假，同行的小伙伴邀请我和王磊一起去华盛顿大学游玩。我们漫步在华盛顿大学，聊着最近的学习、生活，两人越聊越投机。华盛顿行程结束后，我们返回了詹姆斯敦的校区，在一起买菜、一起做饭、一起谈天说

## Unexpected Love and a Desired Life

After the one-year stay in the United States, I had a deeper understanding of myself. A lot of students chose to prepare for the entrance examination for graduate schools. I took a reflective look into my heart and realized it was not what I wanted. With the exchange student experience and a background as an English major in the education field, I didn't have a hard time with job hunting. I also applied my principles in the process of job hunting. What were the methods adopted by the team? Was there a focus on innovations? My priority went to these questions and the income was not my first concern. I decided to be a teacher.

The ability to think critically is an important part of American education, which runs through all the courses there. Every article the student writes should be a presentation of the student's own thinking. This is the educational idea that I have learned in the United States.

Whenever my students win prizes in the national English competitions, I always feel extremely proud of them, just like how I felt about myself when I learned in 2008 that I was selected to be a member of the CSC-SUNY 150 Program.

Now the night is deep and I am writing the article for the 10th anniversary of the CSC-SUNY 150 Program.

My daughter is running a high fever. Her rather critical condition makes me distracted. But I also feel deeply obliged to the program and I want to share my experience with others. I have gained a lot from that year's stay in the United States. My husband and my daughter also rank

地中，我们恋爱了。

2018 年，是我们相处的第十个年头，相爱的第九个年头，结婚的第四个年头。2008 年的美国之行是我和我先生永远难以忘记的。我们在美国邂逅爱情，也在美国见证了彼此的成长。真实面对自己，勇敢活出自我，时刻保持辩证思维，让我们的生活和工作更加纯粹快乐。

一个人发呆时，想起自己在宿舍煮饭时搞得全宿舍烟雾探测器巨响而忍俊不禁；心疼那个为了交论文而挑灯夜战的自己；无比感激玛丽琳数次邀请我们到她家做客；感谢我的好朋友贝基和萨曼莎不嫌弃我蹩脚的英文，依然真诚地和我交朋友，一起逛街闲聊的时光帮助我渡过詹姆斯敦漫长的冬天。感恩所有因"CSC-SUNY 150 奖学金项目"而认识的爱心人士。

十年，我们的爱，一直都在。

among the list.

My husband Wang Lei is the best gift from CSC-SUNY 150 Program. At the spring break in the United States, other students from the program invited Wang Lei and me to University of Washington for a visit. We strolled on the campus of University of Washington, chatting away. We found out that we really hit it off. Back to our own campus after the trip, we often shopped and cooked together, and we fell in love.

Our stay in the United States would always be a treasured memory in our hearts. We had not expected love but it just came by, and we also witnessed each other's personal growth.

Taking a look back at that year in the United States, I couldn't help smiling. In my mind's eye, I see myself cooking in the dorm and the smoke triggering off the smoke detector; I see myself staying deep into night to work on the course papers. I am very grateful to Marilyn for her kind invitations to her house. I am also grateful to my good friends Becky and Samantha for the happy time together while chatting and window-shopping. I am grateful to all the caring people in the CSC-SUNY 150 Program.

In the past ten years, our love has always been there.

# 在一起，创造奇迹

## Together, We Created Wonders

唐兴林 / 四川师范大学　纽约州立大学新堡社区

Tang Xinglin / Sichuan Normal University　SUNY at New Paltz

在童话故事《夏洛的网》里，威尔伯每次遇到困难时，夏洛都会在网上织出鼓励它的文字，帮助威尔伯走出困境。"CSC-SUNY 150 奖学金项目"也是这样的一张网，中美两国政府和社会各界爱心人士一起用心编织，把对我们 150 名学生的关怀和支持，在这张网上汇集成"爱"和"力量"，鼓励我们努力向上生长！也正是这张网，把我们 150 个孩子紧紧联系在了一起。

In the fairy tale Charlotte's Web, whenever Wilbur gets stuck, Charlotte would write something encouraging on the web to help him get out and move on. The program, CSC-SUNY 150, is just this kind of web, woven by the Chinese and American governments, as well as caring people from all walks of life. This is a web of "love" and "strength" to show their care and support to us 150 students, and encourage us to strive on. It is just this web that made the 150 students a closely connected group.

### 我是大山的孩子，因地震到了美国

### A Boy from the Mountain Area

我的家乡平武县位于四川西北部，是青藏高原向四川盆地的过渡地带。那里高山耸立，碧水蓝天，是少

My hometown Pingwu County is located in the Northwest of Sichuan Province, a transitional zone from Sichuan Basin to the Sichuan-Tibet Plateau. Pingwu is a beautiful place where mountains soar high into the blue sky and water flows clear and cold. People of different ethnic groups live there, and giant pandas live there, too. I was born in the mountains and grew up there.

数民族聚居的美丽小城，也是国宝大熊猫的故乡。我是大山的孩子，从小生活在大山的怀抱之中，上山采药、放羊、砍柴、挖野菜，这些都是我童年生活的剪影。与大自然的紧密接触，塑造了我的性格：既有大山的沉稳和担当，也有溪水的清澈和灵动。

平武山区的教育是落后的，教育资源十分短缺。小时候，我不知道读书何用，一天到晚就知道玩儿。想着长大以后自己也会和村子里大多数人一样，扛上行李外出打工赚钱，然后盖房子娶妻生子。我的父亲和母亲都是朴实的农民。升入初中，父亲便经常叮嘱我，"要使劲念书，这样以后才会有出息。"我信以为然，开始努力成为别人眼里的"好学生"。后来，我升入县城的高中，再后来又如愿以偿考上了大学。可即便是在收到大学录取通知书的时候，我依然不知道课本上所说的"知识改变命运"这句话到底是什么意思。

2006年，我第一次走出大山，坐了近七个小时的大巴车来到成都，开启了我的大学生活。校园里的一切让我备感兴奋，城市的繁华更是让我目不暇接。这一切给在大山里生活十多年的我带来了人生的第一次冲击，我告诉自己一定要更努力。大学的生活令我感到充实和快乐。我发奋学习，

In the midst of mountains, I looked for herbal medicine, worked as a little goat herd, collected firewood, and picked potherbs, which were the snapshots of my childhood life. The mountains made me what I am: calm, dependable and resourceful.

In the mountain areas of Pingwu County, the education is on the backward side, and the education resources are scarce. When I was a little boy, I didn't know that education could make a difference, and just hung out all day long. I thought I would grow up like most other young men in the village—pack up one day and make a living somewhere with the ultimate goal of having my own family. My parents are artless farmers. When I was a junior high student, my father often said to me, "Make an effort with your education, and try to make something out of yourself." I shared my father's view. I began to work hard and became a good student. I went to the county for my senior high, and finally realized my dream and won a place at university. People often say that knowledge can change one's fate. When I got the admission letter, I still didn't know what it was really about.

In 2006, I packed up and left the mountain for the first time. I took a long-distance bus. After almost seven hours' riding, I arrived at Chengdu, and started my university life. Everything on campus was exciting to me, and the prosperity

没日没夜地泡图书馆，看书、写作业、准备各种考试，周末做兼职赚钱。那时，我心里琢磨着，这样读完四年大学，毕业后找到一份好工作，有一份稳定的收入就满足了。那个时候，"知识改变命运"对于我来说或许就是这个意思吧。

2008 年 5 月 12 日，汶川发生了特大地震，我的人生也由此发生了转折。我万万没有想到自己会因地震去到美国。大地震之后，教育部、国家留学基金委员会和纽约州立大学联合发起了中美人文交流历史上具有里程碑意义的"CSC-SUNY 150 奖学金项目"。纽约州立大学提供全额奖学金，邀请来自四川地震灾区的 150 名大学生到美国学习，目的是为四川灾后重建培养建设者和领导者。该项目在当时受到国务院领导人温家宝、刘延东、美国副国务卿内格罗蓬特等国家领导人的高度重视。由于大学期间我的学习成绩优异，所以被学院推荐成为全省两千多名候选人之一。通过国家留学基金委组织的面试后，我有幸获得了赴美学习的机会。

## 在美国的 284 天

2008 年 8 月 15 日到 2009 年 5 月 25 日，在大洋彼岸发生了太多难

of the city proved to be something that I had not seen before. I had been living in the mountains all my life, and all this was the first shock I ever had. I made up my mind that I would work harder. My life at university was happy and rewarding. I studied very hard. I was at the library whenever I could, reading, doing homework and preparing for all kinds of exams. During weekends, I would do part-time jobs to support myself. At that time, what I had in mind for a satisfying end was that I would graduate as an honor student, find a good job and earn a decent income. That was how I understood knowledge could change one's fate.

On May 12th, 2008, an unprecedented earthquake struck Wenchuan County. The track of my life changed, and I never expected I would get an opportunity to go to the United States because of the earthquake. After the earthquake, the Ministry of Education, the National Overseas Study Fund Committee and the State University of New York jointly launched the meaningful Sino-US cultural exchange CSC-SUNY 150 Program. The State University of New York provided the funds and invited 150 college students from the earthquake-stricken areas to go there for a one-year study. The program was highly valued by Chinese leaders Wen Jiabao and Liu Yandong, Negroponte, American Deputy Secretary of State and other leaders from both countries. There were more than 2,000 candidates, and I became one of them. After a successful interview with the National Overseas Study Fund Committee, I became one of the 150 students.

### 284 Days in the United States

I was in the United States from August 15th

忘的故事。每次翻开影集都能带给我许多的感动。

### 初来乍到

2008 年 8 月 15 日，我人生第一次坐飞机竟然飞了超过 12 个小时，从四川到了纽约。飞机落地，纽约州立大学副总校长罗斯德到机场迎接我们。大巴车把我们带到了繁华的曼哈顿，很多以前只在荧屏上见到的场面像幻灯片似的映入我的眼帘。记得电影《海上钢琴师》里面，当巨轮上的人们透过迷雾看到自由女神像的时候，他们使劲欢呼、拥抱。站在窗前，望着远处的自由女神像的那一瞬间，激动、感慨、欣喜、迷惘，各种思绪交织在一起。我心想自己能有这样的机会来到美国终究是幸运的。

150 名同学中，我是唯一分在新堡校区学习的。新堡是一个美丽的小镇，它的美不仅是夏日如火的晚霞或者那秋日如画的彩林，而更多的是来自这个小镇人们内心的温暖。学校的国际项目中心是我在新堡的家，每位老师都像亲人一般，他们给了我无微不至的关怀和照顾。初来乍到时的孤独和忧虑，在这个充满爱和温暖的大家庭里迅速地融化了。短短一周的时间里，我便融入了学校的生活。国际项目中心为我们国际学生提供多方面

in 2008 to May 25th in 2009. There are too many unforgettable memories, and every time I open the photograph album, my heart is filled with warm feelings.

### Just Arrived

On August 15th, 2008, it was my first time to travel by air. It was a 12-hour flight from Sichuan to New York. When the plane landed, Charles Nicholas Rostow, vice president of the State University of New York, went to the airport to greet us. The bus took us to Manhattan, and many scenes that I had only seen on the screen unfolded before my eyes. In the movie *The Legend of 1900*, when people on the ship saw the Statue of Liberty through the fog, they cheered and hugged. I looked out of the window at the distant Statue of Liberty, and at that moment, my heart was filled with excitement, emotion, joy, confusion, and all kinds of thoughts. I was lucky to be here.

Of the 150 students, I was the only one who studied in New Paltz campus. New Paltz is a beautiful town. Its beauty is not only in flamboyant sunset in the summer or the picturesque forest of colors in fall, but also in the warmth from the hearts of the people in the town. The Center for International Programs was my new home in New Paltz. All the faculty members were so nice and gave me all the care and support I could use. As a newcomer, my loneliness and worry quickly melted in love and warmth from this big family. Within one week, I mingled into the school life. The Center provided a wide range of help and support for our international students, as well as a broad platform for our participation in school and community services. It was this platform that enabled us international students to enhance our understanding of each

的帮助和支持，也为我们参与学校和社区的服务搭建广阔的平台。正是有了这样的平台，我们国际学生才能增进对彼此国家和文化的了解，对美国有了更全面的认识。

### 多元的跨文化交流

新堡有来自世界各地的国际学生，大家彼此非常友好，相互学习，共同成长，建立了深厚的友谊。当时在新堡有接近 20 名中国留学生，我们互相关心，彼此照顾，如同家人一般。短暂的相处后，我们成立了新堡首个中国留学生协会。每逢中秋或者春节，我们组织形式多样的活动，并邀请当地社区的朋友一起参与我们的节日活动，增进对彼此的了解。

除此之外，我们还利用课余时间和其他国家的学生一起开展跨文化交流活动。印象最深的是"THE BIG THREE PARTY"（大三国），这次活动是中国、日本和韩国留学生一起策划的，目的是向美国学生展示中日韩三个国家的传统文化。活动中有个节目很有趣，三个国家的学生各选一首对方国家的歌曲，并且用该国语言进行演唱。我们中国学生演唱的是韩国的《阿里郎》，韩国学生演唱日本的《樱花》，日本学生演唱中国的《茉莉花》。为了这次活动能完美呈现，中央音乐学院的两位同学充分发挥自

other's countries and cultures, and to have a more comprehensive understanding of the United States as a superpower.

**Cross-cultural Communication**

There were international students from all over the world in New Paltz. They were very friendly to each other. We learned from each other, grew up together and became very good friends. At that time, there were nearly 20 Chinese students in New Paltz. We were like a big family. We cared for each other and took care of each other. After a short time together, we established the first Chinese Students Association at SUNY New Paltz. During Mid-Autumn and Spring Festival, we organized various activities, and invited friends from the local community to participate in our festival activities to enhance mutual understanding.

In addition, in our spare time, we carried out cross-cultural exchanges with students from other countries. The most impressive one was The BIG THREE PARTY. This event was planned by the students from China, Japan and South Korea. The purpose was to present the traditional culture of the three countries to American students. One interesting program stood out in this activity. Students from the three countries were to sing a song from the other two countries. Our Chinese students sang the Korean song "Arirang"; Korean students, the Japanese song "Cherry Blossom"; and Japanese students, the Chinese song "Jasmine Flower". In order to present a wonderful performance, two students from the Central Conservatory of Music gave full play to their professional expertise and gathered us together for rehearsal in their spare time. The event was very successful and was highly evaluated by the university and local

己的专长，把大家召集在一起排练。活动非常成功，得到了学校和当地社区的高度评价。

### 象征中美友谊的小松树

2009 年 4 月 25 日，在时任纽约州州长助理胡思源叔叔的安排下，时任州长大卫·彼得森邀请我们去他家里做客。我们 43 位学生代表受到州长夫人的亲切接待，她还和我们一起在官邸后院种下了象征中美友谊的小松树。其实，我们 150 名地震灾区的孩子能有如此好的机会到美国学习，和纽约州的大力支持密不可分。

离开美国前夕，胡叔叔将州长写给我们的一封信送到我们手中。州长在信中说："年轻一代将成为未来世界的领导者，中美两国青年要彼此多交流、多学习。"从州长的信中我能真切地感受到他对中美两国青年增进彼此了解所寄予的厚望。时光飞逝，十年过去了，胡叔叔也退休当了爷爷，想必州长官邸后院的那棵松树已经长高了。

### 我的老师贝丝

贝丝是新堡分校国际项目中心的副主任，在新堡学习期间，她和她的家人给予我很多生活、学习上的关心和帮助。离开美国之后，我们仍然保持联系。每当她从新闻上看到四川发

communities.

**A Small Pine Tree as a Symbol of Sino-American Friendship**

On April 25, 2009, with the arrangement of Mr. Hu Siyuan, then the Assistant to the Governor of New York, the Governor David A. Peterson invited us to his home. 43 student representatives were cordially received by the Governor's wife. She planted a small pine tree with us in the backyard of the mansion to symbolize the friendship between China and the United States. The fact that the 150 students from the earthquake-stricken areas had such a good opportunity to study in the United States was inseparable from the strong support of the people of New York.

On the eve of our leaving the United States, the governor wrote a letter to us, and Mr. Hu gave it to every one of us. In the letter, the governor said, "The younger generation will become the leaders of the future world, and the youth of China and the United States should get to know each other more and learn more from each other."

生泥石流或者洪涝灾害时，都会在微信上问候我的家人是否平安。

今年夏天，我从四川大学研究生毕业，收到贝丝和她的家人的祝贺。她在信中说："我知道，你将继续以积极的方式影响人们。谢谢你在这一年与我们分享你的生活，我们非常珍惜与你的友谊。"

纽约州立大学新堡分校是我的母校，近几年来它们在北京、四川和重庆都有很多国际合作项目，只要新堡有老师出差来到四川，我都会抽出时间接待他们。"给予就是收获"，我打心底希望新堡的老师们到四川也能感受当年他们给予我的那份温暖。

### 我的朋友安

安是一个特别善良的人。她和丈夫丹以及他们的女儿、女婿一起在新堡经营一个很大的农场。2008年的平安夜，我和朋友去她家做客认识了她，后来我们成了很好的朋友。我喜欢和她分享我的故事，她也给予我很多鼓励和支持。离开新堡的时候，她送给

I sensed his great expectation for the youth of China and the United States to enhance mutual understanding. Time really flies. Ten years later, Mr. Hu has retired and is a grandpa now. For sure, the green pine tree in the backyard of the governor's house must be taller than before.

**My Teacher, Beth**

Beth was the deputy director of the Center for International Programs at New Paltz Campus. During my stay there, she and her family took care of me and gave me a lot of help. After leaving the United States, I still keep in touch with them. Every time she gets to know that some natural disaster that occured in Sichuan from the news, she would send me a WeChat message to ask if my family is safe.

This summer, I got my master's degree from Sichuan University and got a congratulation letter from Beth and her family. She wrote: "I know that you will continue to influence people in a positive way. Thank you for sharing a year of your life with us. We are grateful for your friendship." In recent years, they have many international projects going on in Beijing, Sichuan and Chongqing. Whenever faculty members from New Paltz come to Sichuan on business trips, I would find time to receive them.

我一张密密麻麻写满文字的明信片，每每看到这些文字，我的内心就充满了能量。她说："圣诞节，你的到来是我们家的一份礼物。因为你在这里，我们的社区变得更加富有，你已经在新堡激起了涟漪。就拿我本人来说，你的勇气、决心、勤劳和谦和，让我备受鼓舞。如果你成为一名教师，你的学生将无比幸运！"

正是因为安的鼓励，我回国后才鼓起勇气选择从事公益，选择和孩子们在一起！

## 过去十年，不忘初心，实现承诺

在美国学习期间我所遇到的人和所经历的事让我至今难忘。纽约州政府、纽约州立大学的 22 所分校以及当地社区，给予我们很多关心和帮助。学校老师更是全力以赴为我们的成长提供支持。我身边的美国同学对他们周边社区所面临的问题都非常热心，积极想办法解决身边的问题，身体力行参与社区建设的方方面面。所有这一切都潜移默化地影响着我，激励着我。

离开美国之前，我们在纽约东河公园里举行了"CSC-SUNY 150 奖学金项目"的结业典礼。一名记者问我："这一年你最大的收获是什么？"

To give is much better than to take. I sincerely hope that when the faculty members from New Paltz come to Sichuan, they will also feel the warmth they gave me ten years ago.

### My Friend, Ann

Ann is a very kind person. She and her husband Dan, with their daughter and son-in-law, ran a big farm in New Paltz. On Christmas Eve in 2008, a friend took me to her home, and later we became very good friends. I liked to share my life story with her. She gave me a lot of encouragement and support. When I left the United States, she sent me a postcard written all over from the top to the bottom. Every time I see the card, my heart is full of energy. She said, "It was such a gift to our family to have you with us at Christmas time. I know that our community was enriched because you were here, and I think that you have created ripples in the waters of New Paltz. I, for example, am very inspired by your courage, your determination, hard work and gracious way of appreciating other people. So I shall pass along many of those qualities you have inspired in me. Your smile and sense of humor fill the air with sunshine. I wish you much good luck as you journey on your path in life. If you do become a teacher, how lucky will your students will be!" It is the encouragement of Ann that gave me the courage to choose to work in public

我回答说："这一年所有人给予我的关心和帮助让我明白了什么是爱，什么是感恩，在以后的人生道路中我将把这份爱传递下去。"

2010年6月大学毕业后，在家人和老师的支持下，我选择做一名志愿者，希望把自己在美国的收获付诸实践。

2010年到2012年，我用两年时间摸底调查了成都市周边一百多个社区的留守儿童数据，并与当地的大学生社团联系，搭建了大学生志愿者和社区留守学生之间的桥梁，从学习和生活上帮助这些孩子们。

2012年到2016年，我用四年时间继续为贫困学生和留守儿童服务，为他们创造了免费参加校外课程学习的机会。孩子们可以在周末和寒暑假免费学习音乐、舞蹈、书画、武术等三十多门课程，我也是其中的一位老师，担任公益课程的教学和管理工作。

2016年，我加入了由联合国教科文组织、中国生物多样性保护与绿色发展基金会以及中国五大植物园联合支持的"观花项目"，担任自然科学课程的设计师。其间，在魏琳老师的带领下，同"CSC-SUNY 150 奖学金项目"的其他几位同学一起，为"5·12"汶川特大地震灾区四川阿

welfare field and work with children when I returned to China!

### A Decade Passed, a Dream Not Forgotten

During my stay in the United States, I met unforgettable people and had unforgettable experiences. The New York State Government, the State University of New York and the local communities showered us with care and support. The faculty members spared no efforts to give us all the help we needed for growing up. The American students I knew were concerned about the local community problems, worked to solve them, and actively participated in all aspects of community building. All these exerted a positive and subtle influence on me, and I was inspired by their examples. Before we left the United States, the "Closing Ceremony of CSC-SUNY 150 Program" was held in East River Park, New York. A reporter asked me, "What's your greatest gain in this year?" I answered, "I got a lot of care and support from a lot of people, and they helped me understand the true meaning of love and gratitude. In the future, I will pass this love on to other people."

I graduated from college in June 2010. With the support of my family and teachers, I chose to become a social worker. I hope to live up to the promise to help other people.

From 2010 to 2012, I made a thorough research on left-behind children in more than 100 communities around Chengdu. In order to help those children with their study and life, I got help from local college students' associations and built a bridge between college students volunteers and left-behind children in the communities.

坝州茂县山区的羌族孩子们策划了"阿坝少年行"公益活动。

虽然在上述公益项目的推进过程中遇到诸多困难，但是大自然赋予我的性格内涵，让我从容应对这些困难和挫折。过去十年，我经历了跨文化、跨学科、跨行业的挑战，这些经历都加速了我的成长。与不同年龄段孩子的接触，也让我对教育有了更深刻的理解。

十年前，安曾鼓励我说："如果你成为一名教师，你的学生将无比幸运！"回顾过去，其实最幸运的是我自己！

## 致未来的我们

亲爱的琳：于我们150个孩子而言，你就是像夏洛一样的朋友。你是我们的良师，更是我们的益友。十年前你和滔伟哥把我们送到大洋彼岸，让我们看更为广阔的世界；得益于此，我们才有站上更大的人生舞台的勇气。我深知"CSC-SUNY 150 奖学金项目"于你而言其分量有多重，在你心中占据何等重要的位置。在过去的这十年，感谢有你一直陪伴我们左右，助力我们奔跑。我们需要你和我们在一起，永远。

From 2012 to 2016, I continued to work for students from poverty-stricken families and left-behind children, creating free opportunities for them to attend after-school programs. These children can learn more than 30 extracurricular courses such as music, dance, painting, calligraphy and martial arts on weekends and in winter and summer vacations. I volunteered my time to work as a teacher. At the same time, I also did the management work.

In 2016, I joined the "Flower Viewing Project" jointly supported by UNESCO, the China Foundation for Biodiversity Conservation and Green Development and the five botanical gardens of China, and worked as a designer of natural science courses. During this period, under the leadership of Ms. Wei Lin, together with several other students from CSC-SUNY 150 Program, I designed the public welfare program "Aba Youth Tour" for the children from Qiang Ethnic group in Maoxian Mountain Area, Aba Prefecture, Sichuan Province, which was an earth-stricken area in the 5/12 Earthquake.

Of course, we had run into a variety of difficulties in the projects mentioned above, but I learned to deal with these difficulties and setbacks in a calm way. Over the past decade, I have faced cross-cultural, cross-disciplinary and cross-industry challenges, and I have learned from the experiences and walked with a steady

致未来的我们："在一起，我们可以创造奇迹！"

pace toward my goal. Having met children from different age groups, I also have a deeper understanding of education. Ten years ago, Ann said encouragingly to me: "If you do become a teacher, how lucky your students will be!" Looking back, in fact, I realize that I have been the lucky one.

## To Us

Dear Lin: For us 150 students, you are just like Charlotte from the fairy tale. You are our good teacher and our good friend. Ten years ago, you and Taowei sent us to the other side of the ocean to see the wider world. Thanks to this, we have the courage to stand on a bigger stage of life. I know how important the program is to you and how important it is in your mind. In the past ten years, thank you for being around us and helping us go forward.

To us in the future: Together, we can make a difference!

# 一年，改变一生

## That Year Changed My Life

文欢／四川师范大学　纽约州立大学科布尔斯基分校

Wen Huan / Sichuan Normal University　SUNY at Cobleskill

我叫文欢，2007 年 9 月至 2011 年 6 月就读于四川师范大学，大二时在美国纽约州立大学科布尔斯基分校学习一学年。

2008 年 5 月 12 日是一个非常特殊的日子，汶川特大地震就发生在这一天，多少人在这一天失去生命，多少人在这一天家破人亡，至今想起，那种难以言表的悲痛仍然沉重。

这次地震之后，美国纽约州政府向重灾区的各所高校在读大二、大三学生发出邀请，选取 150 名灾区学员以全额奖学金的名义到纽约州立大学的各个分校学习。对于重灾区的孩子们来说，这是一份抚慰，也是一份惊喜！何其有幸，我成为这 150 名学生

My name is Wen Huan. I studied at Sichuan Normal University from September 2007 to June 2011. During my sophomore year, I studied at the State University of New York in Cobleskill, USA.

May 12th in 2008 is a date that can never be forgotten. The Wenchuan Earthquake happened on that day. It took away so many people's lives and made their families incomplete. Whenever I think about it, it still weighs heavily on my heart.

It is because of the earthquake that the government of New York State offered funds and opportunities to invite 150 college students from the earthquake-stricken areas for one-year stay at the State University of New York as exchange students. The invitation came as a comfort and was a surprise for us. And it also symbolized the continuing and deepening friendship between the peoples from the two countries.

It was a comfort and surprise for kids of the earthquake-striken areas! And I was lucky enough

中的一员；唯有努力学习，才不辜负这次机会。

到美国的第二天，纽约当地华侨组织就邀请我们享用了一顿丰盛的中餐。让我们备感温馨的是，他们还给我们每人准备了一个50美元的红包，就像我们在家过年领红包一样。我们抵达美国的第一时间，就感受到了同胞的温暖。也是在这一天，中国驻美国大使彭克玉邀请我们到大使馆，分别见到了我们即将前往的纽约州立大学各个分校的校长和老师。我们18名学生被分到了科布尔斯基分校。

校长唐纳德·津盖尔和我们在校期间的主管老师乔纳森·莫雷尔，对我们的关心和照顾无微不至，尤其是乔纳森·莫雷尔就像我们的爷爷，所以我们也都亲切地称他为"爷爷"。

初到一个完全陌生的环境，"爷爷"对我们的关心事无巨细。为了让我们尽快熟悉新的学习环境，到科布尔斯基的第一天，"爷爷"就带我们逛了美丽的校园，给我们介绍学校的各个部分；帮我们安排所需的学习书籍和用品，怕我们不能负担有些自费的资料，还专门向学校申请给我们免费发放。放假了，"爷爷"就带我们去了解商业区的生活设施；担心我们无聊，就经常请我们去他家里做客，或者带我们去奥尔巴尼、波士顿、佛

to be one of the members of the program. I made up my mind that I would study hard and make a good use of the opportunity.

On the second day in New York, the local Overseas Chinese Association threw a big welcome party for us. Every one of us got a Red Packet as a gift in which we found 50 dollars. It felt like the celebration of Spring Festival when we got Red Packets as gifts from family members of the older generation.

It was also on that day that we were invited by Ambassador Peng Keyu to the Chinese Embassy in New York to meet the presidents and the faculty members from different campuses of SUNY. I was then assigned to SUNY-Cobleskill with other 17 students.

Here, I would like to speak in capitals about Mr. Donald Zingale, the president of Cobleskill, and Mr. Jonathan Morell, our supervisor. They gave us all the care and support we could use, and Mr. Jonathan Morell was like a grandpa in our eyes. We called him "Ye Ye", which means grandpa in Chinese.

Although we were new there, we felt welcomed and not at a loss. Our grandpa, Mr. Jonathan Morell, should have all the credit for it. He attended to everything. On the first day we arrived there, he showed us around the campus

罗里达等地游玩。"爷爷"对我们的关爱，让我们内心无比温暖和踏实，也充满了对他的感激之情。

在科布尔斯基留学的这一年，我们不仅收获了知识，还收获了友谊，也有了从未有过的体验，开阔了我们的眼界。

记得项目要结束的时候，我们都希望回刚举办了奥运会的北京看看，"CSC-SUNY 150奖学金项目"的组织人魏老师和滔伟哥哥欣然答应，帮我们一一安排事项，虽然最后因为遇上非典没去成，但还是很感谢他们！

记得最后要离开的时候，彭克玉大使邀请我们去大使馆吃饭唱歌，当

and introduced everything we needed to know. The books and the like we needed were provided for free under the arrangement of Mr. Jonathan Morell lest that we could not afford it.

When holidays came, Mr. Jonathan Morell would take us to downtown for a visit. He often invited us to his house for holiday time and also took us for tours in Albany, Boston and Florida. He filled our hearts with loving care and we felt very grateful.

During the year at Cobleskill, we learned a lot and made a lot of friends. All these new experiences proved to be an eye opener for us.

I can remember that when the program was drawing to end, we offered to go to Beijing, where the Olympic Games was just closed. The program organisers Ms.Wei and Brother Taowei were glad to promise us and arranged everything for us. Although we didn't make it just because of the Sars, I would like to offer my sincere thanks to them.

时的热闹和不舍记忆犹新。感谢彭克玉大使自始至终关心我们。

感谢我在科布尔斯基的老师和同学，教授我们知识，给予我们关心和帮助，让我们顺利完成了一年的学习。

站在更高的起点，我们"CSC-SUNY 150 奖学金项目"每个人的生活轨迹都发生了变化。我们当中，有的人在国内继续攻读学位，有的人本科毕业后又回到美国继续留学生活，也有的人本科毕业后就参加了工作。

时间飞逝，转眼到了 2018 年，十年时间过去了，我们都不再是当年那个年轻的我们，我们现在基本都是孩子的妈妈或爸爸了。回想以前在美国留学的生活，所学到的知识和观念，

Thanks to Mr. Peng Keyu, then the Chinese Ambassador in New York, attending to us all the way through the program. Before our departure from the United States, Mr. Peng Keyu invited us to the Chinese Embassy for a farewell party. We had dinner and sang songs together. I could still see it clearly in my mind's eye that how happy and sad we were at the same time.

Thanks go to my teachers and fellow students in SUNY-Cobleskill for their care and help. Because of all of you, I was able to complete my study and enjoy my stay there.

Taking this program as a higher start, all of us have changed the life path. Some furthered their study for Master's or Doctor's degree; some returned to the US to resume their study-abroad life; some found a job.

Time flies. We are ten years older and almost all of us have become mothers and fathers. We are proud to share our stories in the United

我们都可以很骄傲地讲给我们的孩子听。

一个十年过去了，在接下来的十年里，希望我们"CSC-SUNY 150奖学金项目"的每一个人，都朝着自己的目标努力奋斗！

States with our children. And what we learned there could be used to educate our children.

Ten years has passed, and in the next ten years, I hope that everyone of the program will strive on towards his or her goal!

# 回望十年

## Looking Backward to the Last Decade

杨轲 / 四川师范大学　纽约州立大学德里学院

Yang Ke / Sichuan Normal University　SUNY at Delhi

　　时间如白驹过隙。眨眼间，如今的我已来到三十而立的人生路口。回首过去，距离 2009 年 5 月 25 日回国已经过去了 3 440 多个日夜，仿若一场梦。在这三十多年的时间里，发生了许多改变我人生轨迹的事情。但我印象最深的，还是 2008 年的大地震以及接下来的"CSC-SUNY 150 奖学金项目"。十年前的地震让太多人的人生航向发生转变，我是其中渺小而又特别的一个。

　　突如其来的 2008 年"5·12"汶川特大地震，使很多人的生活发生了变化。对我而言，意义重大的"CSC-SUNY 150 奖学金项目"叩响了我的门。这场大地震后，我和其

How time flies in the blink of an eye. Now, I am standing on the intersection of life at my age of 30. Looking backward, I have spent over 3,440 days and nights since I came back to China on May 25th, 2009. All stories happening there resemble a dream. Over the past 30 years, I have met several things that have converted my life track; however, what has made me impressed most is the earthquake hit in 2008 and the CSC-SUNY 150 Program. One decade ago, this earthquake transformed the life path of various people, of whom I was just a tiny and special one.

The violent earthquake hit the land suddenly in 2008, leaving a large number of people's life a world-shaking change. For me, the CSC-SUNY Program significantly came into being. Due to this earthquake shaking the whole world, 150 students, including me, from 13 universities in Sichuan, gained the opportunity to exchange in the State University of New York for free.

他来自四川 13 所高校的 149 名同学一起，得到了免费到纽约州立大学交流学习的机会。现在回想起来，当时一切都发生得太快。那时我不曾料到，一个小小的决定会改变我的人生轨迹。从地震发生时的恐惧万分、惊慌失措到后来的悲伤难过，从获知能参与"CSC-SUNY 150 奖学金项目"的惊喜不已，到抵达美国纽约时的懵懵懂懂，我的心绪如同海潮般起起伏伏。3 个多月的时间，现在回想起来仍然如梦。之后留学美国 10 个月的经历，对我的世界观、人生观、价值观产生了极大的影响。

"世界这么大，我要去看看。"在参与"CSC-SUNY 150 奖学金项目"之前，我只是一个普通家庭的普通学生，来自四川的一个小市镇。虽然2008 年，通过网络我们可以瞬时了解这个世界上各个地方发生的事情。但通过电脑显示器看见的那些画面，有时候遥远得像一个故事，我只是一个旁观者。帝国大厦、时代广场、中央公园等，对于我而言，只存在于想象和影视文艺作品中。我从未梦想过有一天我也能漫步其中，切身体会异乡的文化氛围。当我身临其境，站在这些影视文艺故事真切演绎、发生的地方时，仿佛戳破了那层原来包裹着我的透明泡沫，看得更远，听得更多，

Looking backward, I find that all things at that moment happened in the blink of an eye. At that time, I didn't realize that this tiny determination would totally change my life track. I was scared and in panic when the earthquake was striking the land, and then I was distressed and grieved. I was excited to learn about the opportunity to take part in the CSC-SUNY Program, but I was muddled when I first stepped into New York, USA. My thoughts went up and down like the sea tides. When I look backward to the past three months, all stories resembled a dream. Those ten months of exchanges in USA has granted me indelible impacts on my outlook to the world, life philosophy and values.

"Since the world is boundless, I need to have a browse of it." Before I joined the CSC-SUNY 150 Program, I was an average student from an average family in a small town of Sichuan Province. Although the Internet prevailed in 2008, and we could learn about what was happening in every corner of the world instantly through the Internet, I was an outsider, in front of the screen of computer, watching those images that sometimes resembled a story far away from my life. For me, all those images, such as the Empire State Building, Times Square, Central Park and so on, were just scenes existing

踏入了一个更加广阔和高远的世界。

在美国留学的这段时间，我深刻感受到了这个世界不断融合的趋势，高科技的进步和发展大幅度地拉近了人与人之间的距离。世界一体化的概念，在我眼中有了更加真实、更加具象化的表现。不论你身处何处，即使是地球的两端，也不再受到距离对人们交流沟通的限制。网络将千里之外的人们紧密相连。在纽约的广场大街上，在西雅图的咖啡馆里，在奥马哈的学校中，来自世界各地的游客、商人、学生聚集到一起，参观、交流和学习。这些新鲜的画面不断闯入我的眼帘，让我如此深切地感受到，全球一体化的浪潮正以不可阻挡的态势汹涌而来。我对自己原先偏安一隅的生活状态愈发感到不安。这世界变化是如此之大，如此之快，它前进的脚步不会停下来等那些停在原地、踌躇不前的人。如果没有坚毅的决心，随波逐流，结局只能是被时代抛弃，被全球化的潮流抛弃。

初到美国，我便遇到了一个小小的考验。因为专业的关系，我需要购买一台相机（建筑专业出去考察需要拍照，在美国我没有买手机）。当时负责照顾我们的克雷格·韦索儿老师了解到这个情况后，从网上帮我找了很多资料，选了三台相机，并仔

in imagination and movies. I had never dreamed that one day I could wander in those places and experience those exotic cultures. When I was standing in those scenarios where all those movies and stories were performed and took place, I seemed to burst the transparent bubble that originally covered me, so much so that I could have a clearer vision, be more informed and step into a wider world.

In my days of exchanges in the USA, I deeply felt that the trend of globalization and the advancement and development of high-end science and technology greatly narrowed the distance between people. Globalization, compared with my early understanding, became truer and more concrete in my perspective. Distance could never constrain the communication of different people, no matter where we were and even though we were scattered in the two ends of the earth. The Internet connected people living within thousands of miles. Visitors, businessmen, and students coming from every corner of the world gathered to attend visits, have exchanges and learn from each other, on the street of the Times Square of New York, in the cafe of Seattle, and in the school of Omaha. Those vivid pictures leaped into my eyes and enabled me to recognize that the trend of globalization came to us irreversibly and ferociously, and I was worried about my original life in which I was content to live in a deserted land. The world changes in a huge and rapid manner and will not wait for those who still stand in the original place and hesitate to step forward. Without stronger determination and more far-sighted visions, anyone can be abandoned by time and the trend of globalization.

When I first stepped into the USA, I

细对比它们的优缺点。在我购买后不久，他还告诉我他发现我买的相机降价了，认真地为我解释了购物网站的规则，并表示这种在一定期限内的降价可以帮我要回这部分差价。后来他不厌其烦地和购物网站沟通，最后帮我要回了与相机差价对应金额的礼品卡，甚至还十分抱歉地告知我他之前把规则搞错了，这种差价不能直接要回现金，只能以礼品卡的形式返还。他的善良和耐心深深地打动了我，让身在异乡的我，也感受到了如在家乡般的温暖。

在美国留学期间，我对美国大学不同于国内的教学方式印象深刻。在国内，同一个班级的同学联系更多也更紧密。而在美国，学校里没有固定

encountered a lesson. Due to the need of my major, I needed to buy a camera (As an architecture major, I needed to take photos in fields. But I didn't buy a cell-phone in the USA). Then, when our teacher, Craig Wesle, who took care of our daily lives, learned about it, he searched a great deal of information in the Internet, shortlisted three different types of cameras and helped me analyze the advantages and the disadvantages of them. Before long after I bought the camera, he told me that he found the camera's price was reduced. He carefully drove home to me the rules of e-commerce websites and said that he might help me get the price difference back within some period. Later, he communicated with the e-commerce website with all his patience, and finally got my price difference refunded in the form of gift card. He was so sorry to tell me that he misunderstood the rule. The price difference could not be compensated by cash but only in the form of a gift card. His kindness and patience

的班级，和室友的关系反而更亲近。
课堂上老师更注意培养学生动手的能
力。作为建筑学专业的学生，甚至可
以参加土建专业修建房屋的课程（当
时学校校长的房屋就是之前某届学生
的作品）。而且，美国课堂上需要学
生讨论发言的机会更多，国内则更注
重听老师讲授。

　　当年的大地震像一记闷锤，重重
地在我的人生里留下印记。从此我对
生命的感受更加具体和真切。我深刻
地体会到了生命的高贵和脆弱，人在
大自然面前是多么渺小与无助，人所
做的一切与大自然的亘古恒常相比，
不过是过眼云烟。有段时间，我甚至
产生了一种彷徨无助的心绪，对人生
的价值和意义感到怀疑。

　　到了美国之后，我从照顾我们的
老师身上学到了另外一种生活方式和
智慧。在美国期间，按照传统，学校
的老师会在各种节日邀请我们到他们
家里做客，与他们的亲朋好友共度佳
节。在校长的家中，我看到了他们圣
诞节的传统"保留节目"。等家中的
小朋友上床睡觉休息后，家中的长辈
围着房屋走一圈，一边走一边摇铃铛，
假装乘坐麋鹿而来的圣诞老人正在派
送礼物。布置好一切，长辈们将小朋
友从楼下叫下来，从悬挂的长袜子中
取出他们的礼物。这时小朋友特别开

deeply touched me and brought me the sense of homeland when I was in a foreign land.

During the exchange in the United States, I was impressed by the different teaching methods of American universities. In China, classmates of a same class usually remained close contacts. However, in the United States, there were not fixed classes and I had close contacts with my roommates on the contrary. In each class, the teacher highlighted the practical skills of students. Even a student majoring in architecture could have a chance to take courses of the civil engineering major (then, the house of the university president had been built by previous students). Moreover, students could gain a variety of opportunities to have their own say in classes of the United States, while in China, the focus of each class was the teacher's lecturing.

The earthquake of 2008 left a deep stamp in my life, as if I had been stricken by a heavy hammer. From then on, I have had a true and concrete sense of life. I have deeply felt the loftiness and fragility of our life and the tininess and helplessness of the human being in front of nature. What humans have done is just a flash in the pan, compared with the immortality of nature. In the past, I even had a sense of hesitation and helplessness and was doubtful about the significance and value of our life.

After I came to the United States, I learned about another life style and wit from our teacher who took care of us. In my days in the USA, traditionally, teachers would invite us to visit their homes and spend every festival with their friends and relatives. In the home of the president, I witnessed their "repertoire" of Christmas. When kids of the family went to sleep, the elder of the family, walking around the house and ringing the

心、特别兴奋，迫不及待地坐在沙发上拆礼物，还神秘地告诉家中长辈他们"听到了圣诞老人乘坐麋鹿的铃铛声"，要求长辈们一起保密。随后，老师向我们介绍，这种温馨有趣的"仪式"在很多美国家庭传承了下来，保留至今。

这个场景一直让我难以忘怀，除了对美国家庭这种别开生面的"传统节日仪式"感到新鲜有趣之外，也让我突然感受到了家庭生活的美好。为自己的小家庭保留一个独有的节日仪式，成了我的愿望之一。如今我已到而立之年，早已组建了自己的家庭，有了可爱乖巧的宝宝。我除了尽自己所能为宝宝创造一个其乐融融的家庭氛围以外，还和家人达成共识，一起创造并保留独属于我们自己的家庭仪式。这种仪式感不知不觉间成了我们家庭成员之间的黏合剂，将我们这个小家庭牢固地凝聚在一起，成为每个家庭成员的精神港湾。

"5·12"汶川特大地震之后很多人获得了新生，其实我觉得我们"CSC-SUNY 150奖学金项目"的同学不仅在地震后获得了新生，还通过美国为期一年的生活和学习迈向了更高的人生台阶，塑造了自己全新的世界观。这些改变浸润在生活中，有些能被明显地观察到，而有些则内化

bell, pretended that Santa Clause was sending gifts on the elk. After getting all the things ready, the elder called all kids to go downstairs and pick up their gift in the socks hanging somewhere in the room. At this moment, kids were happy and excited. And sitting on the sofa, they were too impatient to unpack their gifts. They would tell the elder in a secret way that they heard about the bells of Santa Clause riding on the elf and at the same time, required the elder to keep it a secret. Later, our teacher explained to us that this interesting ceremony had been kept and carried forward in many American families.

This scenario has lingered in my memory. With the fresh sense of and interest in this special traditional festival ceremony of American families, I suddenly felt the happiness of a family. So I wished that I might keep and engage in a unique festival ceremony for my own small family. Now, I am at my ripple age and have my own family and a cute baby. While creating a cozy and happy atmosphere of family for our baby, I have made a consensus with my family members that we need to get together to create and keep our own family ceremony. This sense of ceremony has quietly become a glue-like tie binding upon our family members together firmly, and become the spiritual harbor of each

成推动我们继续前行的动力。十年的时间，我成长了许多。目前我从事建筑设计行业，参与设计了很多项目。虽然生活状态与理想还是有一定的差距，工作繁重，但是这是建筑行业的共性，目前看来还无法改变。我更赞同活在当下的生活态度，更珍惜自己现在拥有的一切。

如今，前往美国留学、游玩的人越来越多。对于想要在美国学习的师弟师妹们，我的建议是首先要学会更加独立。大学生作为一个成年人，要锻炼自己处理实际问题的能力，不能再想着随时向家人求助。其次，身处异国，要尊重当地人民的文化和生活习惯，很多美国人都有宗教信仰，作为留学生可以不参与但是要给予足够的尊重。生活中大部分事情都需要清楚地表达自己的态度，有话直说更容易与美国人沟通。对于寄宿家庭，最开始的交流肯定是困难的，毕竟文化环境、生活习惯之间有太多不同之处。这时候最便捷、能减少误会的方法就是请一个有两边生活经历的人来沟通，尤其是有留学经历的师兄师姐。学生作为一个数量庞大的群体，其包容性、接纳性是很强的，也是沟通起来难度最小的。信息技术的发展、社交网络的兴起，拉近了不同文化人们之间的距离，只要有勇气、不害羞，

family member.

An abundance of people claimed that they gained rebirth after the earthquake in 2008, but in my opinion, our classmates of the CSC-SUNY 150 Program not only gained the rebirth after the earthquake, but also stepped to the higher ladder of our life after the one year of living and learning in the United States, from which we have shaped our new outlook of world, life philosophy and values. Those changes penetrate all our life, some of which can be obviously observed, but some of which cannot. They have silently become our endogenous impetus to push us forward. Over the past decade, I have grown up. Now, I am engaging in the business of architecture design and have taken part in several projects. Although there is a wide gap between the life and the ideal, and the workload is heavy, it is the common feature of the architecture industry beyond my control. I couldn't agree more with the philosophy of living at the present moment, emphasizing and cherishing what I have.

Nowadays, there are more and more people who would like to go to the United States for further study or for a tour. To all schoolmates who want to do so, my suggestion is that you need to learn to be independent at the outset and not always reach for a helping hand from your family. Besides, living in the overseas, you need to respect the culture and the living habits of the natives. Many American people have their religious belief, so as an international student, you must respect them even if you don't join them. You need to express your attitude in your daily life. Acting your way directly can help you better communicate with American people. If you live in boarding houses, your exchanges at first

沟通其实不是特别困难。

如今回想起过去的种种，我时常感到自己很幸运，成为"CSC-SUNY 150 奖学金项目"的一员。"CSC-SUNY 150 奖学金项目"不仅为我们打开了一扇通往世界的大门，更以此为起点衍生出了许多珍贵的缘分。我们在这个项目中交到了真心朋友，我们彼此鼓励、相互扶持，共同学习。因为"CSC-SUNY 150 奖学金项目"，我们心中为自己树立了一个人生准则：做一个乐观通透、积极向上的人。要对身处困难之中的人伸出援手，把这份属于"CSC-SUNY 150 奖学金项目"的精神财产不断传承下去。

must meet several difficulties, due to differences in cultural circumstance and living habits. The easiest and most effective way to solve this problem is to invite a friend with life experience in both countries to help you to communicate, such as your elder schoolmates with such experience. Students are of a large group and with strong inclusiveness and adoption, so it is easiest to communicate with them. Furthermore, with the development of information technology and the growth of social media, the distance between people of different cultures has been narrowed. If you can take your courage and guts, communication with others is just a piece of cake.

Nowadays, when I look backward to all the days in the past, I always feel that I was lucky to be a member of the CSC-SUNY 150 Program. This program has not only opened for us a door to a wider world, but also derived many cherished chances and relations from it. Through this program, we have made many bosom friends, who always encourage each other, help each other, and learn from each there. It is the CSC-SUNY 150 Program that has helped us to establish a code of life in our mind: to be optimistic, honest and active people. We need to lend our hands to persons trapped in the difficulties and carry forward the spiritual legacy of the CSC-SUNY 150 Program.

# 忆往昔——十年，四记

## Looking Backward: Four Chapters for the Past Decade

周涛 / 四川师范大学　纽约州立大学奥尔巴尼分校

Zhou Tao / Sichuan Normal University　SUNY at Albany

### 灾难——回望故园三千里，风尘满目泪沾衣

2008 年 5 月 12 日下午，当我从剧烈晃动的教学楼冲出来时，身边一片喧嚣，四周仿佛天塌地陷。之后一条条来自媒体的灾情报道证实了大家的猜测：四川地震了。虽然家人朋友平安，可看着新闻里惨烈的画面，看着那么多失去家园和至亲痛哭的人们，即便素不相识，心中也是一片黯然。无论是否受灾，无论受灾轻重，那个夏天的四川人常常泪流满面。

一夕之间，大家心中多了一些沉甸甸的东西，即便如我这般懵懵懂懂，也觉得我们活着的人是受了上天眷顾，但不能就这样心安理得地享受，

### Worries & Sadness from the Catastrophe in My Hometown

On the afternoon of May 12th, 2008, I rushed out of the heavily shaken teaching building, and found myself surrounded by a sea of noise from panicking people as if the heaven had fallen down and the land broken into pieces. Later, the reports on the disaster from media affirmed to people's guess: an earthquake hit Sichuan Province. Although my family was safe, watching those tragic images on the TV and finding many people losing their home and family members whom I did not know, I felt very sad. Whether stricken by the disaster or not and whether having lost more or less, people in Sichuan always dropped tears in that summer.

Over a night, everyone took a heavy burden on the heart. Even though I was a student, I felt that we people still alive were receiving a favor

我们应该为伤痕累累的家乡做点什么。但当时一个大一的孩子，该做些什么呢？

## 缘起——后又去国三千里，千江浩荡一溪起

由于四川在"5·12"汶川特大地震中遭受巨大创伤，在教育部和多方人士的努力下，美国纽约州立大学提供了150名交换生名额给来自四川灾区的青年学生。经过层层考试，我幸运地成为其中一员，被安排至纽约州立大学奥尔巴尼校区学习。在这里，我度过了毕生难忘的留学生涯。在这一年里，我既体验了远离家人、独自成长的艰难，也体会到了各方关怀带来的感动。

背井离乡总是艰难的，首先是生活上的障碍。初入异国，日常的衣食住行都要逐渐适应，这是不小的挑战。其次是学业上遇到的困难。初次接触

from the Heaven. However, we should not take it for granted that we were entitled to a better life. We needed to make some contributions to our hometown. For a freshman student in a university, what could I do?

### The Chance
### —Leaving Home for a Foreign Land

Since Sichuan Province was hit heavily by the earthquake in May 12th, 2008, and with efforts of Ministry of Education of PRC and people in different fields, the State University of New York in the United States provided a opportunity of 150 exchange students to young students of disaster-stricken areas in Sichuan. After several rounds of examinations, I was shortlisted as one of them. I was assigned to the State University of New York at Albany, where I spent my unforgettable days of studying abroad. Over that year, I felt the hardship of being far away from my families and being independent in life and also experienced care and touching moments from all walks of life.

It was hard to live far away from my family. Firstly, I met obstacles in daily life. When I first stepped into an overseas land, it was a challenge to adapt to clothing, diet, accommodation and transportation. Secondly, I met difficulties in my study. When I was first exposed in the language context of English only and western teaching methods, my Chinese classmates and I didn't know how to deal with them. In China, people always had such a fixed concept of strict senior high school life but easy circumstance of university. However, in Albany, I experienced course pressure as big as that of the junior year of

全英文的语言环境和纯西方的教学方式，我和同去的同学都有些无所适从。在国内，我们习惯的是严格的高中生活和宽松的大学环境，但在奥尔巴尼，我却体验到了堪比高三的课业压力：课堂教学多以讨论形式展开，考试也常用论文代替，讨论和论文的素材则来源于大量的课外阅读任务。语言和文化的不同带来的是阅读和理解障碍，抱着词典挑灯夜读，几乎成为常态。

在这样的"煎熬"中，我也感受到了来自多方的关怀。为促成项目落地奔波一个夏季的魏琳老师，在同学们分赴各校区后，继续操心大家的生活和学习；幽默风趣的哈格特教授是个中国通，总是用脑袋里满满的中国故事为我们一解乡愁；和蔼的哈特曼教授虽然不善言辞，但总会在节日来临时，邀请我们去他家中做客，亲自烹制美味的大餐；严肃的德不来希教授虽然会毫不留情地指出我论文中的问题，但也会耐心地讲解修改技巧；一向干练的丹尼尔老师，也会在我们面前显露柔情的一面，常柔声细语鼓励我们。

也正因此，才有了2009年回国时大家在眼泪中依依惜别的场景。虽然不舍，但我们知道，祖国和家乡还有更重要的任务在等着我们。2009

senior high school in China. Classroom teachings were often conducted through discussions, paper writing took place of the test, and the source of the class discussion and the paper writing came from a lot of reading after class. The difference of language and culture brought me with obstacles in reading and comprehension. It was my routine that I read to deep night with a dictionary at hand.

In this "hardship", I also felt cares from different people. Madam Wei Lin, who spent a summer time on promoting the success of this program with all her efforts, was still concerned about the life and study of each student, after we were assigned to different schools. Professor Hargett, who was a humorous China hand, was always ready to tell Chinese stories kept in his mind to cure our nostalgia. Although our kind professor Hartman was not so talkative, he always invited us to his home and cooked for us in the days of festivals.

The strict professor Deblasi pointed out problems in my paper directly, but he still gave me several suggestions for revision. Even our sophisticated teacher Danielle would show gentleness to us and encouraged us in his gentle voice.

Therefore, we all dropped tears before leaving for China in 2009. Although we were

年，回国前夕，我写下一篇《三别赋》，告诉自己，不能忘了使命。

## 迷茫——心怀南山隐逸梦，身在浮世宦门中

也许是冥冥中注定，原本一心想成为教师的我，毕业时考上了四川省2011年的选调生，成了一名公务员。孤身来到陌生的农村环境，住在简陋的宿舍里，听着不甚熟悉的方言，学习处理琐碎的党政办事务，我渐渐迷茫起来：这样日复一日的重复劳动，真是有价值的吗？身边有人劝我说，习惯就好。也有曾经的同学、老师认为基层公务员并不适合我这个曾经的"文学青年"，留美期间结识的老师也曾递来橄榄枝，建议我重回校园深造。

我自己也在动摇，一度感到迷茫失落，随手写下过一首小诗："宦门寂寥不生草，人情凋零无知交。只为斗米命难却，常提秃笔无风月。"在这样的纠结中，我想起了哈格特教授与我讨论人生道路时曾经说的话："我完全理解你，也全力支持你，不管你做什么，不管你前行的方向是哪里。我百分百信任你，你一定会找到你前行的方向。不过，千万千万不要误信任何一个让你降

reluctant to leave, we knew our motherland and hometown needed us to take greater responsibility. In 2009, before we came back, I wrote down an article called "Ode to Three Farewells." I silently told myself that I needed to keep my mission in mind always.

### The Contradiction Between My Ideal & the Reality

Maybe it was the arrangement of my destiny. I had planned to be a teacher, but I passed the civil servant examination of 2011 and became a civil servant. I came alone to a strange village, lived in a simple dormitory room, heard unfamiliar dialects, and learned how to deal with trivial affairs of party and government office. I was gradually confused. Was it worthwhile to repeat all this work day by day? Someone persuaded me to get accustomed to this lifestyle. Besides, some of my classmates and teachers reckoned that I, once a "literature young person", could not adapt to the grass-root civil servant. The teacher who I got along with in the United States, also extended to me an olive branch and suggested me to go back to school for further study.

I once felt reluctant, lost and frustrated. I wrote down a complaint sighing at the loneliness and helplessness because of the contradiction between my ideal and the reality. In this psychological conflict, words from Professor Hargett came into my mind, when we were discussing life philosophy:"I understand and support you completely, no matter what you do and what direction you take. I have absolute confidence in you, and I am positive that you will

低目标的'建议'！"

老师对我的决定给予了全力支持，那我自己又怎能轻易动摇呢？刚跨入行业门槛，若轻易说离开，未免太过草率。更重要的是，我始终记得，成为参与灾后重建的一支青年力量，是我们赴美学习的最大目标，而人民公仆这一角色，恰恰是参与建设的中坚力量。所以，我决定坚持下去。

## 新程——夜静山空倾耳听，茂林深涧有清溪

我开始踏踏实实沉浸于工作中，把所有新任务当作成长的历练。2014年，由于深感管理理论知识不足，我决定考研，经过努力考取了四川大学公共管理学院的MPA（今年已顺利毕业），希望从理论上加深对地方政府管理的认识。

find your way. And never, never, never listen to people who advise you to lower your goals for any reason!"

My teacher fully supported my decision, and how could I easily give it up? Since I just stepped into the threshold of my business, it would be too hasty to quit my job. More importantly, I always kept in mind my goal of studying abroad in the United States to be the young power to underpin the post-disaster reconstruction. In this sense, the role of civil servant was the hardcore of the post-disaster reconstruction. Therefore, I was determined to continue my original journey.

### A New Journey

I immersed myself into my work with all my heart and soul, treating all new tasks as a chance for my growth. In 2014, due to lacking in knowledge of management, I determined to apply for a master degree. After my hard work, I was admitted to the program of MPA of School of Public Administration, Sichuan University. Now, I have successfully completed my postgraduate study. I hope I can strengthen my understanding of local government management in terms of theory.

In accordance with the cultivation plan of a young civil servant, after a short period of working in the grass-root government of town, I took rotary positions in the organization departments of municipal party committee and provincial party committee respectively. I took part in work related to grass-root party building and cadre affairs, and then went back to the township government to be in charge of civil affairs, public health, social security, and culture,

按照选调生培养方案，在一段时间的乡镇工作后，我又前往市委组织部、省委组织部轮岗学习；先后参与基层党建、干部工作，后来又回到乡镇，分管民政、卫生、劳动保障、文化等工作。在这期间，经历了多种重角色转换，案头的书也一变再变：从自己最喜欢的《古文观止》，变成业务必需的《公共政策分析》《党组织选举手册》《民政政策文件汇编》《基层党务工作实用手册》……

在一个个加班的夜晚，在研究生答辩前最疲惫的时刻，我常常想起在美国抱着词典挑灯苦读的日子。那时的苦读，是因为知道自己肩负着家乡的殷切期盼，不敢辜负；如今的苦读和坚持，是因为知道，"为灾后重建而努力"不只是口号，还需要信仰和能量。

etc. During this period of time, the books on my table have varied with the frequent changes of my roles in work. Once, my favorite book was *The Finest of Ancient Prose*, but nowadays, books necessary for my work are always at hand, such as *Public Policy Analysis, Manual on Party Organization Election, Collection of Policies and Documents on Civil Affairs, Practical Handbook of Grass-Root Party Affairs*, etc.

At each night of working extra hours and at the most tiring moment before my oral defense of the graduation in the post-graduate program, I always recalled the days when I read deep to the mid-night with my English dictionary in the United States. At that moment, I worked hard, because I knew I had to shoulder the responsibility and expectations of my hometown. Today, I work hard, because I know that "working hard to serve post-disaster reconstruction" is not only a slogan. It needs our belief and energy.

**Appendix:**

### Three Farewells

(Three farewells means that my hometown fellows paid forever farewell to their lost friends and relatives; I paid temporary farewell to my hometown, due to leaving for the United States for studying abroad; I paid regretful farewell to friends made in the United States since I had to come back to China. A farewell could not only produce one's sad mood but also stimulate one's fighting will, and the latter is just the most cherished.)

We paid forever farewell to those passed away.

The year of 2008 witnessed the sudden

附记:

## 三别赋

(三别,即在家乡所见的父老痛失亲友之永别,自己因赴美留学而与家乡的暂别,离美归国与所交友人的憾别。别,能生哀绪,但亦能激斗志。后者,是为其最令人珍惜之处。)

黯然销魂者,惟别而已矣。

戊子见山崩地析,风云变色,然骨肉分后恩义在,丝缕相牵斩不断。此恨绵绵生,生生断人肠。

穆穆相祭,泪眼唯能与冷石相望。青烟生,入九天,带不走思人泪零落,反引得寒雁鸣西风,凄切至凉,孤声无应。执黄花,有暗香绵延,慰帖思人心,然牵不归、引不回,离人魂。

一别,黄泉人间两茫茫,今生来世发苍苍。悲兮?怜兮?日月盈仄,时光飘渺,纵星移物又如何,沉沉思心总不忘。当日笑语,今朝泪眼,一个别字切断。

后又去国三千里,稚子远游怀乡情,谁明?隐隐乡愁,似千江雾霭,挥袖拂不走,顺水流。诉与清秋月,只觉清秋寒。月不语,牵来浮云遮望眼。

二别,离情别绪处处散,清秋冷月独相伴。

一年期至,已丑当归。抬望眼,

disaster with the fallen mountains and broken lands. Although our friends and relatives passed away in the disaster, our memories and prayers always went along with them. The grief lingered long in our memories and broke our fragile hearts.

Standing in front of the tombs of lost families and friends, we could only stare at the cold tombstone, with tears dropping down. The smog of burning incense flew to the heaven, which could not take away our sad tears but brought wild gooses crowing to the cold west wind. We picked up a yellow blossom at hand, feeling the light fragrance creeping outside. We wrote words to pay prayers to our lost families and friends, but could not wait for their coming back.

The First Farewell went to my deep sorrow when we were parted by the boundary of life and death. Was it of great grief or sympathy? Even if all stars had changed their position on the heaven, my missing to all lost friends and families would not have been deserted. The farewell witnessed our laughter in the past and my tear at present.

Later I traveled thousands of miles away from my homeland to the United States. Who could understand the feeling of a young person in a foreign land? My nostalgia flowing like the mist along the river was hard to be dispelled by waving sleeves.

The Second Farewell was for my sorrow of parting lingering only with the company of the chill autumn and cold moon.

I would come back in 2009, after ending my one-year exchange. Upon departure, we stared at the eyes of each other and shook hands. Standing in this scenario, I sighed that farewell for leaving brought such a great grief to us. In the whistling wind, we felt greater sentimental emotions.

手相执。眼前情景，当值一声叹：黯然伤神者，惟别而已矣，此地此时泰风猎猎，倍增其愁矣。

三别，难得新交成挚友，无计短聚终归散，岂能无憾？

然思及年光有限，料其难禁抛掷流散；且故园殷切相望，断壁参差待整，心为之振。速速意决绝，即即归家去。誓要立于苍天厚土之间，手执利镰长镐之器，破荆斩棘，重整故园。别此不当叹，故土方为根。放船千里，千古文人梦；远游千山，不尽士子愁。今已愁罢，明尚可追。吾唯愿，归蜀地。复愿，锦江千里，天府万顷，此后无别无离恨，无分无思愁。唯有天地世人长相守。

幸而天公不造绝地，造物不生死息。遂早有，蜀地多沃野，蜀人为乐民。沉吟间抚昔，仰首后望今：庭中，桑叶桃枝沃若生；屋内，浅笑和语日日密。更有举国相倾来助，万人合力来援，物力齐聚，思心合一，幽幽别恨，已去大半。蓬勃心志，暖如青阳之谷风，流连此间；盛如朱明之赤日，照临四方。别后有重聚，劫后生新息，清心得道，多难兴邦，人间至理矣。

The third farewell was for that regrettable parting with my new friends.

Since youth was limited, and the reconstruction of my hometown called me back, I made a determination to come back and spare no effort to rebuild my hometown. Since my root remained in my hometown, it was unnecessary to sigh for leaving. Over the past thousands of years, men of literature dreamed to travel thousand miles away, but those distant mountains and rivers couldn't separate them from the nostalgia of those homesick travelers. Now it was time to pay farewell to the sadness of parting, and to pick up our enthusiasm to pursue a bright future. I was looking forward to coming back to Sichuan. I wished that life here would be more peaceful with less sad farewells to or separation from our loved ones. Wish a forever company with them.

The Heaven never seals off all the exits, and all things on the earth come and go naturally from generation to generation. Since the ancient time, Sichuan has enjoyed abundant lands and optimistic residents. Nowadays, in the yard, mulberry trees wear full green leaves and peach trees wear full fruits. In the house, there are always laughs and smiles. United as one, people from all walks of life in our country brought assistance and goods to help us rebuild hometown, so that we almost forgot the grief and sadness brought by the disaster. Those undoubtedly brought a vigorous energy to us as warm as the gentle wind and the warm sunshine. Since then, we have had a reunion after being parted and a rebirth from the disaster. A simple philosophy of the world is that a pure heart makes a just cause, and much distress regenerates a nation.

西华大学

Xihua University

# 感恩有你

## Thanks for Having You

陈玲／西华大学　纽约州立大学布法罗分校

Chen Ling / Xihua University　SUNY at Buffalo

一天下午，电脑右下角突然弹出了一个提醒：你有一封来自琳纳特的邮件。我急忙点开，邮件来自一位美国的老太太，她仍旧亲切地问候我："玲，希望你一切顺利。"时间倒带，2008年的经历清晰再现。

2008年的大学暑假跟往常一样——兼职，泡在图书馆，仿佛大学生活就是如此，唯一不同的是，中途穿插着几轮特殊面试——我们这群孩子幸运故事的开始。几轮面试过后，学校老师通知我们可以去美国念书了。

对于一个农村孩子来说，去美国念书简直就是不可能发生的事，但这一切就这么简简单单又轰轰烈烈地开始了……

In one afternoon, a piece of news suddenly popped up on the right corner of my computer screen. It read, "You have an e-mail from Lynnette." I harshly clicked it, and found it from an old American lady. She kindly said as usual, "Hope you doing well, Ling." This immediately brought me back to those days in the US, and the special experience in 2008 clearly emerged in front of my eyes.

I spent my summer vacation of 2008 as usual, taking part-time jobs and sitting in the library, and this seemed to be what university life should be. But the only difference was that there were several rounds of special interviews in that summer vacation—the beginning of our group of lucky kids. After several rounds of the interviews, teachers of the school informed us that it was ready for us to go to the United States for further study.

As for a child from a rural family, it seemed

## 初识美国

就这样，我和同学们来到了美国。这里有只能在电视和杂志上看到的白宫、帝国大厦和自由女神像，林肯纪念堂和华盛顿纪念碑前总是有人驻足，五角大楼比想象中更威严肃穆……

本来只存在于概念中的东西突然呈现在眼前，不再是画面、图片、文字，而是实实在在地呈现在眼前的实体。此刻我终于理解什么叫"百闻不如一见"，也终于明白为什么不但要"读万卷书"，更要"行万里路"。

短暂游览之后，我和其他 16 位同学一起来到了纽约州立大学布法罗州立学院。布法罗的天空很蓝，像梭罗笔下瓦尔登湖那样蓝。和煦的微风吹在脸上，亲切得让人快要忘记这是在一个陌生的国度。

初到异国他乡的兴奋与激动完全战胜了行李的笨重、旅途的疲惫和离家的伤别。我就像一个刚出生的孩子，怀揣着对一切的好奇，开始了这段为期一年的美国留学之旅。

美国学生太热情了，记得我们刚刚到达宿舍大楼时，国际学生宿舍的管理员们就给我们准备了当地有名的布法罗鸡翅。听着他们一口纯正流利

impossible to go to the United States for study, but this journey began in a simple but exciting way.

### First Touch to the United States

My classmates and I came to the USA. There was the White House, the Empire State Building and the Statue of Liberty that could only be seen on the TV or magazine. People always stopped in their tracks in front of the Lincoln memorial and the Washington Monument. The Pentagon was more solemn than our imagination.

All those things that originally existed in my mind were actually present in front of my eyes. They were not images, pictures, words, but entities in front of us. At that moment, I suddenly got the sense of "Seeing is believing," and understood the reason why "one needs to not only read 10,000 books, but also travel 10,000 miles to know the world around us."

After our short travel there, the rest of the 16 classmates and I went to SUNY-Buffalo. The sky in the Buffalo was as blue as the Walden Lake depicted by Thoreau. When the gentle wind blew on my face, it was so kind that I seemed to forget I was living in an overseas land.

Because it was the first time that we stood on the foreign land, we felt too excited to notice the heavy luggage, the tiring journey and the painful departure with our families. I, like a newborn child curious about everything, started a one-year trip to study in the United States.

American students were of great hospitality. I can remember that when we arrived in the dormitory building, the dorm supervisors prepared for us the Buffalo chicken wings, a

的英语，我觉得自己似乎有点口吃。躺在床上，一整天的疲惫与不适完全消失，满心期待着未来一年丰富多彩的生活：会发生什么样的故事？会遇到什么样的人？心里一边祈祷着明天快点到来吧，一边又祈祷时间能过得慢些，再慢些。我希望自己在美国度过的每一分、每一秒都有意义。这就是一个少女全部的小心思。

## 渐入佳境的学习生活

8月25日，布法罗州立学院正式开学，略显紧张的我见到了陌生的老师和同学。正式上课时，老师的专业英语一度让我摸不着头脑，完全进入无字幕美剧节奏，冲击力还是蛮大的。毕竟我们是去学习的，而且我学的是理工科，在开始的一段时间比较吃力。课后，在和老师交谈时，他鼓励我积极参与课堂讨论和发言。渐渐地，在老师和同学的帮助下，我对周围的一切都熟悉了起来。和大家一起做题、复习，一起去图书馆。他们会给我讲解不懂的单词，我也会教他们几句汉语。就这样，我们渐渐成了好朋友。

其实初到一个地方，环境和同学都是陌生的，大家需要一段时间去适应。在学业方面，我们上课要多做笔

special local delicacy. When I listen to their fluent English, I seemed to be a little bit stammered. Lying on the bed, I was looking forward to the abundant one-year life here in the days ahead and my tiredness of the whole day totally vanished. What kind of stories would happen? Whom would I meet? I expected the fast arrival of the next morning but hoped that the time here could be as slow as it could be. It was the thought of a young girl that each second and minute in the United States could be meaningful.

## Gradually Adapting to Learning in the United States

The new semester of SUNY-Buffalo formally began on 25th, August 2008. In class, I was totally confused and shocked when I heard the fluent English spoken by our teacher. It seemed that I were watching an American drama without any subtitles. It was difficult for a math and science major like me to catch the contents of lectures at the very beginning of my journey, let alone I had almost everything to learn in further study. After class, I exchanged my feelings with my teacher and he encouraged me to take an active part in class discussions and activities. Gradually, with the assistance of teachers and classmates, I was familiar with my surroundings. I got together with others to do exercises, review the course, and go to the library. American students would explain those difficult words to me, and I would teach them several sentences of Chinese. So we became friends.

Actually, when we firstly came to the new place, the surrounding and classmates were quite new and so strange that we all needed a period

记，下课多泡图书馆，生活方面主动参加各种活动、多交流。很多美国老师和同学也都了解我们这群来自中国的学生，给予我们很多帮助。

在所有的学习课程中，让我印象最深的是化学实验课。我和我的搭档总共完成了11个实验。由于配合默契，效率很高，每一次我们都能得到一个不错的分数。尽管后来我并没有从事相关专业的工作，而是投身于商业地产，但那段做实验的日子依然是我在美国学习期间的一段难忘经历。

除了化学课，我们还给学习中文的美国学生补习中文，因此艾丽莎和我成了很好的朋友。她喜欢周杰伦的歌，我便成了她的翻译；她经常开车带我去看美国电影，遇到不懂的单词时，她就翻译给我听。期末，在校长家里，校长给我们颁发了证书，并亲自送我们礼物作为纪念。我们也成为布法罗州立学院2009级校友，享受到如此高的待遇，我们心里十分感激。

美国的大学生不分年龄、国籍，都在一个班上课；学习上他们更看重知识的接受度，不太看重考试分数；在选择专业时更重视个人兴趣而非发展前途。这也是值得我们国内教育学习的地方。

of time to adapt ourselves to them. In our study, we needed to take more notes in class and more frequently go to library after class. In our daily life, we needed to actively take part in various activities and exchanges. A variety of American teachers and classmates had learned about us, so they gave us a great deal of understanding and help.

In all my courses, I was impressed most by the chemical experiment course, in which my partner and I finished 11 experiments in total. Due to our cooperation and high efficiency, we got a high score each time. Although I didn't engage in the relevant jobs, and instead in the commercial housing industry, those days of making experiments in the USA are still a piece of unforgettable memory of my journey to the United States.

At the same time, we 17 Chinese students also helped those American students who were learning Chinese to learn Chinese better, so Elisha and I became good friends. She was fond of songs of Jay or Zhou Jielun, a Chinese pop singer, so I translated the lyrics for her, and in turn, she became a translator of difficult English expressions to me. In the end of the semester, the president of the college granted the certificate to us at home and gave us gifts. We also became one of the Alumni of 2009. We were very grateful to this honor.

In the United States, students of different ages and nationalities take courses in the same class. In the process of learning, they highlight the adoption of knowledge, instead of scores. In choosing majors, they emphasize the personal interest, instead of development perspective. These are worthwhile for us to learn from.

## 我的美国爸爸妈妈

课堂生活是丰富多彩的，课余生活也是如此。

我们利用课余时间参加了学校的各种活动。如"亚洲之夜"，参观了尼亚加拉大瀑布，游览了华盛顿和加拿大的多伦多，生活不再枯燥乏味。

学校还给我们每个人安排了一个寄宿家庭。一对中年夫妇琳和约翰进入我们的生活，他们经常带我们去参加各种活动；邀请我们参加他们家里的每一个节日；当时正值美国总统选举，他们还带我们去给奥巴马投了选票；带我们一起到餐厅吃饭，到教堂听音乐，游览市中心。当他们对我说他们是我的美国爸爸妈妈时，我心里酸酸的，原来自己早已开始想家了。

琳和约翰生活上给予我们足够的关爱。万圣节，我们一起在家"装神弄鬼"，站在门口给前来索取糖果的小孩发巧克力。到了圣诞节，他们还特意提前为我们准备了精美的礼物，在圣诞节当晚给了我们一个大大的惊喜。那也是我收到的最为珍贵的礼物——琳送给我一本精美的自制相册，里面记录着我们一起生活的点点滴滴；约翰则为我准备了一个刻着自己名字的小雪花。约翰说，这样就可以让我在回到中国之后还能回想起布

### My American Mother and Father

Life is colorful either in class or after class.

I made most of my after-class time to take part in various school activities such as "Asia Night", visited Niagara Falls, and took a short journey to Washington and Toronto in Canada; therefore, my school life was not boring any more.

The school arranged a host family for us each. A middle-aged couple of Lynnette and John came into our life. They always took us to join in several activities, invited us to take part in their family festivals, to restaurants for supper, to churches for listening to the music, and to the downtown for fun. In the presidential election, they even took us to vote for Obama. When they told us that they were our American father and mother, I was a little sad, since I began to miss my home.

Lynnette and John tried their best to take care of us. On Halloween, we played costumes, dressed in strange clothes and gave chocolate to kids who came to ask for candies in the doorway. On Christmas, they prepared delicate gifts for us, and gave us a big surprise on the Christmas Eve. These gifts were the most valuable ones for me— Lynnette gave me a delicate self-made album that

法罗这个小镇和他们这群可爱的人。

临走的那天，琳和约翰到寝室为我送行，泪水从我眼中滑落。琳说我是世界上最好的女儿，我让她觉得她是世界上最好的美国妈妈。因为美好的感情，我们舍不得离别；因为纯真的友谊，我们更加懂得珍惜。离别是为了再次相见，我会记住这句话的。如今我怀孕了，自己的孩子即将出生，更深刻地领悟到为人母的心情，我更感念当初琳和约翰在那段异国他乡的日子里，他们代替爸爸妈妈给予我的温暖和关爱。

回到国内毕业后我参加了工作，和经历了数年爱情长跑的一位异国男友结婚，如今一个新生命即将降临，一切都按部就班进行着。在美国的留学经历和如今简单而幸福的平淡生活也更让我懂得珍惜和感恩。

时间很短，故事很长，感谢为整个项目付出的每一个人，正是有了你们的付出才有了"CSC-SUNY 150奖学金项目"，我们一定不忘初心，感恩前行！

had recorded all stories about our living together, and John gave me a small snowflake with his name engraved on it. John said that even after I came back to China, those presents might remind me of the small town of Buffalo and this group of lovely people.

Before I left for China, Lynnette and John came to my dormitory to say goodbye to me. I could not help dropping my tears. Lynnette said that I was the best daughter in this world. For me, she was the best American mother. We were reluctant to leave, due to our bosom relationship. We learned more about how to cherish each other, due to our pure friendship. I will keep in mind the saying that being apart is aimed to meet again. Nowadays, I am pregnant and will have my maternity leave. I am going to have my own baby, so after I deeply perceive the sense of being a mother, I miss Lynnette and John more. In those days of overseas land, they acted as our father and mother to give us warmth and cares.

After I graduated and came back to China, I started to work. I got married with my foreign boyfriend, after we fell in love with each other for a long time. Now, a new life is to be born. All is as usual. My journey to the United State for further study and my present simple and happy life make me more understand thankfulness and cherishing.

It is impossible to pour out the whole story within such short time. However, I would appreciate each and everyone who has made contribution to this program. It was his or her efforts that made the CSC-SUNY 150 Program come true. We need to keep our original intention to go further with thanks.

# 匆匆已十年，责任肩上挑

## More Responsibilities with the Ten Years Passing by

王隆攀 / 西华大学　纽约州立大学布法罗分校

Wang Longpan / Xihua University　SUNY at Buffalo

我叫王隆攀，来自汶川县耿达镇，2010 年 7 月毕业于西华大学，现工作于阿坝州，是一名普通的公务员。

"5·12"汶川特大地震已经过去十年了，我也越过弱冠，进入人生的而立阶段——从一名 21 岁的青涩大学生成长为 31 岁的成熟青年，有了自己的家庭，拥有一份稳定的工作。十年前的那段时光仿佛离我很遥远，但有时又仿佛近在眼前。

### 灰色记忆中的一束光

对于 2008 年的记忆，我的脑海中首先浮现的就是那一张张失去亲人后悲伤无助的脸庞。那场灾难让我真

My name is Wang Longpan, from Gengda Town, Wenchuan County of Sichuan Province, graduated from Xihua University in July 2010. Now I am an average administrative staff, working in Aba Autonomous Prefecture.

The Wenchuan Earthquake has passed for one decade, and I have grown form a 21-year-old young university student into a 31-year-old mature young man with my own family and a stable job. Time of 10 years ago seems to be far away from me, but sometimes, it lingers on in front of my eyes.

### A Beam of Light Shooting into My Gray Memory

When I recall the year of 2008, several faces of hopelessness and grief emerge in my mind at the outset. That catastrophe makes me realize that we humans are tiny and powerless in front

正感受到了在大自然的力量面前，人类是如此的渺小。灾难发生以后，社会各界捐资捐物、出人出力，共同帮助灾难中的人们，又让我看到了团结与爱的无限力量。

那一年，本应只有灰色的记忆和血色的悲哀，但是偏偏有一束光照进了我的生活。当我接到"CSC-SUNY 150 奖学金项目"入围电话通知的那一刻，真是万分欣喜，对于连省内的城市都还没去过几个的我来说，留学是一个想都不敢想的奢望。

当父母听到这个消息时，他们非常高兴我能有这样一个机会去见识一些新的东西。但他们有支持，也有反对。在他们的观念里，没有发达与否之分，只是觉得遥远就充满了不安全与未知，但最终还是一致同意支持我。

## 并不轻松的大学生活

第一次办签证，第一次坐飞机，第一次出国，第一次见到大海，第一次身临电影大片里的著名场景——时代广场……不敢相信有太多梦幻般的事情真的一件接一件发生在自己身上。

凡事都有两面性，梦终究还是被紧跟着的语言、饮食、文化等各方面的冲击和压力拉回现实。我对美国的了解基本是通过电影获得的，在电影

the mighty power of nature. After the disaster hit the region, people from all walks of life donated goods and strength to help residents in the earthquake-stricken region. Seeing this, I realized the fact that unity and love boast infinite power.

There ought to be only gray memory and bloody grief in that year, but there was a beam of light that shot into my life. When I received the phone call to inform me of being shortlisted by the CSC-SUNY 150 Program, I was really excited. It was a luxury dream for me, since I hadn't even left for other cities in our province.

Naturally, my parents were delighted to know that I took an opportunity to broaden my horizons, when they heard about the news. However, they still had some worries to frown up my decision, though they supported me. In their mindset, they only believed that there was danger and uncertainty in a remote place, irrelevant to development. Finally, they all supported me.

## The Uneasy University Life Abroad

There were several "first times" of applying for visa, taking an airplane, going abroad, seeing the ocean and visiting the Times Square that was a famous scene in several high box-office movies. I could not believe so many dreamy events having happened upon me one after another.

Every coin has its two sides. The dream was pulled back to my reality, due to various impact and pressure followed by the language, diet, and culture. I had gained the impression of the United States, basically from movies. In the movies, life in the university of the USA was easy, with small number of courses to take. However, in fact, there was a large number of courses and heavy

里，美国的大学生活比较轻松，没有那么多的课程。但事实是，美国的大学课程很多，学习任务也比较重，再加上我们语言、文化的差异，大学学习并没有想象中那么轻松。

布法罗学院根据我们的情况，设置了相应的课程和项目来帮助我们尽快适应这里的学习和生活环境。开学不久，学校就组织大学新生到农庄露营。我们走进深山，燃起篝火，烤上棉花糖，品尝地道的比萨。不同肤色、来自不同国家的同学围坐在一起，有说有笑，闲扯八卦。肤色、种族、语言、文化的不同阻挡不了喜爱交流的青春本性。

美国大学课堂实行小班制，大学以学生自己选课为主，一个课堂的学生，有各种肤色、各种文化背景，甚至年龄段也不一样，有的课堂上甚至有六七十岁的学生，也有很多在职人员。

进入正式学习阶段后，首先是选课。不同的课程有不同的学分、不同的导师，课程设置也十分灵活，甚至可以选择舞蹈、烹饪、瑜伽等课程，且大多数课程都十分注重培养学生的团队精神、合作意识和创新能力。通常，老师会把学生分成不同的组，各个组确定一个题目，最后的成绩需要全体组员合作完成后才能获得。课余，

workload in the American universities. Due to the difference among our languages and cultures, learning in the university was more difficult than my previous imagination.

Buffalo State College prepared corresponding courses and projects to help us quickly adapt to the environment of learning and living there, on the basis of our individual situation. Not long after the new semester began, the school organized freshmen to go camping on the farm. We walked into the mountain, lit bonfires, roasted marshmallows and tasted pizza. Classmates of different colors and from different countries sat around, laughing and chatting. The difference among the color, race, language and culture could not pale the essence of youth of enjoying exchanges.

In American universities, students were encouraged to select their own courses. Each class was designed for a small group of students who had different skin colors, cultural backgrounds, and even ages. In some classes, there were even students in their sixties or seventies and those who had formal jobs already.

When the formal learning started, I needed to select courses first. Different courses had various credits and supervisors, with flexible course designs. You could even choose courses such as dancing, cooking, Yoga, etc. Several courses highlighted students' team spirit, such as cooperative awareness and innovation ability. Usually, teachers divided us into different groups and gave each group a topic. The final score would be achieved through the cooperation of all members of the group. After class, the school would organize us to take part in several activities, such as outdoor barbecue and visits

学校还会组织我们参加野外烧烤聚会、参观艺术馆展览等活动。周末，寄宿家庭经常会邀请我们去家中小聚，偶尔还会一起去看场美式足球、保龄球比赛。

渐渐地，我也适应了当地的学习和生活。这次经历让我感受到，在出国前应该做好充分的准备，特别是文化、语言的准备。出国以后应该尽量去结识美国本土的学生朋友，了解当地学生的生活、学习方式，参加更多的社区活动，充分了解当地的文化，尽量融入当地的生活。不要因为学校华人多，就整天待在自己的华人小圈子里，只有融入美国的环境，才能更快地适应和成长。要知道中美两国的学生其实都有各自的优势。

## 我眼里美国人的优点

美国学生除了学习，也十分注重生活。他们周末大多会去郊游，或者参加一些社区活动，以此来丰富自己的生活，注重在社会实践中不断提高自己，以便将来走出校门更好地适应社会。在活动中，他们注重培养自己的独立思考能力和语言表达能力。

留学生活非常充实，但也留下了一些遗憾。我在美国期间觉得想学又没能真正学会的是他们思维的方式。

to art exhibitions, etc. In the weekend, our host family would invite us to take a gathering at home and watch American football or bowling games.

Gradually, I adapted to the life and learning there. This experience has made me realize that we need to make sufficient preparations before we go abroad, in particular for language and culture. After stepping into the overseas land, we need to get along with native students of the United States, learn about the authentic ways of living and learning of native students, participate in more community activities, experience local culture, and try to engage in the local life. We should not only stay in the small circle of Chinese students, due to a large number of Chinese living there. Only when we get involved into the American circumstance, can we quickly adapt to the circumstance and achieve growth. Actually, students in both China and the United States boast their own advantages.

### Americans' Strongpoint in My Eyes

Besides learning, American students also attach importance to life. In the weekend, they would go for a trip or take part in some community activities, in order to enrich their lives. They highlight the social practice to improve themselves, in order to better serve the society after graduation. In several activities, they would emphasize the ability of independent thinking and language expression even from their childhood.

Although my days of my exchange in the United States were rich and abundant, there were still some regrets. During my days in the

美国学生有十分独立的思考能力，不是人云亦云，有愿意主动接受别人批评的态度，也有评判或者是辨别老师教学方式、教学内容的意识，敢于挑战老师的权威，有主动锻炼、培养思考和辨别是非的能力。

## 服务家乡

这段经历也给我带来了观念上的变化，我开始有了对社会的整体思考。我意识到自己不应该只是在自己的小圈子生活，还要抽出时间来尽一些社会责任。

2010年毕业后，我立志回乡服务，报名参加了"大学生志愿服务西部计划"项目，被分配到九寨沟县开始了为期两年的志愿服务工作。在我最初的认识中，回到家乡阿坝州当一名公务员，对个人、对家庭、对社会的服务来说都是最直接、最有效的途径。其间，最让人难忘的是九寨沟县方舟孤儿院孩子们童真的笑脸，以及大山上留守老阿妈煮的一碗清汤面。

2012年志愿服务期满后，我参加了选调生考试，被分派到阿坝州马尔康市的一个乡政府工作，亲眼见证了这些年国家教育、医疗、养老等惠民政策在基层的落地，真切地看到了农牧民群众脸上洋溢出的幸福感和获

USA, what I desired to learn but failed was the way of their thinking. American students were characterized with their ability of independent thinking and critical sense. They had a good attitude to actively accept others' critics and an awareness to judge the teaching methods and teaching content of teachers. They dared to challenge the authority of teachers and were willing to train and foster their ability of critical thinking.

### Serving My Hometown

This experience brought to me the change of my mindset. I began to have a holistic consideration for our society. I realized that I should not live only in our small world, but I needed to spare some time to assume my social responsibility.

After my graduation in 2010, I was determined to come back to my village and serve my hometown, so I applied for the "University Graduates Voluntary Service for the West" project, and I was assigned to Jiuzhaigou County for 2-year voluntary service. To myself, my family and my social service, it was the best and most effective way for me to come back to Aba Autonomous Prefecture as a civil servant. During

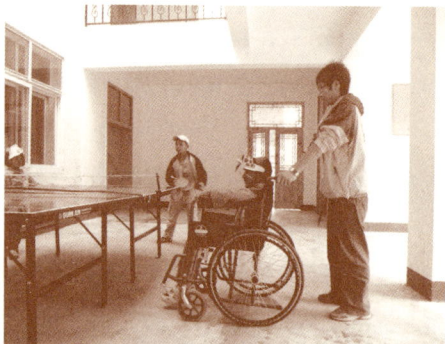

得感。

2015 年，我被选派到州级机关工作至今。目前我还处于学习上升期，遇到了很多好的领导和导师，虽然工作很平凡，但我会继续努力，希望取得一些突破，让自己成长起来。

如果没有这趟美国之旅，我想自己现在应该不会在这里，而是会选择去大城市工作，去追求财富以及舒适的生活环境。"CSC-SUNY 150 奖学金项目"给予我帮助，我也应当承担起社会责任。

弹指一挥间，匆匆已十年。如今，我已是两个宝贝的爸爸了。这趟美国之旅，让我认识到人类其实是社会性的群体，我们的个体成长也是社会的一部分，我们是互相联结不可分的。个人成长以后有义务去回报社会，不能仅仅为了自己生活的舒适。一位老师曾嘱咐我们："既然接受了这次宝贵的机会，那么就要勇于承担这份责任。"

my 2 years of voluntary service, what made me unforgettable was smiles on the faces of kids in Fangzhou Orphanage of Jiuzhaigou County and a bowl of simple noodles cooked by an old left-behind mother.

After I completed my voluntary service in 2012, I took part in the civil servant examination and was assigned to working in a grass-root government of Maerkang City, Aba Autonomous Prefecture. I witnessed the implementation of favorable polices of education, health care and endowment, etc. in the grass-root rural areas by our country and felt the sense of happiness and achievement of farmers and herdsmen.

Since 2015, I have worked in the government of our prefecture. At present, I am still in the process of learning and in the line of promotion, and have met several good leaders and supervisors. Although work is busy, I will continue to work hard to make some breakthrough, so as to be grown up.

Without my journey to the United States, I believe that I would not stay here and might have gone to metropolis to pursue wealth and a comfortable living environment. Since the CSC-SUNY 150 Program granted me much assistance, I should shoulder the social responsibility so as to live up to this fortune.

How time flies and ten years have passed by! Nowadays, I am a father of two babies. This journey to the United State has made me realize that humans are a social group and our growth is a part of the society, and no man is an island. At the same time, when we are grown up, we have the obligation to serve the society, instead of only pursuing comfortable and material life.

In my days of working in the grass-root

在基层工作的这些日子，我更加懂得群众生活的难处和艰辛、期盼和愿望，因此也更加坚定了我服务家乡人民的理想和信念，争取在平凡的岗位上书写一段不平凡的人生。

government, I have deeply touched the difficulties and hardships, as well as wishes and expectations of poverty-stricken people. Therefore, I am determined to serve people in my hometown and try my best to lead a glorious life in my average working position.

西南交通
大学

Southwest Jiaotong University

# 美国归来这十年

## The Ten Years after Returning from the United States

蒋沥辉 / 西南交通大学　纽约州立大学德里学院

Jiang Lihui / Southwest Jiaotong University　SUNY at Delhi

2008 年 5 月，四川经历了一场可怕的地震。全国各地都团结起来支援四川地区，帮助四川地区重建。远在大洋彼岸的美国纽约州立大学 22 个分校也为 150 名四川地震重灾区的大学生提供了为期一年的免费学习机会。这个"CSC-SUNY 150 奖学金项目"特别注重培养这些灾区青年的领导能力，帮助他们回国后能够迅速返回地震灾区，服务当地民众，为受灾地区的经济发展做出贡献。我当时就读于西南交通大学，有幸成了这个项目的一员。从得知这个消息到最后成行，一共只有一个多月的时间。

In May 2008, Sichuan met a terrible earthquake. All parts of the country were united to support Sichuan and helped it to be rebuilt. Twenty-two branches of State University of New York in the United States also provided a one-year free learning opportunity for 150 college students in the earthquake-stricken areas of Sichuan Province, and paid special attention to cultivating the leadership of young people in these areas so that they could serve the local people and make outstanding contributions to the economic development of those earthquake-stricken areas quickly after returning home. I was studying at Southwest Jiaotong University and had the honor to be a member of this program. We started our trip only a little more than one month after we got to know this program.

## 克服不适应，这是我成长的第一步

第一次出国，心里有恐慌也有期待，更多的是感恩。刚刚到美国的时候，有一些不适应，在饮食、语言和课堂学习上，都遇到了很多困难。我记得那时候最害怕上的是历史课，历史老师语速很快，加上我本来历史科目薄弱，上课听不懂，很自卑，不能跟同学们很好地交流，上课也不能很好地参与课堂讨论。但是幸运的是，学校有一个学习中心，如果我们在学习中遇到问题和困难，都可以到学习中心去寻求老师的帮助。那时候下课，我就常常去学习中心，那里的老师特别细心地帮助我们，随着时间的推移，我慢慢地适应了全英语的课堂，而且还可以和同学们一起参与课堂讨论了，我感到特别开心。

日子就这样慢慢地以全新的方式在我的面前展开。每一天我都能学到许多新的东西，感受着美中教育理念的巨大不同。课堂上，我们自由地与老师交流自己的想法和观点，似乎没有哪个答案是错误的，所以我不担心自己会说错或者做错。在小说鉴赏课上，这种感觉尤其明显。小说鉴赏课大概是这样的：每两天我们会读一篇小说，或长或短，然后写一篇读后感，

## Overcoming Inadaptation, the First Step in My Growth

It was my first time to go abroad, but there was more gratitude than panic and expectation in my heart. When I first arrived in the United States, there was some inadaptation. I had problems with the diet, language and study style there. I remember what I was most afraid of at that time was history lesson. The history teacher spoke very fast. In addition, I was weak at history in China, and this caused more difficulties when I first arrived in the United States. I couldn't understand and communicate well with my classmates nor know how to express my ideas in class discussions, so I felt inferior to others. But fortunately, there was a learning center. If we encountered problems and difficulties in learning, we could go to the learning center to seek for help from teachers. At that time, I often went to the learning center after class. The teachers there helped us very carefully. As time passed by, I slowly adapted to the English-only class, and was able to participate in class discussions with my classmates. I felt very happy.

Time passed by with all brand new things. I was able to learn a lot of new stuff and feel the differences of American educational ideas. We could share our ideas and opinions with our teachers freely. It seemed that no answer was wrong, so I was not worried about saying or doing wrong things. In my novel class, this feeling was particularly strong. Novel appreciation class was probably like this—we would read a novel, long or short, in less than two days, and then hand in a reflection to the teacher. The teacher read it carefully and wrote comments. And we could discuss in the next class about the

老师认真阅读后写下评语；下一节课全班讨论，不管是对于作者、小说里的人物，还是由小说想到的关于自己的人和事，都可以交流。我们听到的永远是老师的赞美和鼓励。尽管每位老师上课的方式不同，但是在老师的鼓励下学习起来却不会特别吃力。除了知识，我们还在交流中学到其他同学的思维方式和他们的价值观。如果用几个词来概括美国的学习生活，我认为是"自主思考""独立创新""交流合作"。

## 行万里路，珍惜这路上的每个人

在美国的一年，我们去了不少地方，如洛杉矶、旧金山等。那些城市特别可爱，像动画片里的房子一样，五颜六色的字母装扮着不一样的店面。我们也去了位于波士顿的哈佛大学和麻省理工学院等世界顶尖大学。因为没有学生卡，我们没有走进哈佛大学的图书馆，但是那严谨的学术氛围足以让我们顶礼膜拜。尽管我们去的时候正值寒假，大雪覆盖了整个校园，但那些刻苦学习的学子们依然在图书馆和教室间穿梭，看着这一切，我的心里充满了敬畏。

除了自然风景，人生路上的风景也因为有了那些珍贵的人而显得更加

author, the characters in the novel or the people and things that came to our minds when reading. There were always praises and encouragements from the teacher. I felt that this was the significant feature of American education. Each teacher taught in different ways, but because of the encouragements from teachers it was not particularly hard to learn. Besides knowledge, we could learn other students' way of thinking and their values towards things and life. As for study in the United States, I think it is characterized by independent thinking, innovation, communication and cooperation.

### Travelling Thousands of Miles, Cherishing Everyone on This Road

We went to many places during the year in the United States, such as Los Angeles, San Francisco in California. They were really beautiful, and the weather was very good. There were many kinds of plants, ranging from the cold belt to the tropical belt. The city was particularly lovely. Stores were decorated by colorful letters, just like the houses in animations. We also went to Harvard University and MIT in Boston—the world's top universities. They were students' dreams. Without the student card we couldn't go into Harvard's library, but the rigorous academic atmosphere was rich enough for us to admire. Although it was in winter vacation when we visited and the whole campus was covered by snow, I was filled with awe when I saw the diligent students shuttling between the library and classrooms.

In addition to the scenery I saw, the scenery in my life was even more beautiful because of those valuable people I have met. The past

美丽。他们像一粒粒珍珠，在我生命的河流里闪闪发光。在学习中心，我遇到了两个特别好的朋友，虽然从美国回来已经十年了，我和他们一直还有邮件往来。一位是前台阿姨凯西，另一位是退休后在学习中心学习数学的伯尼叔叔。

每次我去学习中心，凯西都会很热情地问我"今天开心吗"，是不是又弄懂了很多问题。久而久之，我在生活中如果有什么问题也会和她分享，她也会给我讲她的孩子们、她生活里有趣的事情，以及她遇到的有趣的学生。伯尼以前在华尔街做咨询顾问，出于对数学的热爱，他退休之后来到德里分校钻研数学。我们常常在学习中心相遇，成了很好的朋友。伯尼教我做美国美食，还送给我好多圣诞礼物。

2009 年 5 月，我们离开前，我满脸泪水地去找伯尼。他说："亲爱的，希望你回去后能够让大家都看到一个积极乐观的你、一个不一样的你。"他的话，给了我面对未来生活的力量。在我们去机场的路上，伯尼叔叔站在路边举着一块牌子向我招手。牌子上面写着"一路平安！我们等你回来！"，那一刻，我的眼泪夺眶而出。

回国后，伯尼叔叔给我寄来过一

experiences were like pearls sparkling in the river of my life. Besides some of my classmates, I made many good friends those days. In the learning center, I met two very good friends, whom I have been keeping in touch with through e-mail in the 10 years after we came back from the United States. One was Aunt Cathy at the reception desk, and the other was Uncle Bernie, who studied mathematics in the learning center after retirement.

Every time I went to the learning center, Cathy was very enthusiastic and asked me if I was happy today and whether I had worked out problems. I shared with her the problems in my life over time. She also told me about her children, the interesting things in her life and the interesting students she met. Bernie used to work as a consultant in Wall Street. Due to his enthusiasm for mathematics he went to Delhi to specialize in mathematics after he retired. We often met in the learning center and became good friends. Bernie would share with me how to cook American food and bring me many gifts at Christmas.

In May 2009, as we were leaving SUNY-Delhi, I went to Bernie with tears. He said, "I hope you will let others see a positive, optimistic and different you when you go back." On our way to the airport, Uncle Bernie stood by the roadside,

张照片，照片上他家院子里的花儿开了。伯尼说，不开心的时候，就看看这些花儿，要像它们一样明媚！

## 带着回忆，继续前行

回国后，我们继续在大学学习和生活，但是在美国学习的记忆常常会突然从我的脑海里蹦出来。那一年特别的际遇、那一年相识的人们，都是我记忆中最美好的部分。

大学毕业之后我当了一名高中英语老师，在家乡的一所高中工作。转眼已经毕业 7 年了，时光荏苒，很多事情都成为记忆，但是这些记忆催促着我继续进步、继续努力。我们"CSC-SUNY 150 奖学金项目"的每一个成员都从心里带着一份感恩，谢谢曾经在灾难之后帮助我们的所有人，谢谢纽约州立大学给我们提供的宝贵的学习机会，给我们的生命带来了不一样的经历。我也把这份感恩和感动化作动力，在工作中认真踏实，用心帮助每一位学生，让他们从我的言语和行动中感受到温暖和力量。

如今，到了而立之年的我们，大都有了自己的家庭，我也有了自己的另一半，也有了孩子。岁月给了我很多，也让我成长了很多。在今后的日子里，我们要好好工作，也要好好生

holding a sign which said, "Safe journey! We are here waiting for you back!" At that moment, tears could not help coming down.

After returning home, Uncle Bernie sent me a picture of flowers blooming in his yard. Bernie said that if I were unhappy, just have a look at those flowers and be as bright as them.

### Moving on with Memories

We continued our study and life in universities. But memories of the people we met and things we experienced that year in the United States often pop out of our minds and became the best part of our memories.

After graduating from college, I have become a high school English teacher and work in a high school in my hometown. It has been seven years since graduation, and many things have just became memories, but these memories urge us to keep on improving and working hard. Every member of the CSC-SUNY 150 Program has always been grateful; grateful to all the people who helped us after the earthquake disaster, grateful to the valuable learning environment and time provided by State University of New York, which have brought different experiences to our lives. I have transformed our gratitude and affection into impetus to work earnestly, to help every student whole heartedly, and let them feel warmth and strength from our words and actions.

Now most of us are in our mid-ages and have our own families. I'm also married and have a child. Time has given me a lot and made me grow up a lot. In the future, we should work hard and live a good life. We should set a good example for students and children. We should

活，为学生、为孩子做一个好榜样，让他们从我们身上看到生活的积极态度，看到人间的爱。生命是一段旅程，需要我们每个人用心体会，也需要我们的学生以自己的角度去丈量。希望我们每个人都坚守内心的准则，用爱宽容地对待身边的所有人和事，也愿我们每个人都能被生活温柔以待。

在"CSC-SUNY 150 奖学金项目"十周年之际，感恩所有帮助过我们的人，愿中美人民的友谊长存，愿我们每一位学子能在生活中努力前行。

also tell them about our past at the right time, so that they can see the positive attitude of life from us, see the true, the good and the beautiful from the people who helped us, and see people's love in the world. Life is a journey. It needs every one of us to experience it carefully. It also needs our students and children to measure it from their own point of view. We hope that each of us will stick to our inner criteria and treat everyone and everything around us with love, forgiveness and tolerance. I also hope that each of us can be treated gently by life.

On the tenth anniversary of the CSC-SUNY 150 Program, I am grateful to all those who have helped us. I wish the friendship between the Chinese and American people will last forever and every student will try his or her best to move forward in their future life.

# 十年之后，在平凡的生活里，笑出勃勃生机

## Laughing out Vigorously in My Plain Life 10 Years Later

吴丹 / 西南交通大学　纽约州立大学普拉茨堡学院

Wu Dan / Southwest Jiaotong University　SUNY at Plattsburgh

> 希望在平平淡淡的生活中，收获一个纯良的自己、诚恳的自己、磊落的自己、热忱的自己。
>
> ——题记
>
> I hope that I can end up finding a kind, earnest, bright and passionate self in my plain life.
>
> —Preface

01

"妈，我要去美国了。"

"啥子啊？"

"学校有个去美国的留学项目，我被选上了。"

"我不信，你莫豁我！"

2008 年 7 月的一个下午，当老师告诉我，我通过了"CSC-SUNY 150 奖学金项目"选拔，即将去美国读书一年时，我和我妈的反应是一样的："你莫豁我！"

01

"Mom, I'm going to America."

"What?"

"There is a study abroad program in the United States, and I was selected."

"I don't believe it. Don't fool me!"

One afternoon in July 2008, when my teacher told me that I had passed the SUNY-CSC 150 Program selection and was going to study in the United States for a year, my mother and I responded the same way, "You don't fool me!"

In order to persuade my parents that this was true, and to convince myself that this "out

为了说服我爸妈这是真的，也为了让自己相信这件"做梦都没想过"的事，我把学校所有的通知、申请流程、留学项目的前因后果仔细给我爸妈讲了一下午，生怕遗漏一处细节，生怕是我理解错了，生怕这只是我一厢情愿的幻想。

整个下午，我妈脸上的每个毛孔都好像在经历一场跌宕起伏的海浪，先从震惊变成怀疑，然后从相信变成惊喜，最后从开心变成了担忧。地震带来的精神冲击还在，那时候的每一次分别，似乎一不小心都会成为永别。

过了很久，我妈挤出一句话："美国好远哦，一年好久哦！"

弟弟在旁边听得云里雾里，一脸好奇："姐，你真的要去美国呀？我们这里的白天，那里是不是晚上？"

我爸倒是挺淡定："这是好事，去！"

02

离开家的那天，我背着书包走在前面，爸妈拉着行李箱跟在后面。我越走越快，他们却越走越慢。

快上车时我回头，发现他们落了一大截。见我回头，他们赶紧跟上来，我妈眼睛红红的："出去小心一点，注意安全，到了马上打电话。"

我笑着接过行李："好的，知

of imagination" thing was true, I carefully told my parents the whole process including the notice from school, application procedures, and the study abroad program the entire afternoon, fearing that I might miss any detail, and making sure that it was not a misunderstanding or just an illusion.

In the entire afternoon, the expression on my mother's face was like an unrestful sea, changing from shock to doubt, then from trust to pleasant surprise, and finally from joy to worry. The effect of earthquake was still in her mind. At that time, every parting was likely to become a farewell forever.

After a long time, my mother squeezed out a sentence, "America is too far away, and one year is quite a long time."

Listening to her, my younger brother got confused, "Sister, are you really going to go to the United States?" "Is our daytime their night?"

My dad was quite calm, "This is a good thing. Take the chance!"

02

On the day I left home, I was walking ahead of my parents with my schoolbag on the back. My parents pulled the luggage and followed.

I walked faster and faster, and they went slower and slower.

When I was about to get on the bus, I turned

道啦。"

当时的我，心里满是对异国他乡的憧憬，想着马上要出国看世界了，再也没有父母在耳边唠叨了，终于自由了，开心着呢。一路从老家到成都，从成都到北京转机，心里都激动得不行。

可是当飞机即将从北京飞往纽约时，我心里突然充斥着一种非常复杂的感情。既希望快一点到美国，又希望飞得慢一点再慢一点。既向往新鲜的生活，又担心遇到困难爸妈不在怎么办？既觉得没人管了自由了，又害怕夜深人静想妈妈。

当时的我 18 岁，在 18 年的人生中，那一刻，才体会到离别的滋味。

多年后，我和妈妈聊天："妈，我最惹你伤心的事是哪一件？"

问完问题，我在脑子里不停搜寻从小到大各种调皮捣蛋、离经叛道的"光荣事迹"，锚定了几件事，等着验证"母女连心"。

我妈却说："最让我伤心的，是你去美国那天，在前面走得飞快，好像巴不得早点离开我一样。"

这一次，我妈笑了，我却哭了。

我突然想到龙应台的《目送》："所谓父母子女一场，只不过意味着，你和他的缘分就是今生今世不断地在目送他的背影渐行渐远。而且，他用

around and found that they lagged behind a great deal. Seeing me looking back, they hurried up. My mother's eyes were red, "Take care and be safe. Call me as soon as you arrive."

I smiled and took the luggage, "OK. I know."

At that time, my heart was full of longing for a foreign country, thinking that I would soon go abroad and see the world, and didn't have to listen to my parents' nagging any more. Finally, I was free and more than happy. I was very excited all the way from my hometown to Chengdu, and from the transfer flight from Chengdu to Beijing.

But when the plane from Beijing to New York was about to take off, suddenly I had a very complex feeling. On one hand, I wished to arrive in the United States soon. On the other hand, I wished the airplane could fly a little slower and slower. I was looking forward to new life but was worried that I couldn't handle problems when my parents were away. I felt freed when there was no parental control; meanwhile, I was afraid I would miss my mother at night.

I was 18 years old at that time. And it was the first time for me to know the feeling of separation in the 18 years of my life.

Years later, I chatted with my mom, "Mom, what's the saddest thing I've ever done to you?"

After asking questions, I kept searching for all kinds of mischievous and rebellious deeds from childhood to adulthood, focusing on a few things, and waiting to verify the "mother-daughter connection".

However, my mother said, "The saddest thing happened on the day you went to the United States. You walked very fast ahead, as if you would like to leave me as soon as possible."

背影默默告诉你：不必追。"

或许妈妈当年就从我的背影读出了"不必追"，而我十年后才读明白：那一年，和父母长长的离别，叫作成长。

03

刚到美国的生活，和预想中一样的是新鲜、自由、刺激好玩；和预想中不一样的是陌生、孤单、困难重重。

第一天去上课，我激动得像个小学生，然后激动地上了一天"英语听力课"，连单词都没听清楚，更别说理解课程内容。

第一次去餐厅吃饭，为了加盐和厨师比画交流了半天，因为他根本听不懂我的"中式英语"，我引以为傲的口语，遭受了致命打击。

晚上躺在床上我很失落。

想起一向聒噪的我，现在连说话的勇气都没有，有些挫败；想起食堂里那些陌生的、难以下咽的食物，有些难过；想起以前遇到困难总会有亲人朋友陪伴，现在异国他乡举目无亲……

我越想越伤心，眼泪就像小溪，顺着眼角哗啦啦地往外淌，止也止不住。

哭过之后心里好受很多，我决定不能轻易认输，以后要靠自己的力量

This time my mother laughed, but I cried.

Suddenly I thought of Long Yingtai's "Seeing Beloved One Off", which reads, "The so said parents and children relationship only means that you are destined to see him walking away further and further. And the back shadow of his figure tells you this silently: never chase forward."

Maybe my mother read "never chase" from my back that year. However, I understood it 10 years later—the long-time separation from my parents that year was called growth.

03

Life in the United States was as fresh, free and exciting as expected; but out of my expectation it was also unfamiliar, lonely and difficult.

I was like a pupil the first day in class, excited to have "listening practice" all day. I didn't catch some English words, let alone understand their meanings.

The first time I went to a restaurant I told the chef to add some salt in my meal. It took a long time because he didn't understand my "Chinglish" at all. I was very frustrated, for my oral English was what I was proud of. Lying in bed I was upset that night.

I was frustrated thinking that I had always

四海之纽

Taking the World as a
Link to Study in USA
川山育纽

战胜困难。

不就是听力和口语吗？我下定决心，两个月之内提高听力，一学期之后能说一口流利的英语。一学期后，我各科全A，还成了数学老师的助教。

不就是吃不惯吗？多尝试几次，说不定就习惯了呢。事实证明，一个月后我就喜欢上了大多数食物，一年长了30磅。

交朋友也没有想象中那么难，我先融入中国留学生，然后和日本、韩国、泰国留学生打成一片，还参加各种社团活动，结交了不少美国当地朋友。

一年后，当我离开美国时，和这些朋友难舍难分，几乎今天哭一场，明天哭一场。当时不知谁说了一句，"此去一别，今生难再相见"，那是我哭得最厉害的一次。

后来，在一次次的告别中，我哭的次数越来越少，不是伤感减轻了，而是我渐渐明白：我们的一生，注定会遇到很多人，会说很多再见，生命

been talkative but now I didn't even have the courage to speak; I was sad thinking of those strange and unpalatable food in cafeteria; and I was thinking about the days companied by relatives and friends when encountering difficulties but quite lonely now in a foreign country…

The more I thought about it, the sadder I was. Tears came out uncontrollably.

After crying, I felt much better. I decided that I couldn't admit my failure easily. I had to overcome the difficulties through efforts.

It's just about listening and speaking. I had made up my mind to improve my listening in two months and spoke fluent English in a semester. A semester later, I got A in all subjects and became a teacher assistant in mathematics.

It's just about eating habits. One would get used to it if he tries. It turned out that a month later, I liked most of the food, and gained more than 30 pounds in a year.

Making friends was not so difficult as I imagined. First, I made friends with Chinese students. Then, I got on well with students from Japan, Korea and Thailand. Besides, I participated in various community activities and made many local American friends.

A year later, when I was about to leave the United States, I had a hard time departing with these friends. I cried almost every day. When someone said, "We probably will not see each other again after the farewell, " I burst into tears and cried my eyes out.

I cried less and less at the following farewell parties. It didn't mean the sadness was alleviated, but I gradually understood: we are bound to meet many people and will say many good-byes. People come and go; only parting is

来来往往，只有离别才是永恒。就像天上的云，聚了又散，散了又聚。人生离合，亦复如斯。

而 19 岁的我，只有经历过这些困难挫磨、悲欢离合，才能长大。

04

在我认识的美国朋友中，基思是让我印象最深的一个。我认识基思的时候，他女儿 5 岁，而他已经 50 岁了，是我们学校的一名老师。基思一家是学校帮我安排的"结对子"家庭，平时照顾我的生活，节假日我去他们家里玩，或参加一些活动，缓解思乡之苦。

我第一次去他家时，基思说，"这将是一段长途旅行。"

他说得没错，从学校到他家，开车需要两个多小时的长途跋涉，因为他家在离学校一百多公里外的森林里。而他每天上下班，都要经历两次这样的长途旅行。

当时的我真的很难理解，"为什么不对自己好一点？"

后来我才明白，住在离学校百里之外的森林里，才是他真正地对自己好。

基思是专攻环境科学的，对大自然有一种近乎偏执的热爱。为了这种热爱，从大学时代开始，他就遍访名山大川。在前四十多年的人生里，他

eternal. Just like the clouds in the sky, they gather and disperse, disperse and gather, and so is life.

At the age of 19, I had to go through these hardships and felt the joys and sorrows before growing up.

04

Of all the American friends, Keith was the most impressive one. When I met Keith, his daughter was 5 years old, and he was 50, a teacher in our school. Keith's was the cooperative family arranged by the school to take care of me. I went to his home on holidays or took part in some activities with his family to alleviate my homesickness.

The first time I went to his home, Keith said, "it's going to be a long journey."

He was right. It took more than two hours to drive from school to his home, because it was located in the forest more than a hundred kilometers away from school. And he commuted two times every day.

At that time, it was hard for me to understand, why not be nice to himself?

Later I realized that living in a forest hundred miles away from the school was his way to treat himself well.

Keith specialized in environmental science

走遍了十几个国家，去看那里的山水草木、风土人情，做项目、搞研究。

到了不惑之年，看过了想看的世界，他就在森林里自己设计盖了一栋房子，从此安定下来，过上了一屋两人、三餐四季的逍遥日子。

在别人娶妻生子的年龄，他在寻访大山，忠于自己的热爱；在别人含饴弄孙的年纪，他才开始组建家庭。

我觉得这样的人生挺酷！

人生的每一阶段，都没有什么事是应该做的，最重要的是你喜不喜欢、愿不愿意。那也是我第一次开始思考自己真正想要的是什么，以后想要什么样的生活。

而基思的一句话我一直记到今天："只要你想做一件事，什么时候开始都不晚。"

## 05

2009 年，从美国回来，我已经大三，在西南交通大学读完本科，后来又念完研究生。

在这五年中，关于地震的记忆，被唤起的次数渐渐变少，我知道它们已被安放在心里某个柔软的角落。但是在这些渐渐淡去的记忆中，有一个细节却慢慢走出来，变得越来越清晰。

地震时，我匆忙跑下楼，最后悔的是没有拿手机，这意味着地震后我

and had a strong passion for nature. For his passion, he had traveled to all kinds of famous mountains and rivers since going to college. In his first 40 years, he had been to more than ten countries, seen the landscapes, plants, local customs, and done projects and research there.

In his forties, he had seen the world, so he decided to settle down. Then he designed and built a house in the forest. From then on, he started a leisurely life with his wife and lived an ordinary life.

When other people were marrying and having babies, he was visiting mountains and stuck to his passion; when other people were playing with grandchildren, he was starting to form a family.

I thought life like that was cool.

There is nothing one has to do at each stage of life. The most important is whether you like it or whether you are willing to do it. That's the first time I began to think about what I really wanted. What kind of life would I like to have?

And Keith's words are still on my mind, "As long as you want to do something, it's never too late to start."

"失联"了，我无法知道家人是否安好，也无法向亲友报平安。

三天后，当我拿回手机，电话、短信都已经爆了。有一个号码，在我"失联"的三天中，给我打了47个电话，发了130条短信。我抱着手机哭了一下午，有对受难同胞的哀婉，有劫后余生的庆幸，有灾难面前亲友携手相伴、互相扶持的感动。

2014年，有个男孩第一次去我家，就对我妈说，"阿姨，你放心，别的女孩有的，她都会有，别的女孩没有的，我也会让她拥有。"

我妈有点吃惊，我把她拉到一边："他就是地震中给我发了一百多条短信的那个人，等了我7年。"

然后，我妈就同意了。

那天晚上，这个男孩对我说："做我女朋友吧。"

我说："好。"

我又问："现在才开始，会不会有点晚？"

他说："不晚，一切刚刚好。"

那种坚信和笃定，让我非常安心。

现在，这个男孩，是我人生最重要的另一半。

他不仅为我们的感情找到了来路，也为我们的未来找到了去路。

2015年，我辞去成都"活儿少离家近"的工作，和他一起成为北漂。

05

I came back from the United States in 2009. I was in my third year in Southwest Jiaotong University, and then I completed my undergraduate courses and later finished graduate school.

Over the past five years, memories of the earthquake have been evoked less and less. And I knew that they had been placed in a soft corner of my heart. But in these fading memories, there was a detail that slowly came out and became clear.

When the earthquake struck, I rushed downstairs and regretted that I didn't take my cell phone. This meant that people couldn't reach me after the earthquake. I couldn't know whether my family was well or not, and I couldn't tell my relatives and friends that I was safe.

Three days later, when I got my cell phone back, it was full of phone records and messages. A number called me 47 times and sent 130 short messages in the three days. I was crying the entire afternoon, feeling sorry for my fellow victims, appreciating my luckiness, and touched by the companionship and mutual support of relatives and friends in face of the disaster.

In 2014, a boy came to my home for the first time and said to my mother, "Auntie, I assure you that she will have all the things other girls have and even more."

My mother was a little surprised. I told her aside. "He's the one who sent me more than a hundred text messages in the earthquake. He's been waiting for me for seven years."

Then my mother agreed.

That night, the boy said to me, "Be my girlfriend." I said, "OK."

我学了 7 年工程，到北京却转行做了互联网，心里有点没底。他说："别怕，现在开始一点也不晚。"

他说的没错，2018 年的我，已经成功转行，在一家互联网教育公司做着自己热爱的工作。

犹记得当年他说："唯好姑娘与梦想不可辜负。"我回赠："唯好儿郎与梦想不可辜负。"

好姑娘和好儿郎，我们都没有辜负。

梦想，我们也不会辜负。

06

2008—2018，回首这十年，好像很长很长，又好像很短很短。

2008 年，是这十年的开端，也是最浓墨重彩，永远无法被忽略的一年。

而这十年，又是我们人生中转折、变化、可能性最多的十年。

这十年，从一个家庭变成一个人，是长大；

这十年，从一个人变成一个家庭，是成熟。

我相信这个十年之后，那群 18 岁的孩子已经真正长大，而且大多数人的生活终将归于平淡，不会一直跌宕起伏，不会都是波澜壮阔。但是只要我们的心脏还在跳动，只要血液里

I asked again, "Will it be a bit late to start now?"

He said, "No. Everything is just fine."

He was so convincing and determined that I felt secure.

Now, this boy is the other half of my life.

He found a way not only for our love, but also for our future.

In 2015, I resigned from my job in Chengdu, and strived with him in Beijing. I studied engineering for 7 years but changed my career to Internet business. I was unconfident. But he said, "Don't worry. It's not too late to start now." He was right. In 2018, I successfully transferred to an Internet education company and did what I loved.

I still remember when he said, "Only good girl and dreams cannot be failed." I responded, "Only good boy and dreams cannot be failed."

We didn't fail to be a good girl and good boy.

And we will not fail to live up to our dreams.

06

Looking back from 2008 to 2018, the 10 years seems like a very long time, but also very short.

还有激情奔涌，只要脸上还洋溢着爱和笑容，在那些平凡的一餐一食之间，涌动着的，就是属于每一个人的波澜壮阔。

在这十年以及今后的每一个十年，希望我们都能在平平淡淡的生活中，收获一个纯良的自己、诚恳的自己、磊落的自己、热忱的自己。

致敬 150，致敬我们的十年！

2008 is the beginning of the 10 years, and it is also the most important year that can never be neglected.

And these 10 years are also with the most turning points, changes and possibilities.

Over the past 10 years, I have grown up from my family to living independently;

Over the past 10 years, I have become mature from a single person to having a family of my own.

I believe that after these10 years, those 18-year-old children have really grown up. Most people will eventually live a plain life, not always with fierce ups and downs, not always brilliant. But as long as our hearts are still beating, as long as there is still passion rushing in our blood, as long as there is still love and a smile on our faces, we are living a brilliant life in our daily routine.

And in these 10 years and every 10 years in the future, I hope that we can end up finding a kind, earnest, bright and passionate self in life.

Salute 150! Salute the 10 years of ours!

# 一晃十年，感谢有你

## My Gratitude to You

杨然 / 西南交通大学　纽约州立大学布法罗分校

Yang Ran / Southwest Jiaotong University　SUNY at Buffalo

十年之前，2008 年 5 月 12 日 14 点 28 分，还是大二学生的我正在西南交通大学犀浦校区的球场上足球课。然而，从那儿之后，我的人生发生了巨大的变化。

地震后，从成都的 8 所高校中选出 150 名地震灾区的孩子赴美留学一年，参加领导力训练，旨在为地震灾区培养重建家乡的"青年领导人"。我有幸作为西南交通大学 16 名获选学生中的一员赴美参加为期一年的留学项目。

于是，就这样，2008 年 8 月 15 日，带着对美国梦的向往，也带着为学院争光的心愿，生平还没有出过远门的我第一次登上了去美国纽约的飞

At 14:28 on May 12, 2008, ten years ago, the world-shaking Wenchuan earthquake took place at my hometown, when I, as a sophomore, was taking football lessons on the field of Xipu Campus in Southwest Jiaotong University. However, after that, it has brought great changes in my life.

Because of the earthquake, 150 children from 8 universities in Chengdu were selected from earthquake-stricken areas to study in the United States for one year and participate in leadership training, aimed at training young leaders to rebuild their homes in earthquake-stricken areas. As one of the 16 selected students from Southwest Jiaotong University, I was honored to go to the United States for a one-year study abroad program.

Therefore, on August 15, 2008, with the longing for the American dream and the determination to make our school proud, I

机。带队的魏老师举止优雅，谈吐不凡，是我们大家的女神。第一次坐飞机，有点兴奋，也有点恐惧，飞机上的一切都令我新奇：起飞的轰鸣声、渐小的房屋和立交桥、苍茫的云海、海上的浮冰……十几个小时后，我们到达了纽约肯尼迪机场，正式开始了我们为期一年的美国之旅。

## 水牛城陌生却温暖

我们一行人在近纽约的纽约州立大学海事学院分校短暂休整后，被分配到了纽约州立大学系统的不同分校。我和其他三个同学一起来到了伊利湖东岸的布法罗分校。到布法罗之前，喜欢吃牛肉的我对"水牛城"（"Buffalo"的音译为"布法罗"）充满了幻想，以为这里满是大大小小不同菜式的水牛可以供我大快朵颐，来到之后发现除了能见到一些铜牛像外，餐馆里并没有什么水牛，倒是鸡翅相当美味。

初来乍到什么都不熟悉，但我们很快感受到了来自学校国际教育办公室的温暖。办公室除了给我们提供全额奖学金、书本费、住宿费以及伙食费，还会每个月给我们额外的零花钱，将我们衣食住行的各方面都安排得很妥帖。

boarded the plane to New York for the first time in my life. Mrs.Wei, the team leader, was graceful in manner and extraordinary in speech, whom we all admired. As it was the first time I took an airplane, I was a little excited but also a little scared. I was curious about everything on the plane—the noise of take-off, the smaller and smaller houses and overpasses, the vast sea of clouds, and the floating ice on the sea. Over ten hours later, we arrived at Kennedy Airport in New York and officially began our one-year trip in the United States.

**The Unfamiliar but Warm Buffalo City**

After a short break at SUNY Maritime College near New York, our group was assigned to different branches of the State University of New York. I went to Buffalo State College on the east bank of Lake Erie with three other students. Before I came to Buffalo City, I was full of fantasies about it. I thought it was full of buffalo of different sizes and they were made into different kinds of dishes. However, when I arrived at Buffalo City, I found that there were no buffalo in the restaurant at all except some bronze statues of buffalo. But Buffalo chicken wing was quite delicious.

When we first came to Buffalo, everything

办公室是我们在美国温暖的小家。斯蒂芬·邓尼特是这个家里和蔼的老爷爷，给我们讲各种有趣的故事和见闻，鼓励我们遵循内心的想法做自己想做的事；约瑟夫·海因卓文像是我们慈祥的父亲，给我们的学习和生活提供各种中肯的建议；玛维思像是一位热心肠的妈妈，喜欢和我们聊天，关心我们生活中的各种细节，我们都亲切地称她为"美国妈妈"。在"家长们"的照料下，我们几个小孩在布法罗开心地成长。

在布法罗一年的学习中，我除了选择和土木工程专业相关的力学课程，也选择了心理学和哲学课程开拓自己的眼界，多一个角度来理解这个世界。一晃十年，尽管当初学的知识大多已经忘记，我依然会用当初在心理学课程中学到的弗洛伊德潜意识理论来分析和理解身边的事。离开美国之前，在约瑟夫和斯蒂芬的建议下，我参加了TOEFL考试并取得了不错的成绩，这也为我之后重新回到美国埋下了伏笔。

## 大家庭里活动多

如果说布法罗的国际教育办公室是一个小家庭，那"CSC-SUNY 150奖学金项目"就是我们在美国的大家

was unfamiliar to me; but we soon felt the warmth from the International Education Office of our school. In addition to providing us with full scholarships, books, accommodations and meals, they also gave us extra pocket money every month, and took good care of our clothing, food, housing and transportation.

The office was our warm little home in the United States. Stephen Dunnett was like a kind grandfather, telling us all kinds of interesting stories and information, encouraging us to follow our heart and do what we wanted to do; Joseph Hindrawan was like our kind father, offering us all kinds of advice in our study and life; Marvis was like a warm-hearted mother, liking to chat with us and caring about the details of our life. Affectionately, we called her our American mom. With the good care from these elders, we grew happily in UB.

In UB's one-year study, I chose not only courses related to my major, civil engineering, but also psychology and philosophy courses to broaden my horizon and understand the world from another angle. In a flash of ten years, although I have forgotten most of what I learned, I would still use Freud's subconscious theory, which I learned in my psychology course,

庭。2008 年末的寒假期间，我们布法罗一行四人和大家庭在纽约集合，看了 NBA 火箭队和篮网队的比赛，为姚明和易建联呐喊助威。之后又一起去华盛顿参加一个短暂的领导力训练项目。在华盛顿我们先后参观了阿灵顿公墓、华盛顿纪念碑、威尔逊国际中心，一起聆听了有关领导力训练的讲座。

这些年来，我一直谨记和反复运用在讲座上学习到的两个原则：不要轻易下结论；像海绵一样去学习吸收新知识。这两点可以作为我在美国学习成果的缩影，从此我在生活中尽量用批判性思维客观地去看待分析问题，凡事不轻易下结论，多从几个角度、多花一些时间去看待身边的人和事，同时保持好奇心，像海绵一样去吸收身边的知识。

朝阳中的新芽

时间过得很快，2009 年秋，一

to analyze and understand the things around me. Before leaving the United States, I took the TOEFL exam on the advice of Joseph and Stephen, and got good results, which prepared for my return to the United States.

### A Lot of Activities in a Big Family

If the International Education Office of UB was a small family, then CSC-SUNY 150 Program was our big family in the United States. During the winter vacation at the end of 2008, four of us and the big family watched an NBA basketball game between Rockets and Nets. We cheered for Yao Ming and Yi Jianlian. Then we went to Washington for a brief leadership training program. We visited Arlington National Cemetery, Washington Monument, Woodrow Wilson International Center for Scholars, and listened to lectures on leadership.

Over the years, I have kept in mind and repeatedly applied the two principles I learned in lectures. 1) Don't draw conclusions easily. 2) Learn and absorb new knowledge like a sponge. These two principles were a small part of what I have learned in the United States. From then on, I try to use critical thinking in my life to objectively look at and analyze problems. I do not draw conclusions easily, but think from some other angles, spend more time observing people and things around me. Meanwhile, I keep my curiosity, learn and absorb knowledge like a sponge.

### Buds in the Morning Sunlight

Time passed by quickly. It was the end of

年的留学生活转瞬即逝。我记得当时的我哭得稀里哗啦，舍不得国际教育办公室这个小家庭，舍不得离开这片土地，并暗自下决心一定要再回来。

回到四川等待我的是大学最后一年的毕业季，由于留学错过的许多很多课程需要在这一年补回来，同时要准备 GRE 考试，所以这一年几乎是在教室和自习室里度过的。还好有好兄弟兼室友，也是"CSC-SUNY 150 奖学金项目"成员江凌龙的陪伴，我们在闲暇时光一起摄影、打网球、玩实况足球游戏，所以这一年的时光除了充实，也有很多乐趣。右图为江凌龙和我一起在西南交大校园里摄影写生的照片。我很喜欢这张照片，朝阳中的新芽提醒着我生命多美好。

## 永怀感恩之心

我想每一个"CSC-SUNY 150 奖学金项目"的同学都怀着一颗想要感恩社会、回馈社会的心，尽管我们的能力有限，但这并不会限制我们尝试去回报社会。我们西南交通大学"CSC-SUNY 150 奖学金项目"的同学们抽出时间，一起去探望了双流安康家园里因为地震而被收留的小朋友。我们这群大哥哥、大姐姐给孩子们上课，讲故事，一起做游戏。看到

the one-year's study in the autumn of 2009. I remember I cried badly. I couldn't bear to leave the small family of the International Education Office, couldn't bear to leave this land. And I decided secretly that I would come back.

The time I came back to Sichuan was my last year of college. Because I had to make up for many courses I missed and prepare for GRE test, I spent almost every day that year in classrooms and study rooms. Fortunately, my good friend and roommate accompanied me, who was also a member in CSC-SUNY 150 Program. In our spare time, we took photos, played tennis, played live football games on computer. Therefore, although I was busy this year, I had a lot of fun. The picture below is a photo taken by Jiang Linglong and me in the campus of Southwest Jiaotong University. I like this picture very much. The bud in the morning sunlight reminds me of how beautiful life is.

**Always Be Grateful**

I think every CSC-SUNY 150 Program student would like to give back to society to express their gratitude. Although our ability is limited, it does not restrict us from trying to do so. Our schoolmates of Southwest Jiaotong University in CSC-SUNY 150 Program visited

小朋友们笑得开心灿烂，我们也打心底里感到开心，希望他们经历伤痛后，依然可以茁壮成长。

和父亲一起踏上映秀这片土地已是地震一年以后，看着远处耸立着重建后的一排排新楼以及眼前被地震摧毁的学校，我心里百感交集。感恩社会八方之力，在短短一年时间完成灾区大部分重建工作，让活着的人们有了安身之处。哀泣逝去的灵魂，怜惜不再成长的生命，愿他们的在天之灵可以安息。如果我们的房子可以修得坚固一点，再坚固一点，大灾大难面前是不是就会有更多的人幸免。作为一个学习土木工程的学生，每一年的 5 月 12 日，我都会想，我究竟可以为我的家乡、我深爱的土地做点什么？

## 再续美国梦

2010 年秋，在顺利拿到本科毕业证后，我又重新返回了布法罗攻

An Kang Home in Shuang Liu for the adopted children after the earthquake. Like their big brothers and sisters, we taught them, told stories and played games with them. Seeing them laughing happily and brilliantly, we also felt happy. We hoped that they could still grow up healthily even after the painful experience.

It was one year after the earthquake that I set foot on Ying Xiu with my father. Seeing the new buildings in distance and the destroyed schools in front of me, I was filled with mixed feelings. Thanks to all the efforts from society, the reconstruction was completed in just one year, and the living people have residences. I wept for the deceased, pitied the stopped lives and wished their spirits rest in peace. If our house could be built more strongly, would there be more people to survive in a disaster? As a student of civil engineering, on May 12, every year, I would wonder what I could do for my hometown and my beloved land.

## My American Dream Went On

In the autumn of 2010, after getting my undergraduate diploma, I returned to UB for my master's degree in civil engineering. And my little family, International Education Office gave me a big gift—graduate assistant in the

读土木工程硕士学位。而我的小家庭国际教育办公室给了我一份厚礼——国际办公室研究生助理的工作。这份工作需要我每周在国际办公室工作20个小时，为国际学生提供学校申请、注册、咨询、档案管理等一系列服务作为回报。我可以每个月领到工资，学校更是免除了我的学费，这让我有充足的零花钱安排更加丰富的生活。

在布法罗的研究生学习阶段，课程信息量大、作业多，复杂的力学理论以及"漫天飞舞"的力学公式让人头疼。我和同学们不得不花大量时间在图书馆讨论，最后依靠大家的智慧一起完成作业。四点一线的生活十分紧凑，我匆忙地奔走在家——教室——图书馆——办公室的路线上。完成白天的课程和工作之后便一头扎进图书馆，很多时候完成作业准备回家已经是深夜一两点，图书馆外的停车场已经空荡荡，一眼便可以望见我的车独自停在停车场中央。布法罗的冬天很冷，大雪覆盖了整个城市，到处都是白茫茫的一片。雪中孤零零的一辆车，这样的景象别有一番风味儿。开车回家，在厨房做完第二天要带的午饭，终于可以结束漫长的一天睡觉了。

布法罗的土木工程学院拥有在业界享有盛名的国家多学科和多灾害地

International Office. This job required me to work 20 hours a week in the international office, providing international students with a range of services, such as school application, registration, consultation, archives management, etc. In addition to my monthly salary, the school exempted me from my tuition fees, and this arrangement enabled me to have enough pocket money to enjoy life.

There was a lot of information and assignments, complicated mechanics theories and mechanics formula for graduate student in UB. My classmates and I had to spend a lot of time in the library discussing with each other and completing homework together. We were very busy rushing from home to classroom then from classroom to library and finally from library to office. After completing the classes and my work I would go directly to the library. Many times, I found it was already 1 or 2 o'clock early in the morning after I finished my homework and went back home. The parking lot outside the library was empty and I could see my car parked alone in the middle of the parking lot. Buffalo's winter was very cold. The whole city was covered with snow. Everything was in white. But it also created a beautiful scene with the white snow and my car in the snow. After driving back home and cooking the lunch for the next day, I could finally go to sleep and end a long day.

震工程研究中心（MCEER），该中心于 1986 年由美国国家科学基金会在布法罗大学成立，以开发新知识和技术来提高建筑物的抗震能力见长。2009 年作为"CSC-SUNY 150 奖学金项目"学生，我非常仰慕 MCEER 的大名。几年后，我终于有幸走进 MCEER 的地震模拟实验室，参加了超高强度混凝土预制件连接的地震性能研究项目，并在导师乔治·李的指导下完成了我的硕士毕业论文（右下图为在地震模拟台上进行的混凝土预制件连接的抗震模拟实验）。

因为地震，我跟随"CSC-SUNY 150 奖学金项目"来到美国，因为"CSC-SUNY 150 奖学金项目"我又选择在美国进一步了解地震。尽管对于如何报答社会，我还没有一条明确的思路，但我感觉自己正在一步步地沿着这个方向前进。希望有一天"CSC-SUNY 150 奖学金项目"里的伙伴们都羽翼丰满，到时候大家齐力回报社会，所有的善因都能结出善果，所有的付出都不会白费。

## 路上的风景也是精神的财富

除了学习和工作以外，我也趁着假期出去旅游，欣赏欧美各地的自然风光和人文风情，结交新朋友，体验

The school of civil engineering at UB has a prestigious MCEER (Multidisciplinary Center for Earthquake Engineering Research), established by the National Science Foundation at Buffalo State College in 1986. It is good at developing new knowledge and technology to improve the seismic capacity of buildings. As a student of the CSC-SUNY 150 Program in 2009, I already revered MCEER. A few years later, I finally had the privilege to walk into the Earthquake Simulation Laboratory of MCEER, participated in the research project of seismic performance of ultra-high strength precast concrete connections, and finished my master's thesis under the guidance of my tutor George Lee (the picture shows the seismic simulation experiment of precast concrete connection on earthquake simulator).

Because of the earthquake, I followed CSC-SUNY 150 Program to the United States; because of CSC-SUNY 150 Program, I chose to learn more about earthquakes in the United States; Although I haven't yet had a clear idea of how to repay the society, I feel that I am moving forward in this direction step by step. I hope that one day the partners in CSC-SUNY 150 Program will be well-prepared, and then we can work together to repay the society, and let all good causes bear good results, all the efforts be rewarded.

不同地方的文化，这些都是我留学期间的珍贵回忆。最难忘的是 2012 年夏天的毕业环美旅行，一辆车，两个人，50 个日夜，19 个国家公园，12 780 英里路程，壮阔的戈壁，秀丽的湖泊，磅礴的冰川，灿烂的银河，一路上看到的每一处风景都印在了我的心里，成了我人生中宝贵的精神财富。

2012 年末，我告别了布法罗回到深圳，开始了土木工程师的生涯；又于 2013 年末辗转至香港，继续从事结构设计工作，并于 2016 年末取得了注册工程师资格。同年，我的女儿出生。家里多了一个甜蜜的小负担，感觉肩上的担子明显重了，但家庭生

## My Wealth
### —Sceneries Seen on the Road

In addition to studying and working, I also travelled on holidays, experiencing the natural sceneries and cultural customs of Europe and America as well as making new friends. All these have become precious memories in my studying abroad period. The most unforgettable was the after-graduation tour around the United States in the summer of 2012. One car, two people, 50 days and nights, 19 national parks, 12,780 miles, we saw the magnificent Gobi, beautiful lakes, vast glaciers and brilliant galaxy. Every scene I saw on the hiking trail was imprinted in my heart and became a valuable part of my life.

At the end of 2012, I left Buffalo and returned to Shenzhen to start my career as a civil engineer. At the end of 2013, I moved to Hong Kong to keep working on structural design and qualified as a registered engineer at the end of 2016. In the same year my daughter was born. Since we have a "sweet little burden," we need to shoulder more responsibilities but also obtain more fun. Now the three of us are living happily in Hong Kong.

活也增添了许多乐趣。现在我们一家三口在香港幸福地生活着。

## 感谢有你

2018 年，转眼"5·12"汶川特大地震已经过去十年，回顾这十年一路走来的轨迹，我有太多要感谢的人和事。感谢纽约州立大学和中国留学基金委给我提供了宝贵的赴美留学的机会；感谢魏琳和陈滔伟老师对"CSC-SUNY 150 奖学金项目"长期以来的悉心指导；感谢"CSC-SUNY 150 奖学金项目"的小伙伴们相互鼓励、一起成长；感谢所有帮助和关注过"CSC-SUNY 150 奖学金项目"的认识和不认识的叔叔阿姨们，是你们的努力让我们的梦想起飞；感谢布法罗大学国际办公室的老师们给我提供再次赴美读研的机会；感谢我的妻子和女儿让我拥有一个幸福的家庭，让我的生命更加完整……

十年前，"CSC-SUNY 150 奖学金项目"是我们梦想开始的地方，这十年中，我们都在为梦想积蓄能量，在十年后或者不久的将来，我希望"CSC-SUNY 150 奖学金项目"可以一起实现梦想，不忘初心，不负众望，回报社会，让这个世界更美好。

## My Gratitude to You

In 2018, the earthquake was ten years ago. Looking back on this decade, I need to express my gratitude to a lot of people and things.

I'm grateful to State University of New York and the China Scholarship Council for providing me with such an opportunity to study in the United States; I'm grateful to Wei Lin and Chen Taowei for their long-time guidance and training in CSC-SUNY 150 Program; I'm grateful to the CSC-SUNY 150 Program partners for encouraging each other to grow up; I'm grateful to those whom we don't even know but have helped and concerned for CSC-SUNY 150 Program, for their efforts to have made our dreams come true; I'm grateful to the teachers in the International Office of Buffalo State College for offering me the opportunity to go to the United States for graduate study again. I'm grateful to my wife and daughter for giving me a happy family and making my life more complete...

Ten years ago, CSC-SUNY 150 Program was the place where our dreams began. In the past ten years, we have been preparing for our dreams. After a decade or in the near future, I hope that students in CSC-SUNY 150 Program can realize our dreams, and keep our original intentions, live up to the expectations, repay the society, and make the world a better place.

# 人生的转折点——回顾美国之行

## Turning Point in Life—A Review of the Trip to the United States

曾修涛 / 西南交通大学　纽约州立大学布法罗分校

Zeng Xiutao / Southwest Jiaotong University　SUNY at Buffalo

现在，回想起在美国纽约州立大学布法罗学院学习那一年的经历，我不禁思绪万千，一幕幕难以忘怀的场景交织在我的脑海里。想到在布法罗的老师、同学和朋友们，想到和他们在一起度过的美好时光，幸福的微笑不禁浮现在我的脸上。

在去美国之前，我的大学生活非常单纯，每天在教室上课，图书馆自

Now recalling the year I spent at SUNY (State University of New York) Buffalo State College in the United States, I can't help thinking about the unforgettable scenes intertwined in my mind. When I think of the teachers, classmates and friends in Buffalo, and of the wonderful time I spent with them, I can't help smiling happily.

Before going to the United States, my college life was very simple, having classes in the classroom, studying by ourselves in the library, and learning English through American dramas. Then due to the radical change in my hometown, fortunately, I was able to participate in CSC-SUNY 150 Program funded by China Scholarship Council and New York State Government and to study and live in State University of New York for a year. After arriving in the United States, many first-time experiences enriched my life—the first time I studied in groups with my American classmates; the first time I spent Christmas with

习，跟着美剧学英语。后来因为家乡
的巨变，有幸在国家留学基金委和纽
约州政府的资助下，加入"CSC-SUNY
150 奖学金项目"，去美国纽约州立
大学生活和学习一年。到美国之后，
许许多多的第一次丰富了我的生活：
第一次和美国同学一起分组作业，第
一次和寄宿家庭过圣诞，第一次到百
老汇看戏剧，第一次滑雪，第一次到
纽约时代广场拍照等。这许多的第一
次带给了我数不尽的快乐和成长。

## 经济学上的启蒙

　　美国是一个先进的国家，有美丽
的风景和现代化的设施。我在这里留
学，也是了解西方文化习俗的机会。
闲暇时间，我选择尽量多出去走走，
多交美国朋友，品尝异国食品。更重
要的是，我了解到了更多更广的信息，

my host family; the first time I went to Broadway
to watch a musical; the first time I skied; the first
time I took pictures in Times Square in New York
and so on. Those many first-times brought me
endless happiness and growth.

### Initiation from Economics

　　The United States is a developed country
with beautiful scenery and modern facilities.
Now that I was studying here, it was also an
opportunity for me to understand western
culture and customs. In my spare time, I chose
to go out as much as I could, to make more
American friends and to taste exotic foods.
More importantly, I learned more and more
information, broadened my horizons and laid a
solid foundation for oral communication.

　　In addition, what influenced me and
changed me most during my trip was the way I
thought and saw the world. Due to my interest
in business, I tried to take microeconomics
and macroeconomics while studying at SUNY.
Through studying in class and communicating
with teachers after class, I have realized that

开阔了我的眼界，同时也为我的口语打下了扎实的基础。

不仅如此，美国之行对我影响最深、让我变化最大的，是思考问题和看待世界的角度的变化。出于对商业的兴趣，我在纽约州立大学学习期间，选修了微观和宏观经济学。通过课上的学习以及课下与老师交流，我意识到，经济学研究的不仅仅是商品、货币等经济现象，整个经济学的基础，其实是对人类行为的深刻分析与刻画。

经济学中提出，每个人都面临选择，那么人们会怎样做出选择呢？对于这一点，经济学中假设每个人都是理性的，而理性的人一定会做出使自己收益最大的选择。人们在做出选择的同时，也是在做着成本和收益的权衡，即选择都是有成本的，或者有机会成本的。每个人的选择都是收益与成本权衡的结果，而个体的持续选择，即构成了实际的行为；所有人的行为，即构成了世界。

我记得当时老师说的这样一番话对我影响非常深刻：经济学是一套看待世界的方法论，这套方法论有超强的解释力，能够解释你们工作中的所有问题，也能够解释你们生活中的绝大部分问题。后来，我用这套看待世界的方法，对于以前很多自己想不通、

economic research is not only about commodities, currency and other economic phenomena; the basis of the whole economics is actually a profound analysis and characterization of human behavior.

Economics brings up that everyone is faced with choices, so how do people make choices? To this point, economics assumes that everyone is rational, and rational people will make the choice which maximizes their own benefits. Meanwhile, when people are making choices, they are also balancing between costs and benefits, that is, choices are cost-effective, or have opportunity cost. Everyone's choice is the result of balancing between income and cost, while the individual's continuous choices constitute the actual behavior, and the behaviors of all people constitute the world.

I remember what the teacher said at that time had a profound impact on me: economics is a set of methodologies for looking at the world. This set of methodologies has super explanatory power which can explain all the problems in your work and can also explain most of the problems in your life. Later, with this way of looking at the world, I found a theoretical basis and a logical explanation for many things that I could not understand and see clearly before. It is this period of study in the United States that has aroused my great interest in this field. After returning home, I have been admitted to graduate school of business and continue to a learn knowledge in this field.

One year's study and life in the United States has given me an enlightenment in economics. It is because of such a learning experience at SUNY that I can be qualified for

看不明的事情，找到了理论依据以及合乎逻辑的解释。正是这段在美国的学习经历，让我对该领域产生了极大的兴趣，并在回国后考上了商科研究生，继续学习这方面的知识。

美国一年的学习和生活，给了我经济学方面的启蒙，在纽约州立大学的这段学习经历，让我进一步胜任在成都外资银行的工作。我也非常高兴找到这份工作，因为它能够帮助家乡的企业更好地融资、经营和发展。这样，家乡的企业有能力为更多人解决就业问题，家乡的人就有更多工作机会，赚取更高的收入，也能过上更好的生活。对我来说，从事金融工作是一件非常有意义的事情。

## 工作中的获益

美国之行让我感受最深的是教学方式的不同。之前我习惯了被动的学习方式，在美国课堂上突然换成主动学习，一时有点跟不上。但是经过老师的启发性引导，我逐渐对讨论、阐述自己的观点产生了浓厚的兴趣。

美国课堂上，老师比较重视课堂讨论。针对某个话题，鼓励学生充分阐述自己的观点和想法，老师再进行评述。以"公司金融"这门课为例，老师在课堂上传授的不仅仅是现有的

the work in a foreign bank in Chengdu. I am also very happy to find this job, because it can help the enterprises in my hometown to better finance, operate and develop. In this way, enterprises in my hometown will be more capable of solving the employment problem for more people. Therefore, people in my hometown can obtain more job opportunities, earn more income and have a better life. For me, engaging in financial work is very meaningful.

### Benefits from Studying Abroad

What impressed me most during the trip is the differences in teaching methods. I was used to passive learning, so I couldn't catch up with the sudden change to active learning in American classes. But after the teacher's inspiration and guidance, I gradually became interested in discussing and stating my views.

In the American classroom, teachers pay more attention to class discussion. They encourage students to fully express their views and ideas of a topic, and then they will comment later. Taking the course "Enterprise Finance" as an example, the teacher didn't merely teach the existing knowledge and theory in the classroom, but also paid attention to the analysis of the comparison between these theories and the actual operation of enterprises. Through the comparative study, students were encouraged to think actively about and discuss some deficiencies in the existing theoretical models and assumptions, and then the teacher would make a comprehensive comment on students' views. In this way, students would learn and understand the content of the course more deeply.

知识和理论，同时也注重分析这些理论与实际企业经营情况的对比。相比于实际情况，鼓励同学们对现有理论的模型和前提假设中的一些不足进行积极思考和讨论，然后老师再针对大家的观点，进行综合点评。这样，同学们会对课程内容学习和理解得更深入。

美国的学习让我对经济学以及如何让企业经营得更好产生了浓厚兴趣。一年的留学生涯结束后，我选择在国内继续完成商科的硕士阶段学习，并进入外资银行工作。美国的留学经历，是我后期学业和择业的转折点，是我人生新的起点。

外资银行对应聘者不限专业，也不限地域户籍，却非常看重个人的性格和发展潜力；青睐那些乐于改变自己、钟爱金融行业、熟悉金融行业相关知识、了解银行各主要部门职责且明确发展方向的学生；也注重应聘者是否有丰富的生活经历、研究课题或者社会活动的经历等。要求应聘者具有团队意识，不失进取精神并勇于承担责任。而这些，都是我在美留学期间收获的宝贵财富。

目前，我在日常工作中会大量使用英文，经常与国外的同事进行交流，对跨国企业提供的银行解决方案进行深入讨论。留美期间大量的英文课堂

Learning in the United States has given me a keen interest in economics and how to operate a business better. At the end of the year, I chose to complete my graduate studies in business in China and after that I was employed in a foreign bank. The experience of studying abroad in the United States is a turning point for my further studies and career selection later. It is a new starting point in my life.

Foreign banks pay great attention to the applicants' personality and potentials, regardless of their majors and geographical residences. Students who are willing to adapt themselves, interested in financial industry, familiar with the relevant knowledge of financial industry, understand the responsibilities of the main departments of bank and clear about their future direction of development, are favored. They also focus on whether the applicants have rich experience in life, research or social activities. Applicants are required to have team spirit, enterprising spirit and responsibility. These are valuable treasures I have learned during my study in the United States.

Now I use a lot of English in my daily work. I often communicate and discuss in

讨论，让我能够更自信地在国外同事面前用英文分析问题，并有效阐述自己的观点。

## 留学美国小贴士

近年来，越来越多的中国学生走出国门，去其他国家留学深造。以我一年的留学经验来看，出国留学特别是去美国留学，需要注意的是，不同的文化环境使得让留学生与美国学生在思维方式、分析问题的角度、与人相处的方式等方面，有非常大的差异。所以持有开放和包容的心态，学会换角度思考，真诚地与美国学生相处，就能够建立和维持良好的友谊。

最后我想说的是，学习不仅仅在于课堂。除了课堂以外，更多地同美国的学生、老师进行接触，参加他们的活动，与他们交朋友。这样，通过在课堂和生活中点点滴滴的接触，才能够更深入地了解美国，才能够在留学期间收获更多。如果在美国迷路，不要犹豫，找当地人问路，美国人很善良，也乐于帮助别人。当然，手上备有一份当地地图就更方便了。

赴美留学，走出家门，需要注意的事情很多，毕竟身处异地，环境、文化、制度种种都有所不同，学会了解这些不同很重要，这样才能过好留

depth with my colleagues about the solutions for transnational enterprises. A lot of English classroom discussions during my stay in the United States have enabled me to be more confident in analyzing problems in English and effectively stating my views in front of foreign colleagues.

### Tips for Studying in the United States

In recent years, more and more Chinese students have chosen to study abroad. Based on my one-year experience, studying abroad, especially in the United States, one should know that due to the different culture, overseas students and American students are very different in their way of thinking, the angle of analyzing problems, and the way of getting along with people and so on. Therefore, we should keep an open and receptive attitude and learn to think in other people's ways, and get along with American students sincerely so that we can establish and maintain good friendship.

Finally, I want to say that learning is not just in classroom. In addition to classroom interactions, more contacts with American students and teachers by participating in their activities and making friends with them can provide us a deeper understanding of the United States, and we can gain more when studying abroad. If you get lost in the United States, don't hesitate to ask the local people for directions. Americans are kind and willing to help others. Of course, it would be more convenient to have a local map with you.

There are many things you should pay attention to when going out and studying in the

学生活，融入留学集体。到了美国后很可能吃不惯当地的食物，所以学会做饭既可以满足自己的口味，又可以节省一定的费用，何乐而不为呢？

回首过往，我的内心充满感激。感谢我的家乡，感谢我的母校，感谢四川省教育厅和教育部，感谢党和政府，感谢美国老师、同学和朋友们，感谢给过我帮助和关爱的每一个人。是你们，让我有勇气面对生活中的种种困难继续前行。是你们，让我的生命翻开了崭新的一页！

United States. After all, it's a different place, different environment, culture and system. It is important to learn about these differences so as to have a better life abroad and integrate well into the group. When you arrive in the United States, you may not be used to local food, so learning how to cook can not only satisfy your own appetite, but also save you some money. Why not?

When looking back, I am filled with gratitude. I am grateful to my hometown, my school, the Provincial Department of Education and the National Ministry of Education; I'm grateful to our Party and Government, to American teachers, classmates and friends, and to everyone who has helped and cared for me. It is you who have enabled me to have the courage to face all kinds of difficulties and move on in my life. It is you who have opened a new page for me.

# 西游东行记

## Journey to the West and East

郑渝鹏 / 西南交通大学　纽约州立大学德里学院

Zheng Yupeng / Southwest Jiaotong University　SUNY at Delhi

2008 年 8 月 15 日，因为"CSC-SUNY 150 奖学金项目"，我们踏上了美利坚合众国的土地。我四下环顾，觉得十分新鲜，长途飞行的疲惫早已消散，行前的嘱托在雀跃中也暂时被放在了一边。在纽约，目不暇接的欢迎与新奇事物"冲击"着我们，与八级地震"等量振幅"的关怀与爱却在所有人小心的呵护中融入我们每日生活的点滴，而对这些背后的努力和付出的体会却是在离开后才真正铺陈开来，让我们铭记于心。

### 西游

8 月底，我和 4 位同学来到纽约

On August 15th, we set foot on the United States of America because of the CSC-SUNY 150 Program. I looked around for all the fresh things and the fatigue of long-distance travel was gone, so were the words said to me before departure. We were "overwhelmed" by dizzying exotica and welcomes. The strength of love and care, as powerful as the M8 earthquake, became parts of our daily life. However, it was only after we left, that we started to think about people's efforts and devotions that contributed to our journey. They will be engraved on our minds.

### Journey to the West

It was the end of August when 3 of my classmates and I arrived at SUNY Delhi. Soon I was exhausted in the English-only environment. Barbra, the assistant of President Vancko, became my buddy and helped me to improve my oral

州立大学德里学院，很快我就在全英语的环境里累瘫了。凡科校长的助理芭芭拉成了我的好友，帮我提高口语水平快速融入校园生活。克雷格与玛丽亚带着我们穿越美国大陆，前往西雅图参观我最向往的建筑。每个节日，我们都会被邀请到老师或者校长家中做客，在万圣节挖南瓜，在感恩节做苹果派，在圣诞节和凡科校长的小孙子一起听圣诞故事。凭借着在行李箱中漂洋过海的泡椒罐头，我还一度被厨师学院的系主任邀请加入厨师学院。如果说家不是一个地方，而是一段时光，那么德里俨然是我们4个中国学生的小家。

248个日与夜，每一天都让我难忘。应华人协会邀请观看姚明NBA球赛，让不是篮球爱好者的我兴奋异常，与"CSC-SUNY 150奖学金项目"的小伙伴们摇旗呐喊。在纽约州州长助理胡思源叔叔的安排下，作为学生代表在奥尔巴尼受到州长夫人接见，并在官邸后院种下象征中美友谊的小树。在纽约大使馆与彭大使共进晚宴的时候，岑参赞的一首《九月九》激起了大家离别时的伤感。而最为难忘的是在美国的两次特别的毕业典礼：一次是我们四位德里的学子穿着特别的学士服，头顶着同班同学为我特殊制作的学士帽站在台上从凡科校长的

English as well as adapt to campus life quickly. Craig and Maria took me to travel across the United States. We headed for Seattle for the architectures I had been looking forward to seeing most. Every festival, we would be invited to our teachers' or the president's homes. We carved pumpkins on Halloween, made apple pies on Thanksgiving. And on Christmas, we listened to Christmas stories with the little grandson of President Vancko. I was also invited by Dean of School of Cook to join them just because of the preserved pepper cans I secretly kept in my luggage. If home was not a place but a period of time, then Delhi was the little home of us four Chinese students.

Those 248 days and nights are unforgettable. Even though I was not a fan of basketball, I was extremely excited and cheered loudly with other fellows of the 150 when I was invited by the Chinese Association to watch Yao Ming play basketball in NBA. Arranged by Uncle Siyuan Hu, the assistant of the governor of New York, the governor's wife received me as the representative of students, and we planted a little tree in the backyard of their house for the friendship between China and America. When having dinner with Consul General Peng at the New York Embassy, Counsellor Cen's song dissolved our sadness of departure. The most unforgettable thing was the two special commencements: one was when wearing the baccalaureate gown and cap made by my classmates, we four students took the graduation certificates from President Vancko. The other was when all the students of CSC-SUNY 150 Program got the certificates for the one-year exchange programs by Hudson River. The two graduation certificates didn't only mean

手中接过来自德里的毕业证书。一次是在哈得孙河边，全体"CSC-SUNY 150 奖学金项目"同学拿到这一年赴美交流的完美答卷。这两份毕业证书并不只意味着为期 248 天的结束，更是对我们每一位"CSC-SUNY 150 奖学金项目"学子未来的期许与鼓舞。

　　在纽约的最后一天，150 名学子在魏老师的带领下共同成立了第一个属于"CSC-SUNY 150 奖学金项目"基金会。我们约定，要将得到的这些帮助与爱传递下去，星星之火可以燎原。

the end of the 248 days, but more expectation and encouragement to everyone of CSC-SUNY 150.

Led by Mrs. Wei, the 150 students established the first Foundation of CSC-SUNY 150 on the last day in New York. We promised to pass on to others the help and love we have obtained.

## 东行

　　别离是开始的前奏。8 年过去，分散在各地的 150 位小伙伴在工作家庭的奔波中忙碌着，虽不时常联络，却因"CSC-SUNY 150 奖学金项目"牵连在一起，未曾忘记毕业时的约定。2016 年的早春，初生的"观花项目"就这样在魏老师的带领下将我和几位同伴聚在了一起。

　　观花项目是由联合国教科文组织、中国生物多样性保护与绿色发展基金会以及中国五大植物园联合支持的公益教育项目。在南京市 43 所小学试行近半年后，在魏老师、许多专家老师以及几位项目同伴的支持下，2016 年的初夏，我将"观花项目"

### Journey to the East

Separation is the prelude of new start. 8 years later, the 150 fellows are in different places and engaged in our work and family. We don't contact very often but we are united as one because of the program and didn't forget our promise on the graduation day. In the early spring of 2016, the "Flower Appreciation Project" led by Ms. Wei brought me and some other students of the 150 together again.

"Flower Appreciation Project" is a public welfare education project supported by UNESCO, China Biodiversity Conservation and Green Development Foundation and five botanical gardens of China. After a half-year's implementation in 43 primary schools in Nanjing, and with the support of Ms. Wei, many experts and teachers and some fellows of the 150, I brought the project to the mountain areas in the summer of 2016. I organized and planned the

带到了大山里，为我的家乡组织了"阿坝少年行"，免费为来自地震灾区茂县的24位羌族的孩子在茂县的黑虎小学带去全新的交流与实践活动。

并非教育专业的我在整个项目的设计与实践中战战兢兢，生怕一丝疏忽与大意辜负了这些孩子的期望，而同时又怕过分的关注对他们造成无形的压力。当年"CSC-SUNY 150 奖学金项目"中，那些关心我们的老师和支持者正是用她们的力量和爱小心翼翼地呵护着我们，我们才能在异乡怡然自得。

在结业典礼时，一个来自石大关乡小学的学生告诉我，她的理想是希望成为我这样的人，为自己的家乡贡献一分力量。我当时竟无语凝噎，一方面自惭自己的贡献太过微薄无法承受这样的赞誉，另一方面却满心鼓舞，感到充满了力量。我想也许贡献并不在于多么宏大，一些小小的改变和付出也许就能成为他人心中一粒小小的种子。

如果说8年前的西行是"CSC-SUNY 150 奖学金项目"的各个参与者为中国、为四川埋下的150粒种子，而8年后的阿坝少年行，则是传递新的"150粒"种子。

"Travel of Juveniles from Aba" and offered free exchanges and practices for 24 children of Qiang Nationality in Hei Hu Primary School in the earthquake-stricken areas of Mao County.

I was unconfident when planning and implementing the whole project because my major wasn't education. I was afraid to miss expectations from those children. Meanwhile, I was worried that too much attention might cause pressure to them. I remembered it was power and love given by those teachers and supporters in CSC-SUNY 150 Program that enabled us to live comfortably in a foreign country.

At the commencement, a pupil from the primary school of Shidaguan Township told me her dream was to contribute to her hometown like me. I was speechless at that moment. On one hand I was ashamed that my little contribution didn't match such compliment. On the other hand, I was encouraged and filled with strength. I thought maybe it didn't matter how great the contribution was, but a little change and devotion would become a seed in other people's heart.

If the west journey 8 years ago was 150 seeds that CSC-SUNY 150 Program buried for Sichuan, then the "Travel of Juveniles from Aba" 8 years later was to pass on another 150 seeds.

## 静待花开

**Waiting Quietly for Flower Blossom**

魏琳老师曾问我在美国这一年最深的感受是什么。十年前我说，在美国的那段时光似乎有着一种说不出的自在，在那里没有无处安放的梦想，似乎所有的小心思、小欲望和小期盼都可以找到安放的位置，并开出花儿来。临别前，克雷格与玛丽亚将我们"送还"到"CSC-SUNY 150 奖学金项目"的大集体中。依稀记得在大巴车上，我抱着玛丽亚哭着说"我现在的脸皮儿比鞋底还厚"。玛丽亚哈哈大笑，似乎她明白这样的厚脸皮儿是挣脱了别人的眼光后学着"做自己"的勇气和信心。

十年之后再回首，"CSC-SUNY 150 奖学金项目"之行并未在 2009 年的那个毕业典礼结束。在这十年之中，那些温暖和爱如同种子一样慢慢破土，滋养着我们，鼓舞着我们，将我们凝聚在一起，把这些温暖和爱播种开来。相信下一个十年，这些爱和温暖将会孕育出更多的种子，而我们只需静待花开。

Ms. Wei once asked me what impressed me most in the year in America. I replied 10 years ago, I was inexpressibly comfortable in America. There was no unrest dreams. It seemed that there were places for all subtle thoughts, desires and expectations. Before our departure from America, Craig and Maria sent us to meet the other members of the group of 150. I remembered I embraced Maria on the bus and cried, "My face now is thicker than the shoe sole." Maria laughed loudly. She seemed to know that "thick face" meant that I had found courage and confidence to "be myself."

10 years later, when I reminisced, the travel of program didn't end with the commencement in 2009. During the 10 years, the warmth and love have been nourishing us, encouraging us and uniting us together to pass on such warmth and love to more people. We believe that in the next 10 years, that love and warmth will bear more seeds. What we need to do is just wait for the flowers to bloom.

西南科技大学

Southwest University of Science and Technology

四海之纽
Taking the World as a
Link to Study in USA

# 纪念那段奇妙的未知之旅

## In Memory of that Wonderful Unknown Journey

陈冰 / 西南科技大学　纽约州立大学阿尔弗雷得陶瓷分校

Chen Bing / Southwest University of Science and Technology　NYS College of Ceramics at Alfred University

我叫陈冰，2006 年至 2010 年就读于西南科技大学，2008 年有幸参加了 "CSC-SUNY 150 奖学金项目"，如今距项目结束已有十年。回忆起当年的经历，就像电影片段似的历历在目。人生能有几个十年？时间似乎过得很快，但却又好慢，一切的一切，还要回到 2008 年。

还记得那年夏天，一群懵懂的少年，通过集体培训，经过大量信息的冲刷，茫然、不知所措地在老师的带领下顺利抵达纽约。一切都非常顺利，这个项目就像有魔法一样，各种手续都是零受阻，我的心情仿佛也如行云流水般，没有什么负担。抵达的那一刻仿佛做梦一样，或许在那之前，我

My name is Chen Bing. I studied in Southwest University of Science and Technology from 2006 to 2010. I was lucky enough to participate in the CSC-SUNY 150 Program in 2008, which was finished one decade ago. When reminiscing, that experience is like movie clips. Life can have a few decades, and time seems to pass quickly, but it is also very slow. Let's go back to the year of 2008.

I still remember that summer, when a group of ignorant teenagers, through collective training and acquiring a lot of information, arrived in New York under the guidance of our teacher. Everything went smoothly. The program was like magic. All the formalities were free of obstacles. My mood seemed to flow like the flow of water; there was no burden in heart. It was as in dream the moment I arrived in New York. Maybe before that, most of us had never thought of coming to such a remote foreign country. At least, I had

们中的很多人都没想过会来到这么远的地方吧，至少我当时没有想过。

"美国"这两个字，说出来很容易，看到这两个字也很容易，手机里、电视上、剧情中、别人的口中，好像这两个字离我们好近，我伸手就能够触碰到的感觉，当我真的踏上那片国土时，我才真正意识到，我脚踩着的这片土地已不叫"中国"，而是未知。

来到美国之后，据自己的专业我们每个人根被分配到不同分校。我被分到了阿尔弗雷得分校。到达分校后，我很幸运地被分配到一个叫"International House"的宿舍，这里有很多来自不同国家的留学生。到这一刻，我才放松紧张的神经。这里的每个人其实都和我一样，身处异国他乡，刚到时，一定也都觉得孤独无依。

never imagined it.

It is easy to speak out the two characters "Mei Guo (America)" and it is very easy for us to see these two characters too. They are in our mobile phone, television, drama, speech, as if the two characters are near to us. It seems that I can touch it when I stretch out my hand. But when I really set foot on this completely different country, I truly realized that the land my feet stepped on was no longer "China". It is unknown.

After coming to the United States, each of us was assigned to different campuses according to our major. My school was Alfred University. After arriving at the campus, I was lucky enough to be assigned to a dormitory called International House, where there were many foreign students from different countries. It was at this moment that I let go of the tension. Everyone there was just like me, in a foreign country and lonely. Soon I got to know a lot of new friends. Several Spanish and French students left a very deep impression on me. They often invited me out

很快我就认识了许多新朋友，几个西班牙和法国的留学生给我留下了非常深刻的印象。这群小伙伴经常带着我玩，有趣的聚会和活动都会叫上我，带着我一起体验了很多之前没有经历过的事情，我非常幸运能认识他们。我积极地融入他们，让相处变得愉快，我觉得自己是幸运的。

大家互相了解后，没了陌生的感觉，很多事都能放得开了。我还记得当年的万圣节，那也是我第一次在国外过节，跟在国内的氛围真的太不一样——化妆、扮演，各种各样新奇的事物让我不知不觉跟随着这里的节奏，体验着这里的快乐。万圣节那天，大家在一起化妆，连自己都快不认识了，真的很开心。我就像个小妹妹，跟着这群哥哥姐姐感受节日的气氛，享受着节日的快乐。类似的活动还有很多，那段时间我经历了好多自己从未经历的事，也真正让我体验到国外与国内的不同。开放包容的精神时时刻刻体现在周围的点点滴滴中，没有拘谨，没有不适应。脚踩的这片土地不再让我害怕和不知所措，反而慢慢变得清晰起来，我也开始用心去感受着身处异国的轻松。我像是在做一个奇妙的美梦，流连忘返，沉醉其中。

很快，两学期的时间就到了。该回家了，该离开美国了，所有曾经的

to play, to interesting parties and activities, and invited me to experience many things that I had never had before. We were very happy together, and I was really lucky to meet them.

After the initial understanding, we became very good friends, and there was no longer strangeness. Instead, we felt very comfortable with each other. I still remember the Halloween in that year, which was also the first holiday I experienced abroad. The atmosphere was really quite different from that in China. The makeup, acting and various novel things made me unconsciously follow the rhythm and experience the happiness. On Halloween, we put on makeup together, until we could not recognize each other; we really had a good time. I was just like a little girl, following this group of older brothers and sisters to feel the atmosphere of the festival, enjoying the festive joy. There were many other similar activities. During that time, I experienced a lot of things I had never experienced, which really made me taste the differences between China and foreign countries. The spirit of openness and inclusiveness was always reflected in the surrounding, and I felt neither stiff nor inadaptable. The ground I stepped on no longer made me scared and confused, but I gradually became clear about my goal. I also began to

相遇相知，到如今都面临分离。也许这一次过后，此生难以相见，但时光不能停留，我也不能永远留在这里。尽管有着太多的难忘与不舍，我愿意再走一遍一年来熟悉的街道，再吃一次最爱的每一道菜，和最好的朋友们再举一次杯，再看看见证我一年成长的宿舍。为了纪念这个项目，2009年5月12日，学校还组织我们来自四川的几个学生在学校种下属于我们的小树，它是我们来过这里的见证。我也希望能把我这一段记忆和感情同这棵树苗一起留在这里，伴随它枝叶丰茂，任凭风吹雨打。

经过一年的留美生活，我最大的收获就是学会了独立，不仅仅学会了生活上的独立，还学会了精神上的独立。因为在很多时候，朋友们不可能随时都在身边帮助你、支持你。例如，在选课的时候，可能朋友们不能在一起上课，有时候会独自一人参与一堂课。身边没有熟悉的同伴，没有了依赖，只能硬着头皮去上课、参加考试等。当然，还有各种问题需要自己解决。

我时常在想我们到底是有多幸运，能让那么多的人无条件地照顾我们、爱我们，让我们无忧无虑地度过这段美好的时光；没有灾难过后的痛苦，让我们更加勇敢地去面对一切事

feel the ease of being in a foreign country. Such a relaxing and pleasant feeling was like a wonderful and beautiful dream, which made me linger on and indulge in it.

Time flied, and two semesters were about to be over. It was time to go home, to leave America. Once we said goodbye to each other, perhaps we would never meet again. As time could not stay still, we couldn't stay there forever. In spite of so many unforgettable moments, I had to say goodbye to this place, so I took a walk through the most familiar streets again, having my favorite dishes again, cheering with my best friends again, and taking a look at the dormitory that had witnessed my growth again. In order to commemorate this program, on May 12th, 2009, students from Sichuan were together to plant a tree on campus, which was a witness of our visit here. I wish I could leave my memory and feelings here with the growth of the sapling, unshaken in the wind and rain.

After one year's stay in the United States, I reaped independence, not only the independence of life but also the independence of spirit. In many cases, friends can not always be around to help and support you; you have to learn to be independent. For example, when selecting courses, it was likely that friends would not select

物，可能这就是来自不同国度的大爱吧。

回想十年前的事情我觉得特别有意思，每过一段时间都回去翻看那时候的照片，想起那时候的故事，甚至每到万圣节的时候我都会想起那张当时化得自己都认不出的脸。一张张笑脸、一页页画面，时常在我的梦中出现。十年前到达美国之前的紧张、即将离开时的不舍，都历历在目。我有时也会想如果当初没有去美国，现在的自己又会是什么样的，命运的奇妙就在于让人捉摸不透，却又乐在其中。

美国大学的课堂与母校的课堂区别是很大的。首先是师生关系，美国的师生关系更像是一个平等的交往关系。课堂互动的时候，美国老师更倾向于选择幽默轻松的教学方式，母校的老师略显严肃。课堂设置也有所不同，美国的一堂课可能只有几个学生，而母校的课堂是不可能出现这种情形的。在美国，同学间的关系较为疏远，而在母校，同学之间的联系非常密切，经常一起做很多事。在美国这种现象很少，他们各自都有不一样的想法，经常独自去完成。

说实话，这段留学经历对我后期择业的影响很大。我是一个工科生，但是后来我选择了从事与语言相关的工作。这段留学的经历使我在选择从

the same course, and you had to go to class alone. With no familiar companions around, no one to depend on, you were forced to go to class, to take exams all by yourself. Therefore, only when you are independent can you cope with difficulties you encounter.

I often wonder how lucky we were to have so many people willing to take care of us and love us unconditionally, and this great love from different countries made us enjoy this wonderful happy time.

It's so interesting to think of what happened ten years ago. I would go back and look at the photos, to recall the old stories, and even the makeup which made me unable to recognize myself at Halloween. The smiling faces and our life there often appear in my dreams. The dread before arriving in the United States a decade ago, and the reluctance to leave are always palpable in mind. I often imagine what I would be like now if I hadn't been to America. The wonder of fate is so elusive, but it also brings happiness to you.

The class in America is quite different from that in China. First, the teacher-student relationship in America is more like a coequal relationship. When interacting in class, American teachers are more inclined to choose a humorous and light-hearted way of teaching, while teachers from my class in China are slightly more serious. The class size is also different, with only a few students in American class sometimes, which is impossible in my Alma mater. In the United States, the relationship between classmates is even more distant, while in my Alma mater, the connection between classmates is very close. We often like to do things together with others, but this situation does not happen very often in the

事相关工作时有了一定优势。这十年来，我的工作总体来说是顺利的。虽然中间也遇到了很多困难，但最后都有好的结果。

虽然目前我只是公司的一个普通员工，刚入职这家公司4个月，所从事的也是自己之前没有接触过的行业。但是通过这几个月的努力工作，获得了公司领导的好评。这一切的美好都与在美期间的经历、见闻是分不开的。这段难忘的留学经历让我能快速适应不同的企业文化。当然，除此之外还有我的自信、不卑不亢与从容应对。

因为这段经历，我接触到了不同的文化，开阔了眼界，同时也让自己在很多方面得到了锻炼和提升，变得独立、自信，也变得更包容。正是因为这些，我在后来的工作中，在接触到不同文化的时候，才能从容面对困难，用心去包容、理解不同的企业文化并融入其中。这十年来，我结婚生子，组建了一个完整幸福的家庭，这也是我所取得的最大成就。

由于文化的差异，与美国友人维持友谊的最好方式就是尊重对方，包括尊重对方的习惯、隐私，当然还有坦诚相待。我相信，不管面对什么样的人，只要真诚地对待他人，一定也会获得他人的真诚相待。虽然在美

US. They like to complete their independent ideas more.

To be honest, this experience of studying abroad greatly influenced my later career choice. I was an engineering student, but later I chose to engage in language-related work. Because of the experience of studying abroad, I had the advantage when choosing to engage in relevant work. Over the past decade, my work has generally gone well. Although I encountered many difficulties in my job-hunting, I overcame them all and the result was satisfactory.

As an ordinary employee of a company at present, I have just been working in this company for four months. The work I am doing now is totally new to me. Through these months of hard work, I have received the company leader's high praise. All this glory is inseparable from my experience in the United States. Thanks to this unforgettable study abroad experience, I can quickly adapt myself to and integrate into different corporate cultures. In addition, I am getting more and more confident.

Because of this experience, I have been exposed to different cultures, which have broadened my horizon. At the same time, I have been trained and improved in many aspects. I have become independent, confident and more tolerant. Because of this, I was able to face the

国留学期间，我们顺利度过了一年，遇到的人都是友好的，但偶尔也会有不好的消息传来，例如枪声。所以出国留学时要注意人身安全。多参与学校举办的一些活动，这样不仅可以交往到不同的朋友，英语水平还会噌噌地上升。美国大学非常强调学生的个性化发展，包括考试的时候大家的答案都不能是相似的。如果相似了，就会判为作弊！想要外出留学的同学们千万不要像我一样腼腆，对待朋友要主动，要大胆去交新朋友。

未来的路还很长，希望在未来的十年、二十年，甚至更漫长的时光里，自己能在变得越来越成熟的同时不忘初心，在某个领域发光发热。能将爱的精神延续下去，帮助别人，就像自己刚到美国时被关怀照顾那样。

能够参与"CSC-SUNY 150 奖学金项目"，我一直都觉得自己非常幸运，它潜移默化地在各个方面影响着我，指引着我。感谢项目中遇到的每一个人、每一件事，感谢这段奇妙的旅程。

difficulties calmly when I came into contact with different cultures in the later work, and I understood and integrated into various cultures. Over the past decade, I've got married, with a baby and a happy family, which is also my greatest achievement.

Due to cultural differences, the best way to maintain friendship with American friends is to respect each other. This includes respecting each other's habits, privacy and, of course, being honest with each other! I believe that no matter what kind of people we face, as long as we treat others sincerely, we will certainly get the sincerity from others. If you go to study in America, take part in some activities held on campus, so that you can not only communicate with different friends, but also improve your English. American universities place a lot of emphasis on individual development, bearing no tolerance of similar answers in exams. If the answers are similar, it's cheating! Students who want to study abroad should not be as shy as I used to be. Take initiative and make new friends.

There is still a long way to go. I hope I can become more and more mature in the next decade, two decades and even longer. At the same time, I will never forget my original intention and I hope I can make a difference in a certain field. To carry on the spirit of love and be willing to help others, just as I was cared for when I first arrived in America.

How lucky I am to be a member of the CSC-SUNY 150 Program, which has influenced and guided me in many ways. Thanks to everyone and everything I met in the program, and thanks for this amazing journey.

# 坚持信念，砥砺前行

## Holding on to Faith and Moving Forward

丁勇 / 西南科技大学　纽约州立大学坎顿学院

Ding Yong /Southwest University of Science and Technology　SUNY at Canton

2008 年，我有幸参加 "CSC-SUNY 150 奖学金项目"，在美国纽约州立大学学习一年。大学毕业后我进入了一家美国石油服务企业，在北京工作两年后，辗转世界各地工作，最后选择和家人一起在成都定居。2016 年步入汽车行业后，我又开始了各地奔波的日子。如今我在美国密歇根工作和生活。

繁忙的工作、快捷的生活节奏和瞬息万变的信息社会，让人变得不太善于回忆。站在而立之年的人生节点上，过去十年的种种在我的脑海中一一掠过，我不禁感慨万千。十年时光，我一步一步走过，人生就是由一个又一个的十年组成。回首过去，珍

In 2008, I was honored to participate in the CSC-SUNY 150 Program and study at the State University of New York (SUNY) for one year. After graduating from the college, I worked in an American oil service company in Beijing for two years, and then moved to some other places around the world and at last settled in Chengdu with my family. After entering the auto industry in 2016, I started to travel around again. Now I am living and working in Michigan.

Busy work, fast life pace and the rapidly changing information society cause people to not do well in recalling. Standing at the turning point of life in my 30s, things over the past ten years have crossed my mind and all sorts of feelings well up in my mind. I have gone through these 10 years step by step, and our life is made up of every ten years. Looking back, cherishing the present and looking forward to the future seems to be the best way to commemorate that period of

惜当下，展望未来，似乎才是纪念那段回忆最好的方式。

2008 年注定是不平凡的一年。从宏观层面来看，2008 年对于国家历史和民族情感是有重大意义的一年。对于那年有幸参加"CSC-SUNY 150 奖学金项目"到海外留学的我们来说，这一年是我们人生的转折点。因为在这特别的一年里，命运的画笔在我们人生的画卷上描绘出了完全不同的轨迹。

我出身于一个普通农村家庭，父母含辛茹苦地送我进大学求知求学。和那个时代千千万万个农村家庭一样，出国留学从来都不是我人生规划的一部分，它遥远得像一个梦。但在我心中，对未来的美好憧憬虽然朦胧，却从未因家庭经济条件的欠缺而放弃。"有朝一日，去见识更高更远的世界"，像一颗深埋在内心的种子，只等遇到合适的土壤、水分和温度，就能破土而出，生出最柔软的绿意。而"CSC-SUNY 150 奖学金项目"的到来，就是滋养这颗种子的阳光和雨露。我多么幸运，梦想终于迎来了得以实现的机会。

我第一次接到该项目的通知时，那种难以置信的激动和兴奋令我毕生难忘。报名之后，经过层层选拔和面试等环节，我和其他 149 名同学一起，

time.

2008 was meant to be an extraordinary year. At the macro level, 2008 is a year of great significance for the country's history and national sentiment. For us who had the honor to study abroad through the CSC-SUNY 150 program that year, it was a turning point in our life. In this special year, the brush of fate left a completely different stroke in our life scroll.

I came from an ordinary family in the countryside. My parents put up with all kinds of hardships to send me to university. Like millions of students from rural families back then, studying abroad was never part of my life plan. It was so far away that it seemed like a dream. But in my heart, although the longing for a bright future was hazy, I never gave up my dream just because of family economic condition. The vision "One day, go to see a higher and farther world" was like a seed buried deep in my heart, and it would break out and produce the softest green color with the right soil, water and temperature. The arrival of the CSC-SUNY 150 Program was the right sunshine and rain that nourished this seed. How lucky I was that the dream I had been looking forward to all day had finally come true.

I still remember the incredible excitement that I had when I first received the notice of the program. After the application, several rounds of selection and interview, together with 149 other students, I finally embarked on the journey of studying in the United States. The dribs and drabs I had experienced with my classmates and teachers during that time always arise in my mind.

During the first month in the United States, we were like the children who just arrived in

终于踏上了留美学习的征程。那段时间，我和身边的同学、老师一起度过的点点滴滴，至今仍记忆犹新。

在刚到美国的那一个月里，我们像刚来到这个世界的小孩，以好奇的眼光去观察陌生的国度、陌生的环境、陌生的文化，每天几乎都有新奇的事情发生。

在美国的大学里，新生入学的前两天是新生环境熟悉日。我们不仅参观了纽约州立大学坎顿校区，熟悉了校园周围的环境，还在奥格登斯堡的雷明顿博物馆里，第一次近距离接触了美国历史初期的印第安历史和牛仔文化。随后，我们又在老师的带领下，爬上了美国排名第五的高山，20 世纪 80 年代奥运会滑雪地——美国纽约州白脸山。立于高山之巅，群山皆在脚下，云海翻腾，天空辽远。在天地之交，在自身的渺小与自然的伟大之间，一览众山小的豪气第一次充盈我的胸膛。

开学第一天，一场隆重的开学典礼宣告着我们美国留学之旅的正式开启。从大教室到小教室，从大课堂到小课堂，从中文到英文，全新的生活环境对我发起挑战。但在老师和同学们的帮助和陪伴下，经过两周的适应和调整，我逐渐习惯并开始了有条不紊的学习生活。我和老师同学打成了

this world, looking at a strange country, strange environment and strange cultures with curiosity. New things occurred almost every day.

In American universities, there is freshman orientation during the first 2 days of a new semester for the students to get familiar with the environment. Not only did we visit the entire Canton campus of SUNY and become familiar with the surrounding environment of the campus, but we also had our first close encounter with the beginning of American history and cowboy culture in the Remington Museum in Ogdensburg. Then, under the guidance of our teacher, we climbed the fifth-highest Mountain in the United States, the 1980s Olympic Games skiing sites—Whiteface Mountain in New York state. When I stood on the top of the mountain, with mountains at feet, clouds writhing and the sky wide and distant, I felt the heroic spirit derived from the grandeur of nature for the first time.

On the first day, a grand opening ceremony announced the official start of our study in the United States. From big classroom to small classroom, from big class to small class, from Chinese to English, the new living environment challenged me. However, with the help and company of my teachers and classmates, after two weeks of adaptation and adjustment, I gradually got used to the well-organized study and life. I got along well with my teachers and classmates and learned the American humorous way of life and manner of doing things. Life and study were compact and full, happy and interesting, like the clear stream flowing down. Every day was filled with joy and expectation.

At the end of October, the first snowfall in 2008 winter arrived in time. It was such a

一片，学会了美国式幽默的生活方式和处事态度。学习生活紧凑充实、愉快有趣，每一天都充满了成长的喜悦和期待。

10 月底，2008 年美国冬日里的第一场雪如约而至。这是我印象里如此美丽的一个冬天，大地上铺了厚厚的一层雪，漫天飞舞的雪花像一个个跳跃的音符，在天地间谱成一段段冬日旋律。大地银装素裹，清雅素丽。而这粉妆玉砌的雪景中，每扇窗户透出的灯火，像天际远处的星星，在夜幕里晕出一朵朵暖意的黄色。

在这样可爱的冬日里，我和其他 5 名同学一起，度过了一段难忘的时光。纽约州立大学坎顿校区里，各式各样的校园活动非常丰富。为了传播发扬中国文化，我们组织了东方中文协会。在留学期间，我们在全校范围内举办了两次大型活动。第一次是 2008 年 11 月初举办的以中国文化为主题的展览。我们准备了丰盛的中国美食，向美国同学介绍中国的经济、历史和文化，得到了校长的高度评价。第二次是在 2009 年春节，我们在全校范围内举办了一次春节联欢晚会。除了丰盛的中国餐，我们还介绍了中国春节的来历等传统节日文化。除此之外，我们还去了当地的小学进行演讲，教美国小朋友学习中文。和那些

beautiful winter, the ground covered with a thick layer of snow, and the flying snowflakes like jumping notes, forming a winter melody between the heaven and the earth. The world was wrapped in silver and became so elegant and beautiful. In the snow scene made of powdery jade, the lights from each window were like the distant stars in the sky, glittering a warm yellow color at night.

In such a lovely winter day, I spent a memorable time with five other students. There were many kinds of activities in the Canton campus of SUNY. To spread and promote Chinese culture, we organized the Oriental Chinese Club. During the whole study abroad period, we held two large-scale activities. The first was an exhibition on Chinese culture in early November 2008. We prepared rich Chinese food and introduced China's economy, history and culture to American students, which was highly supported and evaluated by the principal. The second was in the Spring Festival in 2009. We held a Spring Festival party. In addition to the rich Chinese food, we also introduced the origin of the Chinese Spring Festival and other traditional festival culture. In addition, we went to the local primary school to give speeches and teach American children Chinese. The precious experience of learning and communicating with those children was one of the most beautiful moments in my memory.

There are many festivals in America. The two most important ones are Thanksgiving and Christmas. The American culture and traditions reflected by these two festivals also impressed me deeply. Before Thanksgiving, people fast for a day and wait for the big dinner at night. The absolute star of the dinner is, of course, the

孩子们一起学习交流的宝贵体验，是我记忆中最美好的片段之一。

　　美国的节日很多，最重要的当属感恩节和圣诞节。这两个节日折射出的美国文化和传统，给我留下了深刻的印象。感恩节前人们要禁食一天，直到晚上才能享用丰盛的晚餐。晚餐的绝对主角当然是美味的火鸡。在圣诞节前夜，美国家庭里的所有成员都要到教堂做礼拜。回到家后，大人会劝小孩早点入睡，等候圣诞老人的到来。第二天清晨，4点左右，小孩兴奋地起床，大家一起聚集在圣诞树下，拆开圣诞老人送来的礼物。小礼物都装在大袜子里，此刻是小孩最高兴的时候，他们会迫不及待地查看礼物，然后玩一整天。

　　2009年1月，作为"CSC-SUNY 150奖学金项目"的一个重要组成部分，青年领导力培训项目分别在克林顿和华盛顿两地举行。参加此次培训，对我来说是很宝贵的一次经历。我不仅对领导模式有了更深入的理解，而且对如何提高团队领导与协作、解决团队中的矛盾有了更直观的感受。这些为我回国毕业后的择业、就业提供了有力的帮助。

　　2009年4月，为促进中美两国人民的友谊，我们作为文化交流使者，在纽约州州长官邸种下了两棵象

delicious turkey. On Christmas Eve, all members of an American family go to church. When back home, adults urge children to go to bed early and wait for Santa. The next morning, around 4 o'clock, the children get up excitedly and gather around the Christmas tree, opening the gifts packages. Small gifts are packed in big socks, and it is the happiest time for children. They can not wait to see the gifts.

Then, in January 2009, the Youth Leadership Training Program, as an important part of the CSC-SUNY 150 Program, was held respectively in Clinton and Washington. It was a valuable experience for me to attend this training. I not only obtained a deeper understanding of the leadership model, but also had a more intuitive feeling on how to improve team leadership, collaboration ability and way to solve the contradictions in the team. All of these have provided big help for my job selection and employment after returning to China.

In April 2009, in order to promote the friendship between Chinese and American people, we, as cultural exchange ambassadors, planted two trees in the governor's department of New York to symbolize the friendship between China and the United States. I, as one of a group of 12 students, then joined the SUNY-Canton Bridge Team and attended the ASCE summit in Buffalo, New York. The steel bridge designed by our team won the first place in New York in the bridge competition. Then, in May, our team won the first prize in the national competition in Las Vegas. The experience of these two awards brought us closer to our American classmates. Our feelings became deeper in cooperation and competition.

征中美友谊的小树。随后我加入了学校 12 名学生组成的桥梁小组，参加了在纽约水牛城（即布法罗）举行 ASCE 的峰会。我们小组设计制作的钢架桥在桥梁比赛项目中荣获纽约第一名。5 月份在拉斯维加斯的全国比赛中，我们小组又荣获全美的项目第一。这两次获奖的经历，进一步拉近了我们和美国同学之间的距离，我们的感情在合作与考验中变得更加深厚。

在美国留学那宝贵的一年中，和大家一起相处的点点滴滴装点了我的留学记忆，留下了珍贵的足迹。我仍清楚地记得，举行毕业典礼那天，大雨倾盆。离别的伤感仿佛被风雨感知，一起落在脚下那片美丽的土地上。虽然工作以后，大家都各奔东西，少有联系，但那份内心深处对彼此的牵挂依然没有随时间的增长而淡去。

当我带着中美两国人民的爱和期望踏上归途，内心除了感恩和留恋，还有一丝对未来的期许。盼望多年后自己能有所作为，有机会回到这里重拾记忆。没想到，人生虽然曲曲折折、跌跌撞撞，但当初的那丝期许却变成了现实，我没有辜负那段美好的时光。

毕业以后，有几份工作供我选择。正当我左右为难、难以抉择的时候，其中一位人事经理提到了工作条

The bits and pieces during the precious year of studying abroad in the United States decorated my memory, leaving precious footprints. I still vividly remember that on the day of the graduation ceremony, the rain poured down. The sadness of leaving seemed to be felt by the wind and rain, floating and falling together on the beautiful land under our feet. Although we drifted apart working in different places after graduation, and rarely contacted each other, the deep concern for each other would not fade over time.

When I returned with the love and expectation of the Chinese and American people, I felt not only gratitude and nostalgia, but also a glimmer of hope for the future. I hope I can make a difference many years later and have a chance to come back and regain my memory. Unexpectedly, although life is full of twists and turns, and stumbles, the expectation has actually become reality, and I have not failed that period of good time.

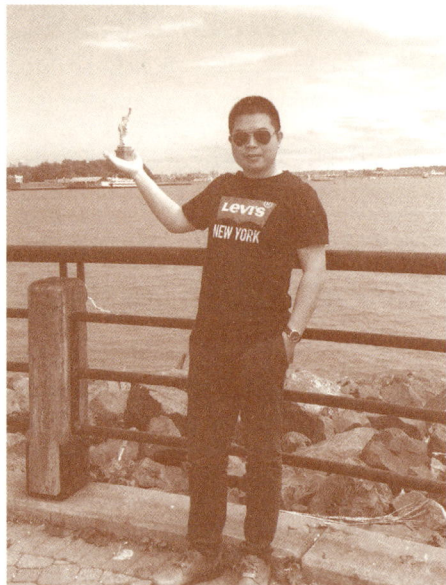

件之一是国际化的工作环境。也正是因为这句话，触动了我的内心，更激起了我心中一个坚定的信念：在一个国际化的工作环境中迅速提升英语能力。机缘巧合之下，我来到了北京。当我拖着一个大行李箱，第一次仰望北京这座温厚包容的城市时，就像当初置身美国纽约，"艰苦奋斗"的信念盖过了一切初来乍到的不适。每次出差，去到不同的地方、感受不同的风土人情和文化氛围、体验不同的生活环境，都能激起我内心对生活的热情和活力。两年之后，我回到成都追求事业，并在这里组建了家庭，完成了生命中的一件大事。

人生，如一片广阔海域，不可能永远平静无波、不起波澜。海浪总是起起伏伏，拍打着礁石和海岸。当人生处于风雨交加的低谷时，依然坚持信念，充满希望，才能最终跨越风浪，迎来真正的云开日出、海阔天空。留学的经历和第一段五年的工作经历锻炼了我、成就了我，给我现在的工作打下了良好的基础。当你把兴趣爱好当作信念的时候，所有的努力和付出就像给信念的种子浇灌雨露、播撒阳光。

后来，我在石油行业的巨浪中失去方向，面临再一次抉择人生方向的重要时刻。我拾起了一直深埋在心底

After graduation, I got several job offers in front of me. While I was in a quandary, one of the HR staff mentioned that one of the working conditions was an international working environment. This touched my heart and aroused a firm belief in my heart: to improve my English in an international working environment. By chance, I arrived in Beijing. When I first looked up at Beijing, a gentle and tolerant city, with a big suitcase, it was like my life in New York in the United States, where the belief of "fight your way" overshadowed all the discomfort of being a newcomer. Every business trip, going to different places, experiencing different local customs, cultural atmosphere, and experiencing different living environments, can arouse my inner passion and vitality for life. Two years later, I returned to Chengdu to pursue my career. I had a family here, which was a milestone in my life.

Life, like a vast sea, cannot be calm forever. Waves always ebb and flow, lapping on rocks and shores. When life is at the trough of ups and downs, adhere to your faith, be full of hope, and you can finally cross the waves and usher in a real sunrise, broad sky. The experience of studying abroad and the work experience of the first five years have trained and accomplished me and laid a good foundation for my current working state. When you take your interests and hobbies as your beliefs, all the effort is like pouring rain and sunshine into the seeds of your beliefs.

Later, I lost my direction in the wave of the oil industry and faced the important moment of deciding the direction of my life again. I picked up the dream and belief that had been buried deep in my heart—the automobile industry, and all of this was inseparable from my wife's unconditional trust and support. As my beloved

的梦想和信念——汽车行业，而这一切都离不开妻子给予我无条件的信任和支持。作为我挚爱的伴侣，她的温柔和理解如命运赐予的礼物，伴随着我度过人生一次又一次重要的考验。

如今总结过去的十年，是最初留学期间培养起来的兴趣、毅力和眼界改变了我的人生轨迹，也是这些力量让我在曲折的路程中始终朝着一个方向不懈前进。过去的十年记忆以"CSC-SUNY 150 奖学金项目"开始，它的美好和珍贵永远不会消失。回忆往昔，我无比感恩相遇过的老师和同学，他们是这份美好记忆中不可或缺的一部分，也是我人生航程中的引领者和助力者。

坚持信念，砥砺前行，我将一如既往，搏击海浪。

companion, her tenderness and understanding, like a gift given by fate, accompanied me through one important test after another.

Now, to sum up the past ten years, it is the interest, perseverance and horizon cultivated during the initial study abroad that have changed my life track, and it is also these forces that have driven me to make unremitting progress in one direction throughout the tortuous journey. The past decade of memory began with the CSC-SUNY 150 Program, and its beauty and preciousness will never end. Recalling the past, I am extremely grateful to the teachers and classmates I met. They are an integral part of this beautiful memory, and also a leader and booster in my life journey.

Holding on to faith and moving forward, I will continue to fight against waves.

# 再回首：感恩那段美国行

## Looking Back: Being Grateful for the American Trip

马洁好 / 西南科技大学　纽约州立大学德里学院

Ma Jiehao / Southwest University of Science and Technology　SUNY at Delhi

2008 年 "5·12" 汶川特大地震发生的时候，我还是西南科技大学建筑系一名懵懂的大一新生。由于地处绵阳的学校受灾严重，我不得不回到同样位于重灾区的家中，和家人们一起度过了睡帐篷、在体育馆躲避余震的一个多月。

没想到的是，灾后这段浑浑噩噩的日子被辅导员突然打来的电话彻底改变了。辅导员只说国际合作交流处让他通知我赶回学校参加一个面试。哪里想到，一回到学校就是参加持续到当天晚上的初步面试，接着是通过初步面试的同学留校进行了一周的有关项目的资料学习和后一轮面试准备，之后就是到成都接受留学基金委

When the Wenchuan Earthquake happened in 2008, I was an ignorant freshman in the Department of Architecture in Southwest University of Science and Technology. The school in Mianyang was so badly hit that I was forced to return to my home in the same hard-hit area and spent more than a month with my family sleeping in tents and gymnasiums to escape from the aftershocks.

Unexpectedly, the day of muddling around after the disaster was completely changed by the sudden call from my college counselor, when he said that I was informed to return to school and attend an interview at the International Cooperation and Exchange Department, I took part in an interview which lasted until night. After that, those who passed the initial interview stayed in the university and prepared for the next interview, learned about the program, and then took part in the CSC interview in Chengdu.

老师们的面试。

记忆中的那一个月，信息量巨大，各种复杂的情绪交织在一起，惊喜、好奇、感激、紧张、恐惧、焦虑、迷茫。当时那个无知的 19 岁的我在最初的压力和焦虑下甚至想要放弃参加这个项目。那时的我根本无法想象，这一项目的背后有多少中美两国的好心人对我们灾区学生的关怀，自己能意外获得这样的机会是何其幸运，而接下来 9 个多月的经历又是何其难忘。

在中美两国领导人的关心下，美国驻中国领事馆、SUNY、CSC、四川省教育厅等两国的各级有关部门都为我们"CSC-SUNY 150 奖学金项目"能在短短一个多月里顺利实现付出了巨大努力。2008 年 8 月 16 日，我们 150 个学生真的站在了美国的土地上！实际上，当时的我仍是懵懂的。在一个小城市生活了十几年的我本就没见过什么世面，异国他乡的一切更是新奇与未知。那时候我也几乎没怎么看过美剧，对美国学习生活的方方面面都太陌生了。

但幸运的是，在美国我遇到了那么多友好的老师、同学。当我们 4 个分到纽约州立大学德里学院的同学初到"Riverview"宿舍的时候，我还天真地以为，这里的宿舍都是这么豪华的。那是一排新修的两层高坡屋顶联

In my memory, I was totally confused in that month, with the huge amount of information coming to me. I had pressure and mixed emotions at the same time: surprise, curiosity, gratitude, nervousness, fear, anxiety and confusion, etc. The funny thing was, as an ignorant 19-year-old girl, under stress and anxiety, I even thought of giving up and quitting the program. At that time, I couldn't imagine how many people from both China and the United States had been involved in this program and showed their concern to the students from the disaster area, how lucky I was to have such an opportunity, and how unforgettable the experience of the next nine months would be.

With the concern of leaders from both China and the United States, the US consulate in China, SUNY, CSC and the Education Department of Sichuan Province had made great efforts to make the program come true successfully in just one month. On August 16, 2008, we 150 students from the program really stood on the American land! But in fact, at that time, I was still ignorant. Having lived in a small city for more than a decade, I had never seen anything out of my small world, and everything in a foreign country was new and unknown. At that time, I hardly ever watched American TV series. I was unfamiliar with all aspects of American study and life.

Fortunately, I met so many friendly teachers and classmates in America. When the four of us who had been assigned to SUNY Delhi first arrived at Riverview, I naively assumed that the dormitories were all so luxurious. It was a row of newly built two-story high-pitched townhouses, each housing eight students, with living rooms, kitchens, dining rooms, four toilets, four double rooms and four single rooms. It wasn't until we

排小别墅，每个别墅可供 8 个学生居住，内都有客厅、厨房、餐厅、4 个卫生间、4 个双人间和 4 个单人间。直到在那里居住了一段时间，我们才得知，"Riverview"别墅区不仅住宿费用昂贵，且只有品学兼优的学生才可以申请入住。早在我们"CSC-SUNY 150 奖学金项目"成行前一个月，德里分校的校长和老师们刚刚得知将有 4 个来自四川地震灾区的学生到德里分校学习一年时，他们第一时间向纽约州立大学董事会提出"我们希望给这几个中国学生最好的宿舍条件，要让他们住最新的、有厨房的宿舍"。这份来自美国校方的真实情谊从我们素未谋面开始一直延续到 9 个月之后我们依依不舍地离开，直到如今，仍深深感动着我、温暖着我。

初到学校，善良的美国老师们总是给我们提供各种帮助。其中最让我们感动的是克雷格。因为他当时是纽约州立大学德里学院的招生服务处主任，主管学生招生入学工作。从帮助我们办理入学开始，他的和蔼友善就给我们留下了深刻印象。于是，开学后我们总是在课间带着一些或大或小的麻烦去敲开他办公室的大门，向他寻求帮助。而他仿佛从不觉得被打扰，总是微笑着迎接我们，帮我们解决学习生活中遇到的新问题，或者就

lived there for a period of time that we learned that the Riverview villa area was not only expensive to live in, but also that only students who were both morally and academically qualified could apply to live there. In fact, the principals and teachers at SUNY Delhi learned the news about the CSC-SUNY 150 Program only one month before we arrived. When they got the news that four students from the earthquake-stricken area in Sichuan would come and stay at Delhi for one year, they first proposed to the Board of Directors of SUNY that "We hope to give these Chinese students the best living conditions, and live in the latest dormitory with kitchens." This sincere friendship lasted from the moment we arrived to the moment we left after nine months. I am still deeply moved up to now.

When we first arrived at school, the kind American teachers always gave us all kinds of help. Craig was the one who touched us the most. As he was the Enrollment Services Dean of SUNY Delhi at that time, he was in charge of the enrollment of students. Since he helped us with the enrollment, his kindness and friendliness left a deep impression on us. So, even after school started, we always went to his office and asked him for help with some big or small problems

只是陪我们愉快地聊聊天。

　　现在回想起来，他那一年不知道被我们这些原本不属于他工作范畴的琐事给打断了多少次。但他和蔼的笑容、一遍遍耐心的解释作答、交谈时有意放慢的语速，总是吸引着我们。我们一次又一次去打扰他，而他竟然也真的把我们的各种琐事都当成自己的事来解决，甚至亲自开车送我们去买生活用品，带我们去申请社会保险号，带我们去纽约市和奥尔巴尼参加活动……我 20 岁生日那天刚好是周末，克雷格和他夫人玛丽亚邀请我们到他们家里做客。我并没有提及我的生日，没想到克雷格夫妇和另外三个小伙伴早就给我准备好了惊喜。能有一个如此难忘的 20 岁的生日，我是多么幸运！在我们心中，克雷格就像是我们在德里的家长，于是在临别之际，我们邀请克雷格夫妇参加"CSC-SUNY 150 奖学金项目"在东湖公园的毕业典礼。2009 年 9 月，我们又邀请了校长坎迪斯夫妇和克雷格夫妇作为我们 SUNY 亲友团的代表到成都做客。

　　为了让我们更好地了解美国文化和他们的家庭生活，在德里很多其他的老师和同学们也会在美国的各个传统节日时热情地邀请我们去他们的家里做客。万圣节时，我们应邀去好友

at the breaks of classes. He never seemed to feel disturbed, always smiling and offering help to solve all kinds of problems in our study and life, or just chatting with us pleasantly.

In retrospect, it's hard to know how many times his work that year was interrupted by our own trivial matters that were out of his responsibility. But his affable smile, his patient explanation and his reduced speech rate attracted us so much, we went to bother him again and again, and he was willing to take our trifles as his responsibility, and even personally drove us to buy daily necessities, apply for the SSN (social security number), and attend New York and Albany activities... One weekend when Craig and his wife, Maria, invited us to their home, it happened that it was my 20th birthday, but I didn't tell them that. I didn't expect that Craig, his wife and three other friends had already prepared a surprise for me. How lucky I was to have such a memorable 20th birthday! In our mind, Craig was like our parent in Delhi. On the parting day, we invited Craig and his wife to our graduation ceremony in East Lake Park. In September 2009, we invited President Candace and the Craigs as representatives to visit Chengdu.

To give us a better understanding of American culture and their family life, there were many other teachers and classmates in Delhi who always warmly invited us to their homes on various traditional festivals in the United States. On Halloween, we were invited to our friend Amy's house to carve pumpkin lanterns. We watched the children in various costumes going from house to house with buckets of candy. On Thanksgiving Day, Teacher Pam from the library invited us to her home to have a Thanksgiving

艾米家刻南瓜灯，看各种扮相的孩子们提着小桶挨家挨户索要糖果；感恩节时，图书馆的帕姆老师邀请我们去她家和她的家人们一起吃感恩节火鸡大餐，那张餐桌上的烛光有着家一般的温暖；圣诞节时，我们又应邀到校长坎迪斯家吃大餐，和她可爱的孙儿孙女们一起在圣诞树下听老奶奶讲圣诞老人的故事。这些走进美国家庭的快乐时光，让我对美国传统文化产生了浓厚的兴趣，也让我和美国朋友们建立了更深厚的友谊。

一转眼，"CSC-SUNY 150 奖学金项目"竟然已经是十年以前的事了。我偶尔会跟一些朋友聊起关于那9个月的一些记忆，聊到那个梦里的某件小事或是某个可爱的人，对别人只是一个个小小的故事，但却印入我的记忆里。

现在回想，参加"CSC-SUNY 150 奖学金项目"似乎已很遥远了，但这段经历带给了我太多甚至当初不曾完全领悟的成长。突然远离家乡，

Turkey dinner with her family.

On Christmas, we were invited to Candace's home for a big dinner. We listened to the story of Santa Claus with her lovely grandchildren under the Christmas tree. These happy times of visiting American families have made me more interested in American traditional culture and helped me build a deep friendship with American friends.

In a flash, the CSC-SUNY 150 Program was ten years old. Sometimes I would naturally talk to some friends about the life in USA during those nine months, and talk about one certain thing or a certain lovely person; for others, it was just a story, but for me, it was true and always made me lost in the memories.

The CSC-SUNY 150 Program seemed a long way off, but the experience has given me so much growth that I did not fully understand at that time. Suddenly being far away from my hometown and familiar friends and relatives, I began to adapt to the new environment and accept all kinds of challenges of life and study alone. The rapid growth brought by this process is hard to describe in words, which has affected my life deeply till now. I learned to respect and understand the differences between people and cultures during my study and life in the United States. I also thought about many issues

远离熟悉的亲友，开始适应全新的环境，独自接受各种生活和学习的挑战，这个过程带给我的迅速成长难以用文字描述，至今仍深深影响着我的生活。在美国学习生活中体验到的各种文化差异让我学着去尊重和理解人与人、文化与文化的不同，也独立思考许多从前不会思考的问题。这部分有关文化差异的体验和思考至今仍影响着我思考很多问题和看待这个世界的角度。此外，国家留学基金委、纽约州立大学，以及许许多多我们不知名的人都对我们项目学生给了许多帮助与关心，美国的老师和同学们也给了我们无私的帮助和真挚的友谊。这些美好与感动至今温暖着我，让我一直心怀感恩与善念，同时激励我更自信、更勇敢地去拥抱生活，热爱这个奇妙的世界。

independently that I had never thought about before. The experience and thinking about cultural differences in this part still influence me to think about many issues and view the world. In addition, the CSC, SUNY and many other unknown people provided the students from the Program with a lot of help and care. The students and teachers from SUNY also gave me selfless help and we built up sincere friendship, which still move me and warm me, making me always grateful and full of good thoughts, and inspiring me to be more confident to embrace life and love this wonderful world.

# 生命中的魔法师："CSC-SUNY 150"项目

## Magicians in My Life: CSC-SUNY 150 Program

杨颖 / 西南科技大学　纽约州立大学坎顿学院

Yang Ying / Southwest University of Science and Technology　SUNY at Canton

　　我又翻开了 2008 年的记忆，时间回到那年的 7 月，我还是西南科技大学土木工程专业大二的一名女学生。距离那场惊天动地的大地震已经过去一个多月了，因为校舍在地震中受到不同程度的损毁，学校停课让学生们在家等候复学的消息。我们是灾区的孩子，我们经历过一场浩劫，可是我们没有悲观哀叹，我们依然坚强，依然对未来充满了憧憬。

　　那时正值盛夏，气温炎热得让人烦躁，但每日的新闻报道却总是让人心痛得如坠冰窟。就在那样一个与往日一样焦躁却又无奈的下午，我睡了一个长长的午觉，一觉醒来却发现竟有辅导员老师打来的 12 个未接来

Coming back to July, 2008, I was then a sophomore in Southwest University of Science and Technology, majoring in civil engineering. More than one month had passed since the 5·12 earthquake. Because school buildings were more or less damaged in the earthquake, school was closed and all students went back home waiting for resumption of schooling. We suffered a lot in the disaster, but we did not lament pessimistically. We were strong and still full of vision and ideals for the future.

It was in the middle of summer, and the heat was irritating. The daily news kept making us heart-broken like falling into ice. In such a restless but helpless afternoon as usual, I took a long nap, and woke up to find that there were 12 missed calls from my college counselor, I called her back nervously, wondering if we were expected to go back to school. I did not expect that it was an opportunity for us to study on the

电！我战战兢兢地给她回了电话，心想是否是学校准备复课了，谁知这竟是一个让我们到世界另一头学习的机会，这让我兴奋不已。正是这 12 个未接来电，开启了我与"CSC-SUNY 150 奖学金项目"奇迹般的缘分，也正是从这一刻起，我平凡的人生轨迹开始有了变化。谁能想到一个连彩票末等奖都从未中过的人，能够得到这样的惊喜呢？

在对未知环境的担心及乡愁中，我们到达了纽约。这是一片令人向往却有些缺乏安全感的土地，这里的一切陌生而又令我充满期待。作为四川人，爸妈最担心的就是饮食不习惯，汉堡三明治、咖啡碳酸饮料刚开始让我的"胃"感觉好新鲜，一段时间后，我就只能依靠"老干妈"解相思之苦。学校知道后，开始为我们准备米饭。你能想象吃多了各种面食的我，

other side of the world. It was these 12 missed calls that started my miraculous relationship with the CSC-SUNY 150 Program, and it was from this moment that my mediocre life path began to change. Who would have thought that a person who had never won the smallest lottery prize would get such a big luck?

Amid the fear of the unknown and the constant nostalgia, we arrived in New York, where everything was unfamiliar and strange to us. As a native of Sichuan Province, I knew what my parents most worried about was the diet. My "stomach" felt fresh at first with hamburgers, coffee and carbonated drinks. But after a period of time, I could only rely on "Lao Gan Ma" (kind of spicy sauce) to help me get rid of homesickness. When the university realized that, they began to prepare rice for us. Can you imagine how excited I was to see rice after eating so much pasta? Later, we started to make our own homemade hotpot that would satisfy my stomach for days. During our stay in SUNY Canton, it was just the love and care from teachers Wei Lin, Chen Taowei, and other CSC and SUNY staff, and also the warm welcome from the New York

见到大米饭时的兴奋吗？后来，我们开始自己动手，一顿自制火锅，可以让我满足好几天。在坎顿期间不论是魏琳老师、陈滔伟老师等所有 CSC 以及 SUNY 的工作人员对我们的贴心照顾，还是纽约华侨对我们的热情欢迎，都极大地缓解了我内心的恐慌和焦虑，让我慢慢地开始用心去享受这趟不一样的旅程，开始新的学习生活体验。

overseas Chinese that greatly reduced my fear and anxiety. I began to enjoy the extraordinary journey.

## 温暖我的那年那人那些事

纽约，这里的人们看似漂泊却又十分坚强，看似繁忙却又饱含激情。宝琳娜女士是我和丁勇、刘小林、鞠丹丹、郑苗以及张光辉几个小伙伴见到的第一位纽约州立大学坎顿学院的校方人员，她作为纽约州立大学坎顿学院的副校长以及校方代表将我们从海事学院接到了纽约州立大学坎顿学院，我们也因此对她从此有了雏鸟情结。

如果说宝琳娜对我们来说是一个母亲的形象，那玛里拉·菲阿科则更像我们的姐姐，她也是这一年中给我印象最深刻的人，不论是带我们到她家过感恩节，陪我们到加拿大游玩，还是随时解答我们的各种疑问，她永远向我们提供帮助，永远是那个亲切

## Those People and
## Years That Warmed Me

In New York, people seemed wandering but tough, busy and passionate. Ms. Pauline was the first SUNY Canton school staff that I met with my friends including Ding Yong, Liu Xiaolin, Ju Dandan, Zheng Miao and Zhang Guanghui. As the vice principal and school representative of SUNY Canton, she took us from SUNY Maritime to SUNY Canton, and we had a juvenile complex for her since then.

If Pauline was just like a mother for us, Marela Fiacco was like our elder sister. She left the most profound impression on me. She not only took us to her home for Thanksgiving Day and took us to Canada, but also answered our questions at any time and always was ready to offer us help. She was all the way the kind sister. She was always there for us Chinese friends in SUNY Canton at almost every significant time during that year. We did a lot of things together and talked a lot. But what impressed me most was a small thing.

的姐姐。玛里拉在这一年中几乎全程陪伴了我们坎顿学院的中国小伙伴的所有重要时刻。我们一起做了很多事情，说过很多话。但我印象最深刻的却是刚到美国不久发生的一件小事。

坎顿是个小镇，镇上的中国人屈指可数，除了镇上的两家中餐厅以及学校里的中国教授就只有我们几个学生了。每到周末就有不同的外国朋友找到我们，刚开始是邀请留学生参加午餐活动，大家相互交流。刚开始我觉得很新鲜，到后来大家都热情地邀请我加入他们各自的社团。那时候的我一方面对没有接触过的事情略感新鲜，一方面又很疑惑，我还不明白这些社团到底是什么，我是否需要，就不断被人劝说加入他们的社团，心中隐隐觉得有一种压迫感，我无法欣然接受，也不知怎么拒绝。

这时玛里拉告诉我，如果你想要了解这件事情，那么就去做；如果你在过程中觉得疑惑或不舒服，那么就停止。一定要考虑清楚，这是你自己的选择，不管你选择哪一个社团，或者不参加，也都是完全没问题的。你可以对他们说不，然后等到你想明白之后再做出自己的决定。

她的这番话如醍醐灌顶，我在过去的岁月中一直好像是活在家人、老师和朋友们对我的认知和期待中，我

Canton is a small town; we were the only Chinese in the town besides the two Chinese restaurants and a few Chinese professors on Canton campus. Every weekend, there were foreign friends coming to us. At first, they invited us overseas students to participate in the luncheon, and we communicated with each other. Later, they began to invite us to join their respective clubs. At that time, I was a little curious about the things I had never been exposed to. At the same time, I was very confused, because I did not understand what these clubs were, and I felt pressure and did not know whether I needed them when they came to ask me to join them.

Then Marela told me that if you wanted to know about it, just do it. If you feel confused or uncomfortable in the process, then stop. You can make your own choice and you have the right to say no to them. Think it clear and then decide it.

What she said was a revelation. I had always been living in the way that my family, teachers and friends perceived and expected from me. I tried to be obedient, a good student, a good kid, and no one ever taught me to refuse when feeling confused. This conversation planted a seed in my heart, and it sprouted and grew. I began to pay attention to my own feelings, which also made me realize that I should be my own master. I learned to listen to my inner voice and real thoughts, and it also made me conscious and courageous to make choices in the coming years.

I was not alone in SUNY Canton together with many people who loved me and helped me such as, Xiaoli, Mr. Feng and his beautiful wife, Maryann, Mr. B, Bill and so on. The days of being together with them are vivid till now.

努力地学习顺从，做个好学生、好孩子，却没有人教过我拒绝。没有人跟我说过，当你内心感到疑惑时，可以理直气壮地说"不"。这次的谈话在我心中埋下了一颗种子，然后发芽、生长。我开始关注自己的感受，这也让我意识到我才应该是自己的主人。懂得倾听自己内心的声音和真实的想法，也让我在未来的岁月中，能够有意识、有勇气去做选择，勇敢地接受和拒绝。

在纽约州立大学坎顿学院我不是孤单的，有好多好多爱我、为我提供帮助的人们，晓丽、冯先生和他美丽的妻子，玛丽安、比尔先生等，与他们相处的画面，到现在都历历在目。他们是让坎顿真正变成家的人。除了对我表达真诚的善意，更重要的是他们身体力行教会了我尊重他人，尊重不同的肤色、文化、思想，"Never Judge"。我体验到了世界的多元，多元才能多彩；学会了真心的体谅和包容，尊重规则以及尊重每个个体的独立性。

## 来激励我的"CSC-SUNY 150"

时光匆匆，回国转眼已经十年，当年的小伙伴纷纷到了而立之年，开始成了工作中的中流砥柱，也开始负

They are the ones who once made SUNY Canton our home. In addition to expressing sincere kindness to me, more importantly, they taught me to respect others, respect people of different colors, cultures and thoughts, "Never Judge". I experienced the diversity of the world and diversity made the world colorful. I learned to be genuinely considerate and tolerant, respect the rules and respect the independence of each individual.

## CSC-SUNY 150:
## My Motivation All the Way

Time flied. It has been ten years since I returned to China. We are in our 30s and have started to become the mainstay of work and begin to feed family. After returning to China, I have emailed to Marela. But since I no longer use the email address, we lost touch. Losing contact with them has been my biggest regret over the years.

I really want to tell them about my changes. I am no longer the sensitive, self-abased and timid girl. I am now a woman who is ordinary but confident, enterprising, and brave enough to meet and overcome difficulties. Over the years, I have earned a master's degree, gained a wonderful love and marriage, and I am dutiful to my parents. I play different roles in my life, and I think my magician has been with me to help me overcome the difficulties of life again and again. I am lucky to have experienced those that year. Only I myself know what I have learned.

During the ten years, I had a job with great pressure but potential for development. My overseas study experience enabled me to successfully enter the management of the

担起家庭的责任。回国后，我跟玛里拉邮件联系过，但最后邮箱很多年不常用也丢了，与他们失去联系是这些年来我最大的遗憾。

我很想告诉他们我的变化，我已不再是当年那个敏感、自卑和怯懦的小姑娘，而是一个依旧平凡，但自信、奋进，偶尔被压力困扰，但勇敢面对的女人。这些年来，我取得了硕士学位，收获了美满的爱情和婚姻，尽我所能孝顺父母。在生活里我扮演着不同的角色，我想我的魔法师一直伴随着我，让我克服生活中的一个个困难。我想我是幸运的，那一年我所经历的，只有我知道。

十年之间，有了一份压力很大但有发展潜力的工作，海外的学习经历让我顺利进入了公司的管理层。因为工作的关系以及不错的英语技能我认识了很多全球各地的朋友，与海外企业及高校有频繁的交流……太多太多的改变和收获，我想这些都因 2008 年那个魔法师。每当新的朋友问起我的经历，我总是说起"CSC-SUNY 150 奖学金项目"，因为我知道，所有这些魔法都是从 2008 年开始的，而 CSC 和 SUNY 正是改变我们的魔法师。

2018 年年初，我带着老公再次踏上了那片土地，我想这也是总结我

company. Thanks to my working field and good English skills, I got to know many friends around the world and had frequent exchanges with overseas enterprises and universities… So many changes and gains, I believe, all come from the magician in 2008. I never talked about my experiences without mentioning the CSC-SUNY 150 Program, because I know that all this magic started in 2008, and CSC and SUNY are the magicians who have changed us.

In early 2018, I stepped onto the land again with my husband, I thought this visit was also an important ceremony to sum up that decade. This time I was no longer a student but a tourist. We didn't go to the east where I was ten years ago, but to the west. Although I went to different cities, I felt familiar as well. We drove to several cities in the west, each with its own charm. I wanted to know more about this land. During the trip, I told my husband about my study

这十年的重要仪式。这一次我不是学生，而是一名游客。我们没有去我十年前去的东部，而是去了西部。虽说是不同的城市，但是陌生中却仍有一份亲切感。我们驾车游了西部好几个城市，它们各有各的魅力，我想更多地了解这片土地。旅行途中，我给老公讲当年在美学习的经历，讲述我遇到的那些人那些事。短短十多天的自由行，让我和老公对美国意犹未尽，我们计划着不久之后带着孩子再赴美国，这一次将去我曾经学习生活的美国东部，继续书写我与美国的缘分。

这个十年已经完结，下一个十年即将开始。下一个十年，我希望成为一个更好的妻子、女儿，为我的丈夫和父母带来幸福，也希望能成为一个合格的妈妈，用自己的实际行动让孩子为我感到骄傲。更重要的是能将"CSC-SUNY 150奖学金项目"学到的一切继续探索、挖掘，成为一个更好的自己，做一个对社会更有用的人。同时将我们得到来自CSC、SUNY、中美两国政府及人民等所有人的帮助和关爱，转化成爱的种子，回馈给需要帮助的人。

experience in America and the people and things I met. After over a ten-day travel, my husband and I made a plan to go to the United States again in the near future with our children. We will go to the eastern United States where I once studied and lived, and continue my connection with USA.

This decade is over and the next decade is about to begin. In the next decade, I hope to be a better wife and daughter, bringing happiness to my husband and parents. I also hope that I can become a qualified mother and make my child proud of me. More importantly, we can continue to explore with what we have learned from the CSC-SUNY 150 Program, and become a better self and a more useful person to the society. At the same time, we will always cherish the help and care we got from CSC, SUNY, governments and people of China and the United States, and will turn them into seeds of love and give them back to others in need.

# 不忘初心　续写故事

## Staying True to Original Intention and Keeping on with the Story

余海意 / 西南科技大学　纽约州立大学杰纳西社区学院

Yu Haiyi / Southwest University of Science and Technology　SUNY Genesee Community College

　　我叫余海意，是来自西南科技大学的一名非典型 IT 男。我不喜欢 IT，酷爱运动交友。2008 年 "5·12" 汶川特大地震后，学校修缮房屋让我们提前归假，我回到老家崇州自学考试项目，虽时时有余震，但也安稳度过了假期。7 月初，我接到老师通知，让我回学校参加 "CSC-SUNY 150 奖学金项目" 面试，那时心中的忐忑和憧憬让我记忆犹新。回学校经过两天面试后成功入选项目，经过一段时间准备后，8 月出发去纽约。生平第一次走出国门，要在异国他乡生活一年，感觉一切都是那么新鲜，我忐忑的心情也随着周围小伙伴和老师的关心而渐渐平复了。

　　My name is Yu Haiyi, an atypical IT man from Southwest University of Science and Technology. I don't like IT. I love sports and making friends. After the earthquake on May 12, 2008, the university let us leave early for the summer vacation due to the building renovation; I returned to my hometown Chongzhou, self-studying for the exams. Although there were aftershocks occasionally, we were safe after all. In early July, I was informed by my teacher to go back and take the interview of CSC-SUNY150 Program. I still remember that I was anxious about and longing for the program at the same time. I passed the interview two days later and I was selected into the program. After a period of preparation, I left for New York in August. When I first arrived in the United States, I felt quite fresh thinking that I would live in this foreign country for a year. My worry gradually disappeared with the concern of my friends and

国外的生活对于现在的我来说，是一次很难忘的经历。首先，我对自己所在的纽约州立大学杰纳西社区学院做一个简短的介绍。美国教学不同于国内教学，以兴趣学习为主。除了基本课程，我选修了我喜欢的篮球和从未尝试的潜水课程。我们6个男生的专业都是工程科学，那边的专业基础课对于我们来说算是很简单的，所以考试全A。因此我们有更多的时间去接触和了解美国的生活。和我们接触的美国同学也发现，我们像他们一样喜欢运动，大家能愉快交流，美国朋友也会问我们关于中国的问题。为了便于对中国文化感兴趣的同学更加深入了解中国，我们在第二学期开设了免费的、系统的中文教学课，吸引了许多美国学生和当地居民。这些课程的目的是教他们学习中文，增加他们对现代中国的认识，吸引他们对中国更加感兴趣。

国内外饮食也有很大差异，学校里有食堂，而且食堂价格公道。美国只有餐吧，东西很贵。吃饭基本就是DIY了，我们的生活自理能力因此提升了一大截。因为没车，辅导员每周三开车带我们去一次超市。起初大家都不会做饭，买了许多加工食品，比如比萨面包放进冰箱，早中晚餐全靠微波炉。后来实在忍受不了没有米饭

teachers around me.

Living abroad was an unforgettable experience for me. First of all, I would like to make a brief introduction to my study at Genesee Community College of the State University of New York. American teaching is different from domestic teaching and it focuses mainly on interest in learning. In addition to basic courses, I took the courses of basketball and diving. We six boys were majoring in engineering science, and the basic professional courses there were very easy for us, so we got A's in all the exams. That spared us more time to learn about American life. When the American students we met found that we liked sports as they did, they invited us to play and we communicated with each other happily. Our American friends would also ask us questions about China. In order to facilitate students who were interested in Chinese culture to have a deeper understanding of China, we offered free courses, teaching Chinese systematically in the second semester, which attracted many American students and local residents. The purpose of these courses was to teach them Chinese, help them understand modern China and arouse their interest in China.

There are also great differences in food between home and abroad. In China, we have our campus canteens offering food at a moderate price, while in America, there are only food bars offering expensive food. So we cooked ourselves, and this improved our ability to take care of ourselves. Since we didn't have a car, the college counselor drove us to the supermarket every Wednesday. At first, because we were poor at cooking, we only bought processed foods, such as pizza and bread, and put them in the refrigerator. Later, we I could not bear the days without rice

和川菜的日子，我们开始学习做饭。原料很好搞定，沃尔玛超市肉菜都有，但是，要学川菜怎能没有川菜的灵魂豆瓣酱呢？我们亲爱的美国文化课老师，开车带我们到水牛城的中国超市买了很多豆瓣酱。经过一周的实践和摸索，我们也会做菜了，于是各种川菜出现在了我们日常的菜单里。学校在乡村，宿舍周围很冷清。除了树，只有松鼠、各种鸟类、狍子、小浣熊之类的动物为伴。

回国后，我们在学校作了几次关于出国交流的汇报，向西南科技大学的同学分享了国外的学习和生活情况。紧接着就面临大三的学业，因为我们大二那年是在美国交换，杰纳西社区学院只是一个大学预科学院，我们在国内大二的专业课在那边没法选修。因此，在紧跟着班上同学学习大三课程的同时，我还需要补修大二欠下的40多个学分的专业课课程。开学一个月，满满当当的课程让我心力交瘁，每天几乎满课，并且作为一个IT男，大三的专业课需要大二的专业课知识才能听懂，于是当时上课几乎就是听天书。后来，室友们了解了这个情况，主动在晚上放弃打游戏和谈恋爱的时间，轮番给我恶补前面的知识。在同学和老师的帮助下，大二和大三的课程在一年之内学完，并且都

and Sichuan food, so we began to learn how to cook. The ingredients were easy to get, like meats and vegetables in Walmart. But how could we cook Sichuan cuisine without bean sauce—the soul of Sichuan dish? Our dear American culture teacher drove us to the Chinese supermarket in Buffalo and we bought a lot of bean sauce. After a week of practice and exploration, we were finally able to make Sichuan dishes by ourselves and a variety of Sichuan dishes appeared in our daily menu. The campus was in the country, and the surrounding of our dormitory was very desolate.

After returning to China, I made several reports on overseas exchanges in our university and shared the overseas study and life with students of the university. Then we got busy with the study of junior year. Because our sophomore year was spent at SUNY Genesee Community College, which was a preparatory college, and it did not offer us the same courses we were supposed to take in our sophomore year, I needed to make up for those courses with over 40 credits while learning the courses for the third year with my classmates. In the first month of the semester, the full classes every day almost made me haggard. To catch up with my classmates

是一次性考过，真的很感谢那时候的同学和老师。这一路走来，要感谢的人太多了，许多人都在我生命中的重要节点教会我很多，帮助我很多。

其实，大学毕业之前，我并没有意向考研或者考公务员。可能是因为我天生性格比较跳脱，不喜欢当"码农"，也不希望从事 IT 行业。毕业时面临两个选择，一个是家人让我去加拿大继续读书，重选医学方向，以后按照家人的意愿进入医疗系统；另一个选择是去自己面试通过的国企工作。因为性格使然，我毅然地选择了工作。

辗转几个地方，从内蒙古到成都，再到雅安、川西三州，印象最深刻的就是在川西。到了川西那么贫困的地方，剩下的只有风景和信仰。如果说自然风景不输国外，而沿途那些虔诚的人们，就像电影《冈仁波齐》里面演的那样，都是去布达拉宫朝圣的人们。我骑行 3 个月，认识了来自全国各地的骑友。

因为工作原因，我当时见到了各式各样的学校，有些学校教室就是一间破破的小屋，屋内老师用不标准的普通话给孩子们上课，没有电灯，就靠窗外的一点点光线看课本，一双双可爱的小手用铅笔慢慢做着笔记。下课时间，孩子们在操场上追来追去。

I had to double my efforts. The teachers and my roommates helped me a lot in those days. With their help, I finished both the courses of sophomore and junior years within one year, and I passed all the exams. I really appreciated the help given by my classmates and teachers.

In fact, before graduating from university, I did not intend to take the postgraduate entrance exam or work as a civil servant. Maybe it was because I was much more active and lively in personality that I did not like to be a "code worker", nor did I want to engage in IT. Upon graduation, I was faced with two choices. One was to go to Canada and learn medicine there, as my family expected. Another option was to work at a state-owned company where I had passed the interview. Because of my personality, I took the second option.

Among the places I have been working at, from Inner Mongolia to Chengdu, from Ya'an to the three autonomous regions in western Sichuan, the most impressive one was western Sichuan. In poor western Sichuan, all that remains is scenery and faith. The natural scenery is truly comparable to that of any other foreign country. The devotees along the way, like those in the movie *Paths of the Soul / Kang rinpoche*, are all pilgrims to the Potala Palace. I spent three months cycling and got to know a lot of people who were cyclists from all over the country.

When I was responsible for the Yili Students Milk in my business, I visited all kinds of schools at that time. In some schools, there was nothing but one shabby old classroom, in which the teachers spoke with strong local accent. There was no electricity, and students read with the sunlight coming from outside,

看到我来，他们主动跑到我面前和我打招呼，看着他们淳朴的笑容，我既开心，又心疼。因为学习环境十分艰苦，但是看到他们开心、努力、快乐的样子，又觉得很幸福。

2012 年初到那边的时候，有些偏远学校的孩子需要每天走两小时山路去上学，每天在学校只吃一顿没有肉的饭，放学后又要走两小时山路回家。我走过许多偏远的学校，有许多学校在大山深处，或者依山而建，到学校的路连车都过不去，车停了还需要走半小时弯弯曲曲的山路。但是见了那些孩子喝着我们提供的学生奶，脸上洋溢着笑容，我觉得自己做的一切都是那么有价值，所以再辛苦、再不易，我也愿意去做。

2014 年 11 月 22 日，四川省阿坝甘孜州康定市发生 6.3 级地震。作为甘孜负责人的我，马上响应进行赈灾支援。因为曾经经历过，所以我更懂得，也更明白那时候灾区人民的心情。当时我冒着大雪和余震将 10 000 盒牛奶于 11 月 23 日晚送到了甘孜州塔公小学。当时我站在残破的小学楼下，想到的都是 2008 年"5·12"汶川特大地震后"CSC-SUNY 150 奖学金项目"对我们的帮助。看着那些孩子脸上的茫然失措和无助的表情，我感同身受，曾经我也遇到过这样

taking notes with their lovely hands. When they saw me coming, they came to greet me with their smiles. I was both happy and heartbroken when finding them living and studying in such difficult environments. But when I saw them happy, I felt happy for them too.

In the year of 2012, children in some remote mountain areas had to walk for two hours each day to get to school. They had only one meal a day without meat. I visited a few schools in mountain areas which were far away from the town. Seeing those children drinking the milk we provided, with a smile on their faces, I felt that everything I did was worthwhile. So I would like to do it no matter how hard it was.

On November 22, 2014, a 6.3-magnitude earthquake hit Kangding, Ganzi Prefecture, Sichuan Province. Being responsible for the Yili Milk business in Ganzi, I immediately responded to the disaster relief. Because I had experienced it, I knew the feelings of the people in that situation. Then I braved the snow and aftershocks and successfully sent 10,000 boxes of milk to Tagong Primary School in Ganzi on the night of November 23. When I stood at the downstairs of the damaged primary school, I was thinking of the help from the CSC-SUNY 150 Program after the earthquake of May 12, 2008. Looking at the disoriented and helpless expressions on the faces of those children, I had had the same feeling. I had experienced such a natural disaster, and there were so many good people coming to help us, bringing us food and tents. I still remember TV news broadcasting about the situation of the epicenter of the disaster area, which was much more dangerous than what I myself had experienced, and relief work was more difficult

的天灾，曾经也有许多好心人来帮助我们，为我们送上食物和帐篷。还记得当时看电视新闻里面播放的震中灾区的情况，比我当时自己经历地震时所处的位置危险得多，救援也更难开展，但是武警战士和医护人员没有一个人放弃，每个人都在竭尽全力救助大家，许多社会各界的爱心人士来帮助我们。我和他们讲，叔叔和你们一样，你们要坚强，未来在等着你们。也正是这份信念支撑着我，在藏区一待就是 5 年。

2016 年底，我辞职回到成都组建了家庭，现在自己创业。当时创业的初衷很简单，为了能更好地照顾家庭。因为老家在四川崇州，自己的一些社会关系都在那边，所以当时在崇州开了一个 300 平方米的进口超市和一个蒙古特色餐饮店。创业起初很难，因为超市投资比较大，所以重心都在这里。进口超市不比传统超市，在每个城市都有供应商，进口产品的各个供应商几乎都在沿海，并且进口产品进货周期极长，库存稍微管理不好就会缺货。

2017 年春节前，我经常飞往外地参加各种进口产品博览会，与各个供应商签订合同，补充线下新品，那段时间比起之前的工作要难许多。现在是移动互联网的时代，实体行业受

to carry out. But the armed police and medical workers didn't give up. There were many loving people from all walks of life coming to help us. Therefore I told those children, be strong and the future was waiting for them. With this strong belief that sustained me, I stayed in Tibet for five years.

At the end of 2016, I resigned and returned to Chengdu. I got married and started my own business. At that time, the original intention was simple, to take care of my family. Because my hometown is in Chongzhou, Sichuan Province, and I have some social relations there, I opened a 300 m² imports supermarket and a Mongolian food and beverage restaurant there.

Prior to the Spring Festival in 2017, I often flew to other places to attend various import products expos, signing contracts with various suppliers, and supplementing offline new products. This is the era of mobile Internet, and entity industries have been affected a lot. It was much more difficult for us than before. In many parties, we business partners communicated with each other. In the next few years, I plan to focus on the catering industry, because no matter how the mobile Internet develops, dining cannot rely on Internet. So next year, we plan to open two Mongolian restaurants, one in Wenjiang and the other in Shuangliu, and a pancake shop in Chengdu. During the last two years of entrepreneurship, I was very lucky to have those partners. We encouraged each other in various adversity and kept moving forward.

My gratitude for CSC-SUNY 150 Program is beyond my words. In the future, no matter how big my business is, I will support one child from Tibetan area to go to school every year. I

到冲击，许多创业的小伙伴们前行十分艰难。在很多次聚会中，大家相互交流，共同进步。我计划在未来几年，把自己的发展方向定位于餐饮行业，因为无论移动互联网怎么发展，吃饭是不能靠网络的。明年，我们计划在温江和双流开两家蒙古特色餐饮店，在成都开一家煎饼店。在这两年创业时间里，我很感谢我的合作伙伴，在各种逆境中鼓励我，不断前行。

对"CSC-SUNY 150奖学金项目"的感谢，千年万语道不尽。未来，事业不管做多大，我会每年支持一个藏区孩子读书，一路前行，不忘初心。

will keep making progress along the way without forgetting the original intention.

# 回顾十年，感恩有你

## My Gratitude to You for the Past

张维维 / 西南科技大学　纽约州立大学普拉茨堡学院

Zhang Weiwei / Southwest University of Science and Technology　SUNY at Plattsburgh

不知不觉已过十年，恍然如梦。但那些经历、那些朋友却实实在在地影响着我的人生。记忆里青涩的我，如今也已成家立业，但十年前的一幕幕仍不时浮现在脑海——地震时剧烈摇晃的宿舍、一片狼藉的教室、惊恐哭泣的同学和倒塌破碎的建筑，即使今日仍能感受到当初的无措和害怕。

这确实是一段不堪回忆的经历。当大家集中到安全区域时，我无法联系上家人。后来通过广播才了解到具体情况。我的家乡都江堰距离震中映秀直线距离 20 公里左右，完全不敢想象家里是什么情况，交通中断、通信中断，我已经不再是无助了，满满的都是绝望。更糟糕的是，震后第二

The past ten years is like a dream. Those friends from that experience have affected my life. I have married and got my own family, but the scenes from ten years ago still come to mind from time to time—the dormitory that swayed violently during the earthquake, the classrooms that were stunned, the students who were crying and the buildings that collapsed; even today I still feel the panic and fear I had at that moment.

This is indeed an experience that I don't want to recall. When everyone moved to a safe area, I was unable to contact my family. Later, I learned from TV about the specific earthquake. My hometown Dujiangyan was about 20 kilometers away from the epicenter. I couldn't imagine what had happened at home. Also, the traffic was cut down, and the network was interrupted. I was more than helpless; I was devastated. One disaster after another, the symptoms of acute nephritis suddenly appeared

天我突然出现急性肾炎的症状，而校医院根本没有药物治疗，附近医院也没有条件进行治疗。熬了两天，尿血症状加剧，终于在朋友的帮助下转到邻近的市进行治疗。

待我回家时已经大半个月过去了。在回都江堰的路上，我想那是我一生中见到的最悲情的都江堰：阴云笼罩，满城的消毒水味道极其浓烈，淌水的路面混合着白色石灰粉，道路两旁满是倒塌的建筑废墟，随处可见穿着白色隔离服的人员在进行消毒工作。一路上我的眼泪就没断过，都江堰不该是这样的，我能感觉到她在哭泣。地震几天后我终于和家里人取得联系，万幸大家都平安，后来我才知道爸爸也是死里逃生，在朋友的帮助下从废墟里爬出来的。我很庆幸，也很感激，朋友就是在你最需要帮助的时候拉你一把的人，感谢我们都有这样的朋友。

"CSC–SUNY 150奖学金项目"是从辅导员那里得知的，当初我并不是很想参加这个项目，一是刚经历这样的大灾难，特别想和父母在一起，也许只有体验过差点失去的心情，才能让我们更加珍惜亲情；二是考虑自身学业方面，也不愿意耽误。后来在老师和父母的劝说下，我参加了。现在回想起来，我觉得很庆幸，庆幸有

on me on the next day after the earthquake, and there was no medical treatment at the local hospital, and it was not accessible to be treated nearby. After two days, the symptoms of hematuria had been aggravated. Luckily, I was moved to the nearest city with the help of a friend and got better treatment.

When I came home, half a month had already passed. On the way back to Dujiangyan, I thought it was the worst condition of Dujiangyan that I had ever seen in my life. It was a cloudy day. The smell of detergent was extremely strong in the city. Mixed with white lime powder, the roads were full of collapsed building debris, and people wearing white gowns could be disinfected everywhere. My tears kept coming down along the way. Dujiangyan should not be like this. I could feel this city was crying. After a few days of the earthquake, I finally got in touch with my family. Fortunately, everyone was safe. Later, I realized that my father had climbed out of the rubble with the help of friends. I was very grateful for having friends like them. As an old saying goes, a friend in need is a friend indeed.

I got the information about CSC-SUNY 150 Program from the counselor. At first, I didn't want to participate in this program, for I just experienced such a catastrophe, and I really wanted to be with my parents. Only when you have experienced the feeling of loss will you know how much you love your family. For another, I was afraid that I couldn't catch up with the class. Later, under the persuasion of the teacher and parents, I decided to go. Now I feel very fortunate to be persuaded to grasp this opportunity. People say this is an opportunity to broaden my horizons, but it is more than that for

这个机会，庆幸我抓住了这个机会。在大家看来这是一个开阔眼界的机会，但对我来说不仅如此。其实我自己知道经历这场地震，我的内心是受到了影响的。此后很长一段时间，每每遇到声音大点的情况，我都会心跳加剧，非常惶恐，夜晚尤其严重，通常半夜惊醒后就难以入睡，也许换个环境，在新的地方，能缓解这种症状。

到美国后，完全不同的生活方式和陌生的环境确实转移了我大部分的注意力。这里的老师和同学们乐观、积极的生活态度极大地感染了我。每天早上食堂阿姨都会对我微笑，问声早上好。通往教学楼的路上会经过一个人工湖，喷泉周围永远都有小彩虹，在阳光的映照下水雾弥漫，充满生机，草坪上时不时跑过一只松鼠，抱着松果一溜烟就爬上树躲起来了。湛蓝的天空没有一丝云，偶尔听到一两声乌鸦叫，都会觉得很惊奇（没怎么见过乌鸦，很好奇）。

到了教室会见到那个让我很佩服的写作老师玛莎，70 多岁高龄的她，每天要坐 30 多分钟的渡轮，然后开40 分钟的车来给我们授课。她思路清晰，笑声爽朗，经常鼓励我们。

我敬佩她，是因为她对待生活的态度：乐观、独立、自信。在我看来，70 多岁的人应该退休在家种种花、

me. I know that my heart has been traumatized by this earthquake. For a long time after the disaster, each time when I heard big sounds, my heart would beat faster because of anxiety. When I awakened in the middle of the night, it was difficult to fall asleep again with the fearful emotion. I was thinking of getting away from this environment, so this symptom might be alleviated in a new place.

After arriving in the United States, my attention focused on completely different lifestyles and the new environment. Teachers and classmates with an optimistic and positive attitude there influenced me a lot. Every morning, the aunty in the cafeteria would give me a big smile and greeted me with good morning. There was by an artificial lake on my way to the classroom. The water in the lake looked beautiful under the sunshine, and a squirrel ran through with a pine cone from time to time. There was no cloud in the blue sky. I would be very surprised to hear one or two crows occasionally.

When I arrived at the classroom, I saw the writing teacher Martha, whom I admired. In her

逗逗孙辈了。但她却说，每个人都应该有自己的生活方式，做自己喜欢做的事，让自己开心才是最重要的。她说和我们在一起，她能感受到年轻人的活力，感觉和我们是一样的。是她教会我，生活需要一种精神、一种态度。

她的授课方式变化多样。她可能收集很多奇特的画作，然后让我们讲述自己看到的内容。因为每个人看到的东西可能都不一样，她也不规定所谓的标准答案，只要能说明自己的想法就好。

另一位对我影响很大的就是我的语法老师。圣诞节，她知道我们不能回家，便邀请我们去她家。初到她家时，我很吃惊。她家里有几个孩子，肤色各不相同。后来我才知道，原来这些都是她领养的非洲孩子。她每年都会去非洲支教，家里的这个小女儿就是她去援教时收养的。因为家里条件不允许，她自己在家给孩子们上课。圣诞节当天，在我们准备午餐时，她丈夫刚上完晚班和早班回家。他们吃、穿普通，但做的事却很伟大。她让我深刻了解到不是所有人都贪图物质享受、追求金钱利益的。有很多东西是物质不能带给我们的，比如怜悯之心、仁爱之心。帮助别人会带给我们比物质更重要的精神力量，一个人很渺小，

70s, she came to school by taking a ferry boat for more than 30 minutes every day, then drove for 40 minutes. Her lecture was easy for us to understand, and she spared no effort to encourage us.

I admired her because of her attitude towards life: optimism, independence, and self-confidence. I thought people in their 70s should have retired at home to plant flowers and gather together with their families. But she said that everyone should have his or her own way of life. We should do what we liked to do. To be happy was the most important thing. She said that she could feel the vitality of young people and being together with us reminded her of her college life. It was she who taught me that life needs a spirit and an attitude.

Her teaching methods varied widely. She might collect a lot of strange paintings, then let us tell what we saw. Because everyone saw something different, she didn't specify the so-called correct answer, as long as the ideas were delivered.

Another person who had great influence on me was the grammar teacher. On Christmas, when she knew that we were not able to go home, she invited us to her house. She taught me that not everyone was eager to enjoy material enjoyment and pursue monetary benefits. There were many things that material could not bring to us, such as compassion. Helping others would bring us more spiritual power than material. People's physical strength was limited, but their spirit would be everlasting.

The nine-month stay with them brought me a lot of shocks and thoughts. We could not always stay in the past. In the long lifetime we would

但其精神却可以很伟大。

和他们短短几个月的交往，真的带给我很大的震动和感触，生活不能停留在过去，人的一生很长，会遇到各种各样的挫折和磨难，我们不能让自己沉浸在过去的伤痛中停滞不前。灾难本身并不会教我们成长，而对灾难的认识、反思才会促进我们的成长。我接受别人真诚的帮助，学会了感恩，也怀着一颗虔诚的心，帮助需要帮助的人。

## 十年蜕变，铸就梦想

十年前我刚上大二，学的是经济学专业。本来应该是按部就班地读书、毕业、找工作，没想到因为地震，有了一个接触不同文化和思想的机会，更没想到我会因为这些，走上不同的人生道路。

2008 年刚到美国，正遇上金融危机。作为一名经济学专业的学生，我不可避免地对华尔街有着浓厚的兴趣，可是真正到了那里，完全没有感受到电视上的那种传奇，一度让我怀疑自己是否走错地方了，再三确认，没有错！大门紧闭的公司，行人寥寥的马路，不太整洁的街道，萧条的感觉扑面而来。这是世界经济最强的国家，这里是金融的中心，可是依然逃

encounter many types of setbacks and tribulations. We can't stick in the past pain. The disaster itself would not help us grow, but the understanding and reflection of the disaster would. Having got a lot of help from others, I am also ready to help others when they are in need. The 150 Program has taught me how to be grateful.

### Dream to Be Achieved in Ten Years

I was a sophomore ten years ago, majoring in economics. I should have lived an ordinary college life graduated and found a job step by step without the earthquake. I would have never had a chance to contact different cultures and thoughts. I'd never thought that my life would be changed that much.

It was the time of the financial crisis when I just arrived in the United States in 2008. As an economics major, I inevitably had a strong interest in Wall Street. When I came here, I didn't feel the legend as it is on TV. I once suspected that I was in the wrong place. Confirmed! No mistake! The closed doors of the company, the pedestrians' roads, the untidy streets, and the feeling of depression lingered in my mind. This was the country with the strongest economy in

不开规则。我不禁想，到底是经济繁荣的结果（表象）重要还是支撑经济发展的体制重要？也许我应该关注的不是简单的如何挣钱的问题。只有一个良性发展的环境才有可能造就可持续的收入增长，制度也许比技术手段更重要。

当初在美国读书时，我写过一篇文章，感叹他们有那么多免费或平价博物馆，能让各阶层的孩子接触到不同学科、广博的知识。当时我的愿望就是自己也能在国内建造这么一个博物馆，天文地理、世界百科全容纳。这些年在国内，每到一个城市，都会特意关注一下当地有没有这样的博物馆。很高兴我们也有，综合性的、专业性的、历史性都有。我常常在那里碰到学校组织学生去参观学习，看到小朋友们围着天体运行演示图讨论的情景，我特别开心、满足。这是国家强大重视教育的表现，我为祖国而自豪。

虽然我没有能力建立一座博物馆，但我可以尽自己的力量为家乡做贡献。大学毕业后，我没有选择从事经济方面的工作，而是做了一名基层法官。我希望为中国的法制建设尽自己的一份力。

要说最满足的事，就是成家并有了一个可爱的小宝宝，现在一岁多了。

the world. It was the center of finance. I couldn't help wondering whether it was the result of economic prosperity (the appearance) or the system that supported economic development that mattered. Maybe what we should focus on was not just about how to make money. Only in an environment of sound development could sustainable income growth be obtained, and institutions might be more important than technical means.

When I was still studying in the United States, I wrote an article about American museums. They had so many museums free of charge or with cheap ticket fee for children from all walks of life to come into contact with diverse and extensive knowledge. At that time, my wish was that I could build such a museum in China, including everything from astronomy, geography, or as many as the world encyclopedia could list. Every time I come to a new place, I will check if there is such a museum in our country. I am very happy that we have different types of general, professional and historical museums as well. I often see students coming to visit and learn as a group with their teachers, discussing something in front of the Demonstration Diagram of Celestial Body movement. It is a sign that our country has become stronger and laid more importance in eduction. I am proud of my country.

Although I don't have the ability to build a museum, I can do my part to contribute to my hometown. After graduating from college, I did not choose to work in economics. Instead, I obtained a bachelor's degree in law and worked as a general judge. I hope I can help the common people with law education.

Speaking of the most satisfying thing,

多多少少受到国外思想的影响，我更注重对孩子兴趣、思维方式的培养，也会比较重视语言沟通教育。得益于老师们乐观、独立、宽容的生活态度，我在处理家庭关系时更随和、平静，不纠缠日常琐事，从容地享受生活。

we have a cute little baby in the family. Now he is one year old, and he is more or less influenced by foreign thoughts, because I pay more attention to the cultivation of children's interests and ways of thinking, and the ability of language communication. Thanks to the teachers' optimistic, independent and tolerant attitude towards life, I am calm in dealing with family matters, abandoning the entanglement of everyday chores and enjoying life more calmly.

西南石油
大学

Southwest Petroleum University

# 爱，让生命绽放华彩！

## Love Enriches My Life

张绵 / 西南石油大学　纽约州立大学法明戴尔分校

Zhang Mian / Southwest Petroleum University　SUNY Farmingdale State College

2018年5月，我又一次来到纽约，回到长岛。此时，距我初次与它相遇刚好过去了十年。时光如白驹过隙，弹指一挥间。在项目十周年之际，我带上丈夫来到我生活学习过的地方。老师们头上又添了白发，朋友们更加稳重成熟。行走在这个陌生又熟悉的城市，往日的种种都历历在目。记忆如此有趣，它总是藏在脑海深处，然后在不经意间蹦出来，给人满满的惊喜与感动……

如果有人问我，当初在纽约留学时最大的感触是什么，那么我的回答是，在那里的每一天，我都是在感恩、感动和坚强中度过的。我们这个

In May 2018, I came back to Long Island, New York again. It was ten years after I first arrived there. How time flies. At this moment, I took my husband back to the place where I had spent days on living and learning, to spend our honeymoon. In the reunion of our old friends, I found that hairs of teachers have turned gray and friends have become more mature. Walking on this strange but familiar city, I could recall stories happening in the past.

If I am asked what is the greatest impression on learning in New York then, my answer is all of my days in the New York was full of thankfulness, touching and strength. Our program was established by the support and assistance of governments of China and the United States, SUNY, organizations of overseas Chinese, associations and churches. Madam Wei Lin in charge of the CSC-SUNY 150 Program once

项目是在中美两国政府、纽约州立大学（SUNY）、各华侨组织、社团以及教会的支持和帮助下顺利实施的。

"CSC-SUNY 150 奖学金项目"负责人魏琳老师曾经说，我们这个项目是个"不可能实现的项目"。是的，从人员选拔、护照签证的办理，到最后到达美国纽约，前后只花了不到一个月的时间，如此神速，不能不说是一个奇迹。中美两国政府和纽约州立大学为这次项目的成功，给了我们最大限度的便利条件。我的美国导师、同学、朋友也在 9 个月的时间里尽他们所能，给我最无私的爱以及最真挚的友谊。

没有系统的培训，没有托福、雅思成绩，我来到了万里之外的美国。有人说，这是初生牛犊不怕虎。其实我知道，如果没有美国朋友们的关怀和帮助，初到美国的我将寸步难行。

## 一、追忆

法明戴尔下雪了。临近期末，大家都在忙着复习、备考，连一向冷清的图书馆也热闹起来，学校的食堂也开始通宵营业，为熬夜的同学提供免费的咖啡和点心。我们在美国的留学生涯接近尾声了。看着匆忙走过的同学，我仿佛也看到了刚刚来到这里时

called the program "an impossible one". It was a miracle that we only took less than one month to complete all procedures and arrived at New York, the United States. To make this program come into being, governments of China and the US, and SUNY provided us with a large number of favorable conditions. My American supervisors, classmates and friends tried all their best to help me over those 9 months, too. Without their help, I could not have moved a single step forward.

### Part One: My Memories on the Past

Snow fell down in Farmingdale. As the end of the semester was drawing near, every one was busy on reviewing and preparing for the final examination, so that the library was full of students. Knapp Hall started to open for 24 hours, to provide free coffee and snacks to students who had to work all night. At the moment when my days for exchange in the United States were to be concluded, watching the schoolmates walking to the classrooms in a hurry, I couldn't help being reminded of the image of myself arriving in school the first day.

### Part Two: First Arrival

In my memory, a group of students full of dreams were shortlisted through several rounds of interviews and screening and finally became members of the CSC-SUNY 150 Program. It was the first time that we would leave home for a destination far away from hometown. In the Chengdu Shuangliu International Airport, Mr. Wang Hong from the International Cooperation Office informed us of several tips in a foreign

的自己，往事一幕幕出现在眼前。

## 二、初到

回想起来，一群心怀梦想的人，经过层层面试、筛选，终于成为"CSC-SUNY 150 奖学金项目"的一员，然后马不停蹄地提着大大小小的行李，第一次远离父母，长途跋涉，到大洋彼岸求学。还记得在双流国际机场时，学校对外合作交流处的王宏老师一直陪着我们，叮嘱在国外的注意事项。随后，已经过了安检的我终于在送行的人群中找到了爸爸妈妈，他们刚从绵竹赶来。我们隔着安检喊话，那一刻，忽然意识到自己真的要一个人远行，百感交集。转过身，眼泪再也忍不住，一滴一滴落下来。

经过 13 个小时的长途飞行，我们终于到达了纽约肯尼迪国际机场。坐在开往 SUNY 法明戴尔校区的校车上，看着远处逐渐清晰的校园，我知道，我的新生活就要在这个花园般的校园里开始了。

## 三、校园生活二三事

在法明戴尔，我对美国式的教学管理有了切身体会。在我们初到的两周里，每天都有两名住宅助理陪着我

country. Not until I went through the security checking, did I find my mother and father squirming in the crowd, who just hurried here from Mianzhu to send me off. We tried to hear each other through the gate. At that moment, I was aware that I was to take a long journey and my tears dropped down when I turned back.

After 13 hours of flying, we finally arrived at Kennedy International Airport in New York and took the school bus to the SUNY-Farmingdale State College. I knew that my new life was to begin on this garden-like campus.

### Part Three: Anecdotes in School

In Farmingdale, I deeply experienced teaching management of American style. In the first two weeks when we arrived in the campus, there were two RA (residence assistance) accompanying us to help us quickly adapt to the life, through whom I made friends. During this period, the school also arranged various activities for us, such as a Hilton welcome party, one-day trip to Manhattan, beach tour, barbecue lunch and cooking Sichuan Cuisine in the university

们，他们的帮助使我们迅速适应了那里的生活，同时也交到了很多朋友。这让我想到母校的"迎新生经验交流会"，其实各国的新生教育方式还是有很多共性的。这期间，学校也为我们安排了各种活动，比如希尔顿欢迎酒会、曼哈顿一日游、海滩游、欢迎烧烤午餐会、在校长家做川菜等。这些活动也是我们与学校领导、导师的非正式见面会，大家在轻松愉悦的气氛下相互了解、认识，为以后在学习和生活上可能的合作打下基础。

在法明戴尔的学习生活并不轻松。法明戴尔实行小班制，一个班二十多个学生，教授经常在课堂上互动，学生也可以随时打断老师提出自己的见解，甚至经常会毫无征兆地开始课堂辩论。初来乍到，我简直无法适应。纽约人说话很快，长岛人说话更是快到极致。虽然教授已经尽量照顾我们放慢语速了，但只要他们讲兴奋时，就又开始"打机关枪"了。

除去语言，我们在这里几乎没遇到什么困难。学校的老师们给予我们很大的关爱和帮助。在这里，我们最常听到的一句话是："如果你遇到困难，请告诉我。"很多教授都曾邀请我们去他们家里做客，他们很愿意了解我们，了解中国，同时也希望通过交谈，让我们更多地了解美国文化。

president's home. Those activities acted as informal occasions for us to meet university administrative leaders and supervisors. We all learned about each other in this relaxing and easy atmosphere, so as to lay a good foundation for our future cooperation in learning and living.

Academic life here was not easy. In Farmingdale, a class only had about 20 students and professors often interacted with students. Students could interrupt the teacher and put forward their opinions in class. When I first came here, I could not adapt to life here. I found New Yorkers spoke fast and people in Long Island spoke much faster. Although our professors were considerate enough to lower down the speaking pace, they would accelerate their speaking pace when they were excited about their topics.

Except for language, we didn't meet other obstacles. Teachers here granted great love and help to us. I often heard the sentence, "If you have any problem, please let me know." Many professors would like to invite us to visit their home. They would like to learn about China and us. At the same time, they hoped we could learn more about the United States through our exchanges. Few American students really understood China. For them, China was an ancient and mysterious eastern country. So in the course of public speaking, my four topics were related to China. I hoped that I could make contribution to popularizing Chinese culture and helping my American classmates to learn about an authentic China. In an overseas land, I could really understand the significance of patriotism and deeply felt that it was important to have a strong motherland to back me up. So I had to spare no effort to popularize the culture of our country and nation.

与他们的交流让我感触颇深，这里的美国同学对中国知之甚少。中国对于他们来说，就是万里之外一个古老而神秘的东方国度。所以在我的演讲课上，四个演讲题目都是和中国有关的。我希望至少我能为祖国文化的传播做一点力所能及的事情，让我的美国同学了解真正的中国。出门在外，我才知道爱国的真正含义。同时，我也深刻体会到，在异国他乡，有一个强大的祖国作支撑是多么的重要。所以我不遗余力地宣传我的国家、我的民族以及文化。

2008 年 12 月 11 日，这是一个特殊的日子。这一天，我们在法明戴尔学习的所有项目同学举行了一场中国文化秀，其中包括中国礼仪、服饰、食物、汉字、历史、音乐和舞蹈。对我的美国朋友们来说，这是一次盛大的中国文化宴。这次文化展示很成功，可谓盛况空前。校长基恩告诉我，从他到学校就任开始，学校的剧场就没有像那天那样座无虚席，无论是媒体还是学校的教授、同学，都高度评价了我们这次表演。法明戴尔掀起了"中国热"，我们很开心。我为自己留学期间设立了两个目标，一是增长见识，提高口语能力；二是传播中国文化，成为中美文化交流的桥梁。项目结束

December 11th, 2008 was a special day when our group of students studying in Farmingdale held an event "Journey to the East" to demonstrate our Chinese culture, including etiquette, garment, food, Chinese characters, history, music, and dance. For my American friends, it was a grand Chinese cultural banquet. Keen, President of the university, told me that the school theater hadn't been fully seated like this since he took office here. Media, professors, and schoolmates thought highly of our performance. We were delighted to see China mania happen in school. I set two goals of my studying in the USA: first, to broaden my horizon and improve my speaking ability; second, to popularize Chinese culture and act as the bridge between cultures of the two countries.

### Part Four: Special Dormitory Life

Kaika, my roommate and a quiet and elegant American girl, often chatted with me. With her assistance, I quickly improved my oral English and she learned more about Chinese culture. Another two girls living next door often came to my dormitory, asking me to teach them Chinese and design for them their Chinese names.

后，这两个目标都实现了。

## 四、别具一格之宿舍生活

我的室友凯拉是一个恬静、优雅的美国女孩，我们经常在一起聊天。在她的帮助下，我的口语能力提高很快，她也从我这里了解了很多中国文化。住在我隔壁的两个女孩儿也很善良、活泼，经常会闯进我的寝室，让我教她们中文，给她们起中文名字。

10 月 14 日，是我 20 岁的生日。在国内，女孩 20 岁的生日是非常重要的。然而在异国他乡，我却没有过生日的兴致。那天，一切都和往常一样，惊喜却接二连三的到来。首先，学校的公共关系办公室主任凯西为我送上了她亲手做的我最爱的甜品"柠檬条"。晚上，同乡朋友斯迪、珍尼瑞和安来到我的寝室，大声嚷嚷着要给我煮寿面。于是，四个女孩儿在厨房里煮起了方便面，那香味老远都能闻到，把正在值班的住宅助理们也吸引过来了。没有蛋糕，简单的一锅面、三个女孩儿和来自外国朋友们真诚的祝福，组成了一个让我终生难忘的生日。

## 五、美国、美国

生日后不久，便是万圣节了。这

My 20th birthday fell on October 14th, 2008. In China, the 20th birthday was very important for girls. Living in the overseas land, I didn't have any desire to have a birthday party. The day started as usual, but I accepted one surprise after another. Director of Public Relations Office Kathy came and sent me my favorite "lemon bars" she made by herself, and Sidi, January and Anne came to make birthday noodles for me. With a single pot of noodles and sincere wishes from so many friends, I had spent a special birthday that would be unforgettable in my life.

### Part Five: USA, USA

Not long affter my birthday, Halloween came. It was the first traditional festival I spent in the USA. I believed that the innovation spirit was fully presented in their festivals. To help us closely adapt to American culture, the school organized a Halloween party in Kathy's house. We were given many stage properties to dress ourselves up. When all teachers saw our costumes, they were astonished. I thought they recognized our innovation. I believed that the essence of American education is to encourage students' innovation spirit in the entertainments

是我在美国过的第一个传统节日。节
日前一个月，各大超市就开始出售节
日用品。稀奇古怪的南瓜灯、吸血鬼
面具、坐在扫帚上的女巫等孩子们喜
爱的万圣节舞会用品应有尽有，看得
我直咋舌。美国人的创新思维在他们
的传统节日里发挥到了极致！校方为
了帮助我们更深入地了解美国文化，
专门在凯西家举办了万圣节聚会。这
还是我们第一次庆祝万圣节呢！打扮
成可爱天使的凯西体贴地为我们准备
了各种各样的化妆品、服装、道具。
老师们看到我们的装扮都惊呆了，我
们的创新能力又一次得到了他们的认
可。在玩耍时学习并激励学生的创新
精神，这就是美国式教育的特点吧。

后来，每到美国的传统节日，学
校都会为我们安排到美国当地家庭共
度佳节。我非常喜欢学校的这种做法。
学习一个国家文化的最好方法不是专
注于书本，而是要亲身体验并享受其
中。

我的美国外婆叫帕特里夏，她退
休以前是学校的副校长，兼任联合国
妇女志愿者协会主席。今年重新见到
她，她已经是学校董事会主席了。这
位慈祥的美国老太太曾经在 1996 年
代表美国出席过在中国举办的世界妇
女大会。终身学习的精神在她身上得
到了充分体现，我特别喜欢她对待人

and games.

Later, when American traditional festivals
came, the school would arrange us to visit native
families to spend those festivals. I really agreed
with this activity. For me, the best way to learn
about the culture of a country was to experience
and enjoy it, instead of reading books only.

I had an American grandmother, Madam
Patricia. Before retirement, she was the vice
president of the university and Chairwoman of the
UN International Female Volunteers Association.
This kind old lady once attended the World
Women Conference held in China in 1996. The
spirit of life-long learning was fully shown on her
life. I appreciated her optimistic spirit and desire
for knowledge. I spent my first Thanksgiving Day,
Christmas, and Easter with her.

生的乐观态度以及她对知识孜孜不倦的渴求精神。我的第一个感恩节、圣诞节和复活节都是在她家度过的。

## 六、感恩、责任

在美国，我体会最多的是关爱。无论是两国政府、学校的老师，还是纽约的侨界、媒体、各华人机构、公益组织，甚至当地教会都给予我们无微不至的关怀。

"CSC-SUNY 150奖学金项目"是一个特殊的项目，它不仅给了我们一次珍贵的留学机会，同时，它也是美国政府和纽约州立大学对我们家乡的人文关怀。在美国纽约，我们是四川大学生的代表，是中美文化交流的纽带，是中华文化传播的使者；回到祖国，我们也带回了善良的美国人民的爱，这是一份超越了国界、种族和宗教信仰的爱。这种大爱、博爱让我们更加相信，世界和平是永恒的主题。正如我的一位美国老师说的那样，世界的未来是建立在各个国家的合作与友谊的基础上的，特别是中国和美国这两个伟大的国家。作为"CSC-SUNY150奖学金项目"的参与者，我们已经荣幸地跨出了第一步，用自己的勤奋、才华、包容和友谊，赢得了尊重和喝彩，也让更多的美国朋友

**Part Six: Gratitude & Responsibility**

In the United States, I gained much care and love from governments of the two countries, school teachers, overseas Chinese, media, overseas Chinese organizations, charity organizations, and even the local churches.

The CSC-SUNY 150 Program is a special one. It not only granted us a precious opportunity to exchange in the United States, but also showed the humanity of American government and SUNY to our hometown. In New York, USA, we were the representatives of university students in Sichuan, the tie of China-US cultural exchanges, and messengers of popularizing Chinese culture. Coming back to China, we have brought back love from the kind American people. This love is boundaryless in terms of countries, races and religions, which makes us strongly believe that peace is an eternal theme of the world. Just as one of my American supervisors mentioned, the future of the world would be built on the basis of cooperation and friendship of all countries, in particular between the two major countries of China and USA. As one of members of the CSC-SUNY 150 Program, I have respects by my hard working, talents, inclusiveness and friendship and helped more American friends to learn about and understand a real China. As a Chinese saying goes, a little fire can kindle the forest. I hope that our members of the program can continue to work out a more glorious story in our own field.

开始了解中国、关注中国。星星之火，可以燎原。期待未来，我们组成的团体能够在各自的领域续写出更加精彩的"中国 150 故事"！

寄语

Words from American Teachers

## 奥尔巴尼分校（Albany）

陈凡平博士
中国研究专业副教授、系主任
研究方向：中国历史和小说中的女性战士、中国历史
　　　　　和小说中的妇女、中国皮影戏、中国木偶戏。

亲爱的韵旭：

感谢你写来的长信和信中所附的有趣照片——真高兴看到它们！不敢相信你们来奥尔巴尼分校学习已经是十年前的事情了。

十年前，接收你们这群来自四川的学生，的确是让人高兴的事——你们是一群积极主动、富有同情心的聪明学生！

看到现在你依然快乐和美丽，我很高兴。作为现任系主任，我谨代表东亚研究系祝福你们永远快乐和成功！

祝好！

陈凡平教授、博士
纽约州立大学奥尔巴尼分校东亚研究系

*Fan Pen Li Chen Ph.D.*

*Associate Professor of Chinese Studies & Department Chair*

*Professor Chen's research focuses on Women warriors in Chinese history and fiction; Women in Chinese history and fiction; the Chinese shadow theatre; the Chinese marionette theatre.*

Dear Yunxu,

Thank you so much for your long letter and the fun photos you attached—I really enjoyed looking at them! I can't believe that it has been 10 years since you were at Albany.

I really enjoyed having the students from Sichuan join us that year—you were such a motivated, compassionate and bright group of students!

It's good to see you so pretty and happy still. As the current Chair of the Department, I would like to represent the Department of East Asian Studies in wishing you continued happiness and success in whatever you do!

With best wishes,

Professor Fan Pen Chen, Ph.D.
Department of East Asian Studies
Hu-211, SUNY-Albany

# 法明戴尔分校（Farmingdale）

我们的中国孩子——我们就是这样称呼法明戴尔分校的"19+"中国学生。这个"+"号代表"CSC-SUNY 150 奖学金项目"的 19 名学生是法明戴尔分校接收的来自其他学校的学生。

我对中国文化和传统极为欣赏，也惊叹于这些年轻人身上每天流露出的愉悦，他们举办的"中国之旅"活动成为校园的一个亮点。

他们尊重他人、与人合作、热爱生活，这些表现都让人赞赏。尽管在地震中遭到不幸，损失惨重，但他们依然保持乐观的心态。

我们一起度过了许多节日，有平安夜、狂欢节、情人节、感恩节等。其中我最喜欢的是万圣节，我提供了许多服装让他们装扮，他们在我那"座无虚席"的家里举办的化装晚会上表现得淋漓尽致。

2009 年 5 月，法明戴尔分校在校园里种下了一棵树，以纪念地震中的死难者。同事们告诉我，他们对在法明戴尔分校工作感到无比自豪。

虽然许多人赞赏我们为这些孩子所做的一切，但我总感到我自己从他们身上得到的更多。在过去的十年里，我一直和孩子们保持联系，这让我很快乐，看着他们结婚生子真是一件幸福的事情。

凯西·科利，　纽约华盛顿港
纽约州立大学法明戴尔分校

Our Chinese children—that is how we have referred to the Farmingdale 19 plus. The plus is because CSC-SUNY 150 Program students from other campuses were attracted to the FSC group and were adopted.

I gained a deep appreciation for Chinese culture and tradition, marveling at the joy these young people expressed every day. Their Journey to China show was a highlight for the campus.

Their respect for others, ability to work cooperatively and their love for life was inspiring. In spite of the tragedy of the earthquake and the enormous losses, they were resilient and optimistic.

We shared many holidays, including Christmas Eve, Mardi Gras, Valentine's Day, Thanksgiving. Halloween was my favorite as I had large trunks of costumes for them to dress up in and they committed completely to an evening of pretending at the 'full' house.

FSC planted a tree in May 2009 to honor those who died. Staff members told me they had never been more proud of working at Farmingdale.

While many applauded us for what we did for our children-by-choice, I always felt that I got more from them. Staying in touch with many of them over the past ten years has brought me much joy. Watching them marry and have children is a blessing.

Kathy Coley, Port Washington, NY
Farmingdale State College, SUNY

丹尼·阿尔切里

　　生物学系实验室经理、副教授，已退休，定居纽约长岛。他获得纽约州立大学石溪分校的生物科学和戏剧艺术硕士学位，擅长写作，是美国戏剧家协会中令人骄傲的一员。他是一名国际剧作家，最近有一部作品在中国制作。他的相关介绍见 www.DTArcieri.com。

## 相遇拉近我们之间的距离

　　记得那是在 2008 年夏天，我收到了学校管理部门发来的一封邮件。邮件告知纽约州立大学法明戴尔分校的教职工，学校邀请了二十多名中国学生来校学习一年。因为一场毁灭性的大地震毁掉了他们的学校和家园，有的学生还失去了亲人。读到此处，我的心都碎了。我知道，得让这些亚洲朋友进入我们的教室和实验室学习，以确保他们不会失学。于是，我激动地自愿提出代表"CSC-SUNY 150 奖学金项目"尽一己之力。

　　不过，我的初衷并非完全是出于学术上的考虑。当然，他们要参加法明戴尔分校的课程学习。但对我来说，更重要的是想邀请来自中国的新朋友走进我们的生活，参观我们的社区、房屋、起居室、餐厅和厨房。我想让他们了解美国人，了解我们的思考方式、我们之间的关系，以及我们所谈论和关心的话题。简而言之，我想让他们了解美国人是如何思考和生活的。

　　重要的是，虽然在此之前我们所受的教育让人误解，但我们应该认识到，我们的生活和思考是相同的。中国人和美国人的追求是一致的：良好的教育和职业、彼此间亲密的关系、长大后成为家人的依靠。希望来访的中国学生能明白我们是同样的人，彼此没什么差别。外貌和语言上的区别意义不大，更重要的是信仰和伦理道德。这些是我们的共同之处，我们的内心是相通的。

　　我知道，中国派了许多出类拔萃的学生来美国留学，有朝一日，他们会成为各行各业的翘楚，会对涉及中美关系的决定产生重大影响。不过，作为其中一员，"CSC-SUNY 150 奖学金项目"中的中国留学生比其他同辈和同事更具优势，他们了解我们，了解美国人。

　　最后，我想这样总结："CSC-SUNY 150 奖学金项目"是我在纽约州立大学法明戴尔分校 38 年工作生涯中的一个亮点。

*Danny Arcieri*

*Laboratory Manager and Adjunct Professor, Biology Department, retired. Holding MA degrees in Biological Sciences and Theatre Arts from Stony Brook University, he lives and writes on Long Island in New York and is a proud member of the Dramatists Guild of America. He is an international playwright with a show produced in China recently. Find him any time at www.DTArcieri.com.*

## Together, We Are the Same!

I remember reading the email from my school's administration in the summer of 2008 telling staff and faculty of SUNY's Farmingdale State College that we had invited approximately two dozen Chinese students to our college for the school year after a devasting earthquake left them without schools and homes. Even family members were lost. My heart was broken. And I knew we had to take our Asian friends into our classrooms and laboratories to save their school year. So, I was very excited to volunteer my efforts on behalf of the SUNY 150 program.

But my motives were not all academic. Yes, they needed to take courses at our school. But what was more important to me was that they came to our homes. I wanted our new Chinese friends to see our neighborhoods, houses, our living rooms, dining rooms and kitchens. I wanted them to learn who Americans were. How we thought, what our relationships were like, what we talked and cared about. In short, how we thought and lived.

And the point was this: although we had all been taught to believe otherwise, we would learn that we lived and thought the same. Chinese and Americans want the same things: educations, careers, loving relationships, security for their families as they grew. I wanted our visiting students to see that we are the same. There are very little differences between us. How we look, the languages we speak have very small meaning. Our beliefs and ethics, however mean a lot. And these things we do share. We are the same in our hearts.

I knew that China had sent us their best and brightest students who would one day be leaders. Leaders in industries and politics. Individuals who would make important decisions concerning the Chinese-American relationship. But the young Chinese members of the CSC-SUNY 150 Program, as leaders, would have a great advantage over their peers and colleagues. They would know who we, Americans are. They would not have to listen to politicians, from both our countries, tell us we are different. It's already happening. The three young students I mentored ten years ago are moving fast in their careers (Hi, Daniel, Andy and Harry!). What's at stake here? World peace! Nothing less.

Let me close by saying in my thirty-eight years at SUNY's Farmingdale State College, the CSC-SUNY 150 Program was a highlight. And I do not think I am exaggerating when I say together we may have saved the world.

# 詹姆斯敦社区学院（JCC ）

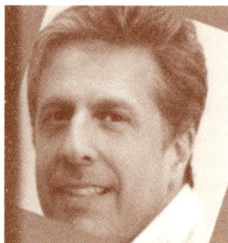

纳尔逊·加里菲（小）

学术创新部执行主任

纽约州詹姆斯敦人，毕业于纽约州立大学詹姆斯敦社区学院和圣博纳旺蒂尔大学，在詹姆斯敦社区学院工作了 38 年，除了全球教育，还负责学院的荣誉课程、应用学习课程、技术强化教学以及与地区高中的合作。

2008 年，纽约州立大学詹姆斯敦社区学院很荣幸地接待了来自成都的 5 名学生。这 5 名学生使我们对中国和中国文化有了更深入的了解。不过，最重要的是，他们使我们认识到，世界各地的人们有许多共同之处，包括希望、恐惧和价值观，但其中最重要的是在全球化社会中，善待彼此，将对方视为同胞的愿望。在 2018 年来谈这一点比 2008 年来说更为重要。我们的许多学生第一次与来自世界各地的代表相遇。自 2008 年以来，我校迎来了更多来自世界各地的国际学生，但我们仍会记得"成都五重奏"小组，以及他们融入我们校园的方式。

祝好！

纳尔逊·加里菲（小）
学术创新部执行主任
纽约州立大学詹姆斯敦社区学院

*Nelson J. Garifi, Jr.*

*Executive Director of Academic Innovations*

*A native of Jamestown, NY, graduate of JCC and St. Bonaventure University and has been employed at JCC for 38 years. In addition to global education, responsible for JCC's honors program, applied learning, technology-enhanced instruction, and partnerships with regional high schools.*

It was a privilege for SUNY Jamestown Community College to welcome five students from Chengdu in 2008. Our five students taught us all so much about their country and their culture, but most importantly they helped us understand that people from all over the world share so much in common including hopes, fears, and values—but most of all the desire to be kind and see each other as fellow citizens in a global society. This is even more important in 2018 than it was in 2008. Many of our students were meeting representatives from another part of the world for the very first time. Since 2008, JCC has welcomed many more international students from around the world, but we will always recall our Chendu quintet and the way they embraced our campus.

Best regards.

Nelson J. Garifi, Jr.

Executive Director of Academic Innovation

Jamestown Community College

## 奥斯威戈分校（Oswego）

黎黎你好，

很高兴知道你的近况。通过学习，你一定感到十分充实吧。

我们都好，戈登大学毕业了，学的是微生物学。在台北的阳明大学读了一年研究生后，决定回到罗彻斯特大学，现在在准备考取执照，取得资格后到临床部工作。

去年和今年，我和潘老师合作取得美国国家安全管理局的资助，办了两次语言夏令营和后续的工作坊，也因此和很多年轻人共事，特别高兴。生活总离不开旅行，这个月到过北加州参加婚礼，去休斯顿作了两个报告，下个月会到新奥尔良参加会议，听听年轻人的讲座，12月去佛罗里达观光或享受阳光，2月到纽约市过春节、吃小吃，希望5月可以带两个学生去密苏里的圣路易市开会，6月到辛辛那提参加论文译审和老朋友聚会，当然还希望从中获得一些有用的信息来撰写我的报告。

十年的时光不长也不短，很高兴大家都过得平安。你们现在是社会发展的动力，加油！两星期前我听了一位十年前到这儿学习的学生的报告，她现在在阿里巴巴做事，和先生一起回到奥斯威戈来分享他们对电子商务的认识。欢迎你写完论文也回奥斯威戈来看看。相信十年的回顾会有感人的故事和启发，预祝成功！

再谈！

箫老师

Dear Lili,

It is so happy to hear from you. You must feel fulfilled throughout the studying life.

All is well with us. Gordon graduated from college majoring in microbiology. After working on his graduate program in Yang-Ming University in Taipei for a year, Gordon decided to go back to the University of Rochester. Now he is working on a certificate, in order to be qualified to go to Clinical Lab.

Supported by Administration of National Security of USA, Pan and I held two summer camps followed with a workshop, and we are so glad to work with many young people. My life cannot live without travelling. I went to North California for a wedding this month, had two lectures in Houston and will be in New Orleans for a coming conference about lectures given by young people. In December, I am going to Florida for sightseeing, or enjoy the sunshine, and in February I may go to New York City to celebrate Spring Festival or take some snacks. I hope we can make the trip to St. Louis in Missouri, with two of my students for a conference. In June, I will be in Cincinnati to grade some papers and gather with my old friends. Then I wish I can gain some useful information from there to write my report.

Ten years has been neither too long nor too short. I'm glad that everyone lived safe and sound. Now you are the impetus for the improvement of society. Go for it! Two weeks ago, I attended a lecture delivered by a student who came here ten years ago. She was employed by Alibaba Group now. She and her husband came back to Oswego to share their ideas about e-commerce. After you finished your thesis, I hope you can go back to Oswego, too. There must be some interesting stories and inspirations in our ten-year review. I hope it goes well!

We will catch up later.

Xiao

# 奥斯威戈分校（Oswego）

十年前，当我们见到来自四川的四位令人称奇的学生时，感到很开心。纽约接收了很多经历了大地震的学生，而奥斯威戈接收了其中四位，他们分别是 Mengtu, Lili, Jian 和 Jian。这些学生把我和安迪介绍给其他老师，分别是温斯洛博士和霍华德·戈登博士，他们都已经离开了校园，前者去了加州，后者已经退休。正是这些学生的主动与热情给校园注入了更大的动力去接受更多的国际学生。

在接下来的十年，我们通过电邮联系，但很少谈及最近的变化。2015 年，我们的朋友 Wenyi Guan Zhuang 安排我们到中国旅行。我们游览了中国的九个城市。那是我们有史以来最远的一次旅行。我们同时，我们很开心见到了之前的访问学者和学生们。我们在成都的接待人叫 Minmin Zhou。她派 Jian 或者 Jack 来机场接我们。结果来的是 Jack，我们七年前的一个学生。与性格腼腆的 Jian 不一样，Jack 的性格外向，与 Amanda 成婚；他们带我们游览这座伟大的城市。Minmin 需要为会议做准备。第二天，Jack 带我们游览了这座古老的城市，我们玩得很开心。Minmin 中午带我们吃了午饭，接下来下午 Jack 带领我们和他的太太 Amanda 一起参观了一座漂亮的庙宇，感受了神奇的中国式按摩，去了熊猫基地，即使雨天也令人赞叹，之后 Jack 还为我们安排了酒店。在游玩回来的第一天晚上，Mengtu 出乎意料来拜访我们。我们相谈甚欢，甚至在房间里叫来夜宵，聊到半夜还意犹未尽。这两位老学生，现已毕业，专注于他们的事业和我们分享了他们的梦想和希望，他们的勃勃生气感染了我们。在我们走之前，我们得知之前一直通过邮件联系我们的 Lili 在德国即将完成硕士学位，另一位学生 Jian 在澳洲学习。在我们离开成都之前，Minmin 帮我们达成了品尝火锅和观看川剧的愿望。

We were happy to meet Four Amazing Students from Sichuan ten years ago. NY accepted many students after the earthquake and Oswego was lucky to meet these four: Mengtu, Lili, Jian and Jian. They introduced us, Andy and me, to other faculty members such as Drs. Winslow and Howard Gordon, both of whom have left the university, the former to California and the latter to retirement. It was their spark of initiative and enthusiasm that gave the campus a greater impetus to reach out to more International students.

In the following ten years, we kept in touch through emails but sporadically responding to their changes. In 2015, our friend, Wenyi Guan Zhuang, arranged a trip for us to visit 9 cities in China. It was the biggest trip we had ever taken and we enjoyed each meeting with our former visiting scholars and students. When we arrived in Chengdu, we looked for Minmin Zhou, our host, who asked Jian or Jack to find us at the airport. He did and there was our student of 7 years before. Instead of shy Jian, we met an enthusiastic Jack who was married to Amanda and they cohosted our visit to this great city. Minmin was preparing a conference, so Jack took us on a trip to the old city the next morning. It was delightful. Then Minmin took us all to lunch and Jack carried on from there. He introduced us to Amanda and we enjoyed many treats: a visit to a beautiful temple, an amazing massage, a rainy but incredible trip to the Panda center, and then he arranged hotels for us. The first evening upon our return from an outing, we were surprised by a visit from Mengtu. We had so much to talk about that we did take out some food to our room and talked till midnight. It was so invigorating to have these two former students, now graduates and interested in their careers, share their dreams and hopes with us. Before we left, we learned that Lili who had emailed us was completing her graduate work in Germany and the second Jian was studying in Australia. Before we left Chengdu, Minmin made it possible for all us to share a hot pot and see some of the Sichuan Opera.

It was the connection that continued a conversation at the hotel for many hours later. In the following years, we were connected on WeChat thanks to Wenyi once again and saw Jack's and Amanda's first child, a beautiful daughter. We heard from Minmin when she came to the States

　　正是我们继续保持联系，才有了后来在酒店长达几个小时的彻夜长谈。在接下来的几年多亏 Wenyi，我们通过微信和 Mengtu 保持联系，并且，我们见证了 Jack 和 Amanda 的第一个孩子——一个可爱的女孩的诞生。去年春天，Minmin 来美国，她为我们带来购于成都一家精品店的阅读台灯，我们非常开心。看到他们在 Jack 的植物企业所表现出的对自然的专注，看到他们为追求更高的学历所表现出的对教育的专注，看到他们为自己的孩子营造充满关爱的环境所表现出的对家庭的专注，我们为这些年轻人的不断进取而感动。我们期待我们之间有限的联系得以继续，好在我们可以通过电邮或者微信联络。

　　祝好！

　　玛丽·安·霍根和安迪·纳尔逊

last spring, she delighted us with a book light from a special store in Chengdu. We are impressed with the ways these young people have moved their lives forward by focusing on nature as in Jack's botanical enterprise and education as they pursue higher graduate studies and family as they create a loving environment for themselves and their children. It is our hope that our connections with them, although limited, will continue. We are very glad to have these inspiring connections over WeChat or email.

Sincerely,


Mary Anne Hogan and Andy Nelson